# HUNTING

*a*

# DETROIT TIGER

**The Mickey Rawlings Baseball Mysteries**
*Available from Kensington Publishing*

# Hunting a
## Detroit Tiger

### TROY SOOS

KENSINGTON BOOKS
www.kensingtonbooks.com

# *Acknowledgments*

A number of people have made contributions to this book, and I'm happy to have the opportunity to express my thanks.

I am especially grateful to Kate Duffy, my editor, for her thoughtful guidance and unflagging enthusiasm; Meredith Bernstein and Elizabeth Cavanaugh, my agents, for their diligent efforts on my behalf; Kelly Tate, for reviewing the manuscript.

For research assistance, I am indebted to Marsha Carey, reference librarian at the U.S. Department of Justice; Sharon Carlson and Pamela Jobin, with the Archives and Regional History Collections of Western Michigan University; Tim Wiles and Scot Mondore, of the National Baseball Library & Archive in Cooperstown, New York; Madeleine Mullin, of the Countway Library of Medicine in Boston; Jessie Rabban and Norman Waksler, of the North Cambridge Public Library. Also helping in the research were Laura Kelly, Cindy Haigh, Nat Rosenberg, Dave Smith, and the staffs of the Burton Historical Collection in the Detroit Public Library and the Government Documents Room of Harvard University's Lamont Library. I am grateful to all of these individuals and institutions for so generously sharing with me their time and expertise.

# Chapter One

## ○○○

*WAR HERO KILLS BOLSHEVIK*

A four-word headline in the morning edition of the *Detroit Journal*. Four words, stark and black. And three of them wrong.

It was true that I'd seen combat in the recent Great War, but I had done nothing heroic. The heroes were the dough-boys who'd been mowed down on the desolate ground of no-man's-land or felled among the splintered trees of the Argonne forest; and the ones who returned home but had sacrificed parts of themselves "over there"—limbs severed by mortar shells, vision seared by mustard gas, minds jellied by the relentless pounding of artillery fire. I had come back alive, intact, and suffering no greater disability than the same one that had always afflicted me: a tendency to be suckered by sharp-breaking curveballs low and away.

The *Journal* was also wrong about Emmett Siever. He was a baseball man, not a Bolshevik. As a journeyman outfielder he'd played for nine teams in five major leagues, from the

1884 St. Louis Maroons of the old Union Association to the 1901 Detroit Tigers club of the fledgling American League. So why the "Bolshevik" tag? Because his most recent baseball activities weren't on the playing field, but in the lecture halls: Siever had been trying to unionize ballplayers—an endeavor which struck me as having less prospect of success than establishing a fan club for umpires.

The most outrageous mistake of the headline, though, the one that provoked my immediate concern, was the way it connected Emmett Siever and me. Because I wasn't the one who killed him.

○ ○ ○

"What do you mean, you didn't kill him?" said the desk sergeant.

I repeated my statement, which I thought sufficiently unambiguous.

The middle-aged cop—Sergeant Phelan, according to the nameplate on his desk—exhaled a long sigh and stared wistfully down at the thick sandwich on which he'd been breakfasting. He reluctantly slid the half-eaten meal aside, then ran a palm between the double row of brass buttons on his uniform, brushing away crumbs of black bread and smearing a gob of mayonnaise into the blue fabric.

I held out my copy of the *Journal.* Suspicion darkened his features. He shot a protective glance at his sandwich as if worried that my presence was a diversionary tactic so that an accomplice could snatch away his salami-on-pumpernickel.

I looked around the small, dismal room. The only other

living creature in the waiting area of the Trumbull Police Station was an inert basset hound curled up in front of a smoky potbellied stove. From within the stove came the muffled hiss of a fire struggling to ward off the spring morning chill. It was a losing struggle, and the odor of burning soft coal did nothing to improve the room's atmosphere.

Turning back to the sergeant—who had the expression of the hound and the shape of the stove—I again tried to force the newspaper on him. After a slow sip from his coffee mug, he took the paper and cautiously drew it close to his broad baleful face. Squinting, Phelan scrutinized the front page like it was a gold certificate of an unfamiliarly large denomination. First the masthead and date—Tuesday, April 13, 1920. Then the major headlines:

*Pickford-Fairbanks Honeymoon Delayed*
*Palmer Blames Primary Loss on Detroit Radicals*
*Railroad Strike Paralyzing Commerce*

"Near the bottom," I said.

Phelan appeared annoyed at the interruption—he probably wanted to linger on the story about Mary Pickford possibly being a bigamist. But he directed his eyes below the fold, and began to read how I'd shot and killed a Bolshevik.

After a minute, he paused to peer up at me. "You're Rawlings?"

This, too, I'd already told him. "Yes," I said with diminishing patience. "Mickey Rawlings. I play for the Tigers."

"Then why ain't ya with the team? Season opener's in Chicago tomorrow, ain't it?"

I held out my right forearm and drew back my coat sleeve

to show him the bandages. "Busted wrist," I explained, then said yet again, "I didn't kill Emmett Siever."

"Sure you did. It says so . . ." He poked a chubby forefinger at the newsprint. "Right there."

For a police officer, Sergeant Phelan had a peculiar notion of what constituted evidence. "I don't care what it says. It's *wrong*. And I want it corrected."

"Then go see the editor or somebody."

"Read the story! It's the *police* who are claiming I did it. That's why I'm here."

Phelan grunted and calmly resumed reading. "He got shot in Fraternity Hall, eh?"

I was tempted to respond, "No, he got shot in the chest." Instead I said, "Yeah. Fraternity Hall."

"Oh! Here, look." Phelan turned the paper for me to see and pointed to the final paragraph of the article. "It's being called self-defense—you're not being charged with nothing. Hell, this story makes you out to be some kind of hero for getting rid of that Red. So what's the problem?"

"Would *you* want to be accused of killing somebody if you didn't do it?"

He pondered a moment. "Well, I don't expect that would bother me as much as if I did kill somebody, and the papers printed it."

The basset hound stirred long enough to issue a loud yawn. Phelan promptly echoed the dog. Resisting an impulse to shake him alert, I said, "There was a cop at the hall last night. He talked to me after it happened. Aikens, his name was. Detective Aikens. Is he here? Can I see him?"

"Don't know no Aikens." Phelan folded the *Journal* and slid it back to me. "You better try headquarters."

"Where's that?" I hadn't been in Detroit long enough to know where police headquarters was. The only reason I knew about this station was because it was across the street from the Tigers' ballpark.

"Bates and Farmer, about a block from Cadillac Square. Can't miss it." He reached for his sandwich and lifted it to his mouth. Apparently, as far as Sergeant Phelan was concerned, I was now headquarters' problem and didn't warrant any more of his time.

"Thanks." I grabbed the newspaper, tucked it under my arm, and turned to leave.

Through a mouthful of food, Phelan mumbled, "Still don't see why you're so worried. What's the worst that can happen?"

When I stepped outside the station house, an icy breeze struck my face; it felt like I was pressing my cheek against a cold windowpane. An eastbound Michigan Avenue streetcar approached, its bell clanging and its wheels squealing as it crawled to a stop in front of me. I was about to hop on when I changed my mind about going immediately to police headquarters.

As the trolley resumed its rattling journey downtown, I stood on the corner, debating my next move. Cold began to numb my skin, while a warm, writhing sensation that I couldn't quite identify started to gnaw at my insides.

I looked across the street to Navin Field's main entrance, a quaint, two-story structure that reminded me of a small-town railroad depot. Behind the entrance, a ramp led to the right-field grandstand of the ballpark proper. Raising my view slightly, I saw the pennants flying proudly above the roof. In nine days, fans would be streaming into this jewel of a ballpark for the Tigers' home opener. I wished I could jump forward in time and onto the diamond—and just play baseball again.

Instead of heading downtown, I started up Trumbull. Exasperating as Phelan's indifference had been, I wanted to believe him, to believe that I could simply ignore the newspaper story, and it would blow over harmlessly.

On the walk home through the quiet residential streets of Detroit's Corktown neighborhood, I worked hard to convince myself that Sergeant Phelan had the right attitude. After all, how bad could it really be? I wasn't under arrest . . . I knew that I hadn't shot Siever, so my conscience was clear . . . And the *Detroit Journal* would certainly have to print a retraction when it discovered the mistake.

By the time I turned from Pine Street onto Grand River Avenue, my head had almost come around to Phelan's way of thinking. But my gut remained emphatically unconvinced. By now I'd been able to identify the cause of the turmoil in my belly: it was fear. Fear of what might happen if the Emmett Siever situation didn't resolve itself as easily as I hoped.

I heard my phone ringing as I started up the steps to my second-story walkup over Carr's Hat Shoppe. It was still ringing when I reached the landing, and continued while I groped for the door key. As I stumbled inside, my nerves jangled in resonance with the urgent clanging.

Before lifting the receiver, I repeated aloud Phelan's final words to me: *What's the worst that can happen?*

## Chapter Two

○○○

"**I** asked you to meet him, not *kill* him." For a long-distance call, the connection was unusually clear—not a desirable quality when the voice being transmitted was the nasal whine of my old muckraker friend Karl Landfors.

Gripping the base of the candlestick telephone, I said loudly into the mouthpiece, "I didn't kill him." I was already weary of making that statement and dejected by the fact that it seemed to have so little effect.

*"Tribune* says you did. So does the *Herald-Examiner."*

Damn! The story wasn't limited to the *Journal,* or even to Detroit. Landfors was referring to Chicago newspapers. Struggling to prevent my voice from betraying my apprehension, I said, "Karl, you've been a reporter long enough to know that just because something appears in print doesn't mean it's true." I then allowed him a few moments to debate with himself whether to defend the integrity of his profession or concede my point.

He came down on the side of reality. "Yes, you're quite right." After a long breath, high-pitched enough to summon dogs, he said, "Tell me what happened. Did you go to the lecture?"

"Yeah, I did." Juggling the phone and trying to avoid strangling myself on the cord, I slipped out of my overcoat while continuing to speak. "It was more than a lecture, by the way. You didn't mention the place was an IWW meeting hall."

"What did you think Fraternity Hall would be—a college dormitory?"

I actually hadn't given any thought to the name of the hall, but I hadn't expected it to house the local headquarters of the Industrial Workers of the World. "Dunno," I admitted. "Anyway, when I got inside and heard the guys talking, it was pretty clear that the place was full of Wobblies. And some of them weren't exactly shy about admitting they were anarchists or communists."

"Why should they be shy about it?"

I decided to pass on the opportunity to debate politics. Landfors was a long-standing member of the Socialist Party and I was— Well, I was more interested in reading *The Sporting News* or *Motion Picture Magazine* than *The Masses.*

Silence lasted until Landfors realized I wasn't going to take the bait. "Okay," he said. "Give me the story. You went to the hall . . ."

"Right. I got there early. Thought I might talk to Siever before it started, but he wasn't around. So I killed time reading pamphlets until the meeting was called to order. First thing we did was sing songs, if you can believe it. Lots of 'em. The Wobblies must be the most musical bunch of radicals anywhere."

Landfors coughed a noise that for him was a laugh. "Then what?"

I switched hands, moving the base of the phone to my left hand and the earpiece to my right. "Speeches. One after another, and most of 'em boring. Then Emmett Siever came out. When the guy who introduced him said Siever was involved in the old Players League, it really brought the house down."

"Why?"

"It was a *players* league. Organized and run by the ballplayers themselves."

"I never knew there was a league like that."

"Only lasted one year—1890. Anyway, Siever's speech was pretty good. Told a few stories about his playing days, then got on to union talk. His said the men who own the baseball teams are the same 'robber barons' who run industry, and that ballplayers are no more special than 'bindlestiffs'—whatever those are."

"Itinerant workers," Landfors explained. "'Bindle' is the bundle they tie to a stick when they travel; it usually contains all their possessions."

"Uh, 'itinerant'?"

A burst of static in the line made his next words fuzzier. "Migrant. Like farm workers who travel from job to job." With a cackling chuckle, he added, "Or like your baseball career."

"Funny, Karl." I wasn't *that* much of a vagabond; I did have a three-year stretch with the New York Giants once, and nearly three full years with the Cubs. "Back to Emmett Siever: he said baseball players are workers the same as everybody else, and they should organize with other workers to protect their rights. Said they should join the one big union—everybody kept using that phrase 'one big union.' Anyway, he got a standing ovation from the crowd when he finished."

"So . . . How did he end up getting shot?"

I turned around to sit against the spot on the parlor stand where the telephone had rested. "Not exactly sure. After his speech, Siever went out a back door to where the offices are. Everyone else started singing again. I wasn't sure if Siever was coming out again, so I got up and walked to the back, too. Figured it might be the only chance I had to meet him. Just as I was about to knock on the door, I heard a 'bang'— sounded like a gunshot, but I wasn't completely sure. It wasn't real loud, and everyone else kept singing. I waited half a minute or so, then I went in to see what happened." After a deep breath, I continued, "I found Emmett Siever in the kitchen. On the floor, shot in the chest, dead. I wasn't with him long when a cop came in, a detective. He asked a couple questions, then he let me go.

"I went back into the main hall. The singing had stopped, and everybody was running around shouting that Siever had been assassinated. Then cops started storming in and it got crazy: the Wobblies yelling 'Raid!' and trying to push the cops out; the cops swinging their billy clubs at anybody who got in their way—it looked like they were cracking heads just for the fun of it. I left and came home as soon as I could."

Landfors sighed. "And that's it?"

"Pretty much."

"Hmm. You're *sure* you didn't kill him?"

What was Landfors suggesting? That I was lying to him, or that it had slipped my mind? I didn't like either implication, but I gave him the benefit of doubt. After all, a friend of his had just been murdered. "I would know, wouldn't I?" was my answer. After a moment, I tried to lighten the conversation, "But enough about me. How are things in Chicago?"

Ignoring the gallows humor, he said, "Let me think about this." The next thing I heard was a click and the hum of a disconnected line. Karl Landfors generally didn't bother with social graces like saying good-bye.

As I hung up, I muttered to myself, "Go ahead and think about it. I'll try not to."

○ ○ ○

What I tried to concentrate on instead was my batting grip. Specifically, on how to increase the number of hands I could use to two.

I unwound the bandages from my right wrist and flexed it gingerly. There was no sharp pain and it appeared only slightly swollen. It felt good enough that I decided to ignore doctor's orders and try swinging a bat.

Determining when to come back from an injury is tricky for a player. Coddle it too long, you can weaken the muscles; exercise it too soon, you can cause additional damage. As a utility infielder, the decision was a little easier for me because time was a luxury I didn't have. A regular player could be out of the lineup for weeks or months with a substitute filling in for him. But there were no substitutes for utility men. If I couldn't play, I'd be off the team. So, no matter what the instructions from doctors, I always followed one simple regimen for recovery from injury: work it out.

Even if it did my wrist no good, I hoped that focusing on baseball for a while would clear my head.

After retrieving one of my Louisville Sluggers from the

umbrella stand near the door, I went to the middle of the parlor and assumed a relaxed batting stance. The room was large enough and the furniture sparse enough that there was little danger of me hitting anything.

I'd rented the cheap, three-room flat "furnished," which my landlady interpreted to mean a bed in the bedroom and a sofa in the parlor. What passed for a sofa was a sagging bed lounge that had shed most of its burgundy mohair. Like the other pieces in the room—an arthritic cane-backed rocker, a lumpish hassock made of carpet remnants, a wooden folding table held together with gobs of glue—it was from the previous century and of no discernible style. Harsh sunlight revealed the furniture's every scar and tear, for there were no curtains on the window—"If you're doing something you don't want people to see, you shouldn't be doing it anyway," she'd explained.

I took a cautious half swing and a flash of pain shot up my arm. The sensation sent me back two weeks in time, to Greensboro, North Carolina. It was while batting in a spring-training game against the Boston Braves that a fastball from Joe Oeschger sailed inside and smashed my wrist. I'd barely noticed the impact at first because of the umpire, who claimed the ball hit my bat and called it a foul tip. With great vigor and no discretion, I pointed out that he was not only blind, but deaf, unable to tell the difference in sound between bone and wood. It wasn't until after my ejection from the game that I noticed my wrist ballooning up to the size of a grapefruit. Manager Hughie Jennings had me see a local doctor, who determined it to be "prob'ly busted or somethin'," and I was sent on to Detroit to let it heal.

As I continued to swing the bat loosely, the pain subsided

to a dull throb. I smiled as I recalled that some of my team-mates envied me the chance to go home early. The Tigers and Braves had decided to cap off their spring-training seasons by barnstorming together in the Southeast. The tour turned out to be a fiasco in every respect. Endless rains kept fans away from the games and turned the playing fields of the ram-shackle ballparks into treacherous swamps. Errors were ram-pant, partly due to poor field conditions and partly because fielders were watching the ground for copperheads and water moccasins instead of paying attention to the ball. More than one pitcher developed arm trouble after hurling sodden, heavy baseballs that were better suited for shot-putting.

My escape from the misery of spring training had afforded me little relief. The swelling and soreness didn't subside for days, and I started to have my first inkling of baseball mortal-ity. Whenever I'd been hurt in the past, I'd never even consid-ered the possibility that I wouldn't recover. But I was older now, twenty-eight, prime age for a ballplayer. Old enough to realize what happens after you reach your peak: you go downhill. If my wrist didn't heal properly, the downhill slide to involuntary retirement would be steep and rapid.

As I took my cuts in the parlor, I found it hurt most when I tried to snap the bat around. It was my top hand—the power hand—that Oeschger had hit, and I couldn't follow through properly. If only I was left-handed like my new team-mate Ty Cobb . . . Hey, why not?

I'd tried switch-hitting before, back when I played semipro ball for industrial teams, but had given it up when I realized that I needed to concentrate my efforts on hitting from just one side of the plate. No reason not to try it again, though. I reversed my hands on the bat handle and crouched in a left-handed stance. It felt awkward at first, but I feigned a few bunts, then some half swings, and it started to seem a little smoother.

Grinning at my own childishness, I then pretended I was Cobb, spreading my fists apart to mimic his split grip and leaning over from the waist in imitation of his stance. I knew I didn't look anything like the powerful center fielder. I was strictly from the infielder mold: five-seven in my shoes, about 150 pounds when holding a bat, and with just enough muscle to loop a base hit one out of every four at bats.

Cobb and I did have one thing in common: we were the only two Tigers who didn't complete spring training. Although the barnstorming tour started in his home state of Georgia, Cobb elected not to participate. His vacation did nothing to endear himself to the rest of the team, but since Ty Cobb had spent the last fifteen years antagonizing his teammates—as well as opponents, fans, and anyone else he came in contact with—neither did it make him more despised than he already was.

The decrepit cuckoo clock on the wall made a grinding noise, and a small bird limped out to emit five groans. Five o'clock. Exactly twenty-four hours ago, I'd left for Fraternity Hall to meet Emmett Siever.

It had come about so innocently. I was new to Detroit, with no friends yet and my teammates still on the road. Karl Landfors phoned and suggested I meet a friend of his who used to be a ballplayer. That's all there was to it. The result: *WAR HERO KILLS BOLSHEVIK.*

Switching back to my natural right-handed stance, I focused on an imaginary fastball knee-high down the middle and took a cut. I swung again, and again, harder and harder, oblivious to the pulsing ache in my wrist. Then I lifted my eyes, looking up to where the pitcher would be and imagining infielders behind him. I wanted to be on a baseball diamond. To forget about the police and the newspapers and the sight of Emmett Siever's dead body. If I could just step onto a ballfield again, everything would be okay.

Laying the bat on the sofa, I went to the phone and made a call to Hughie Jennings at the Sherman House Hotel in Chicago. A bellboy tracked him down and the manager got on the line. I asked him if I could come and join the team.

Jennings hesitated. "Doctor say you can play?"

"Not yet, but I'll be seeing him again tomorrow. Even if I can't, I'd like to be with the club. Work out some, maybe warm up the pitchers if you want . . ."

"Well, I don't think Navin is gonna pay for you to come out here if you can't play." Tigers owner Frank Navin was a renowned nickel-nurser.

"I'll buy my own train ticket," I offered.

"There'd still be hotel and meals to pay for."

I wasn't even worth room and board? "I'll pay for that, too, if Navin won't."

Jennings paused again. "Well, it ain't just Navin that's the problem." He cleared his throat. "I don't want you getting hurt."

"I'll take it easy—"

"I don't mean getting hurt on the field. It's in the locker room I'm worried about. The other players are out for your scalp."

"Why?"

"They think you killed Emmett Siever."

Jeez. "I didn't kill him, Hughie! The newspapers got it wrong!"

"Yeah, well, I think it'd be better for you if you stay in Detroit. Maybe by the time we get home, the boys'll have calmed down."

I didn't want to push it with Jennings. "Okay. If that's what you want."

"Take care of that wrist, kid. If they're still as pissed as they were this morning, you might have to use your dukes."

After hanging up, I went back to swinging the bat. Left-handed, with a split grip. Maybe I didn't look like Ty Cobb, but I now had one more thing in common with him: my teammates hated me.

# Chapter Three

## ○○○

**A**t the same time that the Tigers were taking the field in Chicago's Comiskey Park for the season opener against the White Sox, I was being tortured in a dark, filthy office in downtown Detroit.

With a strong two-handed grip, Dr. Wirtenberg twisted my right wrist. He'd already poked, prodded, and squeezed the damaged joint, and was now giving it some kind of final test, apparently to see if he could unscrew my hand from my arm. "Seems to be getting better," he mumbled, releasing his hold on me.

The doctor's lips were drawn back, not in a snarl but as a precaution. Clamped in his stained yellow teeth was a burning cigar stub so short that it threatened to set his equally stained gray mustache on fire.

"Am I okay to play?" I asked, fighting the hope in my voice.

His eyes squinting against the smoke that shimmied up his face, Wirtenberg pulled the wet, crumbly cigar from his mouth, handling it with far greater care than he'd shown my wrist. In a nasal voice that sounded strongly of the Bronx, he said, "Think you'll need another appointment. Maybe two."

Something about his manner gave me the impression that the additional visits were more for his benefit than for mine. "Tigers pay you for each visit, right?"

Wirtenberg nodded. "That's the arrangement I have with Mr. Navin."

"How much?"

"I don't see where that's any—"

"How about if I pay you myself for two more visits and you give me a clean bill of health?" I wanted to be free to join the team and play ball as soon as I could. Besides, two more treatments by this guy and I'd be out for the season.

The doctor gave the smoldering cigar a mercy killing, crushing it out in an iron bedpan on the corner of his desk. Sprinkles of cigar ash, as well as a more uniform layer of dust, covered everything in the room, including some grimy medical instruments. I'd been in minor-league locker rooms that were more sanitary.

Wirtenberg removed his pince-nez and polished the lenses with his necktie. "Sounds reasonable," he agreed. "It's four dollars a visit, so you owe me eight altogether."

I suppressed a laugh. The fee he'd quoted was probably double what he really got from Frank Navin. Judging from the condition of the office and knowing Navin's reputation as a tightwad, my guess was that the team physician was selected solely on the criterion of lowest rates. It wasn't even a requirement that the doctor be a Tigers fan—tacked on the wall next to Wirtenberg's diploma was a New York Yankees pennant.

"Give you five," I counteroffered.

"Six."

"Five."

"Close enough."

I pulled a bill from my wallet. "Do I pay you or the receptionist?"

"Me."

The doctor tucked the money in his vest pocket, then scribbled a note to the effect that I could play baseball again. Handing me the slip of paper, he said, "Was probably just bruised anyhow."

As I rolled down my shirtsleeve, I noticed how red and swollen the wrist had become as a result of his examination. If it wasn't bruised before, it sure was now. "Should it be bandaged again?" I asked. I knew the cotton wrapping was only for protection in case I banged my hand on something; it wouldn't help the healing process.

"If you like." He made no move to do the wrapping.

After loosely winding the bandage myself, I pulled on my coat, put the note in a pocket, and started to leave. I was more convinced than ever that one of the best ways to stay healthy is to avoid doctors.

"Oh!" Wirtenberg said as I reached the door. "I read about you in the paper yesterday." When I turned back to face him, he asked in a confidential tone, "Tell me: why did you really kill that fellow?"

I started to say "I didn't—," then caught myself. What was the point of denying it, I thought. No one believes me anyway. "Because he was a Yankee fan," I said.

O O O

Two people were in the waiting room outside.

One was the doctor's receptionist, whose nose was buried in the latest issue of *Collier's*. It remained there as I passed her desk; her response to my "Good-bye" was "Uh-huh."

The other person was a bulky, thick-necked man wearing a loose khaki sack suit. He rose from a bench near the door, pulled himself to a height of about six-four, and studied me carefully. In a raspy voice, he asked, "Mickey Rawlings?"

I acknowledged that I was, and tried to figure out who he could be. The man's head was crowned by an oversize tweed golf cap, a thin yellow bow tie was embedded under his lowermost chin, and a green automobile duster was draped over his left forearm. Bright red socks were visible between the tops of his heavy black work boots and the high-riding cuffs of his trousers. Physically, he looked like a wrestler, but all I could determine for certain was that he had no fashion sense.

Forming a toothy, mechanical smile, he said, "Let me shake your hand."

I held up my bandaged wrist and started toward the door. "Sorry. Can't."

He slid in front of me, the unconvincing grin still on his face. "A mutual friend asked me to take you to lunch."

"Who?" If the mutual friend was Karl Landfors, declining the offer might be the best thing to do. I seemed to bring his friends bad luck.

"Frank Navin."

Navin? That was a surprise. I'd never met the Tigers owner,

not even to sign my contract. Navin was my boss, not a friend. "And who are you?" I asked.

"Hub Donner. Shall we go?"

The name was unfamiliar to me. "Uh, yeah, sure." I was wary, but curious to find out what this was about.

With a gesture at the door he stood aside for me to go first.

Down three flights of stairs, we emerged on Gratiot Avenue and into a thick, overcast day with a bone-biting chill in the air. It felt more like midwinter than the first day of baseball season. Donner slipped into his automobile duster and I fastened the belt of my double-breasted ulster. He pointed to a glossy new Model T runabout parked at the curb. "We can take my car."

As he grabbed the handle of the passenger door, I said, "Let's walk." Something in the back of my mind warned me that getting into a stranger's automobile might not be the wisest thing to do, even if the stranger did claim to be a friend of Frank Navin. In fact, the mere notion of a baseball owner having a friend sounded suspicious.

A hint of a genuine smile twitched the corners of Donner's mouth. "Fine by me," he said. "It's not far. Thought we'd eat at the Tuller."

Half a block from Wirtenberg's office, we turned west on Madison Street, our heads low and shoulders hunched in defense against the bitter wind. Most of the heavily bundled men passing by us wore derbies jammed low on their foreheads. I was in a straw boater; it was my personal custom to wear the summer hat from opening day through to the end of the World Series, and I wasn't about to break the tradition just because of a little cold weather.

Donner became aggressively chummy as we walked, jaw-ing and joking like a Rotary Club luncheon speaker. He accompanied his punch lines with slaps on my back, and often draped his big hand over my shoulder. I shrugged it off every time.

By the time we crossed Randolph, fat snowflakes were dancing in the air but not yet sticking to the sidewalk. And I had already tired of Hub Donner's company.

The Hotel Tuller was an imposing structure, about fifteen stories high, filling Park Boulevard from Bagley to Adams. There was something forbidding about its stately appearance; the very bricks seemed to suggest that only those of wealth or importance were welcome within. I wondered if the man-agement still maintained the policy that finer hotels used to have of refusing service to actors or ballplayers.

Either the policy had been abandoned or I wasn't recog-nized as a baseball player, for we entered without incident. After checking our coats and hats, Hub Donner directed a fawning maître d' to give us a window table in the Men's Grill. The ground-floor restaurant, with its dark wood paneling, polished brass, and plush carpeting, had the ambience of a gentlemen's club. Although it was on the late side for lunch, almost all the tables were occupied, and it was several min-utes before the maître d' could accommodate us. We settled into leather chairs next to a window overlooking Grand Cir-cus Park. The view of the park, where naked trees shuddered in the wind, was often interrupted by pedestrians walking past.

Sitting across from each other, I took a closer look at Donner. He reminded me of movie actor Erich von Stroheim in one of his evil Hun roles. Donner's close-cropped salt-and-pepper hair looked more like a five o'clock shadow than a hairstyle. Creasing his scalp was a patchwork of vivid scars; I assumed he was proud of the marks, or he would have let his hair grow out to cover them.

Scanning his face, I caught his dark steady eyes and saw that Donner was sizing me up, too. Literally sizing me up. "So you're the fellow who killed Emmett Siever," he said. "Smaller than I expected."

"If it makes you feel any better," I said, "maybe the guy who really shot him was bigger."

Donner chuckled as if to show he'd only been pulling my leg.

When our waiter came, Donner took it upon himself to order for both of us: porterhouse steaks, double thick, rare, with potatoes and onions. I interrupted that I wanted mine well-done. He let me name my own drink, ginger ale, while he opted for coffee, black.

As the waiter scurried away with our orders, Donner fingered a ridge of scar tissue that ran for several inches over his right ear. I'd seen enough similar marks during the war to know that it was a bullet wound. I also knew that most fellows who had them didn't like to be asked about their scars—the stories of how they got them were usually too grisly or too embarrassing for them to want to repeat. Hub Donner was drawing attention to his, though, almost pleading for a question.

I went along. "War wound?"

Donner laughed as unconvincingly as he smiled. "Yes, but not the one you were in." His words sounded as if they passed through broken glass on the way out of his throat. "Union wars. Bullet was from one of Bill Haywood's miners

in Colorado, summer of '05. Haywood's boys play for keeps."
The smile again. "But so do I."

To everyone else, the radical labor leader was "Big" Bill
Haywood; Donner wouldn't even concede him his size. "The
other scars from bullets too?"

He shook his head. "Nah. Just got nicked up a little—
pipes, ax handles, bricks. Kid's stuff."

Hub Donner was doing all he could to impress me with
his personal toughness. But to what purpose?

"You said Mr. Navin asked you to meet me," I reminded
him.

Donner nodded. "That's right. He—" The waiter
appeared with our drinks and made a production of setting
them on the table. Donner waited until he was again out of
earshot before continuing. "Mr. Navin thought you might be
of some help to him—and to baseball." For God and country,
the way Donner made it sound.

I stifled the groan that swelled my lungs. "Help him how?"

"Simple." Donner took a gulp of his steaming coffee. "Let
the American League publicize the fact that you're against
a players' union."

"But—"

"You won't have to do much. There'll be some articles
written under your name for the newspapers and some magazines. Don't worry—somebody will write them for you. You
just have to agree to let your name be used."

"I don't—"

"Of course, we'll start with the Emmett Siever incident.
The way I see it, you were at the meeting to confront him,
tell him you didn't believe in his goddamn union. Brave of
you to do it right in Fraternity Hall, by the way, with all them

anarchists there. Hey! That's the way we'll present it: you met him on his home field. Give it the baseball slant." He thought a moment, brushing his palm over his stubbly head. The grating sound it produced was similar to his voice. "Maybe you can make some speeches, too. Can you talk in front of an audience? Again, we'll get somebody to write them for you."

Donner was beginning to sound more like an adman than a muscleman, and I was starting to realize that he had brains to go along with his brawn. "No, I don't like to talk in front of people," I said. Now, how to get out of the rest of Donner's plan? Or Frank Navin's plan, or whoever came up with this bright idea.

Massive steaks, with onions and potatoes heaped around them, were placed before us. Hub Donner fell to with his knife and fork, shoving large chunks of bloody meat into his mouth. I pushed my potatoes around with a fork as I thought over Donner's proposal. My appetite was diminishing fast.

Donner made a sucking noise as he tried to draw out a piece of gristle stuck between his teeth. Waving his knife around the room, he said, "What do you think of this place?"

"It's okay."

"You should have seen the Ponchartrain in its heyday. *That* was a hotel. Couldn't walk more than ten feet in the Ponchartrain bar without bumping into somebody with an automobile named after him. Henry Ford, Louis Chevrolet, the Dodge brothers, Ransom Olds, they were all regulars there." He paused to use the tip of the knife on the stubborn piece of meat. "But those days are gone. The car men all meet at the Detroit Athletic Club now. Rest of the city's business leaders come here, but it ain't like it was at the

Ponchartrain." He shook his head. "Me, I don't like change. I like things the way they used to be."

"Who *are* you?" I asked. "What do you do? You work for Mr. Navin?"

Donner pointed his knife at my plate. "Eat up." After putting another piece of steak in his own mouth, he said, "I'm what you might call a personnel coordinator. Factory owner or somebody has trouble with his employees, he calls me in and I coordinate them."

"You're a union buster."

"Damned right I am. And proud of it. No way I'm gonna see Reds and Bolsheviks destroy this country."

"I thought Reds and Bolsheviks were the same thing."

He looked taken aback. "Yeah, well, whatever. All I know is they're ruining everything made this country great. Used to be a man felt lucky to have a job and appreciated a chance to support his family. Now nobody wants to work. You know how many men are out on strike right now?"

"Four million, the papers say."

"That's right. More than one worker in ten is out on strike, living off the labor of honest men. And it's not just miners and mill hands no more. Now you got railroads, police departments, the whole goddamn city of Seattle striking." He shook his head with disgust. "People just don't want to work no more."

Donner paused to finish his steak, and I chewed on some fried onion. It occurred to me that it might be fun to lock him in a room with Karl Landfors and let them lecture each other until one of them dropped. It also occurred to me that he hadn't answered my question about whether he worked for Frank Navin. "Who hired you?" I asked.

"The American League."

"A union's okay with the National League?"

Donner laughed. "Nah, they hired their own personnel coordinator."

"Oh."

He laid down his knife and fork. "It's to save your job, if you think about it. Public's already mad at baseball players. You boys go forming a union, and it could kill the game."

I'd heard of a hundred things that were going to kill baseball, but the game always survived. "Don't see how that could be," I said.

Donner launched into a history lesson. "Two years ago: country's at war, boys are dying overseas, everybody at home is making sacrifices. And what do the ballplayers do? Threaten not to play the World Series unless they get more money. What the hell kind of patriotism is that?" He slammed a palm on the table, then waved away the waiter who came scurrying to see what the matter was. "And last year even worse. Country's getting back to normal, looking forward to the Series again, and the damn White Sox sell out to gamblers."

"That's not true!"

"It ain't been proved yet, but everybody knows it."

I felt a heavy sadness. I'd heard the rumors, too, that the 1919 World Series hadn't been on the level. But I didn't want to believe it.

I'd noticed that Donner had never asked for my views on organized labor. I don't think it mattered to him. And I wasn't going to volunteer my opinions—especially since I wasn't quite sure how I felt about the union issue.

Lunch finished, Donner lounged back in his seat and folded his hands over his belly.

"Thanks for the meal," I said. "But I really don't want to get involved with this union business one way or the other. What the papers said about the other night was a mistake. I just want to clear it up and forget it."

"Sorry to hear that," said Donner without a note of sorrow in his voice. "Mr. Navin's gonna be disappointed."

I let the implied threat pass. "The season's starting, and I got to concentrate on baseball." I held up my bandaged wrist. "Got to get this thing healed and get back in shape. If I'm playing lousy, I'm off the team and no help to Navin anyway."

"Very well," said Donner. "I'll pass that along—to your boss. I think you'll change your mind soon."

I forced a smile. "I'll let you know if I do."

Donner returned a grin as devoid of sincerity as mine.

# *Chapter Four*

ooo

A hundred times in the last year and a half, I'd suffered through a recurring nightmare: I was back on the battle-field, standing alone above a muddy trench full of German soldiers, firing down on them with my Springfield rifle. The dream never varied. In it, I never noticed until I started shooting that my targets, although dressed in the uniform of the Kaiser's army, were merely unarmed boys playing soldier. And once I began firing, I couldn't stop—every time I attempted to pull my finger off the trigger, the weapon would go off, putting another bullet in another boy. The rifle never ran out of ammunition, and I could never pull myself out of the dream, until all of the boys were lying dead in a bloody heap.

I was aware that I was having the dream again, but something was wrong about it—something was different. I wasn't shooting at kids dressed like soldiers this time. My targets huddled in the trench were white-haired men in old-fash-ioned baseball uniforms—all of them looking like Emmett Siever. Something else was different, too: I was waking out of it while some were still alive.

The telephone rang again and I realized why my dream had come to a merciful end. I stumbled from my bedroom to the dark parlor, rushing to pick up the receiver.

"Mickey Rawlings?" The voice was muffled, as if the speaker was gagged or holding a handkerchief over the mouthpiece.

I paused to let the last vestige of sleep drain from my head. "Yeah, this is me."

"Saw you with your pal Hub Donner yesterday. Guess we know which side you're really on."

The struggle to both distinguish the words and comprehend their meaning was too much for me. "What are you talking about?"

"Now we know why you killed Emmett Siever."

"I didn't— Who is this?"

"A friend of Siever's. You're gonna find out he had a lot of friends."

"But wha—"

"And we're not gonna let you get away with his murder." The caller made an effort to be sure his next words came through clearly. "The cops may have let you off the hook, but we won't. His death will be avenged."

Although it seemed futile to explain myself to an unknown voice on the telephone, I said, "I *didn't* kill Emmett Siever, and I barely know Hub Donner."

"Whatever Donner paid you, it wasn't worth it. We're gonna throw you from the train." Then there was a click as he hung up.

I collected myself enough to be sure that this call was no dream. But who in real life threatens to throw you from a train? That seemed an odd thing to say, and I could make no sense of it. I pictured Pearl White tied to the railroad tracks in one of her movie serials, and briefly wondered if that was what the caller meant.

Although sunrise hadn't yet come, I knew I wouldn't be falling asleep again. Instead of going back to bed, I went to the kitchen. As I filled the coffeepot with water, I thought of other threats I'd received over the years. They'd involved fists, bats, knives, guns, even a sword once. And those were all before I went to war and had to face cannons, machine guns, and poison gas. But being thrown from a train? That was a new one.

○ ○ ○

After two cups of black coffee and a hot bath, dawn was starting to light my apartment and the caffeine was beginning to clear my head.

I made a quick trip to the local newsstand and returned with the Thursday morning editions of the *Journal,* the *Free Press,* and the *News.* Sitting on the least tattered spot of the parlor sofa, I sipped a fresh cup of coffee and began reading the papers.

As usual during baseball season, I went to the back pages first. The sports section described in detail the Tigers' 3–2 opening loss to Chicago. Not really a bad start, I thought. The game did go eleven innings, and the White Sox—despite their surprising loss to Cincinnati in last fall's World Series—were still the best team in baseball. Holding them that close was something of an achievement.

Reading about the ball game made me long to be back with the team. The home opener wouldn't be for another week, and staying in Detroit by myself for that long seemed interminable.

Moving to the front pages, I was relieved to see that there wasn't another word printed about me or Emmett Siever. Most of the headlines were about the national railroad strike:

*Palmer Paints Rail Strike Red*
*Strike Chiefs Under Arrest*
*Senate Urges Action to Break Railroad Strike*

The only local news to make the front pages was a growing feud between the U.S. Treasury Department and the Detroit police. Treasury agents were accusing the police of graft, claiming they'd been paid off by rumrunners to turn a blind eye to the booze coming over the river from Canada. Detroit mayor Jim Couzens defended his police department as "above reproach" and charged that the federal "interlopers" were incompetent to enforce prohibition and were seeking a scapegoat for their own failures. I found this report encouraging—it sounded like I wouldn't have much trouble getting a beer in Detroit.

I went back to the articles about the railroad strike to see how travel would be affected. I was happy to read that strikers were only targeting freight, not passenger trains. Baseball teams would still be able to go from city to city according to schedule.

The strike stories did contain some troubling statements from Attorney General Mitchell Palmer, however. Palmer claimed to have evidence that "Reds"—the catchall term for Wobblies, unionists, anarchists, foreigners, communists, and a host of others—were planning a May Day bombing campaign, and he was vowing to use "any means necessary" to prevent it. I had the feeling that whatever this labor war I'd been drawn into was all about, it was only going to get worse.

*We're gonna throw you from the train.* I couldn't forget those words.

I set the newspapers down next to me and took a swallow of coffee. Okay, somebody saw me with Hub Donner, assumed I'm working with him to bust the players' union, and figured that's why I killed Emmett Siever. Was it one of my teammates—the ones Hughie Jennings said were mad at me? I couldn't see how—they'd all been in Chicago while I was meeting with Donner. Besides, the Tiger players I knew would make a more direct threat—involving a baseball bat, not an anonymous phone call.

My guess was that the caller was a probably a Wobbly, somebody who'd been at the IWW hall and was angry about Siever's death.

Damn that Hub Donner and his strong-arm approach. Sometimes a little stealth is called for. He should have been discreet, met me in a quiet place, out of view . . .

Jeez. I finally got it. The scheming sonofabitch *wanted* me to be seen with him, and for people to think we were pals. The backslapping, going to one of the city's most famous hotels, specifying a window table so we could be easily seen.

That's why he was so sure that I'd change my mind about working with him. If the Wobblies thought I was in league with Donner, then I would have to go along with him just to protect myself from the IWW.

I flung the papers on the floor. Like hell I would.

○ ○ ○

"Can't miss it," Sergeant Phelan had told me. As I walked through downtown Detroit, though, finding police headquarters turned out to be something of a challenge. Part of the problem was that I hadn't been to the city since 1912, the last year I'd played in the American League. There'd been so much growth since then that I had difficulty finding the old landmarks.

Another problem was street names. As the auto industry turned the city from a frontier town to a major metropolis, respectability had become important. Red-light districts, once considered essential entertainment, were no longer quite so desirable. Loath to eliminate them, however, Detroit came up with a novel way of lessening their notoriety. I'd heard from other ballplayers that as certain streets became infamous for brothels and blind pigs, instead of shutting down the whorehouse and unlicensed saloons, the City Council simply changed the names of the streets.

During my search for the police station, I discovered that Croghan was now Monroe, and Champlain had been rechristened Lafayette East. Finally, using Cadillac Square as a reference point, I did work my way to the drab stone building that served as headquarters for the Detroit Police Department.

The desk sergeant inside the bustling front room was more lifelike than his counterpart at the Trumbull station house, but no more helpful in leading me to Detective Aikens.

"Don't know nobody by that name," the sergeant said. "What's yer business with him?"

"It's about the Emmett Siever shooting Monday night. Detective Aikens handled the case, I believe."

"Don't think so." He called across the room to another uniformed officer. "Hey Vern! The Siever shooting. That's Mack's case, ain't it?"

At Vern's affirmative return yell, the sergeant said to me, "Detective McGuire's the man you want to see. Let me check if he's in." He reached for a telephone, and after a brief conversation with McGuire, gave me directions to a second-floor office.

Walking along the upstairs hallway to McGuire's office, I checked the names on each door looking in vain for "Aikens." When I came to the one with *Det. Francis McGuire* lettered on the frosted glass, I rapped on *Francis*.

"Come in!"

I stepped inside to see a smallish man seated at a desk covered with papers and file folders. He was probably about thirty, but his long, rust-brown hair was uncombed and his face so mottled with freckles that he had the look of a twelve-year-old boy.

"I'm Mickey Rawlings," I said. "Desk sergeant said you'd see me."

"Sure will." He stood up, offering his hand. "I'm Detective McGuire. Call me Mack. I don't stand on ceremony." McGuire flashed an easy smile, causing the freckles to move around like a kaleidoscope.

I hesitated only a second before returning his grip. The swelling of my wrist was down, and a handshake couldn't be any worse for it than what Dr. Wirtenberg had done.

"Have a seat," McGuire offered. "Oh—and close the door, please. Don't want to let the heat out."

I did as he asked, though I could detect no heat. Despite a radiator clanging and gurgling behind his oak swivel chair, the room was chilly. McGuire was dressed for the cold, in a heavy three-piece tweed suit. I kept my overcoat on as I settled into the room's only other chair. Space was so tight in the tiny office that my shoulders were wedged between the side of a file cabinet and a coat rack.

"I actually came to see Detective Aikens," I began. "But nobody seems to know him."

McGuire sat rigidly, hands folded on his desk like a well-behaved schoolboy. "Afraid I can't help you there. I've never heard of him either. Anything *I* can do for you?"

I didn't understand how the police could have a disappearing detective. "Aikens was the officer who first showed up when Emmett Siever got shot. He's the one I talked to."

McGuire shook his head. "Sorry, don't know the man. There's no detective by that name on the Detroit police force."

"He's a big fellow, about six-one, over two hundred pounds. Kind of a droopy face, nose like Babe Ruth's." I searched my memory for anything else I could recall about Aikens. "He nods his head after everything he says."

"Sorry."

"He showed me his badge. Said he was with the Detroit P.D."

"Sorry." McGuire spread his hands. "Afraid you're stuck with me."

What the hell, I figured, what did I care which detective was in charge of the case. "Okay. The reason I'm here is that the papers are saying I killed Siever."

McGuire leaned back. "Yes. In self-defense. So what's the problem?"

"I didn't kill him for *any* reason! Why would Aikens have let me go if he thought I did?"

"I couldn't answer that. Like I said, I've never heard of—"

"Yeah, I know, you don't know any Aikens."

McGuire shrugged. A loud metallic belch came from the radiator.

"Things is," I said, "I'm getting all kinds of trouble about this. People read the papers, and they believe I did it. All I want is for the police to tell the papers that I didn't do it."

"I'm afraid that's impossible. According to the report, you did do it."

"Then whoever wrote the report got it wrong."

"No, that's not possible, either. I wrote the report."

"But you weren't there. You never even talked to me!"

"Take it easy, Rawlings. I didn't need to talk to you. The situation was thoroughly investigated, and it was clear what happened: Siever pulled a gun on you, and you shot him in self-defense. Case closed."

Case closed? It was never open, as far as I could tell. "Wait a minute," I said. "Why 'self-defense'? How did you come up with that?"

"Would you prefer that we charged you with murder?"

"No!" I thought a moment and tried another angle. "Okay, what did I shoot him *with?* I didn't have a gun."

"You must have. You couldn't have shot him without one." McGuire ventured a small smile, but I saw nothing humorous in the situation. "And of course Siever's was in his hand."

"It was?" I searched my memory. I was sure I hadn't seen a gun anywhere near Siever's body.

"You were there. You must have seen it." McGuire's jaw shifted. "The report's written, and the case is closed, Rawlings."

I was still picturing Siever as I had found him. There'd been no gun in sight. "Emmett Siever did not have a gun in his hand."

McGuire smiled again, the freckles twisting themselves into a new pattern. "Right. And you didn't shoot him."

I clenched my right fist. The resulting pang stopped me from doing anything more with it. Good thing, since slugging a police detective in his own office would be a very stupid thing to do.

Hunching over his desk, McGuire began rifling through the stacks of papers. He pulled a photograph from a folder and slid it to me. "See for yourself."

I picked up the black-and-white print and forced myself to look at the unsettling image of Emmett Siever's bloody corpse. His body was basically in the same position as when I'd seen it in the kitchen of Fraternity Hall. With one exception: clutched in Siever's right hand was a long-barreled revolver.

How did it— No, don't get interested, I told myself. So somebody planted a gun on him, what concern was that of mine? Don't get involved.

But I was already involved. If somebody went to the trouble of planting a gun, what else might they do to maintain the story that I killed Siever? I was torn. From painful experience, I knew how ugly it could be to get mixed up in a murder case. On the other hand, it was also probably the only way to keep myself *out* of trouble.

It started to dawn on me that McGuire might not be an adversary. "How does a case get opened again?" I asked.

He tilted back in his chair and interlocked his fingers over his vest. "Well, now, that's hard to say. The department doesn't like to reopen investigations. We have other cases to move on to, you know. As far as I'm concerned—and more importantly as far as my captain is concerned—I'm off the case." He paused. "Of course, if some new evidence was to come up . . ."

"How do you find new evidence if you're not investigating anymore?"

"I won't find it. Somebody else would have to, and then bring it to me." He smiled again. "I think I've probably said all I can on this matter." He drilled me with a look that told me a bit more.

I understood him perfectly. "Thank you."

We stood and shook hands. McGuire added, "It would have to be very strong evidence."

"It will be," I said.

*Chapter Five*
○○○

**E**arly Saturday afternoon, two days later, a volunteer showed up to help me obtain evidence about Emmett Siever's murder. Not that I'd asked for his help; nor had he offered. He'd simply phoned to say he was coming, and I knew that what he was really telling me was that I had an ally.

The 1:20 train from Chicago pulled into Michigan Central Depot at precisely 1:19 and Karl Landfors stepped down onto the platform. While a porter put two pieces of luggage next to him, Landfors checked his pocket watch. A satisfied look brightened his angular face, as if he was personally responsible for the prompt arrival. He very well could have been; knowing his irksome nature, I wouldn't have been surprised if he'd nagged the engineer into complying with the schedule.

After Landfors tipped the porter—the man's exaggerated "Thank you, suh!" and deep bow suggested the tip was a miserly one—we exchanged perfunctory handshakes, and I hoisted the larger bag, a leather-bound canvas coat case. "Thanks for coming," I said.

Landfors reached down for an alligator Gladstone bag, grunting as he picked it up. "It's not entirely because of you that I'm here." With a thin forefinger, he pushed his horn-rimmed spectacles higher on his long nose. "Emmett Siever has a daughter— Or is it had? She's still alive, so it might be present tense. But of course he's dead, so he no longer has her. Perhaps past tense, then." He sighed. "Anyway, I want to pay a call on her."

I smiled at his determination to pretend that it wasn't concern for me that had prompted his trip. "Too bad you couldn't have made it to his funeral," I said. "Hardly anybody went."

"Did you go?"

"No. Read about it in yesterday's *Journal.* The way the paper put it, there weren't enough people there to field a baseball team. Whoever wrote the story tried hard to make it sound like there's no loyalty among radicals." I shifted the bag to my other hand. "The paper also mentioned me again as the one who killed him."

As we walked out of the train station, Landfors said, "I feel somewhat responsible for your predicament, and I will do what I can to help."

"Thanks. I appreciate it." I hailed a cab—like almost every other automobile in this city, a black Model T—and gave the driver my address. Once Landfors and I were seated inside the standard-issue Ford, I said, "You're not responsible for what happened, though."

He brushed lint and dust from the lapels of his severe black suit. They weren't necessarily mourning clothes; Landfors always dressed as though he was going to a funeral. "In a way, I am." Landfors pulled a handkerchief from his breast pocket and dabbed his cheeks and forehead. "My motives in asking you to meet Emmett Siever were not entirely pure."

"What do you mean? You knew something was going to happen to him?"

"No, no. Nothing like that. It's just . . . Well, in the past, you and I have been on the same side in some pretty tough battles."

"We sure have." There'd been a few scrapes that we'd barely come out of alive.

"In some ways we seemed to think alike," he went on. "I was hoping, I suppose, that you might take an interest in politics . . . and the labor movement. It's been a tough time for us—for progressives—since the war, and we can use you on our side. I always had the feeling you were sympathetic to the cause, and I thought if you got to know Emmett Siever, a former ballplayer, you might want to become active. Pretty stupid of me, huh?" He turned his head to me, his eyebrows arched above the rims of his glasses.

I wasn't angry at Landfors for trying to get me involved in his passion. It seemed only fair, since it had been largely because of my influence over the years that he'd become a baseball fan. "No, not stupid at all," I said. I didn't know how to explain to him how I felt. "I just don't trust any kind of organizations right now. All these different groups wanting to control how people think and act, each group claiming to have a lock on patriotism. It's as bad as it was during the war; except now instead of 'Huns' it's 'Bolsheviks' who are supposedly gonna destroy the country. I want things to go back to the way they were before the war—those were good times, everybody seemed to get along with each other. Sorry, Karl, but I'm not going to have anything to do with either side in these political fights. Hell, I'm just trying to fit in with the Tigers, and that's tough enough—especially now."

During the remainder of the ride, I told Landfors of my conversation with Hughie Jennings and that it looked like it would be even harder than I expected to get along with my new teammates. I also filled him in on my meetings with Hub Donner and Detective McGuire.

The cab swung onto Grand River Avenue and let us off in front of my landlady's hat shop.

We climbed the shaky staircase to my rooms. "This apartment ain't much," I said as I opened the door. When Landfors had phoned and told me he was coming, I'd insisted that he stay with me. It hadn't occurred to me until this moment that he might not want to.

Landfors stepped inside, his face souring as he looked around. "Not quite like the house you had in Chicago. I liked that place better." He took off his derby; sparse brown hair, almost as threadbare as my sofa, was plastered to his bony head. Landfors wasn't yet forty years old, but looked more like fifty. He was one of those serious guys who'd probably skipped childhood entirely to hasten his entry into middle age. His aging process had been further accelerated by three years on the front lines in Europe, first as a war correspondent and then an ambulance driver. What had taken the greatest toll on him, however, was the loss of his new bride in the 1918 Spanish influenza epidemic.

"I liked the other place, too." I put the suitcase next to the sofa. "But I'm always gonna be moving, and I don't want to let myself feel too settled again." In Chicago, I'd been renting a cottage and had filled it with new furniture of my very own. It had been my first real home in many years, and

I hated having to move. But when the Cubs sold me to the Tigers, I sold the furniture and came to "Dynamic Detroit," as the city boosters called it. And I'd finally accepted the sad fact that utility infielders don't get to settle down until they're retired utility infielders.

While I went to the kitchen for ginger ales, I called to Landfors, "I had another phone call, too, before I went to police headquarters. Anonymous, some guy trying to disguise his voice. Said Siever had friends, and they were gonna 'throw me from the train.' " Back in the parlor, I handed Landfors a bottle of Stroh's. With Prohibition having become the law of the land on January first, the brewery had switched to the production of soda pop and ice cream. "Have any idea what that's supposed to mean?"

Landfors took a long swallow of soda pop. "It's a Wobbly expression." He hiccuped and thumped his chest with his fist. "Migrant workers travel on freight cars. Wobblies riding the trains check to see if the bindlestiffs have IWW membership cards. No card, no ride. The Wobblies throw them off the train."

"Nice recruiting method."

"The IWW has done more than anyone to improve the lot of migrant workers. It's only reasonable to expect them to do their part by joining up and supporting the fight. This is a war we're in, Mickey. All's fair."

That attitude was one of the things that had me down on causes. True believers were willing to do anything for their side to win. And Landfors was a true believer. Although we did think alike in certain ways, the two of us also had some distinct differences.

"Does 'all's fair' include killing people?" I asked.

"No." Another hiccup. "Not usually."

I'd have preferred the answer to be a definitive no. "That fellow who called to say they're going to throw *me* from the train . . . should I be worried?"

"Probably. But not too much. If they were really going to do something, I doubt if they'd call you ahead of time." Landfors sounded as unconcerned as Sergeant Phelan.

Carrying the bottle of pop, he began to prowl the parlor, poking his nose here and there and wrinkling or bobbing it depending on whether he approved of what he saw. One of the few items to garner an approving nod was a set of Mark Twain books that I'd brought with me from Chicago. Stronger approval came when he saw the literature I'd been given at Fraternity Hall stacked on the phone stand. From the pile— which I'd meant to throw out—he picked up a red booklet entitled *IWW Songs to Fan the Flames of Discontent.* "The 'Little Red Song Book,' " he said, smiling. "Some good ones in here: 'Joe Hill,' 'Solidarity Forever,' 'Casey Jones' . . ."

"Yeah, and we sang most of them. I thought I was in a church choir."

Landfors chuckled. "Music is powerful. And a lot of people the IWW is trying to reach can't read—but they'll remember songs. Wobbly writers use mostly Christian hymns—that way the music's already familiar—and put labor lyrics to them. It gets the message across quite effectively."

It figured there was a strategy behind the sing-alongs; radicals were generally too serious to enjoy music for its own sake. "The singing *was* pretty rousing," I admitted. Pointing at the sofa, I said. "This is just for tonight. Tomorrow you get the bed."

"I don't need—"

"I bought a ticket while I was waiting for your train. I'm going to Cleveland tomorrow. First thing I need to do is be with my teammates again, face them in person at least and try to make things right if I can. It's only for three days, then we're back here for the home opener. Besides, I can use a few days to think over what to do about this Siever thing."

Landfors rubbed his nose. "If you're leaving tomorrow, we better do something special tonight. I'll take you to a nice dinner."

"Thanks, but I was thinking something a little different. You friendly enough with the Wobblies to get us into Fraternity Hall?"

"I suppose so."

"Great. I want to go back and see where Emmett Siever was killed."

Two images of Siever remained vivid before my mind's eye. One was the dead, bloodied man I'd seen in person, slumped on the kitchen floor at Fraternity Hall. The other was the photographic likeness that Detective Mack McGuire had shown me in police headquarters—the one in which Siever was gripping a revolver, a revolver that most definitely had not been there when I'd found him. Those images were only pieces of the picture—and in the case of the photograph, it was a false one. What I needed was a fresh, objective view of the entire crime scene.

○ ○ ○

We walked to Fraternity Hall, through a neighborhood that had been largely taken over by the automobile industry. A few well-kept older homes remained, but most of the buildings on First Street were of recent construction: institutional rooming houses to accommodate workers new to the city, and brick factories that manufactured everything from magnetos to headlamps.

Near Bagley, between a ten-cent-a-night rooming house and a Detroit Edison substation that emitted a humming noise, we arrived at the plain, concrete block building where I'd come to meet Emmett Siever five days earlier.

Karl Landfors pressed the doorbell. After a long minute, the same wiry old man who'd taken my two bits admission on Monday night creaked open the door. He pulled a short-stemmed cherrywood pipe from his mouth and scrutinized our faces. "Cards, please."

Landfors produced several cards from his wallet; they all featured the color red either in the ink or the paper. The old man examined the cards, nodded, and handed them back. "Welcome," he said, stepping aside to let us into a large vestibule. Low tables along the walls were covered with stacks of pamphlets, newspapers, and handbills. Tacked above them were crude posters illustrated with brawny, bare-armed workmen; they carried slogans encouraging workers to join the "One Big Union," and one, with a drawing of a wooden shoe, advocated "Sabotage" if wages weren't satisfactory: "Good Pay or Bum Work. The IWW Never Forgets!"

Offering Landfors a gnarled hand, the man said, "Stan Zaluski. Happy to have you here, Karl. I've read some of your pamphlets. And your pieces in *The Liberator,* of course. Powerful writing. We need more like it."

Landfors grinned as he returned Zaluski's grip. I wondered if he had authored any of the literature on the tables.

A compactly built man who seemed familiar to me

appeared in the open doorway to the main hall. He had the complexion of a ghost—almost no pigmentation in his skin, and hair that was blond to the point of white. If he was a baseball player, he'd doubtlessly be nicknamed Whitey. He leaned against the jamb, hands plunged deep in the pockets of his loose-fitting white duck trousers, looking me up and down. "Check the other guy, too," he said.

"I intend to, Whitey." Zaluski turned his attention to me. "Need to see your card, too, if you don't mind."

I squelched a smile at hearing the pale man's name. "I don't have one."

Landfors spoke up. "This is Mickey Rawlings. A good friend of mine."

"Rawlings!" Whitey squawked, his body jerking erect. "Son of a bitch!" He turned his head and called into the hall, "C'mere guys! The bastard that killed Emmett is here!" Immediately I heard chairs being scraped and shoved, and the rumble of heavy footsteps approaching.

Zaluski glared at me. *"Rawlings?* You got some nerve showing your face here."

A half dozen men gathered behind Whitey. They muttered curses at me, but did nothing more than look menacing. They seemed to be waiting for the little man to take the lead.

Whitey fixed me with cold, pale, pinpoint eyes. "Murderer always returns," he said, as he slowly drew his right hand from his pocket. "But when you come back here, you don't get away again." Flicking open an ivory-handled straight razor, he stepped toward me, the other men pressing his back.

The glinting blade looked deadlier than a bayonet. I knew how much a razor could hurt as a shaving tool; as a weapon, it terrified me. Besides, I'd been trained to protect myself from the thrust of a bayonet. I had no idea how to defend against the slash of a straight razor.

I shot a look at Landfors. His eyes were wide and his mouth agape. This wasn't a battle of words like he was used to; he wasn't going to be much help in a physical brawl. Then a quick backward glance at the door. I had no doubt that Whitey would be on me before I could get it open. I'd rather face him and fight than have my throat cut from behind.

Whitey took another step closer, waving the razor in a tight side-to-side pattern. I hunched my left shoulder, drawing my arm as high into my coat sleeve as I could, preparing to block the blade with my forearm. Then maybe I could move close enough that he couldn't swing the razor. I had no idea what to do about the other men, but at least they appeared unarmed.

The crowd behind Whitey abruptly parted as a large, snowy-bearded man of about sixty came through from the main hall. His impressive paunch, covered by a red flannel shirt, acted as a cowcatcher to push the others aside. Green suspenders curved around his gut and attached to worn, baggy dungarees. "What's going on here?" he demanded, looking from man to man through small wire spectacles perched on his bulbous nose.

Whitey didn't divert his gaze from me. "This is the bastard who killed Emmett Siever. Gonna give him a little justice."

"No you're not," the larger man said. "Not here."

"But—"

"I said not here! Put it away."

Whitey hesitated, like a kid who doesn't like being told

what to do and so stalls in sullen defiance. But then he closed the razor and jammed it back into his pocket.

The large man turned to Landfors and me. Although he resembled a department-store Santa Claus, his bass voice was far from jolly when he said, "What the hell you doing here, you scrawny-assed son of a bitch?"

I was trying for an answer when Karl Landfors spoke up. "Leo Hyman, you fat-assed Bolshevik. Good to see you, too."

I immediately tried to pretend that I'd known all along that it hadn't been me Hyman was addressing.

Teeth became visible through long strands of mustache, and Hyman stepped forward. He and Landfors shook hands; firmly but not warmly, I noticed. "You in charge here, Leo?" Landfors asked.

Hyman nodded.

"The reason we're here," Landfors said, "is Mickey tells me he didn't have anything to do with Emmett Siever's death. I believe him, and I want to help him find out who did. I'd appreciate it if you'd let us in so he can walk me through what happened that night."

Whitey spoke up, "You're not letting them in here, are you?"

Hyman turned. "That's my decision to make." Jerking his head toward the doorway, he said, "All of you get back to work. You too, Whitey."

The other men went back into the main hall. Stan Zaluski sat down in a chair next to one of the tables and puffed at his pipe until smoke billowed from the bowl.

Whitey was the last to leave. "Better frisk them first," he said before strutting away.

"That's Whitey Boggs," said Hyman. "Head of the Relief Committee. Good man, but a little high-strung."

"How about it, Leo?" Landfors said. "Can we look around?"

Hyman thought a moment. "Sure. Come on in."

Landfors and I stepped around the literature tables and into the main hall. It was about the size of one of the storefront nickelodeons I used to frequent, dimly lit, with unpainted concrete block walls. At the far end was the door that Emmett Siever had passed through just before he'd been shot.

Whitey Boggs stood in the center of the room, supervising the other men, who were setting folding chairs into circles of eight to ten each.

Hyman hooked his thumbs in his suspender straps and leaned back to counterbalance his belly. "I don't see where it would do any harm for you to look around. Those fellows are gonna be watching you, though, so don't try anything out of line. And if you want to go in the back, I gotta go with you."

"Thanks, Leo." When Hyman left, Landfors said to me, "Let's have it. From the beginning."

I glanced around. On Monday night, the chairs had all been lined up in rows facing a small platform to the left. Other than that, it looked basically the same as I remembered. It also felt the same; there was a clamminess in the air that came from being encased by concrete. The only decorations were more IWW posters, which failed to give the room any feeling of warmth.

"Okay," I began. "Like I told you before, I came early hoping to talk to Siever but he wasn't around. There were a lot of men—and some women, too—milling around . . . jaw-ing with each other, handing out pamphlets, nothing unusual. Then there was a call for order, and everyone took their seats."

I now remembered where I'd seen Boggs before. Pointing to the stage, I said, "Whitey Boggs was the fellow running things. I don't remember seeing Leo Hyman. Anyway, first thing we did was sing those damn songs. Then Boggs introduced the speakers, about eight of them." Among them, there had been an electrician who'd recently been fired from the Fordson tractor plant, a Peninsular Stove metal worker, and a longshoreman from the Riopelle Street docks. They'd all spoken of "one big union" and used the same slogans. They had sounded so much alike, that I'd stopped paying attention after the third speech.

I started walking across the bare cement floor toward the back door, with Landfors following. "Emmett Siever was the last to talk," I said. "He seemed to really be saying something—didn't just spout slogans. He came across as reasonable instead of radical. Tell you the truth, I kind of liked listening to him myself." I chose not to add that I didn't necessarily agree with everything Siever had said.

"And then?"

"Siever's speech was the last one. Something that sounded like a Salvation Army band struck up 'Solidarity Forever' again, and everybody started singing. Except for Siever. He left the stage and went out that door. After a few minutes, I followed him and waited a little while to see if he'd come back out. Then I heard a 'bang'! With the music and the singing being so loud, it took a moment till I realized it was a gunshot. Nobody else seemed to notice. Anyway, that's when I went through to see what happened."

We'd reached the door in question, and Landfors called to Leo Hyman, who was speaking to several other men near the entrance. They all stopped to stare at Landfors and me.

When Hyman rejoined us, Landfors asked him, "Can we see the offices?"

Hyman caressed his beard. "Sure. It's not locked. Go ahead."

I pushed in the door and led the way. We stepped into the middle of a narrow hallway that ran the length of the building. Across the hallway were a number of closed doors which I assumed were the offices. "This is the way I came," I said, turning left.

"Why?" Landfors interrupted. "Did you hear something?"

I thought about the question. "No, just the singing and the band. I guess I turned this way because that's the way the door opened." It was hinged on the right and swung in, so the easiest direction to go was left.

"See anyone?"

"Not till I went back there," I said, pointing toward the end of the corridor.

Landfors nodded for me to proceed. Hyman maintained silence as he accompanied us.

About ten feet down the hall, we came to a large kitchen. Black iron kettles simmering on a couple of old-fashioned wood ranges gave off a rich, spicy smell. One woman stirred the pots while two others diced potatoes at a butcher-block table piled high with small loaves of dark bread. They all paused from their activity until Hyman said to them, "Please go on with your work." To us, he said, "Getting ready to serve dinner. Got a lot of folks needing soup and bread these days."

I barely registered the dinner preparations. Pointing to the floor in front of an enormous icebox, I said softly, "That's where I found Emmett Siever." The sight was still vivid in my memory. Siever's aged face had been handsome even in death; not one strand of his carefully groomed silver hair was out of place, and his chiseled features had softened to an expression of peaceful contentment. His gaunt body, however, had looked far less serene: arms and legs splayed, a white shirt dripping crimson from a gunshot wound to the chest. My stomach began to experience the same queasiness that had run through me that awful night.

Visualizing the way I had found him, I knew for certain that Siever had no gun in his hand. I decided to tell Landfors about that later, because I wasn't sure how much to say with Leo Hyman there. "I was bent over looking at Siever," I continued, "when a guy in a dark suit came up behind me. Showed me a badge, said he was Detective Aikens of the Detroit Police. He barely looked at Siever—didn't have to because he was obviously dead. Aikens asked my name, what I was doing there—I told him I was looking for the toilet—and then he sent me away."

"He just let you go?" Landfors said.

"Yeah. I sure wasn't going to argue with him about it. I went back in the main hall and heard people yelling that Siever'd been assassinated. Then cops started busting in, swinging their clubs. Some of the Wobblies tried to fight them off. I didn't know what to do, so I pushed my way to the door and went home as soon as I could." I started walking back along the hallway.

Hyman said, "It's been getting bad again, Karl. Ever since Palmer lost the primary here, they've been rousting us, harassing us every way they can. Almost as bad as the raids in January."

Recalling the headline about the attorney general's loss in the Michigan presidential primary, I said, "Palmer's blaming the loss on Detroit radicals."

They both looked at me with surprise.

"It was in the paper," I said.

"They cover that in the sports page?" Landfors ribbed me.

"Politics *is* a sport," I said. "You just don't have to be in shape to play it."

Hyman chuckled and patted his gut. "Your friend might have a point there, Karl." Turning serious again, he went on, "Palmer's afraid he's losing his power. The raids were his last glory." I also knew from the papers that the Palmer raids over the winter had rounded up ten thousand "undesirables," and that many were still in prison awaiting deportation. "People are finally getting tired of his scare tactics." Hyman pursed his lips. "Some are even bothered by the fact that the raids were unconstitutional."

"Palmer says there'll be bombings come May first," I said. "Says Bolsheviks are planning a revolution to take over America."

Landfors spoke up, "He's crying wolf once too often."

I gestured to the end of the hallway opposite the kitchen, past the row of office doors to an open space. "What's down there?"

"Work area," Hyman answered. "Where we make picket signs and such. Got a small printing press, too."

"And in these rooms?" I asked, referring to the ones along the hallway.

"Just offices and storage. And a toilet. No bomb factories if that's what you're thinking." It wasn't what I'd been thinking, but Hyman stopped and opened one of the doors anyway. "Don't even lock them anymore. Just keep the doors closed to keep from having to see what's inside." The office was wrecked: desk and chairs overturned, drawers and papers strewn on the floor. "The cops keep tossing the place. Doesn't pay to keep cleaning the mess."

"Something bothers me," I said. "How did Aikens get here so fast? And the other cops, too."

Landfors stared at the wreckage. "They were probably watching the place."

"All the time," said Hyman. "Of course, we watch them, too." My face must have shown something, because he smiled and explained, "We all spy on each other. Neither side does anything that the other doesn't know about."

The three of us went back into the main hall. I remembered the anonymous phone call I'd gotten, and that someone must have seen me with Donner. "Are your people keeping an eye on a fellow named Hub Donner?"

"Ah, Donner," Hyman said, his eyes twinkling behind his spectacles. "An old and cherished enemy of my people."

"Huh?"

"Donner's been fighting us for years. Capitalists pay him a lot of money to keep honest men from eating. The last few years, he's been with the Ford Service Department out at the Highland Park plant."

"A repairman?"

Hyman and Landfors both laughed. Landfors said, "More like military service. It's Ford's private police force."

"Union busters," put in Hyman.

As we walked to the front exit, I noticed the Wobblies were all clustered there staring at us.

"Anything else I can do for you?" Hyman finally asked.

"Think we're all set," said Landfors. He raised his eyebrows at me.

"All set," I agreed.

Hyman said good-bye and Landfors and I started toward the door. To my relief, the men made way for us to pass through, shooting nothing more deadly at us than angry glares.

I expected that when I met my teammates in Cleveland, they'd be looking at me much the same way. Except they'd be holding baseball bats.

# *Chapter Six*
○ ○ ○

The pallid grass of League Park was patchy and tentative, perhaps not quite convinced that spring had arrived. The clay of the base paths, still frozen, seemed equally uncertain; pebbles bulged from its terra-cotta surface like wary groundhogs checking to see if they should go back into hibernation.

There was no sunshine to brighten the view of the diamond; low, dark skies were threatening rain, possibly the same storm clouds that had caused two of the scheduled games in Chicago to be postponed. Now they'd drifted over to Cleveland, following the Tigers team. I didn't consider myself superstitious, but the current weather pattern couldn't be considered a good omen for the new season.

Although the playing ground wasn't yet in prime condition, it was the Elysian Fields compared to the parks we'd slogged through during the spring-training tour. For me, it was enough that it was a major-league ball field, the first one I'd been on since last September.

Not that I was doing much. I stood alone in foul territory,

between first base and the visitors' dugout, watching the other Tigers go through pregame warm-ups.

Several were lined up for batting practice. Ty Cobb, who had to be first at everything, was already in the cage; as he sprayed line drives around the park, he repeatedly cursed the pitcher for not throwing the ball exactly as he wanted.

Along the right-field foul line, starting pitcher Howard Ehmke, a tall right-hander who threw the sharpest curveball in baseball, warmed up with catcher Oscar Stanage.

Tossing the ball near Ehmke were my rivals: the infielders. For me to break into the lineup, one of them would have to be injured or in need of rest. The Detroit infielders were discouragingly healthy, but I hoped to benefit from their spotty playing records. Second baseman Ralph Young had a career batting average of only .200. Rookie Babe Pinelli, slated for third base, had yet to prove himself a major-league player. Donie Bush, the Tigers veteran shortstop, was starting to slow down, and his range wasn't what it used to be. On the whole, I thought I had a good chance of playing fifty or sixty games this year, and possibly earning a starting position.

But it looked like I had no chance of touching a baseball today. I fidgeted in my road flannels, scraped my spikes at the hard ground, and started slapping my mitt against my hip. My wrist wasn't good enough for me to take batting practice, but I did want to throw the ball some. The problem was that no one wanted to play catch with the man who killed Emmett Siever.

My teammates hadn't welcomed me back with open arms, but at least they hadn't greeted my arrival with firearms either. Dutch Leonard was the only one who'd been openly hostile; among other things, he'd asked if I felt like a hero for gunning down a sixty-year-old man. I'd tried to dismiss Leonard's words; the burly pitcher was known for having a disposition as nasty as Cobb's, and this was nothing out of the ordinary for him. He failed to rouse the other players against me and eventually dropped the goading. The Tigers, who seemed to enjoy quarreling among themselves as much as the Wobblies liked sing-alongs, had so many factions and internal squabbles that they couldn't even cooperate long enough to gang up on me. Not on short notice, anyway.

Hughie Jennings had been indifferent to my return to the team; he did little more than grunt when I'd reported to him. The Tigers' manager was entangled in his own battles, especially with Frank Navin and Jack Coombs. Navin had hired former Athletics pitcher Coombs to coach the pitching staff, and Jennings took it as a challenge to his authority, convinced that Navin was planning to give Coombs the managing job. As a result, Jennings paid even less attention to the players than he used to, and they took advantage to pursue their own petty wars.

A low rumble of thunder came from the direction of Lake Erie. I suddenly realized how dim things really looked.

It had been so different a year ago. When the 1919 season opened, the nation was celebrating its victory in the Great War, rejoicing in the safe return of those doughboys who'd survived and honoring the memory of those who hadn't. The major-league baseball owners, who'd spent most of the war trying to exempt their players from serving, deftly tried to change history by crediting ballplayers with winning the war. Opening Day ceremonies at Cubs Park included a lengthy eulogy for Eddie Grant, my teammate on the 1914 Giants, who'd been killed in the Argonne. The Chicago players who'd served, such as Grover Cleveland Alexander and me, were singled out for lavish praise during the team introductions. It was such a promising spring. Returning to the National League Champions, the chances were strong that by the end of the season I'd finally realize my ambition of playing in the World Series. But came October, the Cubs were twenty games behind the pennant-winning Cincinnati Reds. A month later, I was sold to Detroit for less than the price of a used Studebaker. I now tried to console myself that perhaps this season would do the reverse: start lousy and end in triumph.

"How about a catch?" came a cheerful voice behind me. I turned to Bobby Veach, our left fielder; he'd finished at the batting cage and retrieved his glove from the bench. Veach was one of the few good-natured men on the Tigers. The kind of guy who, if he was captain of a sandlot team, would always pick the kid brother nobody else wanted.

"Sure," I said. "Thanks." That's what I'd been reduced to: the pathetic kid nobody wanted to play with.

We walked out on the right-field grass and started exchanging casual throws, gradually increasing the distance between us. Bobby Veach was an easygoing Kentuckian who always acted apologetic about being in the major leagues— despite coming off a season in which he'd batted .355 and led the league in hits, doubles, and triples. That kind of performance was almost expected of a Detroit outfielder. The saying was, "Put a Tiger uniform on an outfielder, and you have a .300 hitter." Unfortunately, there was no corresponding adage for utility infielders who wore the Old English "D" on their jerseys.

The distance was too long to talk, and all I was doing

was playing catch, the same as a million kids could do, but that simple act felt good—it gave me hope.

○ ○ ○

The Detroit outfielders didn't do much hitting during the first six innings. They did do a lot of running, chasing after doubles and triples banged out by the Cleveland batters. It was no easy task, for League Park had a peculiar outfield. The furthest corner of center field was the deepest in the majors, stretching more than five hundred feet from home plate. The right-field fence was less than three hundred feet down the line, but more than forty feet high, with a screen of chicken wire and steel girders atop a concrete wall. A ball batted into the screen was in play, and could carom unpredictably—Tris Speaker drove a double off one of the girders which ended up being fielded by Bobby Veach in left-center.

On the Tigers bench, with our team down by eight runs and their interest in the game waning, Dutch Leonard and Chick Fogarty turned their attention to me. Fogarty was a lumbering second-string catcher who had trouble remembering that the signs were one finger for a fastball and two for a curve. He'd latched on to Leonard during spring training, serving as a combination sidekick and errand boy.

Leonard gave me worse than Fogarty did, calling me, "war hero" as if it was an expletive and asking if I planned to murder any more old men. Fogarty followed Leonard's lead like an echo. Then the two of them sat on either side of me and tried to squeeze me between them—a bush-league maneuver that I didn't think even happened in the minors anymore. I steeled my body against the squeeze and ignored their words. I kept reminding myself that Leonard was a lefty and therefore not a rational person, and Fogarty was merely parroting his roommate. The more I ignored them, the louder and uglier their taunts became.

At the end of the seventh inning, Hughie Jennings pulled himself off the bench. On his way to the third-base coach's box, he said, "I'm sick of the noise coming from over here. Put a sock in it!" Jennings stepped out of the dugout, then added, "Rawlings, go coach first. That ought to keep things peaceful."

I squirted out from between Leonard and Fogarty like one of Dutch's spitballs. Reflexively, I reached for my mitt, then dropped it when I realized I didn't need a glove. Trotting to first base, I felt empty-handed but full of authority. This was my first time coaching in the big leagues. From utility player to coach seemed quite a promotion, for whatever reason and however temporary.

While Cleveland's Stan Coveleski warmed up on the mound, it dawned on me that I didn't know exactly what a first-base coach was supposed to do. I'd seen them in action, of course, but all I could remember was that they clapped their hands a lot and dispensed pointless chatter like "Way to go!" or "Let's get it started!"

I felt naked and conspicuous in the coach's box. Looking around, I directed my attention to the Indians on the field. Several of them had been teammates of mine on the 1912 Red Sox: Tris Speaker, now the Indians' center fielder and manager; third baseman Larry Gardner; and Smoky Joe Wood. Wood was no longer a pitcher and no longer smoky; he was now an outfielder, and with the exception of Babe Ruth, the best hitting ex-pitcher in the game.

When Bobby Veach came to bat, I looked over to Hughie Jennings for guidance as to what a base coach should do. Jennings went through his trademark routine, first bending down and pulling tufts of grass from around the third-base box, then standing on one leg and issuing a rebel "Ee-yah" yell. He seemed twenty years older than when I'd seen him eight years ago. The cry was a hoarse echo of what it had once been, and the old manager appeared to have trouble keeping his balance on one leg. And I still wasn't sure what I was supposed to do.

After Veach popped out to short, Ty Cobb came to bat. "Let's get it started!" I yelled, clapping my hands.

Cobb did, dragging a bunt single. It wasn't the best way to try to start a rally when behind by eight runs, but it did boost Cobb's batting average—which was usually more important to him than the outcome of the game.

Nonetheless, I said, "Way to go!" when he reached first base. Improvising, I clapped my hands again and added, "Way to get things started."

He shot me a lethal look and hissed, "Shut up, busher, or I'll knock your goddamn teeth out." Ty Cobb epitomized the sort of team spirit that existed on the Tigers.

I tucked my hands back in my pocket and shut up. But I silently hoped that Cobb would get picked off or thrown out stealing.

Neither happened. He was left stranded at first, and we went on to lose the game 12–4, our third loss in a row. At least the defeat had nothing to do with my base coaching.

○ ○ ○

After the game, I went directly to Public Square and checked into my room at the Hotel Cleveland. I was to share it with Lou Vedder, a rookie pitcher who hadn't worked a single inning in the majors. He'd seemed a nice enough kid during spring training, lacking the cocksure attitude typical of most young pitchers. I briefly considered taking Vedder to dinner, but decided it wouldn't be fair to him—the other Tigers would have given him a hard time for associating with me. So I unpacked quickly and left the room, with the vague intent of catching a movie.

When I stepped out of the hotel elevator, I spotted Hughie Jennings in one of the lobby's oversize wing chairs. It was a manager's job to watch the comings and goings of his players, and make sure they were all in by curfew. What he usually did was use his post in the lobby to hold court, talking baseball with everyone from players and writers to fans and hotel staff. Jennings seldom attracted an audience anymore, though. He sat alone, his eyes directed at the carpet, raising them hopefully now and then at passersby. A newspaper was in his lap, not quite concealing the silver pocket flask underneath it. It was no secret on the team that Jennings was ailing and boozing, and each of those factors contributed to the other.

I'd noticed in spring training that Hughie Jennings had become virtually a baseball outcast. Few of his own players were on speaking terms with him, and he was often ridiculed in print as a has-been. I hated to see him treated that way. Jennings had been star shortstop for the celebrated Baltimore Orioles of the 1890s. Later, in his first three seasons as manager of the Tigers, he led the team to three straight pennants from 1907 to 1909. But in baseball you don't get to keep your job based on what you accomplished in years past. Jennings was now no longer a winner, his health was poor, and at age fifty-one he was about to be discarded from the game.

There was a bare flicker of a smile as I approached him. Jennings's once fiery red hair was fading to gray, the twinkle was gone from his Irish blue eyes, and he rarely grinned. But he looked pleased that his utility infielder was still speaking to him.

"Hi, Hughie," I said, taking an armchair across from his. "Thanks for letting me coach first today."

"Hell," he said. "My grandmother could be a first-base coach, and she's dead. Kept you out of trouble, anyway."

Ignoring the comparison with his deceased grandmother, I said, "I can play now, whenever you want me to. Got a note from the doctor saying my wrist's okay, and it felt fine when I was throwing with Veach today."

"I'll keep that in mind." He drew out the flask and took a swallow, then tucked it back under the paper. Prohibition wasn't taken too seriously in this part of the country but no sense taking chances. Jennings exhaled sharply, the scent of whiskey filling the air like spray from a perfume bottle.

"By the way," I said. "I was wondering. When we talked on the phone, you said the guys were real pissed at me. Any of them in particular?"

"You think I got nuthin' better to do than listen to them babies bellyache? They piss and moan about every damn thing. Was never like that in the old days." He wiped his mouth with the back of his hand. "Used to be a player didn't think about nuthin' but baseball." His dim eyes grew dreamy, and I thought he was about to launch into stories of the "old days."

As much as I would have liked to hear them, I realized I might be able to direct his recollections to a more useful purpose. "You were playing about the same time as Emmett Siever," I said. "Did you know him at all?"

Jennings nodded. "We were teammates once. Came to mind when I read about you killing him."

"I didn't . . ." I dropped my protest when I realized Jennings wasn't listening anyway.

"My first season," he went on, "with Louisville, 1891. A bum team, no pitching staff. Same as I got now—how the hell am I supposed to win a pennant without a goddamn pitching staff?"

"Got to have pitchers," I said. "So what about Emmett Siever?"

"He was an outfielder. But we already had a solid outfield: Patsy Donovan, Farmer Weaver, and Chicken Wolf. Siever hardly got into a game all year. So he did his playing at night—whorehouses and saloons. From what I heard, he'd always been like that—knew the red-light districts better than he knew the ballparks. And him with a wife and baby girl at home. Shameful, if you ask me." He paused for more whiskey. "Patsy Donovan, he turned into a fine hitter. And his little brother—Wild Bill—was about the best pitcher I ever had. Couldn't have won them pennants without him. Him and George Mullin. If Navin would get me pitchers like Donovan and Mullin, I'd win him a goddamn pennant. But can't—"

"Can't do it without pitchers," I finished. "You remember anything else about Emmett Siever?"

"We never played on the same team after that one year, but we saw each other from time to time. Even met his wife once—sweetest little lady you ever saw. Shame what happened."

"You mean about him running around on her?"

"I mean about her dying. In childbirth, trying to give him a son. Her and the baby both. After that, Siever changed his ways for a while, but then took to feeling sorry for himself and went back to whoring and boozing."

When Jennings took another pull at the bottle, some of it leaked down his chin. Embarrassed for him, I turned my head and saw a foursome of Tigers get out of the elevator. Dutch Leonard was one of them, with Chick Fogarty on his heels. Leonard pulled up short, elbowed Fogarty, and nodded in my direction. They probably thought I was trying to play teacher's pet in talking to the manager. After a lingering look at us, they went into the hotel dining room.

Trying to elicit a little more information from Jennings, I asked, "Siever was never active in unionizing back then?"

"Hell no," he snorted. "Barstools and bordellos, that's where he was active. And sometimes on the ballfield. There wasn't much union talk anymore anyway by the time I came up to the bigs. Players League had just folded, you know."

I murmured that I did know.

"Damn fools, if you ask me. Monte Ward and Tim Keefe were the ones behind it. Complaining about the reserve clause and saying ballplayers were treated like 'slaves.' We made damn good salaries for 'slaves'—hell of a lot more than you could ever make in the coal mines." Jennings coughed, long and hard. After he caught his breath again, he said, "Baseball is the way it is, and you don't go trying to change it—that only causes trouble and nobody likes trouble. Keep your nose clean, and you're set for life. After you stop playing, you can be a coach. Then, if you got brains, a manager. And—" His face furrowed, and I could tell that he was wondering what came after managing. "All I need is a couple good pitchers," he murmured.

I soon took leave of Jennings and left the hotel to find a meal. Strangely, having learned what a scoundrel Emmett Siever had been, I felt less guilty about taking his life. I had to remind myself that I really hadn't killed him.

One thing I was clear on: it was unfair that a man like Siever could do what he'd done and be remembered as a great guy while Hughie Jennings could give thirty good years to baseball and be discarded like an old scorecard.

I wondered what Jennings would do if Frank Navin fired him. Would he end up a night watchman or a bartender like so many other former stars?

Then my thoughts turned to myself: what would *I* do if I could no longer get a job in baseball?

○ ○ ○

I walked through Cleveland's theater district, a spaghetti dinner sitting heavy in my stomach, still fretting over just about everything. Amid the vaudeville and burlesque houses were movie marquees advertising Mary Pickford's *Pollyanna*, Gloria Swanson in Cecil B. DeMille's *Why Change Your Wife*, and *The Sporting Duchess* starring Alice Joyce. None of them tempted me. What I needed was something to make me laugh.

At Ninth and Prospect, I came to The Strand, which was featuring Harold Lloyd's latest comedy *Haunted Spooks*. I was about to enter when a poorly lit marquee half a block away caught my eye. Headlining at Grand Vaudeville was *Serial Queen Marguerite Turner*. I grinned so broadly at seeing the name that the muscles in my cheeks ached. Margie Turner!

Harold Lloyd forgotten, I rushed to the Grand's ticket booth and paid thirty cents for a third-row seat. I walked into the half-empty theater as the Four Harmony Kings were perpetrating a barbershop quartet rendition of "How Ya Gonna Keep 'Em Down on the Farm After They've Seen Paree." The shabby interior, reeking of mildew and perspiration, smelled almost as bad as the music. A smattering of applause greeted the end of the song, and "Eccentric Comedian Milo" came out to perform bird imitations. I sat through three more acts until the card on the easel read:

> MARGUERITE TURNER
> *Recreating Scenes from*
> *"Dangers of the Dark Continent"*

The curtain parted to reveal a jungle set consisting of potted trees, hanging vines, and a backdrop illustrated with birds, snakes, and monkeys. The painted creatures on the canvas sheet were more frightening than the live, ancient, shaggy-maned lion that stood in the center of the stage. The heavy chain attached to one of the animal's unsteady legs eliminated any sense of danger.

From the wings, a young girl in a frilly pink dress walked out twirling a parasol. The lion roared something like a yawn, and in fine melodramatic style the girl squealed, "Help! Help!" A rolled-up newspaper poked out from behind a potted plant and smacked the lion's rear paw, causing him to roar again.

Bounding into the scene came Marguerite Turner, wearing jodhpurs and a pith helmet. "Get back!" she warned the passive beast.

At the sight of Miss Turner, I stopped wondering why a little girl would be strolling through the jungle with a parasol in the first place. My complete attention shifted to the actress I had known as Margie.

It had been six years ago, when I was playing for the Giants and Margie was making pictures with the Vitagraph Studio in Brooklyn. I'd watched her film scenes for the serial that she was now "recreating"—I'd even gotten bit parts in a couple of them. The movie versions hadn't been much more realistic than the portrayal on the stage, but Margie Turner was very real—and very special. We'd had an incredible time together until her career took her to Hollywood.

Margie moved slowly toward the lion. She then sprang at him, her helmet falling off. Her long brown hair tossed from side to side as she wrestled the big cat hand to hand. The little girl put her hand over her eyes, but there was no cause for fear. The lion looked pleased that someone was playing with him.

I went back to thinking of the times Margie and I had had together—at Coney Island, in the movie studio, at the ballpark. The romance had been more magical than anything the movies could create. Despite the fact that a friend of hers had been murdered and we'd had to track down the killer.

The lion made a playful swat with its paw, and the girl screamed. Margie pulled a revolver from its holster and fired at the animal. The report of the cap pistol was so feeble that some in the theater laughed. The big cat rolled over, supposedly dead, but looking like he wanted his belly rubbed. Margie untied the girl, who gratefully hugged her rescuer. The curtain fell and the audience applauded—not as enthusiastically as they had for Milo's bird imitations but louder than for the Four Harmony Kings.

When Josie Flynn's Female Minstrels took the stage, I debated whether to leave quietly, grateful that some fond memories had been rekindled, or take the risk of meeting her again and possibly having those memories diminished somehow.

The debate took all of about a minute.

I found the usher, a teenage boy with a spectacular case of acne, sweeping the lobby floor. I told him I wanted to see Marguerite Turner.

"You and every other stage door Johnny," he said.

"You don't understand. I'm a friend of hers."

"Yeah, you and every other stage door Johnny."

"Can you give her a message?"

He looked me over, probably to determine what I could afford, before naming his price. "Sure. For half a buck."

I thought I was dressed well enough to be charged a dollar, but wasn't going to argue. Putting two coins in the boy's hand, I said, "Tell her Mickey Rawlings would very much like to see her."

He hesitated. "Mickey Rawlings . . . the one who killed that Red in Detroit?"

Why doesn't anyone ever say "Mickey Rawlings the baseball player?" I wondered. "Uh, no," I said. "That wasn't me."

The kid looked skeptical. "All right, I'll tell her. Wait here."

I checked my watch half a dozen times in the ten minutes

until the usher returned. "She's coming," he said. "Soon as she's dressed." Picking up his broom, he resumed relocating trash from one corner of the floor to another.

It was another fifteen minutes until Margie Turner appeared. Her lithe figure was cloaked in a white middy blouse with a slightly crooked black tie and a provocatively short blue skirt that fell to only mid-calf. I stared at a face that was more beautiful than I remembered: heavy-lidded, dark, laughing eyes; full, bemused lips; a tawny complexion framed by long, flowing, chestnut hair.

"Hello, Mickey." The throaty voice sent a tremor through me.

"Hi. You look . . . great."

The usher snorted, and I heard him mumble, "What a smooth talker."

"Would you like to . . . go to dinner?"

She smiled. "It's almost ten o'clock."

"Oh, how about . . ." C'mon, Mickey, think of something.

"A walk?" she suggested.

"Yes." I let out a breath of relief and offered my arm.

Outside in the cool spring night, Margie said she was staying at the Winton and suggested we walk in that direction. I agreed, silently hoping that the hotel was a long distance away. Seeing her on stage had brought back memories; her touch on my arm had triggered a tingling of my heartstrings.

We strolled slowly, oblivious to the downtown crowds, chatting easily about nothing of importance. I was immediately comfortable with her, as though we were *meant* to walk side by side. We'd gone more than a block before I noticed she was limping. "Did the lion hurt your leg?" I asked.

"That sweet old cat? No, he couldn't hurt a fly." She

patted her right hip. "Fell off a camel two years ago making a desert movie. Studio put me on morphine till the picture was finished. Then I had an operation to put my hip back together. It feels fine now, but I walk a little funny. That's why I'm doing vaudeville. The studio fired me—told me people don't go to the movies to watch cripples." She tried to laugh it off, but her voice cracked. "Nobody in Hollywood would take me."

"I'm sorry. I think you look wonderful."

"You too. As handsome as I remembered." She patted my arm. "I read about you in the papers. About shooting that man in Detroit." With concern in her voice, she asked, "Are you in trouble?"

"No, just a misunderstanding." I didn't want to go into it with her. Being with Margie again had me thinking of the happy times before the war. I yearned to go back to those days of innocence, for things to be the way they used to.

We talked little the rest of the way, and mostly of what we were both doing now. No questions about the past six years; no inquiries about other sweethearts.

In far too little time, we reached her hotel. I coaxed her into circling the block once, and then once again, before I said, "I'll be here two more nights. Would you like to go out tomorrow?"

"I'm sorry." She shook her head. "Tonight was our last show at the Grand. We're leaving for Toledo in the morning."

I was too disappointed to say anything.

"It was nice seeing you again though." She planted a kiss on my cheek. "Good night."

I didn't return the good-bye until she'd passed through the hotel door.

I trudged back to the Tigers hotel. I'd been on my own for most of my life, and never really minded being alone. But after parting from Margie Turner, I found myself feeling more lonesome than I ever had before.

Back at the Cleveland, I saw Hughie Jennings asleep in his lobby chair. When I stopped at the front desk for my room key, the clerk handed me a note along with it.

I unfolded the torn scrap of paper and read: *You'll never be part of this team. Leave before it's to late.* The spelling of "to" made me think it was genuinely written by one of my teammates.

If the message was supposed to scare me, it didn't succeed. Nothing they might do could be worse than losing Margie Turner again.

# Chapter Seven

ooo

**C**obb's Lake reflected afternoon sunlight directly into my eyes, causing me to squint as I stepped into the batter's box for practice. The body of water, more of a puddle than a lake, was Navin Field's most notorious feature. Conceived by Ty Cobb and created by the Detroit groundskeeper, it was designed to help the Georgia Peach successfully lay down bunts. Before each game, the area in front of home plate was flooded so that bunted balls would die in the mud and fielders attempting to grab them would slip. After a few innings, most of the water usually soaked into the ground. For now, fresh from the hose and with the earth too hard to absorb it, Cobb's Lake sat a motionless pool, its surface barely rippled by the westerly breeze.

I'd had to fight for a turn at the plate, the same as a rookie just up from the bush leagues. If Bobby Veach hadn't let me in ahead of him, I likely would have come to blows for a chance to hit—and was fully prepared to resort to that if necessary. Once in the box, I assumed a left-handed batting stance to go easy on my right wrist. I didn't expect to hit well; I merely wanted to swing a bat in a setting more realistic than my parlor and get used to facing a live pitcher again.

That pitcher was my road roomie, Lou Vedder. After my too-brief encounter with Margie Turner, I'd spent most of the remaining Cleveland visit in the hotel, doing little more than mope, pine, and sulk. I'd talked just enough with Vedder to learn that he was from Oakville, a small town southwest of Detroit, and that a contingent of his family and friends would be coming to our home opener. Hughie Jennings was doing Vedder a kindness by letting him throw batting practice so that his fan club could see him pitch in a big-league ball-park—until game time, when Dutch Leonard would take over.

The odd thing was that there was also a batting practice *catcher:* Chick Fogarty. By having a catcher behind the plate, Frank Navin didn't need to stock up on as many baseballs, and saved himself a few dollars.

I swung awkwardly at the fat tosses Vedder lobbed up, poking a few loopers over the infield and mostly hitting routine grounders toward third. My wrist held up fine, and after getting around on one of his pitches enough to pull a decent line drive between first and second, I declared a victory of sorts and called it quits.

Dutch Leonard yelled from where he was warming up, "Wanna see if you can hit *my* stuff, busher?"

I looked around and saw the other players watching me. No way was I going to back out of his challenge. "Don't see why I couldn't! Everybody else can!"

Leonard walked out to the mound and Vedder stepped aside. I took my place in the box, expecting that I'd have to use my ducking reflexes more than my bat.

Chick Fogarty cackled, "Watch yer head, kid. Dutch might be a little wild today."

His control turned out to be fine. He put his fastballs exactly where he wanted: at my nose, behind my neck, and a couple at my ear. I evaded each throw without giving him the satisfaction of hitting the dirt.

Then he aimed one at my knee and I skipped back just in time. "Nice dance," said Fogarty as he cocked his arm to return the ball. On impulse, I snatched it from his grip, reared back, and hurled the ball at Leonard as hard as I could. See how he likes it, I thought. Taken by surprise, Leonard flung his hands up and ducked instead of catching the ball in his glove, which earned him some hoots from the players.

I left the box, and turned my back on the fuming Leonard. As I walked to the bench, our baby-faced bat boy came running up to me. "Mr. Navin wants to see you," the twelve-year-old said breathlessly, pointing to a box seat on the third-base side of the field.

Handing the boy my bat, I veered over to the owner's box. Prior to this moment, I'd only seen Frank Navin in photographs. Round, bald, and bespectacled, the team's former bookkeeper still looked more like an accountant than a magnate. Navin was a smaller, nearsighted version of the man seated to his right: Hub Donner, professional union buster.

When I reached the railing, I said, "Hello, Mr. Navin. You wanted to see me?" I avoided looking at Donner.

"Think you're Ty Cobb, batting left-handed?" Navin said. I had the impression it was supposed to be good-natured kidding, but I couldn't be sure from his expression. Navin wasn't known as "old poker face" for nothing.

"Wish I was." I smiled my best aw-shucks smile. "I'm trying to learn to switch hit." I didn't mention wanting to save stress on my wrist. If Navin thought I was damaged goods, I might be dropped from his payroll.

Donner patted the arm that I'd draped along the railing. "Well, you got a ways to go from the looks of it!"

"Yeah. Guess so." I kept my eyes on Navin and took my arm off the railing.

After a moment's silence, the Tigers owner said, "Mr. Donner tells me you're reluctant to do what he asks." His tone was decidedly not good-natured.

I abandoned my smile and tried to adopt an expression as innocent as the bat boy's. "Well, yeah, I am. See, I don't know anything about politics or unions, and I want to keep it that way. I don't want to get involved on either side." I looked Navin straight in the eyes, and said with total honesty, "All I wanna do is play ball."

Navin's fleshy face tightened. "That's understandable, I suppose."

Grinning for no apparent reason, Hub Donner broke in, "What is *not* understandable is why you went to Fraternity Hall again." Donner's severe tone was at odds with his jovial expression. "Going once to confront Emmett Siever, that's fine—commendable even. But last Saturday you went again. That can start to look like you're in sympathy with the Wobblies, and that's bad. Don't you think, Mr. Navin?"

"Very bad," Navin agreed.

Leo Hyman had been right: Donner—or an associate of his—did have Fraternity Hall under surveillance. Or somebody was following me.

"I wouldn't recommend going there again," said Donner. "Would you, Mr. Navin?"

"No, I wouldn't."

"Okay," I said. "I get the message."

Donner's body convulsed with an inexplicable belly laugh. "One more thing," he said. "You seem to be chummy with a Karl Landfors—a known Red. Staying at your place, isn't he?"

"Yup."

"Well, I recommend you find some new friends." He emitted a genuine chuckle. "Dutch Leonard ain't gonna be one of them from the looks of it, but there's gotta be other guys you can pal around with. Landfors is only going to bring you trouble." He merely glanced at Navin this time, and the Tigers' boss silently nodded agreement.

I faced Donner directly. "Karl Landfors has been a friend of mine for years. Saved my life once, among other things. To me, that counts for a lot. I don't care what his politics are, and he don't care that I haven't any at all. So if it's all the same to you—and even if it isn't—Karl Landfors will be welcome in my home for as long as he wants to stay."

"Loyalty is admirable," said Donner. "Just be careful where you place it. You might come to regret your choice of 'comrades.' Consider yourself forewarned."

Shifting my gaze to the Tigers' owner, I said, "Anything else, Mr. Navin?"

"No, son." He didn't look angry, or pleased. Navin's lips were taut and horizontal, not giving me a clue to his frame of mind. Barely perceptibly, they finally twitched up at the corners. "Let's see if we can win this one today," he said.

As I turned away, I realized that Donner had done it again.

The smiling and laughing, patting my arm—it must have looked to anyone watching that we'd been having a friendly chat. Half a dozen Detroit Tigers stood around the batting cage, with malice in their faces and their bats held high. And these were the players who'd already taken batting practice.

○ ○ ○

After a few Opening Day speeches and ceremonies, wheelchair-bound Charlie Bennett was rolled out to a spot behind home plate. An enormously popular catcher with the Detroit Wolverines in the 1880s, Bennett's career had ended when he fell beneath a train and lost both legs. When a new baseball field was erected on the corner of Michigan and Trumbull in 1896, it was christened Bennett Park in his honor. That lasted until Frank Navin bought the Tigers and rebuilt the park in steel and concrete. When it reopened in April 1912, on the same day as Boston's Fenway Park, the Detroit home grounds had a new name: Navin Field. All that was left for Charlie Bennett was an annual appearance to catch the ceremonial first pitch. To me, that illustrated one of the differences between players and magnates: ballplayers earn their honors; owners buy them.

The game got under way, and the fans settled back for what promised to be a fine pitching matchup: Dutch Leonard against Chicago's Eddie Cicotte.

With Leonard on the mound and Chick Fogarty unable to think for himself, I was left in peace on the bench. Through the first few innings, I studied the players on the field, mentally cataloging their tendencies for future reference: did they play deep or shallow, were they pull hitters or did they hit to the opposite field, how far could they hit, how fast did they run.

When I looked at the White Sox, though, I couldn't stay focused on their mechanics. I remembered what Hub Donner had said about the Sox throwing last year's World Series. He wasn't the only one to say it; there'd been stories in the press and rampant rumors. Who on the Chicago team could have been involved, I wondered. Certainly not Joe Jackson, Eddie Collins, Ray Shalk, or Buck Weaver—they were all too upstanding. Cicotte and Lefty Williams, who'd pitched like a couple of sandlotters in the series, were the most likely candidates, I thought.

I shifted from wondering who to imagining why. Why would a major-league ballplayer conspire to lose baseball's most important event? I wouldn't know *how* to play to lose, and couldn't fathom any player doing so, no matter how much money gamblers might offer him. Once you're on the diamond, in the throes of a ball game, there's only one way to play: all out, to win.

Some of the present game action did filter through to me. Cicotte was pitching strong, holding the Tigers scoreless through the first three innings. Dutch Leonard wasn't faring as well; he gave up three runs in the first, two in the second, and one in the third. Despite the improving trend, Hughie Jennings sent him to the showers and began a parade of the younger pitchers, giving them one inning each. Jennings and pitching coach Jack Coombs bickered constantly, the manager refusing to take any of Coombs's suggestions.

Going into the top of the eighth, with Chicago ahead 8–1, Jennings sent Lou Vedder to the mound. I was happy for the kid that he was getting to make his major-league debut in a no-pressure situation.

When Vedder started off by giving up a double to Buck Weaver, I cringed. When he walked the next batter on four pitches, I shook my head. Don't blow it, kid. Jennings cussed, and Coombs gloated.

C'mon, I silently cheered Vedder on, put it over the plate. He went into his stretch, then staggered backward, clasping a hand to his eye.

"Balk!" cried the plate umpire. The White Sox runners each advanced a base.

Jeers and catcalls and more than a few laughs came from the stands. At this point, Jennings should have sent Jack Coombs to talk with Vedder and settle him down. Instead, the manager pointedly looked away from Coombs and turned to me. "Rawlings! You're his roomie. Go see what the hell that kid's problem is."

I bolted from the bench and ran to the mound, with as little idea of what to say to a pitcher as how to coach first base. Vedder's face was lowered and his shoulders sagged. This had to be damned embarrassing for him, with his friends and family watching.

Plunging my hands in my back pockets the way a manager would, I said, "What happened, kid?"

"Couldn't help it, Mick. A bug flew in my eye."

Not knowing what to say to that, I kicked my spikes at the ground in the belief that it was a very manageresque thing to do. The crowd murmured with impatience. I lifted my head to the grandstand; twenty thousand pairs of eyes looked back at me, and I realized how scared Lou Vedder must feel as the center of attention. "A bug flew in your eye,"

I repeated. "Look, kid, if you're gonna pitch in the big leagues, you gotta learn to catch 'em in your mouth."

He bobbed his lowered head. "Okay. I'll try."

"Just throw the ball over the plate," I said.

Back in the dugout, I reported to Jennings, "No problem. He'll be fine." I kept my eye on Vedder, who was staring after me. Then his whole body appeared to relax and he smiled, perhaps having finally realized what I'd said. He wiped his mitt over his forehead and proceeded to retire the next three batters in a row, two of them on strikeouts.

Jennings left him in there for the ninth inning, and again Vedder shut down the White Sox hitters. The final score of the Tigers' sixth consecutive loss was 8–2, and the fans were merciless in their booing. It was no consolation that their jeers weren't directed at me. I wanted to be playing for a winner. Even if I wasn't actually playing.

○ ○ ○

On the walk home from the ballpark, I entertained the notion of dropping my queries into Emmett Siever's murder.

I wondered if it might be best to do exactly what I'd claimed to Donner and Navin—concentrate on baseball and stay out of labor conflicts. If I stopped nosing around, showing that I was on no one's side, then perhaps both sides would realize that I wasn't a threat and leave me alone.

It didn't take long for me to realize that wishful thinking wasn't going to make my problems disappear. What had me in trouble wasn't what I was going to do in the future, but what people thought I had done to Emmett Siever last week. The IWW would still want revenge—to throw me from the train, as the phone caller had phrased it. Nor did Hub Donner appear likely to let go of the change to capitalize on Siever's shooting by using me for antiunion propaganda.

The only way for me to get in the clear was to find out who really killed Emmett Siever. That should satisfy the Wobblies, Hub Donner, and my teammates. It struck me as odd that the police weren't on that list. The police should have been the most interested in solving his murder, but they were the only ones content to leave the case alone. More than that, they'd gone to the trouble of planting a gun on Siever so they could dismiss me as having killed him in self-defense. Why would the police care about me? Why plant the gun? Why invent the self-defense story?

When I entered my apartment, Karl Landfors was sitting primly on the sofa, one hand holding a hardcover book close to his face. He lowered it enough to peer over the top. "I think it's obvious who killed Emmett Siever," he said, smirking.

I hung my jacket on a nail in the back of the door and hooked my straw boater over the resulting lump. "Not to me," I said. I stepped into the kitchen and was annoyed to discover that there was no ginger ale left in the icebox. In its place were bottles of Moxie that Landfors must have bought. I opened one of them and brought it into the parlor. Seating myself in the rocking chair, I took a long swallow. It tasted like carbonated vegetable juice—the perfect beverage for Karl Landfors, I thought.

My houseguest used a dust-jacket flap to mark his page and put the book on the coffee table. Looking exasperated, he said, "Aren't you going to ask who it is?"

I twisted my head to see the title of the book: *Main Street* by Sinclair Lewis. "That any good?"

"Yes."

Landfors was getting peeved, and I felt pleased at having brought that about. He was such a natural irritant, that it was fun to outdo him now and then. But I wasn't cruel enough to torment him for long. "Okay, Karl. Who done it?"

His face made a rapid transition from peeved to smug. "Aikens. Or whatever his name really is. Except for you, he was the first person in the back room after it happened—he probably just stayed there after he killed Siever. And there's no real Detective Aikens on the police force. Why would he impersonate an officer if he didn't have something to hide?"

I took another sip of the Moxie and craved a beer. "I don't think it's him, Karl, whoever he really is." I'd already considered the possibility of Aikens being the shooter.

"And why not?"

"Two reasons. For one thing, if he shot Siever, why didn't he just leave? There was a back door. Why didn't he use it to get away? If you murder somebody, I'd expect the natural impulse is to get away as fast as possible. Why stay around with the corpse?"

"Maybe the door was locked."

"Don't see how. There was a crossbar on the door—on the *inside* of the door. I saw it when we were there with Leo Hyman. That would keep people from coming in, not from leaving. All the killer had to do was lift the bar, and he's out."

Landfors frowned. "You said 'two reasons.'"

"The second thing is that Aikens must be some kind of official, even if he's not with the Detroit Police."

"And how did you deduce that?"

"How else did the cops know to pin the shooting on

me? Aikens was the only person who talked to me after it happened. He must have been the one who told the cops I was back there."

"Oh." Landfors picked up *Main Street* and cracked it open. With thorough indifference, he asked, "Did you win today?"

"No. We got clobbered." His attention had already gone back to Sinclair Lewis. "Say, Karl . . ."

"Yes?"

"You said Emmett Siever has—had—whatever—a daughter living here."

"Yes. Constance."

"Could you take me to see her? I'd like to tell her that I'm sorry about her father, and tell her I didn't have anything to do with his death." I also wanted to find out if she knew anything about the gun that her father supposedly tried to shoot me with.

"Sure," said Landfors. "I think she lives in Hamtramck."

"You *think?* You said you were going to pay a call on her. Haven't you seen her yet?" It had been ten days since Siever's death and Landfors had been in Detroit for five.

Landfors pushed up his eyeglasses and looked sheepish. "Actually, I'm not very good at that sort of thing." That was true, I expected; Landfors generally exhibited the social graces of a cigar-store Indian. Laying down the book, he stood and rubbed his hands together. "Let me phone her and find out if she'll see us."

OOO

At Landfors's insistence, we stopped for a light dinner at Kelsey's Cafe next to the hat shop downstairs. Since I didn't cook, I'd already come to think of the little restaurant as my dining room.

This evening, struggling to think of a way to convince Constance Siever that I hadn't murdered her father, I had little stomach for the pea soup and ham sandwiches the waiter served us. Landfors managed to eat twice as much as me while doing three times the talking.

He drew up short when I told him what I'd learned from Hughie Jennings about Siever's past. Chewing thoughtfully, he said, "Perhaps some men make better martyrs than they do human beings."

"How long did you know him?"

"Actually, I really only knew *of* him. I'd only met him once or twice"

"You told me you and him were friends."

"I suppose I did exaggerate our relationship a bit." Landfors dabbed a napkin at the corners of his mouth. "I'd heard good things about Siever, that he was a clever strategist, an articulate speaker, and was completely dedicated to the cause."

"The 'cause' being the ballplayers union of the IWW?"

"*That's* the point," Landfors said, crumbs falling from his lips. "There is no difference! Working people are working people, no matter what their trade. That's what I admired about Emmett Siever: he was willing to use whatever prestige he had as a baseball player to help not only ballplayers, but anyone else who labors for his bread. One big union. That's the only way for *any* worker to protect his rights." Pointing to my sandwich, he asked, "Going to eat that?"

I told him to finish it and resumed my efforts to compose what I would say to Siever's daughter. I wondered if I should bring her flowers, and if so what kind. What blossom do you bring to a woman who thinks you killed her father?

Unable to resolve the flower question by the time we caught a streetcar for Hamtramck, I gave up on the idea. All I would give her would be my sincere condolences on her loss and an emphatic denial that I'd had anything to do with creating that loss.

As the swaying trolley rolled north, Landfors explained to me that Hamtramck was an independent village embedded within the city of Detroit. Traveling up Joseph Campau Avenue, Hamtramck's main business thoroughfare, Landfors pointed out the massive Dodge Brothers automobile plant to our right; the sound of its machinery was audible over the clatter of the trolley and brackish fumes billowed from its forest of smokestacks.

We hopped off about ten blocks past the plant and walked west into a residential neighborhood of small, single-family dwellings. According to Landfors, they were occupied primarily by Polish immigrants who worked on the Dodge assembly lines.

Near the Lumpkin end of Wyandotte Street, we found the Siever home, a well-kept clapboard bungalow painted a pinkish beige with white trim and red awnings.

Landfors paused at the door to check his watch. "Five to eight." He continued to stare at the watch face. When I realized that he intended to wait the five minutes, I rang the bell myself. Somewhat startled at the departure from the schedule, he snapped the watch shut and tucked it in his vest pocket.

The door was opened by a tall, lean woman wearing an ankle-length green plaid skirt with a white shirtwaist buttoned up to her long narrow throat. The woman's fair face, though not unattractive, was sharp and angular. The short style of her ash-blond hair made her appear even taller than the five-nine or five-ten I estimated her height to be. "You're early," she said.

Landfors shot me a look of reprimand.

"Well, no harm. We were just about to break, so come in." Her manner was brusque and businesslike.

We followed her into a small foyer. I noticed a small black emblem pinned above her left breast; to determine what it depicted would have required a closer inspection than politeness permitted. Landfors and I removed our hats, and I waited for him to make the introductions. He seemed stalled, so I nudged his ribs to get him started. "I'm Karl Landfors," he said. "Are you . . . ?"

"Constance Siever. Call me Connie." She shook his hand firmly, then turned to me. "And you must be Rawlings."

"Mickey," I said, offering my own hand. She ignored it.

"As I said on the telephone," Landfors began, "Mickey would like to talk to you. About your father."

"Very well." She poked her head into the parlor, where about a dozen ladies were seated around a long dining table. "Let's break now," she said to them. "We'll resume in ten minutes." To Landfors and me she said, "We'll talk in the kitchen."

The Siever kitchen had all the hominess of a Woolworth's luncheonette: utilitarian furniture, institutional stove and ice-box, plain white crockery. We sat at a small table next to a window overlooking a barren backyard.

Connie Siever didn't offer any refreshments. She said to Landfors, "I'm so glad you're here. I've always wanted to meet the man who wrote *Savagery in the Sweatshop.* A truly great book—right up there with *The Jungle,* in my opinion."

Landfors flushed.

Somewhat incredulous, I said, "You read it?"

"Several times."

I couldn't stop myself from blurting, "All the way through?"

She laughed and nodded.

I was impressed; I'd tried many times to work my way through the ponderous, muckraking tome and never got beyond the second chapter.

Landfors didn't appear to notice my reaction to her literary achievement. His eyes were riveted on Emmett Siever's daughter. I nudged him again. He coughed and finally spoke up, "Mickey has something to tell you, Miss—uh, Connie."

She turned to look straight at me. "Then why doesn't he do it?" Her eyes were a vivid green and fairly glowed with the light of intelligence.

I began hesitantly, "I know the newspapers say I'm the one who shot your father, uh, Miss Siever." It seemed too familiar to call her "Connie." "But I want you to know it's not true. I never even got to talk with him. I did hear him give a speech, but that was it. He sounded like a smart and decent man. And I'm very sorry that he's dead."

"Do you feel better now?"

"Well, I just . . . All I wanted to do was tell you . . . Uh, no, actually I still feel lousy. But I give you my word *I didn't kill him.*"

She stiffened slightly, her posture and demeanor starting to resemble that of an ice sculpture. "I don't know you. Why should I take your word for anything?"

Landfors piped up, "I've known Mickey for years. If he says he didn't do it, that's enough for me. In fact, I'm the one who asked him to go to the hall to meet your father. I wouldn't have done that if I didn't trust him."

"If he didn't kill my father, then who did?"

"I don't know," answered Landfors.

I shook my head, silently echoing him, before venturing a question. "The reports said he was shot in self-defense. Supposedly your father had a gun. Do you know if he carried one?"

"Yes, I do know. No, he never carried one."

"Own one?"

*"He* didn't. I do. Two of them: shotgun and a hunting rifle. Care to see them, Sherlock?"

"Uh, no, that's okay, thanks." A series of questions ran through my mind. How well did Connie really know her father? When had he reentered her life? Had they lived together in this house? And: Who had raised her after her mother died? Instead of giving her the opportunity to point out that those matters were none of my business, I said, "No more questions. Again, I'm sorry for your loss." From outward indications, I was sorrier than she was about it.

Connie Siever hesitated, then changed the subject. "Have you seen Leo Hyman yet?" she asked Landfors.

His lips tightened. "Briefly. At the hall."

"You two should make up," she said. "Leo's one of our best. I've known him since the Lawrence strike back in 1912." I knew from playing in Boston that year that the successful strike of textile workers in Lawrence, Massachusetts, was the IWW's biggest victory.

"Your work with the mill hands has been an inspiration," said Landfors.

It was Connie Siever's turn to blush. She and Landfors were clearly turning into a mutual admiration society, and I felt I was becoming witness to the mating ritual of radicals.

Okay, one more question. "Did your father live here with you?" I asked.

"Yes." She gave me a cold glare that discouraged any further questions. I returned a polite smile of surrender, and she shifted her attention back to Karl Landfors.

"What are you working on now, Connie?" he asked. Her name came off Landfors's lips easily now.

"The Suffrage Amendment." She darkened somewhat. "The loss in Delaware was a terrible disappointment. Only a few states left, almost all of them in the South. I'm setting my sights on Tennessee—their legislature votes on ratification in August." She nodded toward the front of the house. "That's what this meeting is about. We're planning a trip to Memphis to organize the women there."

Left out of the conversation, I occupied myself with trying to identify the black ornament pinned to her shirtwaist.

"Only need one more state," Landfors said. "I'm sure it will pass."

"You know there's no such thing as a sure thing going up against the established order."

"Yes, that's certainly true."

She checked the kitchen clock—more than the allotted ten minutes had passed—then leaned toward Landfors. That movement enabled me to see that the pin she was wearing was the figure of a black cat. "Would you mind giving us a little talk?" she asked him. "Some of the women are new to this, and a little timid. I'm sure a few words from you would be very rousing for them."

"Well," Landfors demurred, blushing a deeper red. I was tempted to throw cold water on his face before he set the house on fire. "It would be an honor . . . if you think they'd really be interested in hearing me."

"Of course they would!" She stood and led us into the parlor, where the women were reseating themselves around the table.

"Ladies, may I have your attention?" They quieted, and she went on, "We're very fortunate to have with us tonight Karl Landfors, a longtime activist and author of one of the classics of modern literature: *Savagery in the Sweatshop.*"

The ladies oohed and ahhed as if Landfors was a baseball star. Connie Siever then waved her hand at me. "And this is his friend Michael." I garnered barely a murmur.

I was as out of place here as Karl Landfors would be on the pitching mound of Navin Field. Using the excuse of a headache, I begged off staying for the talk. There were no objections from any of the women—nor from Landfors— and I left to catch a streetcar for home.

On the ride back to Detroit, I summed up what I had learned. One thing was that Emmett Siever hadn't owned a revolver—according to his daughter. The other thing I'd learned was that his daughter didn't seem to care very much that he was dead.

# Chapter Eight

○○○

**F**riday was an off day in the schedule, an opportunity to sleep late and linger in dreamland. Unfortunately, the dreams I'd been having lately were ones that I preferred to avoid. After a fitful night with little rest, I was up for good an hour before dawn. I envied Karl Landfors sleeping soundly on the sofa.

After a cursory run through my morning bathroom routine, made simpler by seeing that my every-other-day shave could easily wait another twenty-four hours, I pulled on some heavy winter clothes, including corduroy trousers that I rarely wore in public because of the noise they made. I buttoned a maroon sweater-coat over a long-sleeved wool undershirt and turned up its shawl collar against the morning chill. My landlady wasn't spending much of the rent money on heat; the radiators were cold and dormant. At one point, I thought they were kicking in, but the sound was only Landfors's breath whistling through his nose.

I brewed a pot of coffee to help generate some internal warmth. Carrying a full mug of it, I felt my way through the dark parlor and sat down in the rocker, taking care to keep the creaky chair still. I held the mug up, warming my face in the steam, and returned to the same thoughts that had kept me awake during the night.

Why had Detective McGuire shown me the photo of Emmett Siever gripping a revolver? Was he a careless cop, letting me see something I shouldn't have? I didn't think so; McGuire had struck me as calculating, not careless. Perhaps it was a warning, as if to say, "We can do whatever we want, and you can't do anything about it." But that didn't jibe with the impression I had at the end of the visit, when he seemed to encourage me to investigate on my own.

My sense was that McGuire had shown it to me so that I'd see for certain that something was wrong. Which raised another question: if the police planted evidence—the gun— why would one of them betray what his own department had done? Why would he disobey orders?

Finding no satisfactory answer to that question, I considered waking Landfors to get his opinion. Seeing him curled up in peaceful slumber, with his glasses off and his balding head bare, he reminded me of an infant—an infant gnome— and I couldn't bring myself to do it.

I needed something else to occupy me for a while. It was still too early to get the morning newspapers, and I wasn't eager to venture out into the cold anyway. The copy of *Main Street* on the table briefly tempted me, but I figured if Landfors liked the book, it probably wasn't very good.

With the gray light of early dawn still too dim for reading, I clicked on the lamp next to my chair and settled for rereading the papers of the last few days. While on my third cup of coffee, I came across one of the stories about Treasury agents accusing the Detroit police of being on the payroll of bootleggers. I read it thoroughly, then flipped through the rest of the papers to study every article on the feud between the federal and local enforcement agencies. I started rocking in the chair, excited that I thought I had the answer to McGuire's puzzling behavior.

The screeching of the rocker woke Landfors, who promptly contributed a foghorn yawn to the din. He reached for his spectacles; once they were securely hooked over his ears, he peered around bleary-eyed. Disappointment that his dreams were over showed on his face.

I stood and stretched. "How'd it go last night?"

His answer was drowned out by an explosion behind me. I spun to see my window disintegrate in a spray of glass shards. The booming report of a gunshot echoed up from the street below. "Get down!" I yelled at Landfors as I hit the floor.

Lying facedown, I heard the squeal of a car speeding away and the tinkle of broken glass raining on the hardwood floor. After a few long seconds, the only sound was of heavy breathing—and I wasn't sure if it was mine or Landfors's. It took a moment more until I noticed the hot prickly sensation running from my shoulder blade to my lower back. The irritation quickly blazed into a searing fire of pain.

I asked Landfors, "You okay?"

"What on earth was that?"

"My guess is somebody put a bullet through the window. And Karl . . ."

"Yes?"

"I think it's in my back."

O O O

Landfors carefully lifted my sweater and undershirt. I obeyed his instructions and lay as still as I could on my belly. Since he'd served in the Ambulance Corps, I trusted his judgment and took his word that the best thing to do for a possible back injury was to remain immobile.

"My, but that's ugly," he said.

"It's bad?"

"No, just ugly. It doesn't look like a bullet wound. Too small."

"Glass?" I hoped it might be merely a fragment from the broken window.

"Don't think so. But it's right at the base of your spine. We better call a doctor."

I thought of Dr. Wirtenberg, with his filthy instruments and rough manner. "Let's not," I said. "You told me you pulled a lot of shrapnel out of kids during the war. Think you can handle this?"

"I can try. There's hardly any blood, so whatever's in there probably isn't very deep."

"Shoulder stings like hell, too, Karl. Can you take a look at it?"

Landfors slowly pulled the sweater and shirt over my head. "You have one more wound next to the shoulder blade. Let me work on that one first before I go digging around your spine." He went to the bathroom. "You don't have much in the way of medical supplies," he called to me. "All you have is some kind of grease."

"Liniment," I yelled back. "Whatever you do, don't put any of that on me." It was a mixture of Vaseline and Tabasco that a trainer had once given me for stiff muscles. It was *not* the thing to put on an open cut.

Landfors took tweezers from his travel kit and heated the tip with a match. It probably made for a more sterile instrument than anything Dr. Wirtenberg had.

Just before he began on the shoulder, I realized there was one sound I hadn't heard: a police siren. "How come there's no cops?" I said. "This is Detroit, not Chicago. How often are there shootings around here? Somebody should have called the cops."

He paused to walk over to the window. "The street's empty," he reported. "Most people are still sleeping. And anyone who did hear the shot might have thought it was a car backfiring."

Landfors then went to work on the shoulder wound. He stretched my skin with one hand, while the other manipulated the tweezers. It felt like my flesh was on fire. "Got it!" he said after a couple minutes of digging. He showed me a bloody BB held in the tip of the instrument. "Buckshot. You're lucky it wasn't close-range. With the distance, and having to go through the window, the damage isn't much. The heavy sweater helped, too, I'm sure."

"Would this count as being thrown from the train?" I said.

"You think it was the IWW?"

"Don't you remember how Whitey Boggs greeted us at Fraternity Hall?"

"They usually don't kill people." Landfors moved down to my lower back and started probing for the pellet embedded there.

The pain was intense. Partly to take my mind off what Landfors was doing to me, I thought over my assumption about the Wobblies. Who else could it be? I was sure it hadn't been one of my teammates: besides the fact that there was hardly a ballplayer alive who'd be up this early in the morning, they just hadn't seemed *that* angry at me. Buckshot . . . a shotgun. Only last night, Connie Siever had mentioned having one. But she hadn't even appeared upset about her father's death—why would she go gunning for me? No, I decided, my initial hunch was most likely the correct one. Actually, Landfors and I were probably both right: it was the Wobblies who shot at me but not with murderous intent.

Through gritted teeth, I said, "This *wasn't* an attempt to kill me, I don't think. Like you said, it wasn't likely to do much damage. If they wanted to kill me, why not wait till I stepped outside? Firing a shotgun into a second-floor window is probably more of a scare tactic."

Landfors dug a little more firmly into my flesh. "Then I would say that this very well could count as being thrown from the train." It felt like he was trying to drill a hole through me; I wished I'd thought to ask him for something to bite on. "Darn," he said. "This one's deeper than the other." The tweezers hit a nerve that caused my leg to twitch like a sleeping dog's.

As he worked, my thoughts traveled back to November 8, 1918, the day after my twenty-seventh birthday. I'd been haunted by the events of that day ever since, and they had colored my reaction to Emmett Siever's murder more than I could explain to anyone else. But I decided to give it a try. "Something I never told you about when I was in France," I said.

"What's that?"

"That stuff in the papers about me being a 'war hero,'

and the things they claimed I did over there, it's all a load of crap."

"As far as I'm concerned," Landfors said calmly,"anyone who fought is a hero."

"No, no—you don't understand." I took a breath. "Here's what happened, what *really* happened. It was November, I was with the 131st Infantry, in France, and we were attacking the Germans at St. Hilaire. Hell, I didn't know anything about being a soldier. The army rushed me through basic training in less than half the usual time, then they assigned me to the 131st, a National Guard regiment. You know why? Because it was from Chicago, and the Cubs' management wanted me with a Chicago outfit—they thought it would make for good publicity."

"I wondered how you ended up in a Guard unit, without ever having been in the Guard," Landfors said.

"That's how. Anyway, it all happened November 8, early in the morning. It was freezing; I remember thinking it was so cold they should have given both sides off that day. Of course, they didn't. My squad was scouting what was left of some village. We split up, combing the area, going through abandoned farmhouses and bombed-out buildings.

"I turned the corner around a barn and there was a German soldier taking a leak against the wall. A boy in a German uniform, I should say, because he couldn't have been more than sixteen years old. However old he was, he saw me and swung his rifle off his shoulder. Mine was at the ready, but I froze. Wasn't till he got off a shot that I took aim at him. My fingers were numb from the cold; I could hardly feel the trigger.

"Finally, I fired. He returned it. I fired again. I swear we weren't more than ninety feet apart, and we couldn't hit each other. I kept trying to aim better and all I could think was that the kid looked as scared as I felt." My voice caught as I continued, "Then I got him. Found out later, it was my last round."

"Consider yourself lucky."

"You know what the first thing I did was?"

"No, what?"

"Tried to see if I could help him, revive him somehow. He was dead, got him in the chest same as Siever was. Just some kid, taking his morning piss, and I killed him. That was my 'heroic' war deed."

Landfors said, "I was there three years, and not much happened the way they say in the recruiting posters or Liberty Bond speeches. Now stay completely still; I almost have this one." A few seconds later, he succeeded in digging the pellet out and stood up. "You have any bandages?"

That was one medical supply I did have, for spike wounds. I told him where to find them, and he returned with the gauze and tape.

As he bandaged the wounds, I went on, "Some lieutenant made up the story that I'd single-handedly wiped out a machine gun nest. Turned out our mission was a flop, so he decided to make up something that would give the unit a little glory. By the time I got back to the States, and the season opened, the Cubs were using me as a poster boy for baseball's patriotism.

"They used me, Karl. From the regiment I was assigned to, to the stories they made up. It was an awful thing, killing that kid. Not something I'm proud of, and I hated the way they twisted things. I tried telling the truth, but nobody wanted to hear it, so I gave up.

"This thing with Emmett Siever is the same. They want to say I killed him, and they want to use me. I'm not giving up this time. I didn't do it, and I'm gonna find out who did no matter what it takes."

"I can understand you feeling that way," Landfors said. "Put your shirt back on."

I'd finished dressing when there was an urgent hammering on the door. It was my landlady, who'd just discovered the glass on the sidewalk and the broken window.

I let her in and tried to calm her down. She wasn't satisfied until I agreed to pay for a new window and not let anyone shoot at me again. I wished I knew how to comply with that second demand.

Landfors then volunteered to clean the mess and board up the window while I paid a visit to the Trumbull Avenue station house to report the shooting.

○ ○ ○

Landfors and I met for lunch at Kelsey's. I took care to sit forward from the backrest. The wounds were tender but not excruciating.

"How did it go with the police?" he asked.

Sergeant Phelan had again been the officer on duty, and turned out to be no more helpful this time than he had when I'd first met him. "I was told that a broken window isn't much of a reason to investigate anything." The morning shooting hadn't been my only reason for speaking to him, however. Phelan did prove himself helpful—though unwittingly so—

when I'd asked him about the feud between the Treasury Department and the Detroit police.

Landfors nibbled at his food.

I thanked him again for patching me up.

He said, "I've been thinking: you might be best off dropping this. True, you have the Wobblies angry at you because they think you killed Siever, but if you go digging into it, you'll have somebody else coming after you: the man who really murdered him. As long as Siever's death is credited to you, he's off the hook. But if he finds out you're looking into things . . ."

"He'll want to stop me to keep himself in the clear. I thought about that, Karl. I don't see that dropping this now would make me any safer. Even if I did, the killer would never know for sure that I wasn't going to bring it up again in the future, so he still might want to kill me, too. No, I'm not giving up."

"I didn't think so," said Landfors.

Changing the subject, I said, "You haven't told me about how it went last night."

He smiled broadly, and a pixilated look came into his eyes. After giving me an almost verbatim retelling of his speech to Constance Siever and her friends, he recounted with relish every word of the adoring praise they'd heaped on him. As he spoke, his demeanor became increasingly distracted, and he repeated his favorite lines often enough that I had the sense of listening to a Victrola with its needle stuck in a groove. It made me wonder—just a little—if people ever tired of hearing me tell about the time I hit a home run off Big Ed Walsh in Fenway Park.

I patiently let him talk on through a dessert of apple pie.

Back in my apartment, I asked a question that shook him partway out of his reverie. "Could you set up a meeting with Leo Hyman?"

"Well, I suppose so. For when?"

"Tonight, if possible. We're leaving for a series against the Browns on Sunday."

Landfors flushed and stammered, "I, uh, I have a date for tonight. I can break it, though, if you want me to go with you."

I didn't need to ask who the unfortunate lady was. "No need. I can talk to Hyman by myself."

He relaxed slightly when I passed up the opportunity to prod him about his date. "Very well," he said as he went to the phone. After he got Leo Hyman on the line and told him what I wanted, Landfors relayed to me, "Tonight's no good for him. Is tomorrow all right?"

"Sure." I remembered that the IWW hall was probably under surveillance. "Not at Fraternity Hall, though. I don't want to be seen."

Landfors nodded and said into the mouthpiece, "Yes, tomorrow night is fine. And the meeting has to be invisible, Leo." After another brief exchange with Hyman, he hung up. "He'll call back to let us know where and when."

"Thanks, Karl. By the way, what's the problem between you and Hyman? Connie Siever said something about how you and him should make up. Did you two have a fight?"

Landfors returned to the sofa. "We've had some differences of opinion." He pushed up his glasses and crossed one leg over the other. "Regarding tactics."

"Tactics?"

He hesitated. "You won't repeat this, right?"

I agreed that I wouldn't.

"Leo Hyman advocates sabotage as a political tactic."

There'd been endless stories about German sabotage during the war. "You mean like blowing up factories and sinking ships?"

"No, no. Nothing that drastic. Hyman goes for a more subtle approach. He's a clever man—used to be an engineer. As a matter of fact, he's quite capable of designing all sorts of complicated devices if he wanted to, but he generally tries to find the simplest way of doing damage. Hyman was the one who discovered that if you put mustard seed in cement mix, the seeds will grow and crumble the concrete. And it was his idea to have assembly workers at Ford put dead rats behind the door panels."

"Dead rats?"

"Yes, the cars are shipped before the rats decompose. Then the dealers are stuck with smelly cars that no one will buy, or the customer returns it. Either way, it's a problem for Ford."

I imagined some poor fellow spending a thousand dollars for a new automobile, taking his family out for a drive, and the smell of decomposing rat ruining the outing. I generally didn't take sides with the combatants in a conflict; I identified with those caught in the middle. "And you don't agree with that approach," I said.

"No. Innocent people get hurt. Imagine a foundation giving way and a building collapsing because of the mustard seed." Landfors shuddered. "Those kinds of tactics only hurt our cause. People have to be won over by words and ideas, not threats. But Leo Hyman feels sabotage is the only real power the workers have, so they have to use it."

I was glad Landfors and I were on the same side on this point. "So . . . where are you and Connie going tonight?"

He blushed. "Dinner. And a show."

"Well, be careful. She might be a witch."

"How's that?"

"She was wearing a pin of a black cat." I smiled to show I was only teasing.

"Oh that." His expression grew a little grimmer. "Well, she sides with Leo Hyman in the tactics debate. A black cat is the sign of sabotage. So is a wooden shoe, by the way. That's where the word came from—a 'sabot' is a wooden shoe. When French farmworkers had a grievance they would throw their wooden shoes into the machinery to jam it. Hence 'sabotage.' "

"Seems to bother you more about Hyman than it does about Connie."

His lips made a thin smile. "I don't expect the subject will come up."

We avoided political discussion for the rest of the afternoon. As evening approached, Landfors fell into a state of almost total confusion, flushed for no reason, took a long bath, and primped endlessly. I wondered when he'd last had a date.

He asked me to lend him a tie with color in it instead of his usual black. I offered him a new suit that I hadn't yet worn myself—a double-breasted, chalk-striped, navy blue worsted with alpaca lining; it had set me back nearly $50. Landfors declined, saying he didn't want her to think he was dressing up for the occasion. He was right: the goal on a first date is to look good, but give the impression that it's your natural appearance—if you're obviously dressing up, the girl might wonder what you really look like.

After Landfors rejected every tie I offered until I reached plain navy blue, I helped him with the knot and ushered him out the door. No matter how he's dressed, I thought, a radical in love is not a pretty sight.

I picked up *Main Street* and settled in for the night, lying facedown on the sofa to ease the pain in my back. I was through the first fifty pages when the cuckoo emerged from the clock and issued eight groans. He seemed to be taunting me with the fact that it was eight o'clock on a Friday night, Karl Landfors was out on a date, and I was home reading a book.

This month couldn't get much worse.

# *Chapter Nine*

ooo

I was alone again the next night, at the soda fountain of Fyfe's Pharmacy, sipping a chocolate ice-cream soda with little appreciation for its flavor. The afternoon game had been another loss to Chicago, extending our "unvictorious streak," as Karl Landfors called it, to seven straight games. Hughie Jennings still attributed the poor start to the team's exhausting barnstorming trip, but that excuse was no longer carrying much weight with the sportswriters or the fans. The simple fact was that our hitters, including Ty Cobb, weren't hitting, our pitchers couldn't get anyone out, and our fielders turned the simplest plays into juggling routines. If we didn't win one of the next four games, the Tigers would end up 0-for-April.

Landfors was off on another date with Connie Siever. All he'd tell me about the first one was that it had been "thoroughly pleasant," but the fact that he borrowed my brightest red tie for this evening showed he was more smitten than his words indicated. He was in such a lovesick daze that I'd made him twice repeat the directions from Leo Hyman on where and when we were to meet.

In accordance with Hyman's instructions, I sat at the end of the counter farthest from the entrance. Through the glass storefront, I watched the traffic on busy Woodward Avenue just north of the Campus Martius. I couldn't get over how much the downtown had grown since I'd been here last. Back then, the city had been one of the smallest to have a major-league baseball franchise, and there had still been a rural character to many of the streets. But times change, especially in Detroit, where the roaring automobile industry sets the pace of progress.

While my eyes watched the passing cars, my mind turned to Margie Turner again. And I got to worrying that I'd missed my chance at "the one." In the last six years, although I'd had enough dates and a few romances, I had never found a girl I was as crazy about as I had been about Margie. What if I didn't find someone like her in the next six years? I would be pushing thirty-five and alone—or settling for someone just for companionship. If I'd only gone to California with her ... It might have killed my major-league career for a while, but I still could have played ball in the Pacific Coast League ... No, I'd made the right choice. Hell, it wasn't really a choice at all. Not a ballplayer in the world would have given up a roster spot on John McGraw's New York Giants to play for the Los Angeles Angels or the San Francisco Seals.

A bright blue Maxwell roadster slid up to the curb. The open, distinctive car was a refreshing contrast to the sea of black Fords cruising by, but not the ideal car to avoid a tail, I thought. I watched as Leo Hyman got out of the driver's side and Whitey Boggs exited the passenger's door. Hyman was again dressed in red flannel and dungarees, the only change being the color of his suspenders: yellow. The sight of Boggs was an unpleasant surprise; I had expected Hyman to be alone.

The two men came into the drugstore without acknowledging me and took seats near the door. Boggs pointed to the menu and the men gave every indication they were going to order something. After a few minutes, they quietly slid off their stools and ambled toward me. "Come with us," Hyman said.

Abandoning my soda, I followed them as they went through the drugstore's small storage room and out the back door into an alley. An empty, four-door hardtop Model T sedan was there, with its engine running. "In the back," said Boggs, opening the rear door for me. I hesitated a moment. Then I figured Karl Landfors wouldn't send me into a setup. I slid into the backseat, Boggs followed me, and Hyman went behind the wheel. He shifted into gear and eased out of the alley. Clever, I thought: if they were being watched, the blue Maxwell would still be under surveillance while they left in this car.

When we turned onto Griswold, Boggs reached into his jacket pocket. I tried to prepare myself in case he pulled his razor. All he took out was a strip of black cloth. "Gonna have to put this on ya."

"Why?"

From the front seat, Hyman said, "No need for the blindfold, Whitey. Landfors vouched for him."

"I don't care what Landfors says. This guy shouldn't know about the place."

Hyman turned slightly. "I said *no.*"

Boggs jammed the cloth back in his pocket. He hunched his shoulders a couple of times, billowing out a cheap, gray

Norfolk jacket that was at least two sizes too large for his slight body. The move reminded me of a cat fluffing out its fur to look bigger.

"Isn't this a bit much?" I asked. "All I wanted to do was ask you a few questions, Leo. Why the production?" To Boggs, I added, "I didn't know you were coming."

"Think I'm gonna let Leo meet you alone? You killed Siever with fifty of his friends right there. No telling what you'd try to pull with Leo if he was by himself."

"That's enough, Whitey," Hyman said.

Removing his cap, Boggs ran a hand through his translucent, limp hair and turned his eyes to the window.

"The reason for the 'production,' " Hyman explained, "is that your friend wanted it that way. Karl said he wanted our meeting to be 'invisible.' "

"Oh, but this isn't necessary. All I told him was that I couldn't go to the hall to see you."

Hyman tugged at his Santa beard. With him behind the wheel, I thought, we should have had reindeer pulling the car. "He shouldn't have used that word then; he knows what it means."

"Well, Karl's been a little preoccupied lately. Probably didn't realize what he was saying."

"No need to go on then," Hyman said. "We'll just find a little place to pull in and talk."

"No," piped up Boggs. "Keep going. Maybe Rawlings doesn't mind being seen with *us*, but I don't want to be seen with *him*."

"Fine," said Hyman, with a shake of his head. He accelerated and we sped southwest on Fort Street. "Weren't you supposed to be taking Norma out tonight?"

"Who's Norman?" I asked.

Hyman laughed so hard his shoulders rocked.

The first color I'd seen came into Boggs's face. "Norm*a*," he said sharply. "She's my . . . she's the future Mrs. Boggs."

"Distant future," said Hyman in a teasing tone. He obviously would have preferred that Boggs had kept his date with her.

I was trying to sort out how much authority each of them had—it's hard to tell with anarchists and communists. My impression was that Hyman was in charge, but he allowed Boggs to have his way at times.

The farther we got from downtown Detroit, the worse the road surface became. My back was starting to ache, and I squirmed in discomfort.

I asked Hyman, "What about the car you left in front of the drugstore?"

"Somebody will have picked it up by now. Whoever was following us—and somebody always is—will have caught on that he's lost us, but it's too late now."

About five miles out of the city, Hyman cut into a cemetery and drove along a winding single-lane dirt road until we came to a small river.

"This the Rouge River?"

"Baby Creek," he said. Nodding his head to the left, he added, "Rouge is right down there." He eased the car over a shaky wooden bridge to the opposite bank which looked like it had been used as a trash dump. "This used to be a nice quiet area—marshes, mostly, great fishing and duck hunting—till Ford got himself a contract to build boats during the war. Boats weren't worth a damn, but the Navy put millions into building that plant. Now it's another part of his empire." Visible beyond the dump site was the Ford Rouge Plant, its blast furnaces spitting smoke and cinders into the orange sky.

Hyman pulled up near a wood shack far from the main buildings of the complex.

"We're meeting *here?*" I asked.

Boggs turned to me. "You have any objection?"

"What I mean is, Mr. Ford doesn't mind you using his property?"

"Not a bit," said Hyman as he killed the engine. "Because he doesn't know about it. Perfect place for us to get together, in his own backyard. They watch our places closer than they do their own."

The shack was the size of a small carriage house. Its bare boards had split and turned gray, and its corrugated metal roof was solid rust. Boggs took a key from his breast pocket, opened the padlock on the door, and led the way in.

"Where'd you get the key?" I asked.

Boggs shot me a look that warned I was being a little too nosy.

Hyman hesitated, then answered, "Whitey used to work for Ford until he got fired for his union activities. But he still has friends with the company. This place isn't used much anymore anyway. It was just for storage during construction."

There was little inside the windowless building: a cot along one wall, some torn cement bags and dented paint cans tossed in the corner, cigar butts and empty bottles littering the dirt floor. In the center of the room was an upended packing crate supporting a kerosene lamp; four boxes were placed around it like a dining-room table for hobos. Boggs lit the lamp and adjusted the flame. Hyman closed the door behind us, and we each sat down on a box.

"Damn," said Hyman. His belly rested on his thighs, and the box was barely visible under his ample posterior. "Wish to hell you had better seats in here. This is murder on my ass." With the low, flickering lamplight shining on his face, he looked like the Santa Claus from hell. After shifting to find a comfortable way to sit, he said, "So what's on your mind, Mickey?"

"A lot of things. For starters, I'm wondering about the raids on the hall. You said *cops* keep tossing the place. But from what I remember about the Palmer raids, it was the *federal* government that carried them out, wasn't it? Not local police."

"You're half-right," said Hyman. "The Justice Department—"

"Anti-Radical Division," Boggs interrupted.

Hyman shushed him with a sharp look. "That's what it used to be called. It's the General Intelligence Division now, a division of the Justice Department. Anyway, the GID did—and still does—coordinate the raids. Local police supply manpower and jail cells. Why?"

"So the federal government *is* involved, at least to some extent."

"Yes. What's your point?"

"During the war, there were thousands of guys who were made some kind of deputy federal agents—"

"American Protective League," said Hyman. "There were *tens* of thousands. Just about any man or boy who ever wanted to play detective or spy."

I went on, "And they reported to the Justice Department

anyone they thought was pro-German or in some way unpatriotic."

"Yes. We were in the 'unpatriotic' category. All union men were."

"Well, I was wondering about Hub Donner. You told me he's fought against unions for years. And he's working as a union buster for at least two businesses right now: Ford and the American League. What I'm wondering is: could he be working for the Justice Department, too?"

"It's possible," said Hyman. "The GID still has what they call Dollar-a-Day men who spy for them and do some of the dirty business they don't want to be connected with." He smiled wryly. "I think Hub Donner would be more expensive than that, though. In protecting capitalism, he turns quite a nice profit for himself. Again: why?"

I wasn't sure if I should tell these men my theory. A look at Whitey Boggs, and the memory of his flashing razor, made up my mind. Giving them another suspect in Siever's murder should reduce their suspicions of me—and maybe discourage any more shotgun attacks. "Seems to me," I said, "Hub Donner is a good candidate for having killed Emmett Siever—a whole lot better than me. Donner's job is to stop the ballplayers union. What better way to stop it than killing the leader? Players are jittery enough about going against the owners, and now they'll really be afraid."

Boggs spoke up, "Somebody will take Siever's place. They can kill us, but they can't stop us."

Hyman stroked his beard. It appeared a darker shade of gray owing to the black smoke filling the room. The only ventilation was chinks between the boards—not sufficient to remove either the smoke or the nauseating smell of kerosene vapors.

I went on, "There's no doubt Donner was keeping an eye on Siever, right? So he'd know where he was that night. What better place to kill him than in the Hall?" It had also occurred to me that that might explain why Donner was pushing me to go public as Siever's killer: putting me in the limelight would keep suspicion off himself.

"Hub Donner . . ." repeated Hyman. "What do you think, Whitey?"

"Whoever it was," answered Boggs, "is gonna pay for it. Emmett Siever was one of the good guys."

That gave me a nice opening for the questions I had about Siever. "Did you know Siever a long time?"

Hyman shook his head. "Less than a year. He was important to us, though. Linking the ballplayers' union to the IWW made us seem less radical and foreign. We're accused of being un-American, but what's more American than the national pastime? You know, a few years ago, there was some talk of ballplayers hooking up with the 'White Rats'—that's the vaudeville union. The players decided not to because they didn't want to be associated with actors. Siever didn't have any such snobbish notions. He believed ballplayers were the same as every other worker."

"I heard his speech," I said. "You say Siever was good for the IWW, but what did *he* have to gain by being associated with *you?* Why did he come to you in the first place—or did you go to him?"

"He came to us," said Hyman. "Through his daughter Connie. She's been active with us for . . . oh, must be going on ten years now. She introduced him to me. Emmett was getting frustrated with the ballplayers—they're a pretty timid bunch when it comes to organizing against the owners. He figured getting some real union men involved would light a fire under them."

Boggs snorted. "The one thing ballplayers *don't* got is balls. Buncha crybabies who ain't willing to stand up for themselves." He leaned toward me. "Who do you got on the Tigers who's doing anything to organize?"

"Hell," I said. "This year we're hardly organized enough to make sure we got the right number of players on the field."

Hyman laughed.

Boggs leaned closer. "You don't got *one* player unionizing?"

"If there was, they wouldn't trust me enough to tell me now."

"And you're not bright enough to figure out who it is on your own?"

I wanted to get Boggs off me. "Okay," I said. "As far as I can tell, Chick Fogarty is the team's union leader."

Hyman grinned. Boggs rolled his eyes at the joke and gave up pressing me.

"You know," Hyman said, "it pains me to say this— because I love baseball—but Whitey's right. Baseball's owners are as mean and stingy and devious as they come. And the players are as meek and gutless as scared puppies."

Not wanting to defend either the owners or the players, I steered the discussion back to Emmett Siever. "You said you didn't know Siever for very long. And I never heard of him being active with the baseball union until a year or so ago. How did he get so involved so fast? Doesn't that seem pretty sudden?" I'd been having difficulty reconciling the drinking, philandering ballplayer Emmett Siever had been with the more recent labor-organizer version.

Hyman said thoughtfully, "Usually it's when a man first discovers that something's important to him that he's the most zealous about it. We need enthusiastic newcomers like that. They keep the movement fresh."

"And you're convinced the union really was important to Siever?"

"Absolutely. Sometimes somebody will come along, full of piss and vinegar, and they turn out to be plants, sent in to infiltrate us. Emmett Siever wasn't one of those. And, of course, we had his daughter to vouch for him."

"If you get plants, how do you know who to trust?"

"We have ways of testing new guys," said Boggs. "Besides, the consequences if they're caught keeps most of them from even trying."

"Why? What happens?"

Hyman answered, "The penalty for treason is the same in every country on earth . . ."

He didn't have to elaborate. "That's what somebody was intending for me yesterday morning," I said. "You wouldn't happen to know who might have put a load of buckshot through my window, would you?"

Hyman and Boggs both shook their heads; I couldn't tell if what I'd said was news to them or not. Neither of them looked distressed to hear it, though.

"Right now," I went on, "I figure it's even. I didn't kill Siever, and whoever shot up my apartment didn't kill me. I'd like to keep it that way. Because if I stay alive, I will do everything I can to find out who *did* kill him."

Boggs said, "I don't see how that's even—Siever's dead, you're not."

Hyman had a small coughing fit. "Let's get out of here. Can hardly breathe anymore." With a heavy groan, he slowly stood up. "If you got any more questions, you can ask them on the way back."

The ride home was slow. Hyman navigated the cemetery road by moonlight; he didn't turn on the headlamps until we were back on Fort Street.

I had no more questions, and my companions had no additional comments. Eventually, I broke the silence by saying to Boggs, "Sorry you had to break your date with Norma for this." I was trying to sound friendly.

"Wasn't worth it," he said. Then, a little more brightly, he added, "But I'll see her for breakfast."

With Landfors dating Connie, and Boggs seeing Norma, the thought occurred to me that maybe I should join the IWW to meet women.

Hyman swung a left on Twelfth Street, and spoke for the first time since we'd left the shack. "I don't know anything about what happened yesterday. But I do know a lot of the boys were upset about Siever, and they figure you did it. I'll spread the word to keep hands off you—for a while. And if you can nail Hub Donner for it, or whoever else was responsible, you're off the hook."

"Thanks. Uh, what do you mean 'for a while'?"

"Two weeks."

"*Two weeks!* We're leaving for St. Louis tomorrow. And we got an eastern road trip coming up soon. I need more time than that. How about two months?"

"Four weeks," Hyman decided. I started to protest again,

but he cut me off. "Four weeks from tonight, we'll meet again, and you better tell me who killed Emmett Siever."

He dropped me off at the corner of High and Fifth Streets, next to Crawford Park. I walked to the fountain in the middle of the park, splashed my face with cold water, and wiped it with a handkerchief.

Then I sat on the edge of the fountain and mulled over what had transpired. It was a pretty successful outing, I thought: I'd picked up some new information about Emmett Siever, was granted a few weeks of peace to investigate, and I'd planted the suggestion of another suspect in Siever's death: Hub Donner.

I felt satisfied with the night's progress until new questions started ricocheting around in my head. Who was "Detective Aikens"? Where had Leo Hyman been when Siever was shot? Who raised Connie after her father deserted her? And most importantly: *how* was I going to solve Emmett Siever's murder in four weeks?

# Chapter Ten

○ ○ ○

Lou Vedder threw without a windup, tossing me three-quarter-speed fastballs that came up to the plate big and fat. Swinging left-handed, I hit them where they were pitched, pulling inside balls up the first-base line and slapping the outside ones to left field.

Like Ty Cobb and Wee Willie Keeler, though not as successful as them, I was a place hitter. Not for me the home runs that Babe Ruth was making so popular. I preferred the strategy of the bunt and the hit-and-run, and the challenge of driving a grounder through the hole and dropping a looper over the heads of the infielders. The fact that I rarely could reach the fences anyway—not even with the new livelier baseball—was only a minor consideration in my preference of hitting style, of course.

I smacked forty or fifty of Vedder's tosses, then called to him, "Let me lay down a few!"

He nodded, and I started bunting his next throws. After each one, I took a couple of steps toward first base to get the feel of running out of the batter's box. It was a little awkward, but since the lefty's box was a step closer to first, I figured I should still be able to beat out more bunts from this side of the plate.

From the dugout, Hughie Jennings yelled, "Let's see some life out there, goddammit!" His anger was directed at a group of Tigers who were talking and laughing near the backstop.

This was supposed to be an off day, and the team resented having to spend it in uniform in Sportsman's Park. Jennings had ordered the extra practice session after we lost yesterday's series opener to the St. Louis Browns, our ninth loss in a row.

I'd had no trouble taking batting practice today; only Ty Cobb batted ahead of me. Most of the other players were making a show of refusing to take the practice seriously; they milled about, chatting casually. Other than Vedder and myself, only the pitchers looked busy, working out under Jack Coombs's tutelage near the right-field foul line. A number of sportswriters had started speculating in print that Coombs would soon take over the managing job from the old Oriole.

At Jennings's outburst, Bobby Veach approached the plate. "Let me hit a few, Mick. Keep Hughie off my ass." I stepped aside and watched while he took his licks. Veach's sharp stroke sent a dozen line drives to deep right field before he tossed his bat aside and made way for Donie Bush.

Bush was a sane version of Ty Cobb—smart, intense, a fiery competitor, but not demoniac like Cobb was. Now on the downhill side of his career, Bush relied more on savvy than speed. His range at shortstop was less, so he'd learned to position himself depending on the pitch and the batter. His bat was no longer as quick, so he'd taken to hitting to the opposite field more. Eventually, though, savvy wouldn't be enough to compensate for the loss of physical skills, and Bush's playing days would be over. As would mine someday.

Clearly as disgusted with our practice efforts as he was with our game performances, Jennings finally yelled, "That's enough for today! Get your asses in here!" As players filed past him to the clubhouse, he added, "You bushers don't deserve to be on a big-league field."

Vedder and I were heading off, too, when I asked him, "You mind throwing me a few more? I didn't get to hit right-handed yet." I wasn't sure how the wrist would hold up, and it seemed the perfect time to give it a try when no one else was watching.

He cheerfully agreed and went back to the mound. I took a few swings to get readjusted to hitting from the right side of the plate, but there was no pain in the wrist and it felt smoother batting from my natural side.

After fifteen or twenty off-speed fastballs, I asked him to put a little more on his pitches. I hit these fairly well, and then he tossed some curveballs that gave me a bit more trouble.

"Okay," I said. "One more. Give me the best you got."

He smiled. "Coming up." Vedder turned his back for a moment, then toed the rubber, went into a windmill windup, and sent a white bullet to the plate that veered sharply down and in. My flailing bat didn't pass anywhere near it.

"What the hell was that!"

Vedder walked in from the mound. "Spitter."

"You got a damn good one."

"Lot of good it'll do me."

"Oh yeah. Jeez, that's a shame." With the spitball being phased out of baseball, only two pitchers per team were allowed to use the wet one this season; on the Tigers, Dutch Leonard and Doc Ayers were the team's designated spitballers. "Well, you got a good curve, too. You'll get a spot in the rotation soon enough."

We were almost at the dugout when I realized I'd left my mitt on the ground near home plate. "You go ahead," I said. "Gotta get my glove."

After I retrieved it, I entered the runway tunnel to the clubhouse, pausing for a second to acclimate my eyes to the dark. I heard Dutch Leonard's voice say, "There he is." I resumed walking, but a little slower.

Leonard and Chick Fogarty were outside the locker-room door, already in street clothes. I tried to push past them.

"Hold on there," said Leonard. "We want to talk to you."

"About what?"

Fogarty grabbed my arm, causing me to drop my bat and glove. I tried to jerk free of him, but his grip was firm. Leonard took hold of my other arm and the two of them dragged me deeper into the tunnel. They released me by throwing me facefirst against the concrete wall. I turned my head just in time to take the brunt of it on my ear instead of my nose.

"Let me explain what it means to be a team player," Leonard said. He nodded at Fogarty, who quickly got me in a bear hug from behind. I felt his jaw touching the top of my head.

Leonard took off his jacket. "Being a team player means you don't go against your own kind like you did with Emmett Siever." He reared back, about to launch a blow at my stomach.

"What's going on here?" interrupted Ty Cobb's southern

drawl. He walked closer and looked at each of us with curiosity. I never thought I'd be happy to see Ty Cobb.

"Just having a little discussion with Rawlings here," said Leonard.

Cobb studied us again. With a faint smile, he said, "Well, fight nice, boys." Then he walked away. *Damn.*

The big catcher tightened his grip around my chest. "Let him have it, Dutch," he urged. Fogarty's chin bobbed on my skull as he mouthed the words.

"You really want to be doing this, Chick?" I asked.

Fogarty started to answer, "Just listen to wha—" I ducked my head forward then snapped it back, nailing him hard on the chin. "Aaah!" he screamed, his arms relaxing enough for me to break loose.

Leonard had a startled look in his eyes. I took advantage to plant a right jab on his nose. "Sonofabitch!" he cried as his hands flew up to his face.

I tried to slip past and get to the clubhouse. Leonard threw out a foot, tripping me. Before I could pull myself up, Chick Fogarty lifted me clear off the floor. "Made me bite my tongue," he said in a slurred voice filled with rage. He gripped me like he was trying to squeeze the life out of me. He did succeed in forcing the air out of my lungs.

"Hold him for me," Leonard ordered.

Fogarty turned me toward the angry pitcher, whose nose suddenly looked like it had an outbreak of gin blossoms. Leonard promptly threw a pair of hard punches into my midsection. With Fogarty squeezing me so hard, I didn't have the strength to brace myself for them.

I tried to slam my heel down on Fogarty's foot, but couldn't reach it, so I settled for kicking his shin.

"Give him 'nother," said Fogarty.

Leonard complied with two more uppercuts to my stomach. "That'll teach you," he said. He picked up his jacket and ran a hand over his hair, smoothing it down. "Okay, Chick, let him go."

Fogarty released me and I sucked in badly needed air. Then he slammed me on the back of my head and I fell to the ground, struggling to stay conscious.

Through my daze, I heard their footsteps as they walked away. I also heard Leonard's voice say, "Little bastard fights back," and Fogarty whine, "He made me bite my tongue."

○ ○ ○

Two hours later, I was walking down Olive Street, in St. Louis's commercial district. My scuffle with Dutch Leonard and Chick Fogarty had left me mildly dizzy and with a bellyache so intense that I felt like I was going to give birth to a vital organ. The good news was that I hadn't damaged my wrist by punching Leonard—which led me to conclude that it was completely healed—and there were no external bruises to mar my appearance.

At Tenth Street, I came to the offices of *The Sporting News,* the weekly sports paper also known as "The Baseball Bible." The purpose of my visit was to learn about baseball unions—from the beginning.

A helpful editor directed me to a storage room used as a "library." Stacked in no discernible order were old baseball guides, magazines, miscellaneous papers, a few books, and, of course, back issues of *The Sporting News* itself.

Sorting through dusty, yellowing publications, I first

looked for material on what I assumed was the earliest attempt to organize players: the Players League of 1890.

In a stratum of papers from that era, I located a Players League Guide, and read the articles in it by League president John Montgomery Ward and secretary Tim Keefe. The legendary John Ward had been a star pitcher who'd successfully converted to shortstop when his arm went bad; and, while playing for the New York Giants, he'd earned a law degree from Columbia University. Tim Keefe had pitched for several New York teams, once winning nineteen games in a row and accumulating more than 300 career victories.

I was surprised to learn that the league had its origins in the Brotherhood of Professional Base Ball Players, organized in 1885 when owners instituted a salary limit of $2,000. Three years after that, the National League set up a classification system: each player would be "graded" and placed into one of five classes, with a salary limit for each class. In addition, lower-ranked players could be required to perform duties such as sweeping out the ballpark or working the ticket booths. When owners refused to meet with the Brotherhood's executive committee to discuss the classification scheme, the players elected to form their own league.

Along with the Players League Guide was a copy of *Lippincott's* magazine dated August, 1887. I thought it had ended up in the stack by mistake, until I saw that it included an article by John Ward entitled "Is the Ballplayer a Chattel?" His answer to that question, and his opinion of the reserve clause, was clear: "Like a fugitive slave law, the reserve rule denies him a harbor or livelihood, and carries him back, bound and shackled, to the club from which he attempted to escape."

In similar language, the Players League manifesto condemned the National League: "There was a time when the league stood for integrity and fair dealing; today it stands for dollars and cents. Players have been bought, sold, and exchanged as though they were sheep instead of American citizens."

Ward's introduction to the Players League Guide declared that the new league was "the representation of all that is manly and honest in baseball. To the player it is a living monument for all time to come." It didn't last nearly that long. Losing money and backers, the Players League folded before the end of its first year. Its surrender to the National League was complete, and the Brotherhood of Professional Base Ball Players collapsed along with the failed league.

I briefly delved into the Players League rosters, noting that Emmett Siever played center field for Ward's Brooklyn team. It wasn't such a rebellious thing to do, since most of the star players were with the new league. Among them were two of baseball's most miserly current owners: Charles Comiskey and Connie Mack.

Continuing my excavations through the old guides and papers, I found that the next attempt at a players union was the Players Protective Association organized in 1900. To avoid being branded as radical, no one from the old Brotherhood was elected an officer of the new organization. The Association was actively wooed and encouraged by Ban Johnson, who at the time was trying to launch the American League and needed ballplayers. Two years later, with his league established, Johnson dropped his support of the Association, and the union dissolved.

It took ten years until another organizing effort was made,

when Dave Fultz started the Baseball Players' Fraternity. Once a mediocre outfielder best known for refusing to play on Sundays, Fultz had gone on to a Wall Street law practice after his retirement from baseball. He outlined the aims of the new players' organization in the November 1912 issue of *Baseball Magazine.* Its stated goals were modest: to demand that team owners abide by contracts, to protect players from spectator abuse, and to provide financial assistance to deserving ballplayers. The Fraternity was not going to challenge the sacred reserve clause, because, according to Fultz, "baseball is a peculiar business and must be governed by peculiar laws."

One of the features that I liked about the Fraternity was that it included minor-league baseball in its membership and goals. "A minor leaguer is just as important to us as the biggest star," said Fultz. It was on behalf of minor leaguers—who could be suspended without pay if they became injured—that Fultz threatened a major-league strike for 1917. He neglected to get the support of the players, though, and the Fraternity collapsed before the season's opening day.

There were a couple points of interest about the Fraternity. One was that Ty Cobb had been one of its four vice presidents. Another was something that I didn't find: any mention of Emmett Siever.

In a thorough check of the records, I found that Siever had played outfield for Detroit in three leagues: with the Detroit Wolverines back when Detroit was in the National League, with the Western League Detroit Creams in 1894, and with the new Detroit Tigers of 1901. But other than his having played for the Players League in 1890, I could find no documentation of his involvement with efforts to form a players' union. Not until last summer.

Emmett Siever had burst onto the labor front from nowhere. But when he did launch his drive for a players' union last year, he was uncompromising in his goals. He intended to openly challenge the reserve clause and stop teams from buying and selling players like commodities.

What I couldn't find the answer to was *why* he'd become so interested and so active.

After leaving the *Sporting News* office, I went to the public library to read more broadly on labor movements and the recent conflicts between labor, management, and government.

To my disappointment, there was little material available on the subject. The library wasn't permitted to carry "radical" literature, so there was almost nothing promoting the labor point of view. Information on union busting efforts was equally sparse because industrialists and government agencies were so secretive about their antilabor activities.

An attractive reference librarian, who appeared to share my frustration at the lack of published material, verbally shared with me what she knew about the IWW, the Justice Department, and the Palmer raids. She didn't say so explicitly, but I gathered from the way she described the opposing sides that her sympathies were with the unions.

I listened closely, absorbed most of what she said, and came away with at least a tentative grasp of the issues. But as hard as I tried, I was unable to decide for certain where my own sympathies lay.

# Chapter Eleven
### ○○○

I'd heard once that a pack of lions is called a "pride." I didn't know if that term also applied to a group of tigers, but if so, it was a misnomer for the humiliated Tigers team that slunk into Detroit's Michigan Central Depot early Friday morning with our tails between our legs.

Hughie Jennings's fearsome lineup of Ty Cobb, Harry Heilmann, and Bobby Veach had been throttled by the St. Louis pitching staff of Urban Shocker, Dixie Davis, and Carl Weilman. In three games against the lowly Browns, the Detroit batting order had managed to put across a grand total of one run. Not only had we extended the winless streak to eleven games, we had now been shut out for eighteen straight innings. The St. Louis sportswriters crowed about their club's successful "Tiger Hunt" in Sportsman's Park in language sure to antagonize both Detroit fans and animal lovers. One of them wrote that the Browns "tamed the toothless felines as easily as drowning a litter of kittens."

Team morale, low since spring training, had entirely evaporated, and internal strife was rampant. Harry Heilmann had developed an inexplicable hatred for amiable Bobby Veach. Donie Bush and Ty Cobb had renewed their fierce ten-year-old feud. Hughie Jennings was no longer speaking to any of his coaches and only a few of his players. Rumors were flying that Jennings would be fired in a matter of days.

The dugout battles left the players too drained to perform properly on the field. My own fight in the Sportsman's Park tunnel was unusual in that it yielded some positive results: neither Dutch Leonard nor Chick Fogarty bothered me for the rest of the series. It also left Leonard looking like he had a snootful for a couple of days and Fogarty sounding like he had a speech impediment.

Although I didn't make an appearance in a game—not even as a coach—I did get in a lot of hitting, thanks to Lou Vedder. The two of us spent our free hours working out at the park. He pitched me enough batting practice that I started to develop a fluid swing from the left side of the plate. Then I caught for him while he tried to come up with another pitch to replace the forbidden spitter. I told him that a fastball, curve, and change-up were all a pitcher needed if he had control, but Vedder got it into his head that he was going to master the knuckleball. He had no more success with that than the Detroit batters had with the St. Louis pitching staff.

Now it was back to our home turf. While my teammates trudged out of the train station, I stopped at a newsstand to see what kind of reception we could expect from the fans—if we still had any fans.

I was happy to see from the headlines that the Tigers' feat in going the entire month of April without a win wasn't the biggest news. Attorney General Mitchell Palmer had managed to capture most of the front pages with headlines like

*Terror Reign by Radicals, Says Palmer* and *Nationwide Uprising on Saturday.* Palmer claimed that that Bolsheviks were planning a May Day revolution: bombings, assassinations, and general strikes. State militias were being called up in response to Palmer's warning, and federal troops were being put on alert. There were other headlines, much smaller, that suggested the scare was of Palmer's own invention, intended to revitalize his campaign for the presidency. The country would find out soon enough whether Palmer was right. Tomorrow was May first.

Whether or not there would be a revolution—which I doubted—I was looking forward to May. It had to mark an improvement over April, a month in which I'd been credited with the murder of a popular ex-ballplayer, had incurred the wrath of owners, teammates, labor organizers, and union busters, and had again lost Margie Turner.

As I left the station, I remembered that tomorrow would also mark one week since I'd met with Leo Hyman and Whitey Boggs. One week gone, with no progress on finding Emmett Siever's killer. Three weeks remained until I'd have to show Hyman some results. Of course, if that shotgun blast through my window had been fired by someone other than Wobblies, trying to meet Hyman's deadline still wouldn't protect me from another attack. I thought of Karl Landfors's warning that the real murderer might try to stop me from exposing him.

Then I thought again of the St. Louis newspapers with their "Tiger Hunt" headlines. The only Tiger really being hunted was me.

○ ○ ○

At my apartment, I found Landfors gone and the icebox empty. I muttered a wish that he would marry Constance Siever and move in with her.

I also noticed that my landlady had replaced the glass in the parlor window. Just when I was thinking that a good thick piece of wood might be the best thing to have over it. What hung over the window instead was my favorite bath towel, which Landfors must have tacked up as a curtain. I renewed my wish about him and Miss Siever in language that would not have made for a polite wedding toast.

Spring had come to Detroit while we were out of town, so after tossing my suitcase on the sofa I opened the window to let in some fresh air. Then I dug under my bed for a dented old biscuit tin that I'd stashed there. I had carried the tin with me when I'd first left home at age fifteen to try and make my way as a ballplayer. Its purpose was to store my "important stuff." The lid had airholes punched in it, and scratched above the holes was the warning: *Beware of Snake*. The tin had never contained a snake, but I thought the warning would discourage anyone from exploring its contents. At first, the container had held nothing more than a few tobacco cards of my favorite big-league players, a photograph of my late aunt, and the old-fashioned fingerless glove my uncle wore when he and I used to play catch—it was his going-away present to me. In the years since, I still hadn't acquired enough additional "important stuff" to need a larger storage box.

I pried off the scarred lid. At the top of the pile inside were my discharge papers from the army and my playing contract for the current season. It was the contract I was interested in.

Unfolding the four-page legal-sized document, I read it word for word. I didn't want to go by John Montgomery Ward's or Emmett Siever's opinions of the terms; I wanted to understand them for myself.

The reserve clause, the single sentence that had caused so much strife over the years, appeared in Clause 11:

> *The club may, at its option, at any time within 90 days after the close of the playing season of 1920, notify the player of its election to have this contract renewed for the succeeding season, and in the event of such notice being given, this contract shall stand renewed for the succeeding season of 1921.*

In his speech at Fraternity Hall, Emmett Siever had said imagine if auto manufacturers had such a rule: a worker on the Ford assembly line could be bound to Ford "in perpetuity." The employee could not seek better wages or conditions at Dodge or General Motors; Ford could simply keep renewing its contract with the worker under terms and salary to be determined solely by Henry Ford. Or, Ford could elect to sell or trade the employee to another company without the worker having any say in the transaction.

The way Siever described the reserve clause, it certainly did not sound fair. Nor could I find any fairness in the wording of the clause in my contract. As far as being sold or traded, the only obligation the Detroit Tigers had was to inform me of the name of my new club and the terms of the transfer.

It was clear from reading the contract that the club had all the options; I had none. Clause 6 of the contract even specified that I had to pay for my own shoes and give the club a $30 deposit for my uniform. On principle, I agreed that players were treated unfairly, and in some ways as "chattels," to use John Ward's word.

But then there was Clause 1:

*The club agrees to pay the player for the season of 1920, beginning on or about the 15th day of April, 1920, and ending on or about the 15th day of October, 1920, a salary at the rate of $3000 for such season.*

Three thousand dollars. More than double what a typical factory worker earned in a year, and I got it for only six months of playing baseball. True, it was a little less than I'd made a couple of years ago, but all salaries had taken a dip after the shortened seasons of 1918 and 1919. What it came down to for me was that I was being well compensated for doing what I loved. Quite simply, I was satisfied.

I put the contract back in the biscuit tin and the tin under my bed. Since we had no game scheduled for Navin Field, and I'd gotten little sleep on the train from St. Louis, I then curled up in the bed for a short nap.

After two hours of sound sleep, I decided to put the day to better use than merely lazing around the apartment. I took a quick bath, then donned a blue seersucker suit, a soft-collar white shirt, and one of the brightly patterned neckties that Landfors had refused to wear.

I next fortified myself at Kelsey's Cafe, downing two cups of coffee and a three-egg breakfast with a side order of flap-jacks at an hour when everyone else was eating lunch. While I ate, I chewed over what my next step should be in probing Emmett Siever's death.

I resented having to do anything at all. If the police had done their jobs, it wouldn't be up to me. It *shouldn't* be up to me. The most I could hope for from them, though, was that Detective McGuire might reopen the investigation—*if* I could bring him hard evidence. If I couldn't make Leo Hyman's deadline and find the killer in three weeks, perhaps I could at least get enough evidence for McGuire to take over for me. Whether that would suffice to keep the Wobblies from coming after me again, I somewhat doubted.

As far as what to do next, it seemed to me that learning more about the victim was the way to go. So far, what little information I had about Emmett Siever had come primarily from his allies—Hyman, Boggs, Landfors, and Connie. I needed another perspective—from one of his enemies. As much as I would have preferred to avoid him, I decided that Hub Donner was the man for me to see.

I tipped the waitress a nickel for a fifteen-cent meal, walked in the fresh spring air to Woodward Avenue, and caught a northbound streetcar.

○ ○ ○

Like its southeast neighbor Hamtramck, Highland Park was completely contained within the Detroit city boundary. As the streetcar entered Henry Ford's company town, it first passed through the neighborhood where his workers lived. Their modest homes all appeared well maintained, but totally lacking in charm. A sterile quality permeated the area, as if the inhabitants were all living in conformity with someone else's design.

Proceeding up Woodward, the first sign of the auto plant

was a *FORD* banner stretched between a couple of towering smokestacks. Minutes later, the factory was visible, sprawling over a vast area. I'd heard the home of the first assembly line called the "Crystal Palace." To me, it looked like an enormous flat-roofed greenhouse. The walls consisted mainly of windows, acres of glass that shimmered in the afternoon sunlight. As the trolley drew closer, the buzz and rumble of conveyor belts and machinery within the plant became audible.

I got off at Manchester and went to the factory's nearest entrance; it turned out to be Ford's employment office, and I was brusquely told that there were no jobs available. I then found the main gate, where I told a guard that I wanted to see Hub Donner of the Service Department. After the guard placed a call to Donner, a second guard escorted me into the office area. The floors vibrated softly from the activities in the plant, and a steady hum filled the air.

Although there was no sign identifying it as such, I knew when we'd reached the Service Department. The area gave the impression of a military headquarters. Smartly dressed, uniformed guards strode around purposefully; they looked alert and businesslike, nothing like what I'd seen so far of the Detroit Police Department. Mixed among them were a few large, disreputable-looking men wearing bad suits and bow ties. In comparison to these bruisers, the uniformed guards looked like Girl Scouts.

Dressed similarly to the other thugs, Hub Donner emerged from a nearby office. He didn't appear jovial as he had at the Hotel Tuller, nor smug as he'd been when sitting with Frank Navin at the ballpark. Royally pissed was how he looked. After dismissing the guard who'd escorted me, he growled, "What are you doing here?"

"I wanted to talk to you about Emmett Siever and the players' union."

"This is where I work for Mr. Ford." Donner brushed a palm over his stubbly scalp. "That other business is for another place and time."

"I didn't know how else to contact you. Besides, you talked to me at Navin Field, and that's where *I* work."

Donner made no verbal reply, but his eyes indicated that he didn't consider our situations equivalent.

"Anyway," I said. "Now that I'm here, can we talk for a couple minutes?"

"Yeah, what the hell." He led me out of the main room, stopping to tell a guard at the desk, "Don't disturb me. This fellow might have some information on sabotage at the Rouge Plant tomorrow."

Donner ushered me into a small windowless room furnished with one table and two chairs. He pointed to one of them. "Sit."

His mention of the Rouge Plant had me a little disconcerted. Did he know that I'd met Boggs and Hyman there? They might have eluded a tail by their trick with the cars, but what if I'd been followed from my apartment?

I decided to volunteer that I'd seen them. If Donner thought I was being open with him, it might earn me some good will. "I met with a couple fellows from Fraternity Hall."

Donner's expression didn't betray whether or not that was news to him. "I told you before it's not wise for you to be associating with Reds."

"I *had* to talk to them. They're the ones mostly likely to know what really happened to Emmett Siever."

"'What really happened' is what the newspapers said happened."

"Told you before, the papers are wrong."

"So you claim."

I studied Donner, trying without success to pick up a hint of what was going on in that scarred heard of his. "It seems to me," I said, "that we have a similar interest in finding out who really killed him. If it turns out a Wobbly killed Siever, the players won't have anything to do with the IWW ever again. And if it turns out Siever was killed by—well, by a union buster, that'll discourage the players from trying to unionize at all. Nobody will want to take Siever's place if they think it could get them killed."

A hint of amusement danced in Donner's eyes. "Are you trying to tell me that you want to help me stop the players' union?"

"Hell no. I'm only interested in clearing myself. The fact that it works out better for you too is just a good reason for you to help me find his killer."

"Having it pegged on you suits me just fine."

"The story that *I* killed Siever isn't making anybody scared of me," I said. "My teammates, for instance: they're mad at me, not scared. Now if it turns out Siever was killed by somebody like you, *that* might make them think twice about going ahead with a union."

"You flatter me."

"Sorry, didn't mean to." We eyed each other uneasily for a moment. I then asked, "How long has the American League had you working on Emmett Siever?"

Donner hesitated before deciding to answer. "Almost a year. Ever since he started agitating."

"Do you know anything about what he was doing before that?"

"Siever was *nothing* before that. A washed-up ballplayer who wasn't much good in his best years."

"What I mean is, was he active with the IWW or anybody?"

"If he was, nobody seems to know about it."

"Hmm." I went on to another question that had been bothering me. "From what I hear, there weren't many players joining up with Siever. Why was the league so worried about him organizing if he wasn't successful at it anyway?"

Donner thought for a few moments. I wondered if he'd ever really considered the *why* of the situation. He might have simply done what the league owners hired him to do and never asked their reasons. "For one thing," he finally answered, "Siever was a radical, and it doesn't take a lot of them to be dangerous. Only needed a few players to go along with him for there to be real trouble. And some players *were* sympathetic to him—still are, most likely." He folded his hands over his belly as if he'd just finished a meal. "Anything else on your mind?"

"Yes. Where were you when Emmett Siever was shot?"

A laugh exploded from his mouth. "Decided you don't like being a hero, so you want to give *me* the glory?"

I stared at him steadily.

His belly still rocking, he said, "I was having dinner with Ban Johnson and Frank Navin, if you really want to know. Ask them if you like."

"No need," I said. The American League president and the owner of the Tigers were pretty strong alibis. "And it wasn't that I thought you killed him," I added, trying to sound conciliatory. "I figured you might have been watching him and maybe saw who went into Fraternity Hall—or who came out the back door."

Intense distaste showed on Donner's face. "I don't got the stomach to go to that place. All them filthy foreigners in there, who knows what I'd catch from them. Can't stand foreigners. Coming here, trying to cause trouble, expecting handouts. Parasites is what they are. It was men like Henry Ford and Andrew Carnegie and John Rockefeller who made America great. Not immigrants coming in to steal the fruits of American labor."

"I thought Carnegie came here from Scotland."

Hub Donner leaned forward and any trace of good humor slowly vanished from his face. "Okay, I played along and answered your questions. Now it's time for you to do something for me—and for the men who put bread in your mouth."

"What do you—"

"This is what's going to happen: you're going to go public against the players' union. Newspaper articles, speeches, the whole thing, just like I told you before."

"And I told you I won't have any part of that."

"Then I hope you got retirement plans."

I tried to appear unconcerned. "So what's the worst that can happen? Frank Navin boots me off a team that can't win a game and ain't giving me a chance to play anyway? Might be a break for me. I'll play someplace else."

"I don't see where that would be such a good break for you. Remember, it's not just Navin—it's the American League. You go against Ban Johnson, and you cut off half your employment opportunities. Leaves you with the Nationals, and you already wore out your welcome with a bunch of their teams." Donner leaned back, a smug look on his face. "You're gonna be lucky if you get picked up by a semipro team in a mill league somewhere."

Jeez. I'd paid my dues in the industrial leagues years ago. I wasn't ready to be heading back down the ranks yet. But I sure wasn't going to go along with Hub Donner, either.

"What I don't understand," I said, resorting to an argument that I didn't really want to make, "is doesn't it make the league look bad that they couldn't get a bigger star than me to go against the union? That would make it seem like all the rest of them were in favor of it."

*"Bigger star?"* Donner laughed. "I wish I could get *any* kind of star. You're a busher, kid. But you're the one who killed Siever, so you'll have to do." He caressed the scar over his right ear. "Tell you what," he said. "I like you. Don't know why, but I think you're an okay kid. Just need to get your priorities straight. I'm gonna give you a break. You take some time and rethink your position. Three days. Give me a firm answer by Monday. And I'll be contacting *you* next time."

I wasn't sure that I wanted to be liked by Hub Donner. I *was* sure that I wasn't going to change my mind. But I agreed to think about it.

Donner walked me to the waiting area and summoned a guard to take me out. "Remember, I'll call you. Don't be coming here again. This is where I do Henry Ford's business, not Frank Navin's."

Three days till Donner's deadline, I thought, three weeks until Leo Hyman's. I was going to have to get a scorecard and start keeping track of who was going to be coming after me, when, and for what reason.

# Chapter Twelve
ooo

**S**unday morning, half past nine. Karl Landfors was still out, hadn't phoned, and I was starting to worry. I hadn't seen him since the previous morning, when he'd left for Constance Siever's house. His dreamy manner and fastidious preparations had given the impression that May Day was more of a Valentine's Day for radicals than a political observance.

When I first woke up and found Landfors missing, I worried that he might have been in trouble—perhaps caught up in another Palmer raid on "Bolsheviks." But after I got the morning newspapers, my worries diminished. According to the headlines, there had been no revolution yesterday. No bombings, no assassinations, not so much as a firecracker. Some papers went so far as to pronounce that the Red Scare was over. I wasn't so sure.

Mitchell Palmer maintained a defiant tone, claiming the revolutionaries had merely postponed their attacks in an attempt to discredit him and lull the nation into a false sense of security. Invoking the appeal that President Wilson had made to him last fall—"Palmer, do not let this country see red!''—the attorney general reaffirmed his intention to stop "the blaze of revolution" while it was still an ember. He also vowed to continue his campaign for the Democratic nomination for president. I briefly wondered if Palmer might try to create a confrontation in order to justify his predictions and regain his credibility; but I decided that was a question for someone with a stronger interest in politics than I had.

Having more or less convinced myself that Landfors's absence simply meant that he and Connie Siever were getting along better than ever, I moved on to the sports pages. Yesterday's game at Navin Field was summed up by the headline *Tigers Handed Twelfth Bump*. A dozen losses without one win. I was starting to wish that it was to be a short season like last year, when the owners cut the schedule to 140 games in the mistaken belief that the war had eroded Americans' interest in baseball. We were now back to a full 156-game season which, on the positive side, meant that the Tigers still had 144 chances to win a ballgame.

The extension of the Detroit losing streak wasn't the day's biggest baseball news. At Braves Field in Boston, the Dodgers and Braves had played the longest game in major league history: twenty-six innings. Nearly three games in one, and all for naught, as darkness put an end to the contest with the score tied 1-1. Joe Oeschger, whose fastball had sent me home early from spring training, pitched for the Braves, and Leon Cadore for the Dodgers. Remarkably, both pitchers went the distance. Their catchers needed to be relieved, but not Oeschger and Cadore, neither of whom allowed a run during the game's final twenty innings.

The Braves-Dodgers marathon brought to mind another pitching duel, another one that I hadn't seen in person but remained the ballgame I remembered most fondly. It took place on July 4, 1905, in Boston's Huntington Avenue Grounds with Rube Waddell of the Philadelphia Athletics matched up against the Boston Americans' Cy Young. I was thirteen years old that summer and idolized the colorful Waddell. I found out the next day that the game went twenty innings, both pitchers going all the way, until Waddell himself drove in the game-winning run.

To my mind, it was the perfect baseball game with the perfect outcome. I replayed it over and over the way some boys reenacted Civil War battles with toy soldiers. In my case, I used the box score and accounts from the game that appeared in New York and Philadelphia papers that my uncle got for me. I was already convinced that I was going to be a big-league ballplayer someday, and readily put myself in the spiked shoes of the men who played that game. One day I might be Socks Seybold or Harry Davis of the Athletics; on another I might be Boston's Freddy Parent or Jimmy Collins. Sometimes I'd let myself be Cy Young, and on special occasions I would be Rube Waddell.

My reverie dimmed. I did become a major-league player, but I never got to meet Rube Waddell. In 1914 he died from pneumonia after helping flood victims in Texas. That ended something for me, but it took years more until I realized what it was: when a boyhood hero dies, it means boyhood is irretrievably lost.

I sighed. I no longer had the innocent faith in baseball that I'd had at age thirteen, and I was angry as hell that I couldn't get it back.

By late morning, I was mad at Karl Landfors for not coming home without as much as a phone call, at whoever killed

Emmett Siever and got me into trouble over it, at Joe Oeschger for nailing me with that fastball, and most of all at Rube Waddell for dying and ending my childhood.

○ ○ ○

Two hours before game time, Frank Navin was alone inside the main gate to his ballpark, stocking the ticket booths. If yesterday's attendance was any indication, there would be a heavy demand for the tickets. Fans came out in record numbers hoping to be present at the first win of the season—but more than satisfied with heckling us mercilessly if we extended the losing streak.

I hopped a turnstile and joined Navin. He was in the process of opening a box of scorecards and sweating from the exertion. Frank Navin was not a typical team owner. Not content simply to observe the team's play from his personal box, he took an active role in the club's most mundane daily tasks. Navin often manned the ticket booths, ushered fans to their seats, or sold them refreshments. I'd read up on him when I was in the *Sporting News* office. Years before, he had been the club's bookkeeper until a lucky streak in an all-night poker game provided him the cash to buy the team. Still a gambling man, he now divided his interests between the Tigers and the ponies.

"Need a hand with those?" I asked.

Navin was struggling to balance a stack of scorecards that came up to his drooping chin. "Over there." He nodded toward one of the concession stands.

I took most of the cards from him and carried them to the booth, placing them on the counter. Navin reached up to put his pile next to mine. "Weather's getting warmer," he huffed.

"Finally," I said. "I hate the cold."

The Tigers owner took a handkerchief from his pocket and mopped beads of sweat from his bald head. The temperature was only in the sixties, so his perspiration had less to do with the weather than with his flabby condition. Still, he was working hard, and to my mind the fact that he was willing to do manual labor made his penny-pinching ways less onerous.

"I have a problem, Mr. Navin," I said.

"If it's money, I can't help. Barely breaking even this year. You signed a contract, and that's all you're going to get paid."

"No, it's not money." I leaned on the counter of the concession booth. "It's Hub Donner. He's really pushing me to help him bust the players' union. I can't do that. I won't go against my teammates." I was supposed to give Donner my answer by tomorrow, but I'd decided to give it directly to Frank Navin instead.

"Then don't." Navin removed his glasses and rubbed the bridge of his nose. "Son, as far as I'm concerned, you signed a contract to play baseball for me, not help Hub Donner fight the union. Just stick to the deal: you play and I pay you for it—but like I said, not a penny more than you signed for."

"The salary's fine, Mr. Navin." I knew that statement would haunt me when it came time for the next contract, but his biggest worry appeared to be that I was going to try to touch him up for a few bucks. "And I appreciate you saying all I got to do is play ball. But Donner says Ban Johnson will kick me out of the American League if I don't go along with him."

"Ban Johnson's in New York. That's a long way from here. Don't you worry about it."

"Donner says he was here a couple of weeks ago. Said him, you, and Mr. Johnson had dinner. You sure Mr. Johnson won't kick me out of the league?"

"Ban Johnson hasn't been out here since January. If he wanted you to help Donner so badly, he'd have told me. So far, he hasn't said anything. If he does, I'll let you know. For now, just worry about baseball."

"Okay. Thanks, Mr. Navin."

I left him with the rest of the scorecards and headed for the locker room, wondering why Hub Donner had lied to me.

O O O

The fans who'd hoped to witness the Tigers' first win of the season were disappointed. Those who'd come to heckle another defeat did so with glee and vigor. A 5-2 loss to the Indians ran our winless streak to a baker's dozen. One hundred forty-three chances left to win a game this year.

Worse than the loss was the fact that I again had to watch the proceedings from the bench. I appreciated Frank Navin saying that all I had to do was play baseball for him, but I wished he would do more—like tell Hughie Jennings actually to put me in a game.

I was in a vile mood by the time I got home, and seeing Karl Landfors asleep on the sofa didn't improve it any. I slammed the door hard enough to trigger a rattling noise in the cuckoo clock.

Landfors woke up with a groan and reached for his spectacles. Once they were securely on his nose, he slithered out from under the blanket. Blinking at me, he asked, "What time is it?"

"I thought you came here to help me find out who killed Emmett Siever, not to court his daughter." I stalked into the kitchen and checked the icebox. Moxie again. I opened a bottle and went into the parlor.

"Well, yes, that's true," Landfors said calmly. He poked a forefinger behind one of the thick lenses and rubbed his eye. "What exactly would you like me to do?"

I gulped some of the pop. First thing I'd like you to do, I thought, is stop bringing Moxie in here. "You could have called," I said. "Thought you might have got caught up in some anti-Red roundup or something."

"That was inconsiderate of me. I apologize." He blinked rapidly. "In the future I'll let you know if I'm going to be late."

I was starting to feel like a heel for yelling at him. Leave it to Landfors to take the fun out of being in a bad mood. I waved off the apology. "Don't worry about it. I'm glad you and her are getting on so well."

Landfors stood up. In his dark, floor-length nightshirt he looked like a folded umbrella. "Thank you," he said. "However, I did come here to help you, and I have been somewhat remiss in that regard." He went into the kitchen, and I heard him filling the coffeepot with water.

"You *have* helped," I said. When he came back in the

parlor, I added, "The problem is there's still a long way to go."

As he swapped his sleeping garment for trousers and an undershirt, Landfors asked, "*Where* exactly is it that you're going?"

That was a good question. "I know where I want to end up," I answered. "With the right person taking the rap for Emmett Siever's murder. That's where I *have* to end up." I thought a moment more. "As far as how I get there, I'm not sure. It seems I'm trying to do two things at once: keep myself out of immediate trouble and meanwhile learn as much as I can that might lead me to Siever's killer."

With a nod at the newly replaced window, Landfors said, "Is that the 'immediate trouble' you mean?"

"It's one of them. Another is getting dropped from the team—and maybe blacklisted—if I don't do what Hub Donner wants me to. There's no way I'm gonna go along with him, and I'm supposed to give him my decision tomorrow. I might have bought myself a little extra time with Frank Navin, though. Maybe he'll keep Donner off my back for a while." I had the impression that Donner was obedient to his bosses. He'd seemed worried about conducting outside business at the Ford plant. Perhaps he'd worry about crossing Navin, too.

"As far as my teammates," I went on, "things have eased up a little. It's this losing streak. The players are numb from it, mentally and physically. Barely have the strength to take the field every day, never mind picking a fight with me. But it can't go on forever, and then who knows what they'll do."

The smell of fresh coffee wafted into the room, and Landfors went into the kitchen. "Would you like a cup?" he called.

The bottle of Moxie in my hand was still half-full, but I decided the sink could have the rest of it, and said yes to his offer.

I glanced back at the window again as Landfors brought in the coffee mugs. "Thanks," I said, and took a sip. For all his flaws, Landfors did make a decent cup of coffee. "As far as the IWW, I think that's where my biggest worry is. Leo Hyman told me that I have three weeks from yesterday to tell him who really shot Siever. He says he'll spread the word to the Wobblies that it's hands off until then, but I don't know if I can rely on that."

"Hyman is a man of his word," Landfors said. He pulled on a clean white shirt and attached a stiff celluloid collar to it. "I have my disagreements with him in certain areas, but I do believe he's a trustworthy man."

"Even if he does tell them to leave me alone, what guarantee is there that they'll listen? I don't expect anarchists are all that willing to follow orders."

Landfors opened his mouth, looking as if he was about to protest, then caught himself. "You might have a point."

"Anyway, that's it for immediate dangers. Now, as far as solving the murder, I think the place to start—"

"Is with the false Detective Aikens." Landfors smiled confidently.

"Uh, no. But speaking of Aikens, I think I have an idea who he is. Well, not who he *is,* but who he's *with* anyway."

A peeved look started to take hold of Landfors's features. "Don't keep me in suspense," he said.

"I think he's with the Justice Department. Specifically, the GID. Leo Hyman told me that during the Palmer raids, the General Intelligence Division coordinated the raids and local police helped carry them out. Remember, the police raided Fraternity Hall the night Siever was killed, so maybe there was a GID man there supervising things. Also, I told you before I thought Aikens had to have some kind of authority because he had to give the police my name. And he did have a badge."

"But you still don't think . . ."

"That Aikens is the killer? No. If he shot Siever, he wouldn't have stayed there in the back room." Besides, I didn't want to believe that a federal agent would kill an unarmed civilian. "He might have seen who did, though. My guess is that Aikens would have been outside the building before the raid, keeping an eye on it. Maybe he heard the shot or saw the killer run out the back door, then he went in to see what happened, and that's when he found me there." I was speculating, and didn't want to include the additional speculation that Hub Donner might have been the man Aikens saw leaving the Hall.

Landfors nodded thoughtfully. "Tell me again what Aikens looks like."

In as much detail as I could, I described the appearance, mannerisms, and dress of the man who had presented himself to me as a police detective. Then I added, "If he *is* with the government, he sure isn't going to want to tell me anything about what he was doing here.

"Anyway, I think the most useful thing to do is find out about Emmett Siever himself. What was there about him that made someone want to kill him?"

"Are you saying Siever is at fault for his own death?"

"No, I don't mean anything like that. Just that he's a part of what happened. Part of the puzzle. And if we know as much as we can about him, maybe we know the motive for shooting him, find who had the motive, and . . . we have his killer."

Landfors looked mollified that I wasn't trying to blame the victim for the crime.

I went on. "I've learned a few things about him. For starters, he wasn't such a great guy. Not always, anyway, certainly not in his playing days. Did you know he ran around on his wife, and after she died he abandoned Connie?"

He nodded, and said softly, "Her grandmother raised her." That answered one of the questions I'd never gotten to ask Connie.

"Another thing," I said, "is Siever's interest in unionizing doesn't go back very far. A year or two at the most. He didn't have anything to do with the players' unions before that. Seems strange to get so active so suddenly."

"It might have been because of Connie. He knew how important the labor movement was—is—to her."

"Leo Hyman told me that she's the one who got him involved with the IWW."

"She mentioned that to me."

"Has she asked anything about her father? Or said anything about who might have killed him?" I wanted to ask Landfors, but couldn't, why she hadn't seemed distraught by her father's death.

Landfors stammered before finding the words, "I'm not entirely sure what she's—what we've—talked about. It always seems we have a lot to say to each other, but I'm never quite sure afterward what it was that we said."

There's something about the lovesick that reminds me of the mentally impaired. "If you have a chance—and if you think you can concentrate on the conversation—could you ask Connie about her father? I think it would help if we knew more about his personal life, and she's the one who would know it best."

He agreed he would, then borrowed a tie and left to see her.

After he left, I went to the window, pulled aside the bath towel and looked out at the cars crawling by on Grand River Avenue. Then I looked straight down, to the sidewalk in front of my building. Another shotgun blast through the window wasn't what had me worried. It was the possibility of a head or belly shot as I stepped outside that scared me.

# Chapter Thirteen

I felt like I had one of Eddie Cicotte's knuckleballs dancing around in my belly. My insides were rocked by spasms of—well, they were spasms of fear, though I preferred to think of them as "butterflies." My legs were jelly, barely able to support my body or lift my leaden feet. That's what the first at bat of the year can do to a body. To mine, anyway.

Staring me down from the pitcher's mound was Cleveland's George Uhle, a burly young fireballer. I faced him right-handed; my wrist was one of the few parts of my body that felt strong, and it was my best chance to get that all-important first hit of the year.

Just meet the ball, I told myself. Get some wood on it . . . Whatever you do, don't strike out. Don't strike out.

Uhle shook off a sign from the catcher, then delivered quickly. I watched a fastball go past me right down the middle. Strike one!

Jeez, it went by fast. I backed out of the box and knocked my bat against my spikes. Ignore everything but the little white ball, I told myself. Forget that Navin Field is packed with screaming fans, forget that it's scoreless in the bottom of the second, or that staying on the club depends on your performance.

Squeezing the bat handle hard, I stepped back in. Meet the ball. Don't strike out. *Don't strike out.*

Next came a slow curve that broke low and half a foot outside the plate. The head of my swinging bat missed the ball by at least that much, and I almost fell over reaching for it. 0-and-2.

Okay, is Uhle going to waste a pitch, or try to get it over with right away?

He went for the strikeout: fastball, belt-high, on the inside corner. I took a hard cut, trying to pull it. The ball ticked the bat handle and fell mere inches in front of home plate, plopping into the muck of Cobb's Lake. I froze for a second, dismayed at the pitiful result—a bunt would have traveled farther. Then I broke for first; no matter how hopeless, run full speed on anything that's hit. Indians' catcher Steve O'Neill fielded the ball and threw me out before I was halfway to the base.

I trotted back to the dugout, surprisingly almost cheerful. I didn't strike out! I didn't strike out!

When I passed Hughie Jennings in the coach's box, he said, "At least you didn't strike out."

In the dugout, Dutch Leonard spat near my feet. "How the hell am I supposed to win a ballgame with *you* in the lineup? Jennings gonna put the batboy in next?"

I didn't respond. I knew Jennings hadn't given me my first start of the season because he thought I could do much to help the team. It was a move to shake things up, to try something new and see if we could pull off a victory.

After Chick Fogarty struck out to end our half of the

inning, I grabbed my mitt and hustled out to second base. I resisted the temptation to gloat to Leonard that at least I'd done better than his buddy Fogarty had.

As for Dutch Leonard, he did have great stuff this game. Through the first three innings, Leonard deftly slid his spitter past the futile bats of the Cleveland hitters. If we could get just one or two runs on the board, we might win our first game of the season. Even though it meant Dutch Leonard getting credit for the victory, I wanted to help bring that about.

My first fielding chance came in the top of the fourth, with two outs and Tris Speaker on third. Cleveland shortstop Ray Chapman hit an easy two-hopper right at me. I casually bent down to field it—and was horrified when the ball bounced low and scooted under my glove, right through my legs. I spun about and retrieved it, but far too late. Chapman was safe at first and Speaker had crossed the plate to put the Indians up 1–0.

I tossed the ball to Leonard, who caught it in his bare hand. Glaring at me, he tucked his mitt under his arm and rubbed the baseball between his palms. Hard, as if trying to tear the cover off; staring at me, as if he wished it was my face in his grip. The sun burst out from behind a cloud, and I felt like I had a spotlight on me. Boos and catcalls from the Monday afternoon crowd registered in my ears. I wanted to dig a burrow under second base and crawl into it.

Leonard finally turned around, and methodically struck out Bill Wambsganss to end the inning. I stayed far away from him in the dugout; he fumed in silence.

We were still down 1–0 in the bottom of the fifth. Two outs, two on: Harry Heilmann on third and Bobby Veach on second. I was the next batter up. As I walked from the on-deck circle to the batter's box, I looked at Jennings. Partly to see if he was flashing a sign, but also because I expected him to call me back and send in a pinch hitter. That was the advice Dutch Leonard was screaming at him from the bench.

Jennings ignored Leonard's pleas. The old Oriole let loose a hoarse rebel yell, "Ee-yaaaah!" Then called, "Bring 'em on in, Rawlings! You can do it, boy!"

I wished that I shared Jennings's confidence. The fact that George Uhle greeted my appearance with a confident grin on his face didn't help.

Uhle promptly blew a fastball by me as I swung late; it was in the same location as his first pitch in my previous at bat. Then the curve, low and away; I again fished for it, and again I missed.

If he was repeating the sequence from last time, the next pitch would be a tight fastball. It was. But this time I didn't try to pull it. I met the ball with an inside-out half swing, trying to push it toward right field. The bat handle shuddered on impact, but my grip was firm. The ball looped its way over the second baseman's head. As Veach and Heilmann raced in to the plate, I tried to stretch it into a double, aware that the right fielder was dead-armed Smoky Joe Wood. His arm turned out to be livelier than I expected, and I was thrown out at second to end the inning.

I ran off the field triumphant. My first base hit of the season, and two RBIs to give us the lead in the game. I didn't have to go all the way to the bench to get my glove. Harry Heilmann brought it out to me as he went to take his position at first base. "Way to go, kid!" he said. Dutch Leonard gave me no such praise, but he had a happy glint in his eyes and a determined set to his jaw. He was going to win this game and I'd given him two runs to work with.

It was all he needed. I got no more hits in the game, though I did steal second after walking in the eighth. Donie Bush had a double and triple to extend the winning score to 5–1.

The fans cheered wildly at the Tigers first win of the season. Somehow, overtones of sarcasm rang through the applause. It's amazing how a crowd can express itself collectively like that.

Until we were in the locker room, the Detroit players all acted is if the win was nothing special. Once in the clubhouse, we celebrated like we'd just won the World Series. The curse was lifted.

My teammates included me in the celebration. Politics and personal grudges were forgotten for the moment. I'd helped win the game, and that's all that counted right now.

I lingered in the locker room, savoring the feel of the game: the stinging raspberry on my left thigh from sliding into second, the mild throb in my wrist from when I'd connected for the game-winning single, the dull cramp of calf muscles that had grown unaccustomed to so much use. Mostly, I was just glorying in the fact that I'd played my first baseball game in Navin Field as a member of the Detroit Tigers.

When I finally did exit the park, I was whistling "Mademoiselle from Armentieres, Parlay-Voo" and almost skipping as I walked. It seemed life couldn't get any better.

Then a throaty female voice behind me said, "Hi, slugger." The sound sent a tingle through me. I didn't have to turn around to recognize Margie Turner.

O O O

Half an hour later, we were strolling through Grand Circus Park, nibbling ice-cream cones. We debated whether vanilla or chocolate was the superior flavor of ice cream, commented on how perfect the weather had become, and verbally replayed most of the ballgame—Margie graciously avoided mentioning my error.

Warm, gentle breezes washed through the park and a soft evening sun filtered through the shade trees. The smell of the greenery provided relief from the odor of automobile exhaust that permeated the rest of the city. Hundreds of people were taking advantage of the fine weather and the downtown oasis. Most of them walked; some sat on the benches that faced the fountain. A few, less particular about their clothes, sprawled on the grass.

Of all the women in the park, Margie Turner was the prettiest. She wore a loose-fitting, sky-blue organdy dress embroidered with white flowers. On her head was a white straw bonnet too small to quite contain her long brown tresses. She swung a beaded handbag as we casually made our way through the crowd. Because of her limp, her hip bumped against me as we walked—and I enjoyed the contact.

"I didn't expect to see you again," I said. "Weren't you going to Toledo?"

"Oh!" She smiled mischievously. "Did I forget to mention that after Toledo we were coming to Detroit?"

I grabbed her ice-cream cone and took as big a bite as I could from it as revenge for teasing me. "Must have slipped your mind," I said, handing it back to her. "How long are you here for?"

"Unlimited engagement. At least two weeks." She looked at me. "You dripped."

I wiped my mouth with my handkerchief.

"You missed it." She touched my arm and we pulled to a

stop. Then she dabbed at my chin with her finger, coming away with a dollop of vanilla. "The Toledo run ended early— our fire-eater set the curtains on fire." She put her finger in her mouth and sucked off the ice cream. "I have all this week off."

She kissed the spot on my chin that she'd just cleaned. Then I kissed her on her lips, full and long. As she responded, I put my arms around her and dropped my cone to the ground. By the time we broke apart, most of it had melted.

When I suggested dinner, Margie suggested that we dine on additional ice cream. Even in dietary preferences we were compatible.

After consuming lavish sundaes at the nearby Statler Hotel, we returned to the park and sat on one of the benches. The shadows had lengthened, most of the people had left, and the air was a little less temperate. I put my jacket around Margie's shoulders, and she snuggled close to me. I was totally content. My muscles had a satisfying ache, my belly was full of ice cream, and my heart was astir.

We talked off and on about nothing in particular, the long silences in between not at all uncomfortable. Among the things we did say, I mentioned that I had a friend staying with me and she mentioned that she had her own room at the Hotel Franklin.

A cool breeze gusted and I felt Margie shiver. I put my arm around her, marveling at how well she fit.

"Would your friend miss you if you didn't come home?" she asked.

The stirring in my heart moved south. "Not a bit," I said.

# Chapter Fourteen

**T**he next three days and nights blended together in a delicious, exhilarating sequence of Margie, baseball, and Margie. We were rarely out of each other's sight, and often in each other's arms. I was so intoxicated with Marguerite Turner, and so oblivious to all else, that it required a conscious effort to check the clock now and then to make sure I'd be at Navin Field in time for batting practice every day.

Margie accompanied me to each game and sat as close as possible to the home dugout. Never the shy type, Margie made her presence felt, brandishing a *Detroit* pennant like she was leading a cavalry charge and cheering louder than any leather-lunged bleacher bum.

Except for the pitching rotation, Hughie Jennings stuck with the same lineup that had produced the season's first win, giving me three more full games at second base. We won the final game with Cleveland and split the first two games of a series with the St. Louis Browns. Despite the distraction of Margie in the stands, I made no more errors and continued to hit. Over four games, I totaled six hits in fourteen at bats, for a batting average of .429. Or maybe .428—I never was quite clear on how to round off. Whatever my exact average, Ty Cobb was batting .203 and *I* was leading the team in hitting. None of my hits was longer than a single, but one of those singles was a drag bunt that I'd laid down left-handed against the Browns' Urban Shocker; it was my first major-league hit batting lefty and gave me hope that I could be a successful switch hitter.

After each game, I showered and changed quickly, then hurried out to meet Margie at the gate.

Our dinners were also hurried. On Tuesday, we picked a restaurant near her hotel; the following nights, we remained within the confines of the Hotel Franklin, eating in the Franklin's café so that we'd have less distance to travel to Margie's room afterward. We ate just enough for sustenance, talked little, smiled a lot, and skipped dessert. Later in the evening we would wash, dress again, and go out for ice cream—then it was back to her hotel. The nights were curiously refreshing although we didn't get much sleep.

I saw little of my apartment, going home only for fresh clothes and to check the mail. I saw nothing of Karl Landfors. So soon after having urged him to do more about Emmett Siever's death, my own interest in it had virtually vanished. The pressure seemed to have eased. Hub Donner's deadline had come and passed, so I assumed my talk with Frank Navin had settled that issue. Leo Hyman's deadline was still more than two weeks away; in the back of my mind I knew the days were ticking by, but I no longer felt an urgency about it.

It was basically wishful thinking on my part. I hoped that my romance with Margie would, like a magic amulet, somehow protect me from danger—that trouble would veer around me the same way that passersby make extra room when a courting couple comes down the sidewalk. It wasn't *impossible* that nothing more would happen to me, but I knew in my bones that it was no more likely than me batting .400 for the entire season.

With Friday an off day in the schedule, Margie and I planned a picnic outing to Belle Isle Park. I probably should have spent the day working on Emmett Siever's murder, but Margie's show would open on Sunday and the run wasn't guaranteed for more than two weeks.

After I left her room Friday morning, I stopped at the hotel newsstand for the *Detroit Journal,* then hailed a cab to take me home for suitable clothes. During the ride, I flipped open the paper to check an ad I'd seen before for the Coliseum of Amusements. I found it listed with the movie and vaudeville shows. The amusement park, near the Belle Isle Bridge, boasted "Rides, Slides, Games." I thought we could go there after the picnic—it might be as close as we could come to reliving some of the times we'd had at Coney Island.

I next turned to the sports section to read about my 2-for-4 performance at the plate in yesterday's game. Next to the account of the game was an article headed *Traitor to the Team?* The "traitor" was me.

The gist of the story was that the Tigers' good fortune was about to end. I was going to publicly criticize the players' union, and the resulting ill feelings on the team would start us losing again.

Whoever wrote the piece was clever about it: there were no quotes attributed to me or to anyone else—nothing that could directly be proved wrong. The story combined speculation, lies, and editorializing to produce something that sounded like news. There was no byline to the piece, but I had no doubt that the man behind it was Hub Donner.

○ ○ ○

I had the cab drop me off half a block from my apartment so that I could pick up the *Free Press* and the *News*. Scanning these papers as I walked up the stairs, I saw that they also carried the story, but in shorter versions.

As usual, Karl Landfors was out. I brewed a pot of coffee and thought about the newspaper stories.

At first, I put part of the blame on Frank Navin for not telling Hub Donner to back off. Then I realized that I had assumed too much. Navin had never said he would intervene with the League's union buster; all he'd said was that he wouldn't kick me off the team if I elected not to go along with Donner.

Thinking about it further, I started to suspect that Donner's main allegiance was to Ban Johnson and the American League, not to the Tigers' owner. The stories in the papers were almost as bad for Navin as they were for me. There's no way Navin would want Donner to be instigating dissension on the team just when we were starting to win. Or maybe the planted stories weren't at the behest of either Johnson or Navin. Perhaps Hub Donner had personal reasons for going ahead with his publicity campaign: to take attention off himself. Whatever Donner's reason, this move was sure to cause more trouble between me and my teammates.

One thing was clear: I was going to have to take on Hub Donner. Even if I couldn't pin Siever's murder on him, I had to find some way to stop what he was doing to me. I pictured Donner as he'd sat across from me in the Men's Grill of the Hotel Tuller, fingering his bullet wound and telling me how rough he could get. Perhaps my bravery had something to do with the fact that I was hitting .400, but I decided to give Donner the chance to show me how hard he could play.

Most of the coffeepot was empty by the time I came up with a plan. It occurred to me that if Donner and the IWW spied on each other, then maybe the Wobblies could tell me where Donner had really been the night Siever was killed. At the very least, I was sure they'd be willing to help me give Donner a little grief. I had wondered for a while why Leo Hyman had given me a reprieve in the first place—what did it matter to him if the Wobblies went after me to avenge Siever's death? Then I realized that he might be giving me the time to cause trouble for his old enemy Hub Donner.

At about the time I should have been leaving to meet Margie, Karl Landfors walked in. He looked like an undertaker who'd been on a three-day binge. His collar was no longer clean, his shirt was wrinkled, and the crease was gone from his trousers.

"Long night?"

He grinned. "And morning." I was glad to see he was no longer blushing about his activities with Connie Siever. "Sorry I haven't been around much."

Struggling to keep a straight face, I said, "Well, I've missed your company. But I understand."

He pulled off his coat and headed to the closet. "I just stopped in for a few minutes. We—Connie and I—are going out again."

As if I'd thought the "we" was Landfors and Ty Cobb.

"No problem, Karl. Say, have you had a chance to ask her about her father yet?"

"Well, I've broached the subject a few times." He found some fresh clothes and started changing into them. "The conversation always seems to go off on another path, though."

"You sweet talker, you."

He paused in his efforts to attach a new shirt collar. "Actually, the conversation—her end of it at least—usually turns to the Suffrage Amendment and her plans to organize in Tennessee."

"Oh."

He mumbled something that indicated he wasn't always happy about Connie Siever's choice of topics.

As he ran a comb over his remaining hair, I asked, "By the way, Karl, can you give me Leo Hyman's phone number?"

He gave me the number without asking why. After Landfors left—in a suit identical to the one he'd arrived in—I phoned Hyman at home and we arranged a meeting for later in the afternoon.

Then I placed a more difficult call. To Margie, to cancel our picnic.

I first tried to get by with saying that "something came up." Her silence urged me to elaborate. I decided I should tell her all, before she had a chance to read the stories Donner had planted. I didn't want her thinking that I was betraying my fellow ballplayers.

Fifteen minutes later, Margie knew almost as much about what was happening with Hub Donner, the IWW, and the players' union as I did. And I had a new volunteer to help me solve Emmett Siever's murder.

○ ○ ○

The projectionist's booth of the Empire Theatre was barely spacious enough to hold two people. With three people in it, including Leo Hyman and his belly, it was uncomfortably cramped.

Stan Zaluski, the old man who took tickets at Fraternity Hall, stood next to the projector, working the machine as it beamed Wallace Reid's latest movie, *Double Speed,* for the Friday afternoon audience. I sat on a stack of film cans, Hyman on a low stool that looked like it was about to be swallowed by his butt.

The dimly lit booth was further crowded by several years accumulation of *Motion Picture Magazine* as well as posters, heralds, and lobby cards for just about every movie since *The Great Train Robbery.* The air was thick with smoke from Zaluski's Cavendish tobacco, and simmering from the heat of the projector's lamp.

"This is nicer than the last place we met," I said. But not by much, I thought.

Hyman brushed his long white mustache away from his lips. "I rather like it myself." Pointing to the small window through which the movie was beamed, he added, "If the conversation's poor, at least there's entertainment."

Zaluski was absorbed in his work, turning the handle of the projector while keeping one eye on the screen and another on a chart in front of him. I knew from a long addiction to movie magazines that the chart told him how many frames per second to crank specific scenes. Chases were supposed to be turned faster and love scenes slower. With a Wally Reid auto-racing picture, just about every scene went at breakneck speed, and Zaluski's sinewy arm was getting quite a workout.

Turning my attention from Zaluski to Hyman, I said, "I really want to go after Hub Donner."

Hyman's brow lifted, causing his spectacles to move up as well. "For killing Emmett Siever?"

"Whether he killed Siever or not—and I think there's a good chance he did—I want to cause him some trouble. Because that's what he's doing to me. Don't get me wrong: I'm not getting involved in your politics or anything. Part of it's baseball, and part of it's personal. Donner's trying to use me to cause friction on the Tigers. And I don't like being used."

"At least you're being honest," Hyman said. "So you want to 'go after' Hub Donner for purely selfish motives."

"Well . . . yes." I didn't like the word "selfish," but I suppose it applied.

"And you want us to help you."

"Not help, really, just a little information."

"Information is the most valuable asset there is in a war," Hyman said. His tone sounded like the one Landfors used when lecturing me about politics or history.

"I'm not in a war. I just have a little battle going with Donner. If you didn't want me to win it, why did you give me the extra time?"

Hyman's face turned implacable. "You have two weeks left."

Zaluski sucked hard at his pipe.

I went on, "You told me both sides spy on each other. So I assume you have somebody who keeps track of Donner.

Do you know where he was the night Emmett Siever was killed?"

Hyman hesitated. "Off the top of my head, no. But then I never thought of him as having killed Emmett. The papers seemed pretty clear on the subject of who did the shooting."

"I already told you the papers—and the cops—were wrong. You must have doubts yourself about what really happened; otherwise, you'd have let Whitey Boggs or one of your other guys kill me already." I gave Hyman a chance to contradict me. When he didn't, I continued, "Donner gave me an alibi for the night Siever was shot, but I found out he was lying."

Hyman turned his head to Zaluski. "What do you think, Stosh?"

Zaluski answered from around his pipe stem. "I don't see where telling the boy where Donner was can do any harm."

"I'll find out for you," Hyman agreed.

"Thanks."

"Reel change," said Zaluski. "Give me some room, fellas."

Hyman and I edged back as far as we could while Zaluski prepared to start the second projector when the film in the first ran out.

Another topic I wanted to explore was Donner's position at Ford. The only time Donner had shown any worry was about doing baseball business on Ford company time. I wondered if I might use Donner's moonlighting to get him in hot water with his bosses at the plant. "I went to see Donner at the Highland Park plant," I said to Hyman. "How much power does he have there? Who does he answer to?"

"He has all the power he wants. He's in charge of the Service Department—his own combination police department and spy service. Only one he answers to is Henry Ford, and I don't expect Ford himself knows all that Donner has going on."

"There were men in plain clothes there. Are they his spies?"

"His goon squad. Were they wearing bow ties?"

"Yeah, same as Donner."

"He makes all his goons wear them—it's how they dress for battle. A bow tie comes undone in a fight; a necktie can be used to strangle you."

Zaluski finished switching projectors. When the next reel was whirring smoothly, he said to me, "Son, you mind cranking this a bit?" Tapping the bowl of his pipe with his free hand, he said, "Need to reload."

"Sure!" I agreed. "But I don't know how."

"Just watch the screen and turn the handle fast enough that it looks right."

I stood and took over the handle, keeping my eye on the infinitely peppy Wally Reid as he raced around on the movie screen. For several minutes, I cranked away. I first did it so that it "looked right." Once I got the hang of it, I turned it just a tad slower and faster, enjoying the sense of power.

With a fresh bowl lit, Zaluski said, "Thanks, son. I'll take it again."

Reluctantly, I gave up the projector and sat back down. I briefly pondered another question I had for Leo Hyman: where had *he* been the night Siever was shot? Probably best not to put it exactly that way though, I thought. "Does Whitey Boggs always run the meetings?" I asked.

Hyman smiled. "When I'm not there he does."

So much for the subtle approach. Okay, shift focus to

make it seem I'm interested in Boggs. "You said he's head of some committee?"

"Relief Committee."

"How many committees you have?"

He smiled again. "Several. Stosh here is head of the Welcoming Committee."

"Means I take the donations," Zaluski said. "Damn!" The film had jumped a sprocket and it took him a minute to get it aligned again.

"How long have you been a projectionist?" I asked.

"I'm not. I only work here once a week. The regular projectionist has a lady friend he meets every Friday. He pays me to cover for him. Been doing it for a couple years now."

Hyman spoke up. "Stosh used to be with Ford. Got fired for unionizing and now he's blacklisted. Can't get a regular job. We have a lot of fellows like that." He added with a small smile, "At least Ford did give him some training for his other career."

"What's that?"

Zaluski answered, "I'm a ventriloquist. Do a little vaudeville and burlesque now and then."

"You learned that at *Ford?*"

"Show him the Ford Whisper," Hyman urged.

Keeping one hand on the projector, Zaluski turned so that I could see his wrinkled face and removed the pipe from his teeth. With his mouth barely open and his lips motionless, he said, "Ford has spotters who watch the men on the assembly line. If they see you talking, they report you. So you learn to talk like this. It's called a 'Ford Whisper.'"

"That's good!" I said. "Can everybody who works there do it?"

"Not as good as Stosh," said Hyman. "Whitey Boggs can't hardly do it at all. Probably what got him fired was that they could see him talking."

"Or unionizing," said Zaluski. "He was active, too. The Ford Service Department gets any hint you might be union, and your ass is out of there. Boggs got fired just after I did."

Through the booth's window, I saw that he was cranking too fast. Angry shouts started coming from the crowd below. Zaluski returned the pipe to his mouth and his attention to the projector.

"One thing I don't understand," I said to Hyman. "Most of the Wobblies are workingmen, right? Factory workers and guys like that. Wouldn't real workers be upset about Emmett Siever, a *baseball player,* getting involved—and getting so much attention?"

Hyman shook his head. "Not at all. We have writers, artists, all kinds of people in the IWW. That's the point: one big union made up of everyone who works, no matter what kind of work it is."

"Even baseball?" I still had trouble sometimes thinking of baseball as "work."

He laughed and nodded. "Absolutely."

"So none of the Wobblies had a personal problem with Emmett Siever?"

"No," Hyman insisted. "Everybody liked him. He was an upstanding fellow."

"Maybe recently. But I heard he was trouble back in his playing days. Even abandoned his daughter after his wife died."

Hyman shrugged. "Not many of us could pass muster if we were judged by what we did when we were young."

"Siever was a hell of a ballplayer," put in Zaluski. "Saw him when he was with the old Wolverines, and again when he came to the Tigers in ought-one. Played with his head. Seemed he knew just where a ball was going to be hit, and he'd be there. Box scores don't give you credit for brains, but he had 'em. Guts too. I was at a game in Bennett Park where I saw just what he had."

"What happened?" I asked.

He took a couple of brisk puffs on his pipe. "Tie game, it was. Bottom of the ninth, one out. Emmett Siever—he must have been forty years old by this time—was on first base and Kid Elberfeld on third. Next batter—Ducky Holmes, I think it was—hits a grounder to second. Easy double play. Second baseman tosses it to the shortstop to get one out, and he relays it to first. But Siever wouldn't get out of the way of the throw. He even jumped a little and took it smack on the forehead. Broke up the double play, Elberfeld scored, and Tigers won."

"Jeez."

"Yep. Siever was out for a week with blurred vision, but that's the kind of player—the kind of *man*—he was." Turning to look at me, he added, "So you can see why friends of his aren't go to let the man who killed him get away with it."

"I'm not gonna let him get away with it, either," I said.

Hyman spoke up. "I got another place to be. You have any more questions for me?"

I thought a moment. "Yeah, one. Who's taking Siever's place? Who's organizing the players' union now?"

Hyman shook his head in a way that said he wasn't going to tell me. Whether or not he knew who it was wasn't clear from the gesture. "I'll get back to you if I find out where

Hub Donner was that night." With that, he stood to leave. "Coming?"

I asked Zaluski if I could stay and watch the movie for a while and he agreed. Hyman reminded me that my grace period had only fifteen more days to run, then he left the two of us alone in the booth.

My impulse in wanting to stay was to ask Zaluski why Hyman hadn't been at Fraternity Hall that night. I realized, though, that Zaluski wouldn't tell me anything Hyman didn't want me to know.

So we settled back and talked baseball. I took over on the projector a few times and Zaluski told me stories about the old Detroit teams—the National League champion Wolverines of 1887, with Dan Brouthers, Sam Thompson, and Charlie Bennett; and the three-time pennant-winning Tigers of 1907 to 1909, with Sam Crawford, Davy Jones, and George Mullin. In return, I told him a few things about Ty Cobb that he hadn't heard before.

The conversation, and the smell of Zaluski's pipe, sent me back to when I was a kid, sitting in my uncle's general store while men gathered around the stove for cracker-barrel baseball talk. My Uncle Matt smoked a pipe, too, and sometimes he'd let me put an unlit one in my mouth.

By the time I left the theater, I was hankering for a pipe of my own and thinking that both Leo Hyman and Stan Zaluski knew more than they would ever reveal to me. The question was: how much of what they knew had to do with the circumstances of Emmett Siever's death?

# Chapter Fifteen

○○○

'd thought it a clever idea at the time. Now I was stuck with the result and not at all comfortable about it.

Eager to see her again, I had phoned Margie the first thing in morning and asked her to the Saturday game at Navin Field. She begged off, with the excuse that she needed to do some shopping. I knew that she'd been a bit annoyed with me yesterday—not for canceling the picnic but because I hadn't told her earlier about the trouble I was in. I then asked her something that I didn't think she'd decline: I told her that we'd been invited on a double date by Karl Landfors and Connie Siever, adding that Landfors was an old friend I very much wanted her to meet. After a slight hesitation she agreed to go. When I tried once more to talk her into coming to the game as well, she firmly said she couldn't make it to the ballpark today.

I attributed my subsequent 0-for-5 batting performance to her absence. To Hub Donner, I attributed the Tigers' coldly hostile attribute toward me. I was sure that every one of them had either read or heard about the newspaper stories. Not one of the players said a single word to me before, during, or after the game. I suspected that the only thing that kept them from committing outright violence was the fact that I'd been helping the team win games. That reprieve was probably soon to end, however, since I'd gone hitless and Dutch Leonard ended up on the short end of a 6-4 score.

At least Karl Landfors came through for me. After I'd explained to him about my story to Margie, he checked with Connie, and they agreed to back me up and join us for dinner.

Hence my present anxiety. Landfors and I were still in my apartment and the mere prospect of him seeing me with Margie had me already feeling self-conscious. The two of them had never met before; I didn't know what they would think of each other. My only consolation was that Landfors would also be with his sweetheart, so he might be equally ill at ease about the double date.

He was certainly concerned about something. I watched Landfors as he fumbled with his necktie. He stood in front of the mirror above the phone stand, tying knot after knot, mangling each attempt, and angrily pulling the tie loose to try again. It was almost six o'clock and we needed to be leaving soon.

I had already primped myself to perfection and put on the new double-breasted blue worsted. "Want me to tie it for you?" I offered.

"No."

Letting the tie hang loose around his neck for a minute, he picked up a yellow paper from the parlor stand. For the fifth time in the hour since the Western Union messenger delivered it, he reread its message, his face darkening the same as it had each time before.

Ever since the delivery boy gave it to him, I'd been badgering him to tell me what it said, to no avail. Landfors looked so troubled that I asked again, "What is it? Anything wrong?" I assumed somebody had died; why else a telegram?

He shook his head the same as he had the previous times I'd asked. "It isn't anything. I hope." Then he turned to me. "And what is it that you're so wrapped up in?"

I'd been looking over a scrap of white paper as often as he'd looked at his yellow one. "Mine's nothing, too." No matter how many times I reviewed my calculations, my batting average had definitely dropped more than a hundred points in one day. It was still over .300—either .315 or .316— and any other time I would have considered that to be a terrific mark. But that brief period of batting over .400 had spoiled me.

Landfors took up the ends of his tie again.

I gave up trying to figure out my exact batting average and directed my thoughts to a subject almost equally depressing: Emmett Siever. "Has Connie said anything about her father yet?" I asked.

He shook his head.

"She was his only next of kin, right?"

Landfors paused from his battle with the necktie, which was never going to look right anyway because it was so twisted and wrinkled. "I believe so . . . why?"

"So she inherits whatever he had?"

His eyes grew wide. "What exactly are you suggesting?"

"I'm not suggesting anything. The reason I'm asking is: if

she inherits his possessions, shouldn't she get whatever Siever had on him when he died?"

Landfors directed his attention back to the mirror and the necktie. "I suppose. Perhaps she's already gotten his effects from the police. Why?"

"The cops claim Siever had a revolver on him. But I know he didn't—not when I saw him, anyway. I figure if Connie could get it back, we might be able to find out where it came from. There must be a serial number on it." The Colt .45 I'd brought home from the war had such a number, and I assumed it must help somehow in tracking a firearm.

"I doubt if the police will release the gun. It will probably have to stay in the evidence room."

"What's it evidence *of?* There was no crime as far as the police are concerned. Remember?"

"Hmm." He made a final assault on the tie and succeeded in twisting a passable four-in-hand. "Close enough," he sighed.

"Anyway, could you ask Connie to get her father's things—including the gun?"

Landfors looked at me blankly.

"Don't have to ask her tonight. Just whenever it seems like a good time."

"Yes, certainly. I'll try to slip it into the conversation." His sarcastic tone and scowling face gave me the feeling this was not going to be a fun evening.

○ ○ ○

The waiter must have thought he was serving at a wake when he came to take our orders. Most patrons of the rooftop nightclub were flirtatious couples and carousing parties who'd come to drink and dance under the stars. Amid the good cheer, our table was an island of gloom.

Despite Margie's and my best efforts, there'd been little conversation during the ferry ride. After awkward introductions, Landfors and Connie barely spoke to us. Margie asked me several times with her eyes what the matter was. I had no answer, other than Landfors's grouchiness was apparently contagious and Connie Siever had come down with a dose of it.

It had been my idea to come across the river to Windsor. I thought it would make for a more relaxed atmosphere, being in Canada, and able to have a few drinks without worrying about Treasury agents swooping in to enforce prohibition. But Landfors and Connie were determined *not* to relax; they sat stiff and solemn, their clothes and bearing making them look like a black-and-white newspaper sketch of defendants at a trial.

The waiter asked again, "What will you have?"

Before Landfors could order us a pitcher of vinegar, I said, "Champagne and oysters. All around."

Margie laid her hand on my arm. "You remembered!"

"No champagne," said the waiter. "Beer. Labatt."

I suspected they did have champagne, but didn't want to waste it on people who didn't look like they'd enjoy it. "Anything but Moxie," I said.

"Beer is fine," said Margie.

The waiter looked at Landfors. "Same for you?"

While Landfors cleared his throat to speak, Connie answered for him, "That will be fine, thank you."

"No oysters, neither," said the waiter. "Pretzels do?"

In one voice, the four of us answered, "Yes."

Margie laughed, and even Connie cracked a small smile.

When the waiter departed, quiet overtook our table again. The only sounds were nearby conversations, the music of a "ragtime" quintet that had no concept of rhythm, and the whistles and bells of barges and ferries navigating the Detroit River.

The silence was almost paralyzing; I looked around, seeking something to comment on in the hope of sparking a conversation. From our location twelve stories above Goyeau Avenue, the lights of Detroit sparkled in the distance, shining brighter than the stars overhead. Candles on the tables flickered in the fresh, outdoor air.

Margie beat me to it. With a twinkle in her eye, she ventured, "Good band."

Taking her seriously, Landfors nodded. "Very."

Connie wrinkled her nose. After another awkward silence, she said to Margie, "I understand you're in show business of some kind."

Of some kind? I thought everybody knew who Marguerite Turner was. She was a *movie star.*

"Yes, I am," Margie said sweetly. "Vaudeville. I wrestle lions and alligators for people who buy tickets hoping to see me get my head bitten off. Our show opens at the Rex tomorrow if you'd like to come."

"No, I'm sorry. I, uh, I have other plans."

"Too bad. There's a fire-breather in the show, too. Sometimes it gets pretty exciting." She winked at me, then asked Connie, "What do *you* do?"

"Connie's a suffragette," I said.

"Suffrag-*ist!*" she quickly corrected me. " 'Suffrag-ette' is

what men call us. It's a diminutive." Landfors bobbed his
head, agreeing with his date.

The band switched to a simpler number, some kind of
fox trot, and couples around us got up to dance. I had an
urgent desire to get onto the dance floor myself. Then it
occurred to me that Margie might not be able to with her
bad leg.

The waiter returned with four overflowing beer glasses
and a large bowl of pretzels.

I lifted mine and said, "Here's to, uh . . ."

"Good times," finished Margie.

I drank deeply and put down the glass half-empty. Margie's was at nearly the same level after her first sip. We looked
at each other, then grabbed up the beers again and raced
to finish them. I beat her, but it ended up close. We slammed
down the empty glasses and wiped our mouths.

Clearly not amused by our contest, Connie Siever took a
dainty sip of her beer. "How did you two meet?"

"I threw a pie in his face," Margie said. "Mickey was with
the Giants back then, and he was making a movie at the
studio where I worked. Poor boy looked so serious about it
that I had to loosen him up." She leaned forward and whispered, "A pie in the face will do wonders."

"I can imagine," said Connie. She shot an appalled glance
at Landfors. I could tell that from now on she was going to
be keeping an eye on Margie for flying pies.

"And how did you two meet?" Margie asked.

Connie lifted her chin. "Karl accompanied Mickey when
he paid a call on me to claim that he didn't kill my father."

"Claim?" repeated Margie. Under the table, she put her
hand on my knee and gripped hard; it felt like she would

have preferred to have been gripping Connie's throat. "If he says he didn't do it, he didn't. Are you saying he did?"

"Not necessarily. But no one else has been caught, have they?"

Margie's fingers dug in more firmly. As I pried them loose, I said, "No. No, they haven't. Not yet."

We all paused while the waiter brought fresh beers for Margie and me. Landfors waved him off when he asked if he and Connie wanted more.

"Well," Connie said, "whoever did it, my father's still going to be dead. Can't change that, so it doesn't really matter, I suppose."

Landfors put his hand on her arm in what he apparently intended to be a consoling gesture. But Connie Siever didn't need any consolation. She seemed totally comfortable with what had happened to her father. And that fact bothered me at least as much as anything else about his death.

I took a swallow of beer and asked Margie, "May I have this dance?"

Her eyes lit up, and she nodded eagerly.

"Excuse us," I said to our company, and took her hand to lead her to the dance floor. I sensed eyes turning to look at Margie. She was stylishly dressed, wearing a belted, golden yellow smock with a long, pointed white collar. Her flowing skirt was emerald green, and a silk scarf of the same color was loosely tied around her neck.

We easily fell into some step pattern that consisted mostly holding each other close and rocking back and forth in time with the music—it worked even better once we followed the rhythm of the same instrument. She bobbed a little with her limp, giving our swaying a syncopated beat.

I caught sight of Landfors and his date in conversation. I didn't know how I came up with the crazy idea for the four of us to get together. We had almost nothing in common.

Margie must have been having similar thoughts. Affecting a snooty British accent, she whispered, "I don't think Miss Siever cares for me at all."

"It's her loss," I replied. "That woman is about as much fun as taking a bad hop to the—uh . . ."

"To the ballocks?"

"That's the spot."

"Her problem is that she's just too serious."

"Perfect match for Karl."

"It's not healthy to be so serious all the time." Margie broke her hands free from me and shot them up under my arms, tickling me till I laughed and squawked for her to stop.

Feigning annoyance, I grabbed her and held her closer and tighter to prevent any further tickle assaults.

"You know," Margie murmured into my shoulder as we resumed dancing, "I worked for the Suffrage Amendment in California. Wrote letters, marched in a couple of parades . . . I loved doing it. Especially when we won. But I'm damned if I'll tell *her* that. I don't need her approval for what I do or who I am."

"No, you don't. And anyway, I think you're—" Failing to come up with a suitable compliment, I said, "Just fine."

She laughed softly. "You sure know how to flatter a girl."

The music stopped. We added to the sparse applause that the band was given, and stayed on the floor for the next number.

I looked again at Landfors and Connie Siever. Their heads were close together in deep conversation. Landfors looked as delighted to be talking with her as I was to be dancing with Margie. I felt a little more kindly to his date; she was making my friend happy. I only hoped that he wasn't setting himself up for a fall.

The next tune was "Let Me Call You Sweetheart," the kind of slow, schmaltzy song I don't care to hear but like to dance to. As the singer crooned the lyrics and we wound our way around the floor, I noticed that Margie's limp produced a marvelous grinding motion against me. There was something I liked even more than slow dancing, and I found myself wishing that we weren't on a public dance floor or stuck with another couple for the evening.

The bandleader announced a break, and Margie and I headed back to the table.

Landfors was finishing a story, ". . . so the Justice Department raids this little Italian social club in New Jersey, and find what they think is a stash of bombs. They put all the men in jail, and send the bombs to be examined. The police can't understand it when all the 'bombs' turn out to be duds. They weren't bombs at all—they were *bocce balls!*"

Connie almost doubled over with laughter. At least she has some kind of a sense of humor, I thought.

Laughing hard himself, Landfors said to Margie and me, "We were just talking about the Palmer raids."

Yup, this was sure a fun couple to spend a Saturday evening with.

Margie and I ordered a couple more beers. When the waiter pointed out to Landfors and Connie that beer didn't taste good if you let it go flat, they agreed to another round, too.

When the fresh brews arrived, Landfors took a clumsy

gulp of his, then said into the glass, "Speaking of Italian anarchists . . ."

Jeez, Karl, you sure know how to enliven a conversation.

". . . I got a telegram today."

"Yes?" Connie prodded him. I was curious myself to find out at last what it said.

"Two men have been arrested in Brockton, Massachusetts. Nicola Sacco and Bartolomeo Vanzetti are their names. Both Italian immigrants, both avowed anarchists. They're going to be charged with murder, but it looks like their political leaning is the only 'evidence' against them."

"That's awful!" said Connie.

Landfors went on, still talking low, "The fellow who sent me the telegram has set up a defense committee on their behalf. And . . . And he's asking me to go to Boston. He wants me to report on whatever happens to these men."

Connie didn't look pleased at this possibility. "Are you?"

"I haven't quite decided yet. I would prefer—"

"What about what *we* were planning?" she demanded.

"Well, as I was saying, I would *prefer* to stay here, but this sounds like something I want to cover. So far, outside the Boston Italian community, these men aren't getting any kind of support. If they're being railroaded, public exposure might be the only thing that can free them." He pushed up his spectacles. "But, as I said, I haven't decided yet."

As Connie opened her mouth to speak again, I asked Margie, "Would you like to dance some more?"

She smiled. "There's no music."

"Oh. Right. A walk, then?"

"We're on a roof."

"A *short* walk?"

"I'd love to."

We worked our way through the crowd toward the east side of the building. A low brick wall topped by a wrought-iron railing ran around the roof's perimeter to make sure the club didn't lose any of its customers to a free fall. The view was splendid: the dark Detroit River, dotted with sparkling lights from passing boats, split around Belle Isle with its stationary lights.

"Now that we're alone," said Margie.

I put my arms around her. "Yes?"

"Tell me what happened last night."

"Oh. Okay." I took her hand, we began pacing along the wall, and I filled her in on my meeting with Leo Hyman and Stan Zaluski. "I don't feel like I'm getting anywhere," I concluded. I didn't mention that I had only two weeks from tonight to come up with something.

"Why don't you ask Connie?" Margie suggested. "Maybe she knows who would have wanted to kill her father."

"Karl's going to ask her for me—eventually. I don't know how much she'll say, though. She might be pretty loyal to the IWW."

"What does that have to do with anything?"

"I think the Wobblies are involved somehow. Not that they necessarily killed him, but they must know something about what happened. They're so protective of themselves that I can't imagine somebody being killed in their own headquarters without one of them knowing what happened. Also, there must be a reason for Siever being killed in Fraternity Hall. Why not someplace easier, like on the street?"

"I don't know." Margie smiled. "But I'll bet you find out."

"Hope so."

For the rest of the night, we left Landfors and Connie to their political talk, while we remained on the dance floor.

Around midnight, the four of us got back on the ferry. It was a smoother vessel than the transport ship that had taken me to France, but I still didn't like being on water. During the journey, Landfors and Connie continued their argument about whether he should go to Boston, while Margie and I cuddled and kissed in the back of the boat.

When we reached the Detroit shore at Bates Street, Margie and I left the two radicals to their arguing and made a beeline for her hotel.

# Chapter Sixteen

**H**ub Donner had done it again. This time he'd made the front page: *Turmoil Tails Tigers* was the headline of a small article at the bottom of the Sunday *Free Press*. According to the story, I was going to denounce the players' union in an upcoming issue of *Baseball Magazine*. A preview of the magazine piece had supposedly leaked out, and the Tiger team was "snarling and clawing" over it.

Donner was trying to produce a self-fulfilling prophecy. On the way to Navin Field, I tried in vain to think of a way to stop him.

When I walked into the locker room, I was immediately aware that something was up. Not one of my teammates looked at me as I sidled my way past the stools to my locker. For a moment, I thought I'd gone to the wrong one—*Rawlings* was no longer chalked above the top shelf. Then fear struck me: was I off the team? I checked the neighboring names: *Pinelli* on one side, *Vedder* on the other. But the name above mine was—oh, it wasn't a new player. The yellow chalk on my locker read: *Judas*. I used my handkerchief to rub out the word.

An expectant silence filled the room. I'd grown used to my teammates not speaking to me; now they weren't talking among themselves, either. They were waiting for something.

After I'd taken off my street clothes, I pulled my baseball pants from their hook. I was about to step into them when I saw the legs had been knotted at the ends. "Pretty bush league," I commented to the room in general. "What's next—short sheeting my bed?"

A few cold, hard glares were the only response.

I flipped the pants over to work the knot loose. Something thudded on my foot. "What the—?" I looked down to see a pigeon. A dead, headless pigeon. "Sonofabitch!" I turned and looked at my teammates collectively. "Who did this?"

There was no answer. A few of them stifled chuckles.

I looked at individuals, from face to face. Most, including Dutch Leonard and Chick Fogarty, appeared amused. Bobby Veach looked sheepish, Harry Heilmann bored, Ty Cobb above it all. Young Lou Vedder next to me was the only one who looked troubled.

I dropped the pants over the bird's body and went to see Jake, our clubhouse man, for a new pair. As I walked away, I heard laughter and talk behind me. The only extra pants available were at least two sizes too large. "Perfect fit," said Jake. "Just make sure you tighten your belt a couple extra notches."

Most of the other Tigers were completely dressed by the time I returned to my locker, but they didn't head out to the field. They remained in their seats, absently punching their gloves, rubbing their bats, or retying their spikes. Something else had to be coming.

I checked my uniform jersey before putting it on, and

looked into each of my spikes for foreign objects before putting my feet inside and tying the laces. Eager to get on to the field, I grabbed my mitt and pulled my cap from the locker shelf. The pigeon's head fell from out of the cap. I jumped back as it bounced on the floor.

The locker room erupted with laughter. It wasn't a "what a swell prank" kind of laugh. There was malice in my teammates' voices.

I looked around and said calmly, "One of you must feel like a really big man, killing a bird. If you got something to settle with me, come after *me*. But I warn you: my neck ain't gonna break so easy."

Chick Fogarty said, "Maybe not. But easy enough."

I flung my glove on the floor. "Come on. Right here, right now."

The catcher slowly drew himself up to his full height. He was the size of a small mountain; if he ever gave up catching, I thought, all he had to do was move back twenty feet and start a career as a backstop. We studied each other for a few moments. There was no anger in his eyes, bewilderment mostly; they changed expression as if he was groping to determine what he should be thinking. And I wasn't really angry at him. Hub Donner was the one I was mad at.

Dutch Leonard urged, "Go ahead, Chick. Give it to him."

Fogarty took a step toward me. Then he ducked his head and kept walking. "Another time," he said, as he passed by and continued out the clubhouse door.

The prospect of a fight gone, the rest of the players started for the door, too.

I wrapped the bird's body in my ruined trousers, scooped up its head with my cap, and tossed the entire bundle in a waste can. I noticed there was hardly any blood from the bird. It had probably been dead already when my teammates decided to behead him. I felt somewhat better that at least it hadn't been killed on my account.

On the way out to the field, I stopped for a new cap. All Jake had was one that was a little too small. Between the cap and the oversize pants, I had the feeling I was bringing the Charlie Chaplin look to baseball.

○ ○ ○

Despite the "turmoil" on the Tigers, we played well enough together to drub the visiting Philadelphia Athletics 9-1 behind the two-hit pitching of Howard Ehmke. The Athletics were the mostly likely team to take our place in the American League cellar, and we'd played with that goal foremost in mind. I'd boosted my batting average slightly by going 1-for-3 with two walks; one of the walks was with the bases loaded, so I picked up a cheap RBI as a bonus.

After the game, I stopped at my apartment before going to Margie's evening show at the Rex.

Karl Landfors was seated on the sofa, meticulously folding his nightshirt. His Gladstone bag and suitcase were open on the floor in front of him, and both were more than half-packed.

Restraining a smile at the prospect, I said, "Moving in with Connie?"

"No." He proceeded to roll a pair of socks. "I'm going to Boston. I decided to look into that Sacco and Vanzetti situation I mentioned last night."

"Oh." I wasn't sorry to have the apartment to myself again. "What's Connie think about you going?"

He pushed up his glasses. "Let's just say that she's less than ecstatic about my decision."

"I'm sorry. You two were getting along so good."

"We *were*. Past tense is correct."

"She said you two had some plans . . ."

"They were *her* plans. Not mine." He jammed the socks in his bag. "Connie Siever is a strong-willed woman. She wanted me to go to Tennessee with her and work for the Suffrage Amendment."

"You didn't want to?"

"I certainly did. But I couldn't resist the appeal from Boston. There are *thousands* of men and women fighting for suffrage. These Sacco and Vanzetti fellows have *no one*. I prefer to work on issues where I can have an impact. On suffrage, I'd be merely one more body in the fray. For these anarchists . . . I don't know what I'll be, but I might be the only help they get."

"You gonna be okay in Boston? I'd hate to see you getting yourself in trouble."

"I'll be fine." He strained to produce a smile. "And, I have a going-away present for you."

"You didn't have to—"

"I found out who 'Detective Aikens' is."

"You did? Who? And *how?*"

A bit of the old self-satisfied look came into his eyes. "As to how, let's just say I was able to pressure certain contacts that I have. And—" He smiled sheepishly, "Well, I did use my contacts, but you set me on the right path by mentioning the GID. Your description of the man was also helpful."

"Let's get to the who," I prodded.

"I have been able to ascertain that 'Detective Aikens' was in actuality Calvin Garrett, special agent with the General Intelligence Division of the Justice Department."

"Jeez. A government agent."

"Yes, the GID used to be—"

I remembered what Whitey Boggs had said. "The Anti-Radical Division."

Landfors looked mildly impressed. "That's right."

"And they organized the Palmer raids, so they're probably still watching the IWW halls."

"I would say that's a reasonable inference."

One thing bothered me: the idea of an agent of the United States government committing a murder. "You don't think Aikens—I mean Garrett—could have killed Emmett Siever, do you?"

Landfors stroked a finger along his nose. "Until last week, I'd have said no. They might deport you, slander you, or frame you. But not murder you. Legally, the GID men aren't even allowed to carry guns. As it turns out, however, they don't need them."

"Meaning?"

He leaned back and took a deep breath. "Eight weeks ago, the Justice Department picked up a couple of men who printed anarchist literature. Just picked them up—didn't charge them with anything. They held the men in the Justice Department's New York office for eight weeks, trying to beat confessions out of them for a bombing. By the way, detaining someone for eight weeks without charges is completely illegal." He swallowed hard. "Last week, one of the men, Andrea Salsedo, was found on the sidewalk, dead. He fell fourteen

stories. The official version is that it was a suicide. I think—
a lot of us think—that he was murdered by his interrogators."

"Damn."

"That's another reason I want to see what happened in
Boston. I don't want another 'suicide' if I can help stop it."

I was stunned by his story. It took a few minutes until I
asked, "How would I get in touch with Calvin Garrett?"

"Don't. Stay away from the GID. They may not kill you,
but they have a hundred other ways to ruin your life."

"But he might have seen who really killed Emmett Siever."

"Perhaps he did. If so, he certainly won't tell you what
he knows."

"No, I don't suppose he would." I sank into the rocker,
trying to figure out how else I could use the information on
Garrett without contacting him directly.

"One more thing," Landfors said. "I did ask Connie to get
her father's personal effects, including the gun he supposedly
had. Perhaps that will give you a lead."

"Thanks, Karl."

He closed the bags and stood up. "If you see her, would
you let me know how she is?"

"Of course."

I accompanied him in a cab to the train depot. When I
returned home to change for Margie's show, I found that
he'd left me with another present: the icebox was stocked
with a dozen bottles of Labatt beer.

I thought more kindly of Landfors as I hurriedly dressed
for Margie's show. I also felt badly for him that things had
hit a snag with Connie Siever. Landfors was always going off
to try to right whatever wrongs he encountered. He seemed
to take them so personally, as if the responsibility for fixing

them was solely his. In a way, I admired his energy and convictions. Perhaps I needed more of those myself.

I'd just opened the door to leave when the phone rang. After briefly debating whether to answer, I picked up the receiver. And was promptly sorry that I did.

"Mickey! Hub Donner here."

"Oh."

"See today's paper?" Donner asked.

"Yes."

"So did your teammates, from what I hear. Looks like you're going to have to pick a side, Mickey. And my side is the one you want to be on."

"Not a chance. What you're doing to me is a perfect example of why players have to stick together. If I join any side, it will be the players' union."

"You think they'll ever trust you now?"

The answer was no. Instead of admitting that to Donner, I hung up on him and left for the vaudeville theater.

○ ○ ○

I spent Sunday night and Monday with Margie, doing nothing that would help determine Emmett Siever's murderer. Most of what we did was intended to sustain us during the separation caused by the Tigers' upcoming road trip.

Tuesday morning, I was home packing for the trip, when the phone rang. Not Donner again, I hoped.

The voice was female and businesslike. "Mickey Rawlings, please."

"This is me."

"This is Connie Siever. I have that item you requested."

"Huh?"

"Karl told me you wanted me to acquire my father's effects. There was one item in particular you were interested in . . ."

"Oh! The gun, yes. You have it?"

"That's what I said."

Not in English, she hadn't. "The police gave it to you?"

"Yes. I had no difficulty at all. Would you care to come by and see it?"

"Sure. Oh—I'm leaving town tomorrow morning. We have a road trip."

"Today then. You remember where I live?"

"Yes, but, uh . . ." Margie and I had other plans for my last night in Detroit. "I have a game this afternoon, and I promised Margie I'd go to her show tonight."

"After the show is fine. And bring her along if you like."

After the way Connie had behaved Saturday night, I couldn't imagine Margie wanting to visit Connie Siever at home. I'd have to go alone then; I couldn't resist seeing the gun. "I'll be there. I'll ask Margie if she wants to come, too."

"Very good. Call me later and let me know what time to expect you." She took a breath. "By the way, have you heard from Karl? Has he gotten to Boston all right?"

"Uh, no. He hasn't called. You haven't heard from him either?"

She hesitated. "No."

I waited a moment to be sure that was all she was going to say. "If I hear from him, I'll let you know."

"No need," she said.

Then why did you ask in the first place, I thought.

After getting off the phone with Connie Siever, I bathed,

dressed, and had my usual breakfast of coffee and cookies. I definitely wanted to see the gun whether or not Margie came with me.

I called Margie at her hotel and relayed Connie's invitation. To my surprise—and mild disappointment—she agreed readily.

$$\bigcirc \ \bigcirc \ \bigcirc$$

"I hope she isn't as ornery as she was the other night," I said as we turned onto Wyandotte Street.

"Sometimes people just make a bad first impression," said Margie. "She deserves a second chance."

"There was no reason for her to act the way she did."

"Maybe she was mad at Karl and took it out on me instead. Or maybe something about me rubbed her the wrong way. Didn't you ever meet somebody and, for no good reason, dislike him right from the start? And then, once you got to know him, found you could be friends?"

I smiled. That was exactly how it had been when I'd first met Karl Landfors. "Yes, that happens sometimes."

"Doesn't mean Connie and I can never be friends," Margie said.

We'd arrived at the Siever bungalow. "Well, let's see what kind of a second impression she makes."

It was a complete reversal from her behavior the other night. Connie greeted Margie with a hug and invited us into the kitchen for beers. She was off to a good start, I thought.

Sitting at the small table by the window, the three of us drank our beers and chatted about the weather. Actually,

Connie did the chatting, and I didn't much care about the weather, but at least she wasn't talking politics.

Margie gave me a "See, I told you so" smile.

Friendly as Connie was being, I didn't want to spend any more of the evening with her than necessary. "You mentioned you have the gun," I reminded her.

She nodded and rose. "Yes, I'll get it."

During the minute she was gone, Margie whispered to me, "I think she feels bad about the other night. That's why she's trying so hard. Be nice."

Connie returned and laid an odd-looking revolver on the table. A zigzag pattern of grooves was machined into the cylinder, and there was a slide mechanism for the barrel and cylinder to move back and forth. I picked up the weapon and read the lettering stamped on the frame: *Webley-Fosbery Automatic*.

"I heard about these," I said. "During the war. It's an automatic revolver. The British used them for a while, but they didn't work if they got dirty. Since there aren't any clean trenches, they had to find another kind of sidearm. I never saw one of these—I heard they're aren't many around."

"How does it work?" Margie asked.

"Not sure," I admitted. "I think it's kind of complicated." The only thing I had mastered about firearms was cleaning them. I asked Connie, "You never saw this before?"

She shook her head no.

"You're sure your father didn't own a gun?"

She looked about to explode at me, but collected herself. "I'm sure. You think this gun is going to lead to my father's murderer?"

"It might. Somebody had to plant it on him. The trick is

to find out where it came from and who could have gotten it."

"You can take it with you if you think it will help," she offered.

"Thanks." No, I decided, better not. Connie had a legitimate reason to have it. If the weapon was to be "found" in my possession, it might only get me in more trouble. "Actually, all I need is the serial number."

She gave me a pencil and a scrap of paper and I jotted down the number.

"I guess we'd better be going," I said. "I have to leave early tomorrow."

"Oh, well, certainly." Connie looked disappointed.

Margie spoke up. "We have time for one more beer."

She and Margie talked while I guzzled the second one and waited impatiently for them to finish theirs.

When Connie walked us to the door, she asked, "If you hear from Karl, will you let me know how he is?"

"Sure," I said. To myself I thought, but this morning you told me not to bother.

As we walked back to Joseph Campau Avenue, Margie explained, "I think she was feeling lonely. That's why I wanted to stay a little longer."

"No problem," I said. But I grabbed her hand and pulled her along in a fast walk to catch the next streetcar.

On the ride downtown, I said to Margie, "I wish the gun wasn't British."

"You have something against the British?"

"No," I laughed. "It makes it harder to trace. I thought I'd start with the manufacturer and see if I could follow through to whoever bought it. Being from England makes it tough."

"Why don't you let me help?" said Margie.

"Huh?"

"You're going to be away, so you won't be able to do anything for a while anyway. Why not give me the number, and let me see if I can find out anything."

"Well . . ." There was no reason not to. I fished the slip of paper out of my jacket pocket and handed it to her. "What are you going to do with it?"

"I don't know," she said. She kissed me on the cheek and added, "I'll try to think of something."

Another thing we had in common: we had the same approach to investigating.

Kneeling in the on-deck circle of Griffith Stadium, watching "The Big Train" Walter Johnson pitch to Donie Bush, I realized that Hub Donner and I had something in common: I also preferred things the way they used to be.

It wasn't only that I yearned for a return to the innocence and optimism that had characterized the American spirit before the war. I also had a specific complaint: I wanted the powers that ran baseball to stop tinkering with my game. I didn't want small changes like the disappearance of collars from uniform jerseys, nor sweeping ones like the juiced-up ball. There should be some constants in life, and baseball was one of them.

Until this year, the Washington grounds were called National Park—a fitting name for the capital's ballpark, though a bit ambitious. Then Senators' manager Clark Griffith was appointed the club's president, and following the example of Frank Navin promptly renamed the park in his own honor. No, I didn't like changes to baseball. Not to the names of the parks, nor to the ball, and especially not to the way the livelier ball was changing the tactics of the game, with every hitter swinging for the fences and making the old strategies obsolete.

Long-armed Walter Johnson was a reassuring constant in the game, a throwback to the old days. He'd been pitching for the Washington Senators since 1907, back when I was still playing semipro ball in a Rhode Island mill league. Every season since then, Johnson usually ended up with the American League titles for wins, strikeouts, and shutouts. And the new livelier baseball wasn't likely to change that.

Johnson went into his windmill windup and delivered. Donie Bush swung wildly for strike two. No, with Johnson it didn't matter how the ball was constructed; no matter what he threw, you were unlikely to hit it and lucky merely to see it.

After Bush fanned, I walked eagerly to the plate. No matter how miserable it was playing for the Tigers, being back in the American League at least gave me a chance to face Walter Johnson again.

I scraped at the hard earth of the batter's box and assumed my stance. I'd faced Johnson only once before, in 1912, and was proud of the fact that I had not struck out. That remained my objective in this at bat.

He wound up, then unleashed a sidearm fastball that seemed to come from the direction of third base. It smacked into the catcher's mitt before I could determine how it got there. "Strike one!" called umpire Brick Owens. My reaction was not disappointment, but a mixture of sheer admiration for his speed and gratitude that it hadn't drilled me in the head.

I choked up higher on the bat. There's only way to hit

Johnson: when his arm starts to move forward, swing the bat and hope the ball hits it. The slow windmill windup again, and the speeding baseball. I swung for the middle of the strike zone—and his pitch went wild, sailing a couple feet over the catcher's head. The sound of the ball buzzing by was too high. "Strike two!" Owens cried. He then added, "Don't feel bad, son. I don't always see them either."

Great. More changes: Walter Johnson losing his pinpoint control and an umpire who admits he doesn't see the ball.

No balls, two strikes. Will he waste a pitch? If I was him, I wouldn't bother. But nothing down the middle, either. I guessed fastball, low and away. That's where I swung on the third pitch and felt the sharp shudder of bat on ball. Just enough to produce a weak pop-up that the second baseman caught to end the inning. Mission accomplished: I did not strike out.

By the end of the eighth inning, Walter Johnson was on the losing end of a 2–1 score. His only weakness was something else that had remained constant through the years: the inability of the players behind him to score runs. The one run Washington had put across was knocked in by Johnson himself when he'd doubled in Bucky Harris.

With two out in the top of the ninth, I had my fourth at bat against Johnson. I was 0-for-3 so far, but he hadn't struck me out once. Donie Bush was on first base, and it would mean an insurance run for Hooks Dauss if I could drive Bush in.

I looked back at Hughie Jennings going through his contortions in the third base coach's box. To my amazement, he patted his left sleeve twice. That was the sign for sacrifice. A sacrifice bunt with two outs? It must be a mistake.

I backed out, scooped up some dirt to dry my hands, and gave him another look. He flashed the same sign: sacrifice. It was ingrained in me that, right or wrong, a manager's orders should be obeyed. But his made *no* sense. I looked to Donie Bush at first base. He must have seen Jennings's sign, for he shook his head, then touched the "D" on his jersey and the brim of his cap. The hit-and-run sign.

Stepping back in the box, I decided to ignore Jennings and go for the hit-and-run. It was the only reasonable play for the circumstances.

On Johnson's first pitch, Bush broke for second base. Washington's second baseman Bucky Harris moved over to cover the bag, leaving a hole on the right side of the infield. All I had to do was poke the ball . . .

The pitch was exactly where I wanted it—on the outside corner—but just too damn fast. I grounded to Joe Judge at first who flipped to Johnson covering for the final out of the inning.

I ran quickly past Hughie Jennings to get my glove from the bench. He was fuming and cussing about "goddamn banjo-hitting road apples who think they're so goddamned smart." The way his blue eyes drilled me left no question as to who the "goddamn banjo-hitting road apple" was.

At least he didn't pull me from the game. I went back to second base for the final inning. When Dauss finished his warm-up throws, Oscar Stanage threw down to second. I fielded it, then flipped to Donie Bush backing me up. He caught the ball and stared at me for a moment. "Don't worry about Hughie," he said. "You did right." Those were the first words any of my teammates had said to me in three days.

Dauss held the Senators scoreless in the bottom of the

ninth, so my failure to drive Bush home didn't cost us the game. But my failure to obey Jennings's orders cost me my temporary starting job. He took me into his office, said what they'd have done to me in the old Orioles days—it involved tar and feathers—and told me I was going to be riding the bench for a while. "Only reason I'm not fining you," he said, "is I know Navin ain't hardly paying you enough to live on as it is."

Back at my locker, I said nothing to my teammates about what had happened. I saw them looking at me when I came out of Jennings's office; they were probably all hoping I'd been traded or released.

As I changed out of my uniform, I realized that Cobb, Bush, Veach, and Heilmann had all struck out today. In fact, Walter Johnson had fanned every batter in our lineup at least once—except me. I was the only one on the team who could say that Johnson had *never* struck me out—and depending on how long Jennings kept me on the bench, I might be able to make that statement for some time to come. That thought improved my mood considerably. By the time I'd showered and dressed, I was buoyant enough that I decided to set a new goal for myself: to get a base hit off the Big Train someday.

○ ○ ○

Karl Landfors had warned me to stay away from Calvin Garrett and the GID. But how could I? Garrett, as Aikens, was the only other person I knew for sure was at the scene when Emmett Siever was killed. Immediately thereafter, at least.

Friday morning, I stood on the northeast corner of Vermont Avenue and K Street, staring up at the intimidating eight-story, stone-block building that housed the U.S. Department of Justice and the Bureau of Investigation. I'd been in local police stations before, and a few municipal buildings, but I'd never been in anything like this. This was a *federal* institution, and the structure's very appearance seemed intended to show that the full weight of the United States government was behind it. This place wasn't going to be staffed by beat cops who could be bribed with beers or low-level civil servants who could be paid off with a few bucks.

I pulled out my watch: quarter past ten, almost two hours until I had to report to Griffith Stadium. I thought of the date: May 14—eight days to Leo Hyman's deadline. There was no question about it: I *had* to speak with Calvin Garrett.

Removing my straw boater as I stepped inside, I ventured through the building's main entrance. Armed guards stood at attention inside the door. They gave me a visual inspection but didn't challenge me. I'd worn a conservative three-button blue serge suit, a stiff white shirt with a high celluloid collar, and a dark green bow tie that I'd bought specifically for this occasion. I wanted to look as innocuous as possible.

The spacious lobby was cold and forbidding. I walked purposefully across the tile floor, trying to give the impression that I knew exactly where I was going. Meanwhile, I cast sidelong glances that failed to detect an office directory or any sign indicating where to find the General Intelligence Division.

At the far end of the lobby, an impeccably groomed and dressed young man sat behind a broad desk arrayed with half a dozen telephones. He surveyed the room like an alert librarian on the watch for anyone dog-earing books or chewing gum. My shoes clattered on the floor as I approached his post. He frowned, and I thought he was going to shush me.

"Can I help you?" he asked.

"I'd like to see Calvin Garrett, please."

"What department?"

"General Intelligence Division."

"I see." The young man pursed his lips. "Do you have an appointment with Mr. Garrett?"

I had phoned earlier to be sure that Garrett was in the building but had hung up when the operator tried to connect me to his office. The only thing I had going for me was the element of surprise, and I didn't want to lose it by warning him that I was coming. "No, but he'll see me."

"Your name?"

"Emmett Siever."

"Let me check." He pointed to a straight-backed chair well out of listening range. "Wait there, please."

I walked over to the chair, but remained standing as I watched the young man place a call. After a minute on the line, he beckoned me with a crooked finger. "What did you say your name was again?"

I again gave him Siever's name and he repeated it into the mouthpiece. After a few seconds of listening, he added with a note of exasperation, "That's what he says." Another pause. "Very well." He hung up and said to me, "Have a seat. Someone will be with you shortly."

I was sure that the someone would be Calvin Garrett.

Minutes later, a hulking man in an unflattering gray suit exited a nearby elevator. The young man at the desk pointed me out, and Garrett approached. He was about thirty years old, with a broad flat nose, dull eyes, and a soft pink face that looked freshly scrubbed. His close-cropped medium brown hair was slicked back with something greasy. "Why the 'Emmett Siever' name?" he asked.

"To make sure you'd see me. Why'd you use 'Detective Aikens'?"

He frowned slightly, then bobbed his head, acknowledging that I had a point. His expression was not that of a deep thinker, but he must have something on the ball to be in his job, I thought. He extended his hand. "Calvin Garrett."

"I know." I returned his soft grip. "Mickey Rawlings."

"I know." He looked around the lobby. In one corner were several armchairs clustered near a potted plant. "Let's talk over there."

"Okay." As he led the way, I added, "I've got a lot of questions for you."

"Fine. We have no secrets here."

"Then why did you make up that 'Detective Aikens' business back in Detroit?"

"I didn't know who you were. Our existence is no secret, but we don't necessarily advertise our presence. You understand."

"Not really. What is it that you do exactly?"

Once we were seated, Garrett crossed his legs and launched into what sounded like a recitation. "The General Intelligence Division is a division within the Bureau of Investigation of the Department of Justice. The purpose of the GID is to compile and maintain information on radicals and their activities in the United States and abroad. In performing this function, the Division acquires such information in cooperation with the Bureau of Investigation, other government agencies, local police departments, the military, and, uh, private citizens." He punctuated the end of every sentence with a nod of his head. "It is the policy—"

I could have read the regulations myself had I wanted to. I interrupted, "In other words, Attorney General Mitchell Palmer runs the Department of Justice. The Justice Department's office in charge of monitoring radicals is the General Intelligence Division, formerly known as the Anti-Radical Division. Palmer is running for president. He was angry about losing the Michigan primary, and blamed it on 'radicals.' A week after the primary vote, a GID man—you—ends up at Fraternity Hall in Detroit. Palmer wanted revenge on the people he thinks cost him the election, so you were sent to crack down on the Wobblies up there. Is that about right?" My tone was more certain than my mind; I didn't want to show Garrett any doubt or fear.

Garrett made a gurgling noise and rubbed his nose with the heel of his palm. I wondered if that habit had contributed to its present shape. "Well, yes, I was there." Not a major admission, considering I knew that.

"My question is: what were you *doing* there?"

He appeared off stride, and his speech became measured. "We have an interest in keeping tabs on radical organizations." He bobbed his head. "The Industrial Workers of the World is one such organization." Head nod. "Therefore, it is in keeping with our mission—"

I tried to interrupt again but failed. Garrett picked up steam and went on a tear about patriotism, free enterprise, and the need to protect American society from "foreign agitators." It sounded like a campaign speech, but I had the impression he believed every word.

Once he had the speechifying out of his system, I tried to convince him that I was not his enemy. "I'm not arguing with what it is you're trying to do," I said. "My problem is that I've been accused of shooting Emmett Siever. I'm hoping you can help get me cleared."

"I don't see how *I* can help," Garrett said quickly.

"You came into the hall just a few minutes after Siever was shot. With the meeting going on in the front, you must have come in through the back door." I paused to give him a chance to confirm this.

He considered his answer before saying, "Yes, I did."

"*Why* did you come inside? Did you hear the shot, or did you see the killer running out the back door or something?"

Garrett rubbed his nose again.

"Look," I said, "if you saw the killer leave, then that puts me in the clear. What's the harm in your saying so? The Wobblies know you spy on them. So what's the big secret?"

"I *thought* I saw somebody slip out the door," he said.

"Did you recognize him?"

"No."

"But you must know it wasn't me. Just tell the cops you saw somebody else. That's all I'm asking. Please."

"I can't do that. It was dark. I'm not positive that I saw anybody at all."

"Well—" I wasn't sure how to persuade him. "You *must* know it wasn't me. Why did you let me go if you thought I might have killed him?"

"I had no authority to detain you. The GID is not empowered to make arrests. The situation at Fraternity Hall was a matter for the police to handle, and I'm confident that they handled it properly."

"But you talked to the police. You told them I was there."

"As I said before, we work in cooperation with local law enforcement."

Calvin Garrett was as forthcoming with useful information as the stone blocks of the building's facade. I tried to steer him away from generalities with a question on the details: "How'd you get inside?"

"Huh?"

"To Fraternity Hall. How did you get in? I don't expect they leave their back door open for anyone to wander in."

His face made an exaggerated show of searching his memory. "As a matter of fact, it *was* unlocked."

I didn't believe him. A question as to whether he picked the lock crossed my mind, but I squelched it when I remembered the crossbar on the door. A lock pick doesn't do any good when the door is barred.

Garrett leaned forward, his dull eyes sharpening. "Now I have a question for *you:* How did you find out who I was?"

It suddenly struck me that letting Garrett know I was aware of his identity might be dangerous for me. "I found out from the Wobblies," I said. "Somebody must have seen you there." If Garrett thought others already knew about him, he'd have no reason to shut me up—I hoped.

"You're in contact with the Wobblies?"

"Some," I admitted. "Just to try to find out who killed Siever. It's the Wobblies who are in contact with *me,* really. They believe what the cops told the papers, and they want revenge."

"Well, you're in a bit of a predicament, then, aren't you?" He didn't sound sorry about it.

"That's why I'm here." I turned my head to look at a

group of men in drab suits walking past us. I tried to guess which ones might be GID agents.

Garrett said, "Maybe we can help each other out."

I didn't want to "help each other out"—I wanted *him* to help *me*. Still, this might be the best offer I was going to get, so I figured I'd better hear him out. "How?"

"You might have some information on baseball's union agitators that we can use." He smiled. "And I might have information that I could pass on to the Detroit police for you."

"Why would you care about the *baseball* union?" I could see the GID being involved in the railroad strikes, or investigating real revolutionaries, but baseball?

Garrett adopted his speech-making tone, "The attorney general feels strongly that the national pastime should not be allowed to go Red. It would tear at the very fabric of American society if—"

"He's doing this for his campaign, isn't he!" Politicians loved to latch onto baseball as a sign of their Americanism. Why the hell couldn't they stick to kissing babies and telling lies about their opponents?

Garrett ignored the accusation. "Someone is going to take Emmett Siever's place. I—we—want to know who that someone is."

"I don't know anything about who's going to try to organize the union."

"Start with your own team. I understand that Chick Fogarty is the Tigers' labor leader. Get friendly with him and see what you can find out for me."

*Fogarty?* Could he really be—I didn't let myself think about it. It didn't matter who was unionizing, I *wasn't* going to help Calvin Garrett or the GID. "I'm not a spy any more than I am a killer," I said.

Garrett started to respond, when a short man with the face of a bulldog and the body of a fireplug scooted up to us. Addressing the GID agent, he said in a rapid-fire delivery, "I was told you were here, Garrett. We have a meeting upstairs in ten minutes. I'll look forward to hearing your report."

"Yes, Mr. Hoover. It's all ready."

"Fine. Don't be late." He spun and walked away as quickly as he'd arrived.

"That your boss?" I asked.

"That's the GID's Chief: J. Edgar Hoover." Garrett stood. "I want to be able to tell him that you'll be helping us."

"You don't always get what you want," I said.

○ ○ ○

What *I* wanted was for Hughie Jennings to have a change of heart, to realize that he'd been wrong yesterday and let me keep playing. He didn't. I was benched for the Friday game while Ralph Young, a former high-school star from Philadelphia, took over at second base.

I found some solace in the fact that I was still on the team at all. Lou Vedder hadn't been so lucky. He'd been dropped from the roster without ever getting to make another appearance on the mound.

Friday night, I was in our hotel room sizing up my new roommate: Harry Heilmann. He was a couple of years younger than me, strongly built, darkly handsome, with an easy manner and a reputation for enjoying the night life. We called him "Slug" because of the way he plodded around the base paths—he could knock a baseball four hundred feet and be held to a single.

Heilmann suffered from no such slowness in his speech. He had the gift of gab, and for the past fifteen minutes had been carrying on a monologue as he paced the room. The main thread was that he wondered where he could find a beer in the capital, but he also wove in complaints about Hughie Jennings making him play first base instead of outfield, admiration for Ty Cobb's ability to place base hits, and contempt for the way Bobby Veach let other players ride him.

Nothing Heilmann said invited comment or conversation. So I didn't respond that Jennings probably had him at first base because he couldn't run, catch, or throw. Nor did I point out that the only player riding Bobby Veach was Heilmann himself.

I did want to talk with him, though. Heilmann was admired on the team—both for his hitting abilities and his sociable nature—and if he and I could become pals, maybe they'd all start to accept me. I tried to think of something to break the ice.

Heilmann stopped in front of the mirror and combed his hair. He muttered that there had to be *someplace* in town where a man could get a drink and vowed that he'd find it if he had to spend all night searching.

I probably should have started with small talk, but ever since Calvin Garrett mentioned Chick Fogarty being the team's union man I'd been thinking about the big catcher. I had previously dismissed Fogarty as nothing but Dutch Leonard's minion. I might have grossly underestimated the man. Large and slow does not mean stupid.

"Harry," I said. I wasn't sure how much he liked being called "Slug."

He paused from his grooming, looking surprised that I was in the room. I think he'd considered me part of the furnishings. "Yeah?"

"Is anybody on the team working on the players' union?"

He tucked the comb in an inside pocket of his double-breasted suit. "Why? You want to shoot him?"

"Funny." I gave him the benefit of the doubt that he'd intended the question as a joke. "Is it Chick Fogarty?"

"What, are you nuts?" He brushed his lapels and headed for the door. "See you later, kid. If you're still up."

I could have used a beer or two myself, and wished he'd asked me along. Left alone, I elected to stay in for the night.

I mulled over my meeting with Calvin Garrett. I hadn't really learned much new from him. *Maybe* he heard a shot, *maybe* he saw somebody leave the back door of Fraternity Hall. All I'd accomplished by my visit to the Justice Department was to confirm what Karl Landfors had already told me: that the "Detective Aikens" I'd met at the murder scene was in actuality Calvin Garrett, special agent with the U.S. government's General Intelligence Division. By talking with Garrett, he now knew that I was aware of his ruse. And he wanted me to help him find out who among the ballplayers were unionizing. On the whole, I thought dejectedly, I probably did myself more harm than good.

Lying stretched out on my bed, I eventually came around to thinking that it had not been a waste of time. For one thing, it was worth checking that Landfors's information was correct. For another, Garrett being at the scene meant that the GID was involved in the Siever case to some extent. I was convinced that Garrett had given instructions to the Detroit police to pin the shooting on me, which meant he was part of a cover-up at the very least. The question was: who were they covering up for? And why?

As the night wore on, my thoughts turned to baseball. They were no more encouraging than the ones about Calvin Garrett. I thought about being benched. And that my 0-for-4 performance against Walter Johnson had sent my batting average plummeting down toward its usual level of .250. About Harry Heilmann not inviting me to go drinking with him. And about playing for a manager who didn't remember what kind of play to put on.

I started to think that Lou Vedder was the lucky one, and I began to nurture the hope that I might soon be traded.

# Chapter Eighteen

○○○

The Tigers team rolled into Michigan Central shortly after noon on Thursday, May 20. By twelve-thirty, I was back at my apartment; two minutes after that, I was on the phone to Margie. I'd called her every day during the road trip, but hearing her voice over a long-distance connection had a frustrating aspect—it emphasized that she was hundreds of miles out of physical reach.

That was about to change soon. Our conversation was brief. Margie said that I must be tired from the trip and insisted on coming to my apartment. I argued that I'd rather go to her hotel; I gave in when I realized that the sooner I let her have her way, the sooner we'd be together.

After a frantic cleanup which even included making the bed, and a trip to the bakery to buy cookies and an apple pie, I truly was tired.

I'd barely made it back from the bakery when Margie arrived. I told her how much I'd missed her, gave her a one-minute tour of the parlor, forced some cookies on her, and told her again how much I'd missed her. She said she'd missed me, too, found some things to compliment about the apartment, ate one of the cookies, and initiated a long kiss. We then sat down on the sofa, which I'd covered with a blanket to hide the bare upholstery.

Margie was smiling, and I started to get the sense it wasn't only because she was happy to see me again. There was always a hint of mischief in Margie's smile, but today it contained something else as well. In a way she reminded me of—a smirking Karl Landfors.

"What is it?" I asked. "You've been up to something."

"The gun that Connie Siever showed us—the one that the police said her father was carrying . . ."

"Yes?"

"I found out where it came from."

"You traced it! How?"

"Well, I didn't *quite* do as you suggested." She looked toward the kitchen. "Do you have anything to wash these cookies down with?"

Damn. I'd forgotten to pick up anything to drink. "Beer?" I offered.

Margie laughed and agreed. After I'd poured us a couple glasses of the Canadian beer Landfors had left me, she went on, "Since it's such an unusual gun, I thought that instead of starting with the manufacturer I'd start at the other end: see if it was used anywhere."

"How?"

"I went to the *Detroit News* and talked to one of their crime reporters. He was very nice; he said he recognized me from my movies. I asked him if he remembered any crimes where a Webley-Fosbery was used. He said there was a notorious case two years ago in Grosse Pointe: a former British soldier shot and killed an elderly couple who caught him burglarizing their house."

"But what does that have to do with Emmett Siever?"

"Well, then I went to the County Building to talk with the prosecutor who handled the case—the soldier was convicted and executed this past winter, by the way."

Why would I care about him, I wondered.

She continued, "I told the prosecutor I was writing a movie about the case. He wasn't much interested in talking to me until I said I was going to make him the hero of the story. Anyway, he let me see the files. And guess what?"

"What?"

"The gun that was used was the same one Connie Siever showed us. The serial number matched exactly."

Somehow, the weapon had gone from a burglar in Grosse Pointe to Emmett Siever in Fraternity Hall. "But the police must have had that gun in the property room," I said.

"Yes. I asked the prosecutor what they did with evidence and he said that's where it would have gone."

"So it was taken from the property room and planted on Siever. It had to be the police who did it—who else would have had access to the gun?"

"No one."

I was astonished at her success. "You did *great.*" This was finally starting to come together. I'd figured the GID was covering something up. Now Margie found out who had carried out the cover-up: the Detroit Police Department. But how—

Margie shifted closer to me and began running her fingernails over my thigh. "I have an hour until I have to leave for the theater."

An hour later, she was on her way to the Rex for her show, and I was contentedly asleep.

○ ○ ○

Detective Francis "Mack" McGuire looked like a tin soldier that had been left out in the rain. He was the color of rust from his bulky tweed suit to his mass of freckles to his unruly hair.

Although Detroit was in the midst of a warm spell, the slight detective huddled in his heavy clothes as if still trying to rid himself from the chill of winter. Bright Friday morning sunlight streamed through McGuire's closed office window, making the room feel like a sauna.

"Last time you came in," he said, "you expressed some interest in the Emmett Siever case. I presume that's the reason you're here today?"

It certainly wasn't to enroll in the police academy. "Yes," I said. "I found Detective Aikens. Had a nice talk with him."

"Really?"

"He's with the General Intelligence Division of the Justice Department. That's where I talked to him—in D.C. His real name is Calvin Garrett." I paused. "But you knew that."

"Did I?"

"When I told you that 'Aikens' had showed me a badge and claimed he was a detective with the Detroit Police, you weren't curious about who was impersonating a cop. You must have known who he really was."

A hint of a smile lifted McGuire's freckled cheeks.

"Was it Garrett who told you to plant the gun?" I asked.

"I don't know what you mean." McGuire's tone was unconvincing.

"You showed me a photo of Emmett Siever holding a revolver. Turns out that gun was a peculiar one: a Webley-Fosbery automatic. It also turns out that it came from the police evidence room." McGuire started to protest. I cut him off. "I checked the serial numbers."

"You're thorough," he said with a smile. "Good quality in an investigator."

"I'm *not* an investigator. I'm a baseball player, and I don't want to *be* an investigator. That's your job."

He spread his hands. "I explained to you last time that my hands are tied after a case has been closed."

"That's why you encouraged me to look into it on my own. And why you put such an unusual gun on Siever. You must have had plenty of guns to choose from, but you picked an oddball. You *wanted* to be caught." I wasn't sure if it was because McGuire wanted the real killer found or to spite Garrett in a jurisdictional dispute. When I'd reported the shooting at my apartment to Sergeant Phelan, I'd asked him about the feud between the police and U. S. Treasury agents; he'd told me that there was no way Detroit cops were going to take orders from "feds." I pressed McGuire on this angle, "You don't like being told what to do by the GID. Garrett told you to plant a gun on Siever, and you sabotaged him by using the Webley-Fosbery."

McGuire's freckles sagged. "Let's just say that I think the laws should apply to everyone the same. I don't like a cover-up for whatever reason."

"You're a fair-minded man."

"No, I'm a lazy cop. It's a helluva lot easier to enforce

the laws evenly instead of deciding who should be exempt from them."

I was sure that McGuire didn't think that simply. He must have been breaking some laws or rules himself by telling me what he had and by showing me the photo of Siever. There had to be more to it. I went on to another question. "What kind of gun was it that killed Siever?"

"According to the official report, you should know that better than anyone."

I wished McGuire would stop playing games. "How about according to the autopsy report?"

"Well, let me see." He opened a brown folder on the desk and looked over a sheaf of papers. "The bullet was a .38."

"What make of gun?"

McGuire hesitated, then announced, "I gotta go to the can." He closed the folder and patted it. Then he rose and squeezed his way out of the office.

As soon as the door closed behind him, I picked up the file and started reading. There had been a .38 slug lodged in Siever's spine—probably a Colt Special, according to the report. But that wasn't all. Emmett Siever had been stabbed in the heart. I read a lengthy, technical description of the wound which was summarized: "such as might be produced by an ice pick or similar instrument."

Detective McGuire pushed into the room again. In mock anger, he demanded, "What are you doing reading that?" and grabbed the folder from my hands.

I was reeling from the new information. As he took his seat behind the desk, I gave voice to my thoughts, "You might have covered up for the wrong killer. You thought

Siever had been shot, you planted a gun on him, told the papers that I'd killed him in self-defense, and figured that was the end of it." The date on the autopsy report was two days after Siever died. "By the time he was autopsied and it turned out he was stabbed, it was too late. You couldn't change the 'official' story at that point. Is that another reason you pushed me into investigating—you don't know who stabbed him?"

"I don't know who stabbed him," McGuire said. "And the medical examiner isn't certain which wound was the fatal one."

"But you do know who shot him."

"To say that I *know* would be stretching it. I wasn't a witness to the shooting, so how can I say I know for sure?"

I was getting tired of the way McGuire played around the edges without coming to the point. "Then who do you *suspect?*"

He thought a moment. "No," he decided, shaking his head. "Sharing my suspicions with you would be inappropriate. And like I told you last time, the case is closed."

"You also said if I find new information . . ."

"Which you haven't yet, have you?"

No, I suppose I hadn't. It was new for me, but not for McGuire. So far, the detective had already known everything I'd found out. He had given *me* some more things to think about though. I tried to remember the list of questions I had wanted to ask him on this visit. There was only one more remaining: "Do you know where Leo Hyman was that night?"

McGuire hesitated again.

"You can't have it both ways," I said. "You can't push

me to do your job for you and then go silent on me when I need help."

The freckles twisted themselves into an expression that indicated he felt he could do whatever he wanted. But he chose to answer. "Hyman was at Fraternity Hall."

"I didn't see him."

"All I know is that he was questioned there after the shooting." McGuire stressed the word "know."

"Thanks." I stood to go. "I'll be back soon."

"I'll look forward to it," said McGuire.

○ ○ ○

On my way home before going to Navin Field, I felt almost relieved that I'd be riding the pines again. I couldn't imagine concentrating on the game. My mind was wrestling with the new information I'd learned, trying to make sense of it.

Why stab somebody and then shoot him—or shoot him and then stab him? Why not simply stab or shoot him repeatedly? The only sensible answer was that there were two killers. Two would-be killers, anyway, one of whom was successful. Okay, so there had to be at least two people involved in the killing—perhaps three, depending on where Calvin Garrett fit in.

I also wondered about Leo Hyman: when and where did he come from that night? Maybe he was the man Garrett saw slipping out the back door, and then he went back in through the front. But why would he kill Siever? And why would Garrett cover for him? I could understand if it had been Hub Donner, someone on the same side as Garrett, but not Hyman—why would the GID cover up for a Wobbly?

When I got home, I called Leo Hyman. "You were going to try to find out where Hub Donner was the night Emmett Siever was killed," I reminded him.

"That's right. Sorry I didn't get back to you. It's a little embarrassing to admit, but he slipped our tail that night. Don't know where he was."

Damn. "Can we get together tomorrow? My four weeks is up and I want to tell you what I have."

"Anything good?"

"I'll let you be the judge."

"All right."

"Where? Not that shack again, please. How about the movie theater?"

"Stosh only works there on Fridays. You don't have a game tomorrow, right?"

"Right."

"Want to see one?"

"Who?"

"The Stars. At Mack Park."

"Sure!" The Stars were Detroit's franchise in the new Negro National League, and I was curious to see how well they played.

Hyman gave me directions to his house, and I agreed to meet him at noon the next day. I also made a promise to myself that I would be very careful when I got there.

# Chapter Nineteen

ooo

**M**y walk to Leo Hyman's house took me into Detroit's east side, an area called Black Bottom. It looked like something I'd only seen on "the other side of the tracks" in segregated Southern cities. Between Beaubien and Hastings was a shantytown, with dilapidated shacks packed closely together. City trash collectors apparently avoided the area; piles of reeking refuse often blocked my path. As crowded as the housing was, the density of people—almost all of them colored—was higher. Swarms of children in ragged clothing congested the alleys, and groups of men and women gathered on the corners.

Farther east, the neighborhood improved, although it was still never going to be mistaken for Grosse Pointe. The homes were small, single-family wood dwellings; they were modest, but well maintained. Many had patches of trimmed lawn and a few had window boxes with blooming flowers. On the corners were sturdier brick buildings that housed barber shops, grocery stores, and doctors' offices. Along the curbs were parked spotless automobiles, almost every one of them a Model T. There were few white faces among the people I passed, and I felt uneasy about being a minority.

Leo Hyman's house was on Monroe Street between Riopelle and Orleans. I thought there should have been a quarter moon cut in the front door—the place wasn't much bigger than an outhouse, and not much prettier, either. Of all the homes on the block, his was the most in need of a paint job and some decoration.

When Hyman let me in, the first thing I wanted to ask was why he chose to live in this neighborhood. I restrained myself, thinking perhaps he couldn't afford any better. It probably wasn't very lucrative to be a professional radical.

The interior of the house was cluttered but not dirty; wires, mechanical parts, and disassembled machines and instruments were everywhere.

"Any trouble finding the place?" he asked. Today he wore red suspenders that were barely visible against his shirt.

"No, the directions were fine. I've never been in this area before, though."

"Neither has the American Federation of Labor."

"Huh?"

"You're wondering why I live in Black Bottom, aren't you?"

"I suppose."

Hyman fluffed out his beard and seated himself on a stool in front of a small workbench. "I'm here because this is where the workers are." With long tweezers, he maneuvered a tiny mast inside a bottle where a miniature ship was under construction. "Negroes have been here since the Civil War—this was the last stop on the underground railroad, you know."

"No, didn't know that."

"Got fifty thousand living in the city now and thousands more arriving every year to make automobiles. This is the new work force, and the IWW wants them to join us. I figure if I live among them, they'll get to know and trust me."

I wasn't sure Hyman would succeed on that score. The more *I* got to know him, the *less* I trusted him. "So you're here for recruiting."

"Exactly. Sam Gompers—'Sell 'em Out Sam' we call him—and his American Federation of Labor aren't interested in these people. A lot of AFL locals won't accept Negroes—or women, or foreigners, for that matter. The IWW takes *all* workers. All people, for one big union."

I wasn't much interested in IWW membership policies. More out of courtesy than curiosity, I asked, "Getting lots of new members?"

He shook his head. "It's been tough. Henry Ford is a popular man in these parts. He beat us to it in trying to win the Negroes over. Ford gives them jobs and pays a whole lot better than they can get anywhere else. You'll see when we're at the game that a lot of colored men wear their Ford work badges on their suits. They're proud of their jobs and not about to jeopardize them by joining a union. I'm patient, though. They'll come around."

"What makes you think so?"

"Ford will do something stupid." He put down the tweezers, picked up a newspaper from a nearby table, and handed it to me. "Look at this."

The paper was *The Dearborn Independent*, dated May 22, 1920. Above the name of the paper were the words "The Ford International Weekly." The main headline read *The International Jew: The World's Problem*.

"Henry Ford doesn't like Jews?" I asked.

"Apparently not." Hyman shook his head in disgust. "Just because of his money and power, Ford can get his prejudices spread around in a rag like this. No one man's whim should carry so much weight." He sighed. "People are contradictions, Mickey. Nobody is all good or all bad. I'll give the devil his due: Ford hires Negroes, ex-cons, cripples and generally gives them all a fairer shake than they'd get anywhere else. But here he is denouncing Jews. Who knows who it'll be next week? Maybe Negroes, and then we'll win them over to our side." Hyman mixed some glue and dabbed it into the bottle, attaching a string to the mast. His hands were as steady as a surgeon's.

I was fascinated with Hyman's deft work. "I hear you used to be an engineer."

"I'm a tinker is what I am. A fine and noble trade."

From the contents of the house, I'd have taken him for a junk dealer. "Who's joining us at the game?" I asked.

"What makes you think anybody's joining us?"

"The first time we met, you brought Whitey Boggs along. Last time, Stan Zaluski was there."

Hyman chuckled. "It's not wise to go into a situation without a second—never know what might happen. Stosh is coming along today, but because he likes baseball, not because I need a backup man. I'm not afraid of you."

"Guess you don't believe I killed Emmett Siever then."

The tweezers stopped moving. "Let's just say I'm not a hundred percent convinced."

"It might have helped me convince other people that I didn't do it if you could have told me where Hub Donner was that night. I don't see how he could have slipped away from whoever you had watching him—a fellow who looks like Donner can't just disappear."

"Hub Donner is big and ugly," said Hyman. "But don't underestimate him just because he looks like a thug. The man is smart." He smiled wryly. "A most worthy adversary."

Hyman sounded like he admired Donner. And I was think-ing that his advice about not underestimating people could also apply to Chick Fogarty.

He laid the tweezers on the bench. "We better be going if we want to see batting practice." He picked up the bottle and studied the ship that was taking form inside. "Ain't never gonna sail, but when I'm done with her she's sure gonna *look* seaworthy."

○ ○ ○

By the fourth inning, I was starting to think that maybe the best baseball wasn't being played in the American and National Leagues.

At first sight, Mack Park didn't hold out much promise. The wooden structure at Mack Avenue and Fairview was like a spring-training ballpark—small, rustic, and shaky. But what was happening on the diamond was exquisite.

Two left-handed pitchers, the Detroit Stars' Andy Cooper and Dave Brown of the Chicago American Giants, were hurl-ing superb shutout baseball. From my grandstand seat, I could tell that both pitchers easily had the stuff—blistering fastballs and wicked curveballs—to make the Tigers' pitching staff. The problem wasn't what they lacked, but what they possessed: dark skin. I'd always thought it unfair that Negroes were barred from Organized Baseball. Now, seeing them play, I realized it wasn't only the colored players who were missing out on something. It was the white players—and fans—who were being cheated as well. I *wanted* to have a chance to bat against these men.

Stan Zaluski and Leo Hyman sat on either side of me. Zaluski sipped a Coca-Cola that he'd "flavored" from a pocket flask. Hyman was keeping count of the innings by consuming a hot dog during each one. I was on my second bag of peanuts and drinking ginger ale. I could tell that Hyman and Zaluski were genuine fans. Like me, they kept their eyes on the game and said little through the first few innings. No matter how many ball games I've seen or played in, I always approached each new game as if something special might happen—a no-hitter, an unassisted triple play, a steal of home.

When Cooper gave up a single to Giants' second baseman Bingo DeMoss, the chance of seeing a no-hitter was gone.

Stan Zaluski said, "It's good to get out to a ball game. I'm gonna have to work all Memorial Day weekend in that damn projection booth, so I better get my fill of fresh air now."

Cristobal Torriente, who I overheard from a fan near us was from Cuba, got up to face Cooper. The left-handed hitter pulled a long line drive over the right field fence—just foul.

"Jeez, they play great baseball," I said.

Zaluski pointed out a portly Negro in the Chicago dugout. "And that man is going to make sure people know just how good they are."

"Who is he?"

"Rube Foster. He started this league. Helluva a pitcher in his day—better than any white pitcher of his time, some would say. Got his nickname by outpitching Rube Waddell in an exhibition game."

Hyman spoke up, "Stosh has been following colored baseball for years."

"I thought this was the first year they had a league."

"First year with a league," said Zaluski, "but they've had

some great barnstorming teams. The Page Fence Giants out of Adrian, Michigan, was one. I remember at the end of the '95 season, they came to Detroit to play a couple of games against the Detroit Creams of the Western League—that was before the Western League became the American League. In the first game, the Giants beat the Creams something like 18-3. Next day, the Creams brought in some National League players as ringers, determined that they weren't going to lose to a colored team again. Giants won that second game 15–0."

I was getting uncomfortable hearing how good the Negro players were. It suggested that playing in an all-white league wasn't something to be so proud of. Moving off the subject of baseball, I said to Hyman, "The reason I wanted to talk to you was about Emmett Siever."

His red cheeks rose in a grin. "I didn't think it was to hear Stosh tell his stories."

"You gave me till today to find his killer," I said. "I've been trying, but I need more time."

The amusement vanished from Hyman's face and he tugged at his whiskers. "I don't think you realize how difficult it's been for me to keep some of our more temperamental comrades at bay."

"I appreciate what you've done, but I need more time. I've made progress, but I haven't pulled it all together yet."

"What progress?" Hyman asked. "Give some reason to give you an extension."

I looked to Zaluski, then back to Hyman. "Well, for one thing, there was an agent from the GID there. I think he's the one who told the cops to pin the shooting on me. As for the gun that was found on Emmett Siever, I can prove it was planted by the cops—it came from their evidence room."

Hyman mulled it over. "What do you think, Stosh?"

Zaluski said, "The boy's trying. Let him stick with it a while."

"Give you another week," said Hyman.

"How about—"

"*One* week. That's it."

Okay. If that's all I could get, I would just have to make the most of it.

We settled back and watched another couple of innings. In the sixth, Stars catcher Bruce Petway threw out a Chicago runner trying to steal second. Petway didn't come out of his crouch; he simply gunned the ball to second on a straight line and on target. "He's got an arm like a cannon," I said.

Zaluski spoke around his pipe stem, "Ty Cobb found that out the hard way."

"They played against each other?" I was incredulous. Cobb had a violent hatred of colored people, and I couldn't imagine him playing baseball with them.

"Exhibition game in Cuba," Zaluski said. "About ten years ago. Petway threw Cobb out *twice* in the same game. Cobb's never played against Negroes since."

"Jeez."

As the game went on, my attention drifted away from it and back to Emmett Siever. A seething sensation started to bubble inside me—anger. I was angry that Hyman and Zaluski could be so casual about things. We could be buddies at a ball game today, and next week they might let their comrades in the IWW kill me. Why the hell should I have to beg Leo Hyman for an extra week? Why should *he* set the timetable for *my* life? Especially when I was certain that he could help me solve Siever's murder if he truly wanted to.

During the seventh inning stretch, Zaluski muttered, "This damned old bladder sure don't hold what it used to," and made another trip to the men's room.

I took the opportunity to ask Hyman, "Where did you say you were when Siever was shot?"

"I said I was somewhere else."

"You weren't in the Hall during the speeches, but I saw you there when I left that night." That was a bluff on my part; I didn't want to tell him I'd learned of his presence from Detective McGuire.

"That was after the cops showed up and the trouble started. When there's trouble I can show up pretty quick."

I pressed, "Where'd you show up *from?*"

Hyman looked at me sternly. "Elsewhere."

I wasn't going to get anywhere with that question. I tried an even less likely tack. "Why don't you just tell me who did it?"

"What?"

"You know it wasn't me. You never even assumed it—everybody else called me 'the guy who killed Emmett Siever.' Even Zaluski thought I killed him. But you never did. The only way for you to know it *wasn't* me is for you to know who it *was.*"

"You're assuming a lot from something I *didn't* say."

"It's not only that. You keep meeting me whenever I ask you to, and you even trusted me enough to go to your secret place by the Rouge Plant."

Hyman shifted uncomfortably. Finally, he said, "Pass the peanuts." That was the most I could get out of him.

*Chapter Twenty*

○○○

**M**onday afternoon, I was in Navin Field, next in line for batting practice. Watching the Tigers players around me, I wondered how well they would do in a game against the Stars. It seemed a terrible shame that there was no chance of finding out.

Our opponents today were Sad Sam Jones and the Boston Red Sox. I was finally slated to start again, relieving Babe Pinelli at third base. The hot corner wasn't my favorite position, but I reminded myself that it's really not bad, either— as long as nothing's hit to you.

Bobby Veach had almost finished taking his swings when our bat boy came up to me. "There's a man wants to talk to you," he said.

I glanced at Frank Navin's box. "Is it Navin?"

"No, some fan, I reckon."

Still looking in the direction of the owner's seats, I realized that Hub Donner hadn't been there in some time. Maybe he and Navin weren't getting along too well lately. "He give you a name?" I asked.

Veach walloped one last drive and said, "You're up, Mick."

"Mmm, yeah," said the bat boy, "but I forget. It sounded like the name of a store."

I had no doubt that this kid was going to work his way up to team president someday. "Tell him he can see me after the game," I said. "I gotta hit now." I stepped into the batter's box and gave the fan no further thought.

He didn't come to mind again until the middle of the eighth inning. I was trotting to the dugout after catching a pop fly for the third out, when one of the ushers hailed me and handed me a note.

I unfolded the expensive parchment. Penned in meticulous script was the message:

*Regretfully, I am unable to remain for the conclusion of the game. If your schedule permits, I would consider it a great favor if you could join me for dinner in the Statler Hotel at 7 p.m.* —*John M. Ward*

John M. Ward. A name like a store. John Montgomery Ward!

○ ○ ○

I canceled my dinner plans with Margie, and at seven o'clock I was seated across from John Montgomery Ward in the Statler Hotel dining room. The Statler was next to the Hotel Tuller, where I had lunched with Hub Donner almost six weeks ago.

Although Ward was about sixty years old, he could have stepped out of one of the tobacco cards I'd seen him on when I was a kid. His hair was graying at the temples and his impeccably trimmed mustache was flecked with silver, but he looked fit and handsome and ready to play ball again if he so chose. It took all the restraint I had not to ask him for his autograph.

"You played a fine game today," he said, pausing from his steak.

"Thank you." I had committed no errors in the field, but only got one hit in four at bats. "Fine" was a generous assessment. Ward's manner was entirely gracious, polite, and genuine; he was a dignified man who maintained nineteenth-century courtesy.

He put down his knife and fork, and directed his dark, piercing eyes at me. "I won't waste your time with idle chatter, Mr. Rawlings. There is a reason I wanted to speak with you. A matter of great importance, I believe."

"Yes, sir?" I hadn't said "sir" since the army; it came out naturally to John Ward.

"You may be aware of my involvement with the Brotherhood of Professional Base Ball Players a number of years back."

"Yes, sir. Actually, I was reading the Players' League Guide a few weeks ago. I also read the article you wrote for *Lippincott's.*"

"I'm impressed," he said, with a tilt of his head. "Not many ball players have an appreciation of their history. Tell me: what is your opinion of what you read?"

I answered honestly, "I think your arguments were very convincing."

"So you are favorably inclined toward a players' union?"

"Well . . . I'm not against it."

Ward smiled. "I take it my arguments were not quite *sufficiently* convincing. Perhaps I should explain my present intent." He brushed his napkin along his mustache, first one side and then the other. "I believe this to be a crucial time, Mr. Rawlings. There is a very real danger, with the present antilabor sentiment in the country, of losing what little ground we've gained in the past thirty years. I believe, however, that if the players remain strong and united, there is also opportunity."

"What do you mean?"

"I believe that the nation will soon tire of the sort of antilabor hysteria that Attorney General Palmer and others are fomenting. Then the pendulum of public opinion will swing in our favor. And we *must* be prepared to ride that pendulum to the ultimate destination: abolition of the reserve clause."

"But why are you talking to me? I'm not active in the union."

"I would like you to *become* active." He studied me for a few moments. "There have been pieces in the newspapers suggesting that you are about to denounce the efforts to unionize. If you were to come out *for* the union, instead, it would demonstrate unity of purpose."

I sought for an explanation to give him, a way to make him understand that I didn't want to be involved *at all*. "Mr. Ward, I respect you tremendously, and I'm grateful for everything you and Dave Fultz and others have done to help baseball players. I'm *not* against the union, and I'll never say anything to hurt it, no matter how hard I get pushed by the owners." Ward gave an approving nod. "But I can't say that I'm *for* it, either."

"How can you not be in favor of protecting your own interests?"

I wasn't sure I could answer that, not even to myself, but I tried to express my feelings as best I could. "I started out playing for factory teams, Mr. Ward. Shipyards, mills, canneries—any industry that would give me a job and let me play on their team. One time, I worked for a cotton mill where it was mostly children operating the machinery. The spindle boys were so small, they had to stand on boxes to reach the spools. And do you know what they did when they got a few seconds off for a break? They'd look out the window and watch the mill's owners playing golf!" I paused to collect myself. "The way I see it, I'm *lucky* to be playing baseball for living. It's what I love to do, and I get paid a good salary for doing it. Mine workers, those kids working in the mills, seamstresses in sweatshops, *those* are the people I sympathize with. I think *that's* where the unionizing effort should go, not to me or to any other ballplayer."

John Ward accepted my comments with no visible sign of disagreement. "That is not an unreasonable argument," he said. "I've heard it many times before. However, may I raise a few points that you might not have considered?"

"Yes, certainly."

"First, there's the matter of principle. No human being should be bought, sold, or traded against his will. No amount of compensation can make such a practice tolerable."

I shrugged. I agreed with him about the principle, but I was able to tolerate it pretty well.

"I realize," said Ward, "that it would take exceptional courage to confront the owners on something as intangible as principle. The owners are much more unified than the players, and, therefore, they are quite effective in making sure that 'agitators' do not have very long careers."

I thought guiltily that my reluctance to buck the owners might have something to do with the fact that I wanted to go on to coaching or managing after my playing days were over. "I *am* going against the owners," I maintained. "Like I said, they want me to go public against the union, and I won't."

"Let me raise another point," he said. "A players' union is good for baseball."

I was always leery of things that were supposed to be "good for baseball." "How so?" I asked.

"It might avert a situation such as the one that transpired during last year's World Series. I believe that the lack of representation for the players contributed to their conspiring to throw the games. Charles Comiskey paid his players half what any other team would have—and even charged them for laundering their uniforms. But the players were not free to sell their services elsewhere. Because of the reserve clause, they were *bound* to Comiskey."

Ward spoke as if it was a fact that the White Sox had thrown the Series. Although the rumors and newspaper stories were growing more numerous and more specific, I wasn't yet ready to accept them as proof. I didn't accept Ward's assumptions about either the Sox' conduct or their motive. "The *reserve clause* is what made them sell out?"

He shook his head. "Not directly. And don't misunderstand me: I do not condone the players' actions for any reason. I am simply saying that the circumstances were ripe for such an occurrence. An example: in 1917, Comiskey promised Ed Cicotte a bonus of $10,000 if he won thirty games. But when Cicotte won his twenty-eighth, Comiskey benched him for the rest of the season. That is an outrageous misuse of power. The Chicago players did have legitimate grievances; they did not have recourse to address those grievances. Total control of their careers rests with Charles Comiskey and the other owners."

"Comiskey was with your Players League, wasn't he?"

Ward frowned slightly. "Yes. Sometimes those who switch sides in a war become the most extreme partisans of their new camps." He shook off whatever thoughts Charles Comiskey had brought to mind. "Allow me to make one final point. I understand you suffered a wrist injury during spring training."

"Yes, but it's all better now."

"What if it wasn't? If your injury had been permanent, what would you do?"

I hesitated. "I don't know. I'd probably try to get a coaching job or something. Or—" I thought a little more. "Or I might end up working in one of those same factories that I did when I was coming up."

"You mentioned a cotton mill," Ward said. "Did you know that Emmett Siever's daughter worked in one of those? Starting at age ten."

"Uh, no, I didn't know that."

"There is no provision in baseball to care for players— or their families—after retirement. It's easy to ignore such things when you're in your prime—young, healthy, living well—but then, like Siever, you discover too late that you have nothing to show for your career."

"Is that why Emmett Siever got involved in the union so suddenly?"

"Let's just say that he finally came around."

I took a sip of water and a deep breath. "Mr. Ward, I respect you—as a player, as a man, as somebody who really believes in his cause. But I just don't feel it's *my* cause. Not enough to go out on a limb for it. If the players really started a union, I'd probably join, but I wouldn't be a leader. I'm sorry to disappoint you. I give you my word, though: I'll never do anything against the union, either."

"I believe you, Mr. Rawlings. And, although I do not agree with your position, I do understand it."

"Can I ask you a question, Mr. Ward?"

"Certainly."

"Emmett Siever was trying to tie the players' union to the IWW. Aren't they pretty radical for baseball players to get mixed up with?"

He answered slowly, "You mentioned a concern about child labor. Do you know who said, 'The worst thief is the one who steals the playtime of children?' "

"No, who?"

"Big Bill Haywood, one of the founders of the IWW. You'd be surprised where you might find your allies. The Wobblies have been in the forefront of some very admirable efforts— including child-labor reform. While I admit that I am not entirely comfortable with the more radical element of the IWW, I will not condemn the organization out of hand, either."

I repeated Haywood's quote to myself and tried to commit it to memory.

"One more question for you," Ward said. "Is your concern for injustices in the mines and the mills merely an excuse to do nothing, or are you working to rectify them?"

"Uh, no, I'm not—I just . . . No."

His face showed disappointment in my response. "I do hope that someday you'll find something to believe in and that you'll fight for it, Mr. Rawlings. If not for yourself and your fellow ballplayers, then perhaps for those children in the mills. I'm sure they'd appreciate having you on their side."

# Chapter Twenty-One

○○○

**M**argie's rose chemise was exactly the right shade to compliment her tawny skin, and sufficiently sheer to reveal every feature of her figure. She sat cross-legged on her hotel room's spacious brass bed, facing me, brushing out her waist-length hair.

I rested back against the pillows, my fingers locked behind my head, watching Margie perform her morning ritual. I was both amazed at how comfortable I felt with this woman and worried that we wouldn't be together like this much longer. Margie would be in town only as long as her engagement at the Rex Theatre lasted. I was only here when the American League schedule had the Tigers slated to play at home. Simultaneously, things seemed so settled between us, yet still so fleeting.

I didn't want to think about it. It was too early in the day to worry about what might happen tomorrow.

The brush snagged in Margie's hair. "Ack!" she cried as she yanked it free. "Someday I'm going to cut this all off."

"Don't do that! I like it long."

"You don't have to take care of it." With a teasing look in her big eyes, she said, "Maybe I'll leave just a strip of hair down the middle, like an Indian."

I played along, recalling a drawing of Friar Tuck I'd seen in an illustrated edition of *Robin Hood*. "Or shaved on top, like a monk's."

She laughed and resumed brushing. I went back to watching her.

I wondered why Margie hadn't asked anything about our future. It was women who fretted about such things, so why hadn't she said anything? Well, I sure wasn't going to bring it up if she didn't.

Besides, I thought, if I didn't get an answer to the Emmett Siever killing, I might not have a future.

"I have a question," I said.

My tone must have signaled it was a serious one. Margie stopped what she was doing and lowered the brush to her lap.

"Am I off base here?" I asked. "Doesn't it make sense that Emmett Siever's death had something to do with the IWW?"

"I suppose so . . ." Her forehead furrowed slightly. "Couldn't he have stumbled across somebody robbing the place, though? Maybe it had nothing to do with his labor activities."

"Who would rob an IWW hall? There's nothing there worth stealing. I think a thief would go for a house or a shop. And if it was a robbery, why would there be a cover-up?"

"I don't know." She started weaving her hair into a thick braid. "When you say it had 'something to do' with the IWW, are you saying you think one of the Wobblies killed him?"

"No, not really. Just involved—somehow. There were at least three people back there: one who shot him, one who stabbed him, and the GID man, Calvin Garrett. And I assume none of those three were in on it together."

"Why not?"

"Well, I don't see Garrett as the type to kill anybody, definitely not with an ice pick. It makes sense to me that he'd be watching the place, and it makes sense that when the killer—or killers—left, Garrett saw them and went inside. And that's when he found me there. As far as the killers, I can't see them being in it together because why try to kill a guy twice—and with two different methods to boot?"

"I don't know why anyone would want to kill him once," Margie said. "Do you have *one* motive for killing him yet?"

"Only to stop the baseball union. And that would make Hub Donner a likely suspect, but there's nothing to tie him to it. I can't pin down where he was at all. Although . . ."

"Yes?"

"If Donner was the man Garrett saw leaving the Hall, that might explain why the GID would cover up for him. They're both on the same side, trying to bust the unions. If it was a Wobbly Garrett saw, he would *want* to pin a murder on him, not cover it up."

"It seems to me that Connie Siever is the person you should speak to."

"No, there's something about her . . . I don't know *how* to talk to her. Maybe because it was her father who was murdered."

"I think she's at peace with that," Margie said. "Give her a try."

As far as I could tell, Connie had always been at peace

with her father's death. That was one of the things that bothered me about her. "Maybe," I said.

"Why 'maybe'?" Margie's voice rose. "You have until Saturday before people start shooting at you again! Connie Siever knows the IWW, and she knew her father. If you think the Wobblies are connected to his death, she's the best person to talk to."

"I suppose . . ." There was no argument against Margie's logic. "You're right. I'll talk to her."

"Good. Connie will be at the theater tonight. You can talk to her then."

"She's going to see your show?"

"Yes. She's really not bad once you get to know her. We're actually getting to be pretty friendly."

"You never told me that."

She playfully slapped my leg. "You think I tell you everything?"

OOO

When I showed up at the Rex Theatre's box office late Tuesday afternoon, I discovered that Margie most definitely did not tell me everything. While picking up the pass she had left for me, I spotted a brightly colored poster tacked on the wall next to the ticket clerk. *ALL NEW PROGRAM,* the heading promised, *Starting July 4th.* A new program meant that the old acts were moving on. It meant that Margie was moving on—and she hadn't mentioned anything about it.

I met Connie Siever in the lobby and we went into the theater, where she suggested sitting in the front. I agreed, although I hoped she would decide to relocate once the

Four Harmony Kings started singing. Her mood was less sour than usual, and her appearance less severe, but I hoped that no one would think the two of us were on a date.

We sat in awkward silence through Shepp's Comedy Circus while the rest of the audience groaned at Shepp's notion of comedy. I wasn't in a laughing mood anyway, knowing that Margie would be leaving in a little over a month.

There were still several acts to endure before Margie was due to take the stage. Since it was soon apparent to me that Connie Siever had no more interest in them than I had, I raised a topic that interested us both. "Are you still active in the IWW?" I asked.

"Very."

"But you don't go to the meetings?"

"Sometimes I do."

"You know what seems odd to me?"

"No, I don't."

"You were the one who got your father involved in the IWW in the first place, but the night he gives a big speech at the Hall, you didn't go to hear it."

"Not that it's any of your business," she said, "but I've heard my father speak many times. One more speech wasn't that great an attraction for me. I've been busy with my own work, trying to get women the right to vote."

"Isn't the whole idea of the IWW that everybody is in everything together—'one big union,' and all that? Leo Hyman was telling me that the Wobblies are the only group that takes in women and Negroes. Why don't you do your suffrage work through the IWW?"

"You're inquisitive tonight, aren't you?"

"I'm always inquisitive. I just usually keep it to myself."

She laughed. "Well, I feel that on women's issues, women should be in the leadership. The IWW accepts women, yes. And some of the leaders are women—Elizabeth Gurley Flynn and Mother Jones, for example. But not in Detroit. Leo Hyman and his men run things here."

"You don't like Hyman?"

"I think Leo does a fine job. But women's suffrage is a higher priority for me than it is for him. So on this issue I work largely outside the IWW."

I'd been hoping to get more out of her about the Wobblies. "Stan Zaluski do a good job, too?"

"He *could* do a lot more," Connie said, "if they gave him a chance. Stan is a very wise man. But hardly anyone listens to him. He's old, and not very strong anymore, maybe, but he's not stupid. They've relegated to him serving as doorman, and a lot of the men treat him like an errand boy."

"How about Whitey Boggs?"

She started to answer, then caught herself. "I think he's done a wonderful job with the Relief Committee. We feed and clothe a lot of needy people because of his work."

"But?"

"Don't repeat this, but the man makes my skin crawl. He's been courting my friend Norma, though, and she seems to like him. I suppose there's no reason I should have to, as long as *she's* happy with him." She turned to me. "Now a question for you, Mr. Inquisitor: have you heard from Karl?"

"He called a few days ago. Gave me his number in Boston, and told me things were getting pretty interesting with—" I'd forgotten their names. "—those Italian anarchists."

"He didn't say anything else?"

Landfors had asked how Connie was, but I didn't know

if I should tell her that. I didn't think he'd have wanted me to. "It was a real short call," I said. "And he seemed pretty wrapped up in what he was doing in Boston. You know how he is."

Sadness slowly came over Connie's face, and her pointed features softened. "I was only starting to know him," she said quietly.

○ ○ ○

Wednesday afternoon, the Tigers closed out the series against the Red Sox with a 2–1 ten-inning win. Howard Ehmke had outdueled Bullet Joe Bush in one of the best games we'd played all season, and I'd scored the winning run on a fly out by Donie Bush. The victory completed a three-game sweep of Boston and boosted our hopes of climbing out of last place.

By the time I left Navin Field and turned up Trumbull to walk home, the elation of the win had worn off, however. I was again thinking about Margie's impending departure and about her secretiveness. I'd dropped a few hints last night trying to lead her into talking about the future, but she didn't say anything about her show moving on.

"Mickey Rawlings!" A meaty hand fell on my shoulder from behind.

I reached up and pushed it off. Drawing to a stop, I turned to face Hub Donner. "What do you want?"

"Let's go someplace where we can talk privately," he suggested.

My instinct was not to be seen with him in public. No, I decided, it would be worse if I was seen going someplace private with him. "Let's not," I said. "You want to talk to me, we'll do it right here." There were stragglers from the ballpark passing by us, pushcart vendors closing up their carts, and newsboys trying to hawk a few last papers.

"How about if I walk along with you?" he asked.

"Fine." I continued on my way, at a brisk pace.

Donner quickly caught up. Matching my strides, he said, "You've been talking to some interesting people lately. John Montgomery Ward, for example. And Leo Hyman again— you even went to his house."

It was no surprise by now that Donner knew where I went; I didn't even feel outraged at being spied upon. "Told you before, I'll talk to whoever I want to."

"We—Ban Johnson and I—have some concerns that you might be thinking of joining the other side."

"Maybe I will." I noted that Donner didn't include Frank Navin among those who were "concerned" about me.

"That would be *very* unwise."

"Look," I said, "as far as I can tell, there's not much happening with the players' union anyway."

"Yes, there is," Donner insisted.

Of course! Donner *had* to claim there was union activity— otherwise there was no reason for him to be on Ban Johnson's payroll. "Why are you pushing me so hard?" I asked. "Planting those stories in the paper, trying to get my teammates mad at me. Why don't you go after somebody big? I'm not that much good to you even if I did go along with what you want me to do."

"Same reason a pitcher bears down a little extra on the lousy hitters: you don't want to let the banjo hitters beat you. I must admit that your stubbornness has become something of an embarrassment for me. I expected—Ban Johnson expected—that you'd have come around by now."

"Sorry to be such a disappointment to you. And to Mr. Johnson, of course." Not that I believed Ban Johnson gave me much thought one way or another.

"If you think I was pushing hard before," Donner said, "I can really play hardball if that's the way you want to go. I could snap your wrist like a twig."

I stopped short. "Maybe you could," I said. "But before you got hold of it, there'd be a lot more marks on that ugly face of yours."

Anger simmered in Donner's eyes while his mouth formed a weak grin. "No reason to go into what-ifs," he said. "I don't think we're at that point yet."

Yet? I didn't see how things could go much further. I resumed walking and turned east on High Street. Donner kept pace beside me. He seemed desperate, and I wondered just what he might be willing to do to get me to turn against the players. Donner wasn't the only one under pressure, though. I had three days to give Leo Hyman something on Siever's death.

"Let's try this a little differently," I suggested. "Instead of threats, you do something for me."

"Such as?"

"Well, I know you were *not* having dinner with Ban Johnson the night Siever was killed. So let's start by telling me what you *were* doing."

Donner barely considered my proposal before dismissing it. "I collect information," he said. "I don't give it."

"Your loss."

We'd reached Crawford Park, and Donner pointed to a bench facing the fountain. "Can we sit a minute?"

Since I still hoped that I might get some information from him, I agreed, and we sat down.

"There's something else I can do for you," he said.

"Yeah?"

"The league has authorized me to offer you an honorarium if you agree to do what we ask."

"Honorarium?"

He withdrew a letter-sized manila envelope from an inside pocket of his jacket and handed it to me. I lifted the flap and saw a crisp new $100 bill. It was the first one I'd ever seen.

"There's a thousand dollars in there," Donner said. "You can walk home with it now. A lot of things you can do with this much money—buy yourself a new car, if you want to."

I rifled through them. There were ten bills. A thousand dollars in cash. I was impressed by the sum, but I felt no temptation. It was with a great deal of satisfaction that I handed the envelope back to Hub Donner.

"Go to hell," I said.

OOO

There had to be a connection. In one way or another, there were quite a few people involved in Emmett Siever's death: the IWW, the GID, the Detroit Police Department, and possibly Hub Donner. The question was: what role did each of them play—what actions had led to Siever's murder, and what actions were taken to hide the circumstances of his death?

It was Margie who suggested a way to find out: start with what they all had in common. They had all been at the scene of the crime.

She was right. I'd gone with Karl Landfors to the back rooms of Fraternity Hall, but that was to retrace my own steps that night. What I needed to do was determine the movements of the killer.

On Friday evening, with less than twenty-four hours to go until Hyman's deadline, Margie Turner, Connie Siever, and I walked together along First Street on our way to Fraternity Hall. Margie was the one who had asked Connie to accompany us. She'd said that Connie's standing with the IWW could ease our way into the hall. In order to get us into the back rooms, Connie came up with the cover story that we were volunteering to help in the kitchen.

We started up the path to the front entrance. I asked Connie, "Can we go in the back way?"

She studied me a moment. "If you prefer." She then led us around the side toward the rear of the building. The first item on my list of questions was: how did the killer get in?

Connie and Margie stopped at a side door near the back. I continued past them, into a broad alley that ran behind the hall. The back wall was solid concrete block, with no doors or windows. Calvin Garrett could only have gotten through the door where the women were waiting for me. Before rejoining them, I gave a quick look over the alley itself. There was enough trash—shells of abandoned automobiles, wooden barrels, and discarded packing crates—to provide plenty of hiding spots for anyone who had the place under surveillance.

"There's a toilet inside, if that's what you're looking for," Connie said.

"Uh, no. I'm fine." I returned to where they were standing. "Okay, you have a key?"

Connie pointed to the door. "What good would a key do?"

She was right: there was no lock, not even a handle. She slapped three times on the wood. Half a minute later, somebody inside asked who was there; at Connie's answer, the door swung inward.

We stepped inside and a small, plain, dark-haired woman lowered the crossbar back into place.

"Hello, Norma," Connie said. "I brought along a little kitchen help."

A smile of welcome flashed over Norma's pale, friendly face. "We can use them," she said. "Expecting a lot of people for dinner tonight."

Connie made the introductions. I paid little attention to what she said, for I was absorbed in studying the layout of the area.

The hallway ran straight ahead, uninterrupted, all the way to the opposite end of the building. On the left was an interior wall that separated the meeting hall from the back rooms; one door, halfway down the corridor, connected the two areas. To the immediate right was an open area that contained an ancient printing press, a workbench cluttered with carpentry tools, and a foot-powered band saw. Piles of handbills, booklets, and posters were on the floor, cans of paint and ink on the shelves, and dozens of picket signs stacked in the corners.

The three women walked ahead of me while I moved

slowly, mentally recording everything I could about what I saw. Beyond the work area, the hallway narrowed. Five offices were to the right, their doors closed, as they had been when I was here with Leo Hyman and Karl Landfors. When we passed the door on the left that led to the main hall, I averted my head; I wished I'd never stepped through it that night in April.

The kitchen was another open area to the right, just past the offices. There were two men and four women hard at work preparing dinner. Norma took charge of us, assigning Connie and Margie to something that involved vegetables, and asking me to watch the soup pots. When I asked what I was to watch for, she changed my task to peeling potatoes.

While I settled down to put my army training to use, Connie said, "Men are so useless. I hate to think what people would have to eat if we let the men do the cooking. The folks who come here for food have enough troubles as it is."

"Men," repeated Margie with a wink in my direction. "What are they good for?"

"Taking out the trash," said Norma.

The conversation turned to the trip Connie was planning to Tennessee. I sensed that my participation in the suffrage discussion wasn't welcome, so I fell to with the potato peeler and looked about the room for hints as to what could have happened the night Siever was killed.

It occurred to me that I had never gone past the kitchen.

I silently got up and walked around the corner. Next to the kitchen was a pantry; its door was open, allowing me to see piles of canned goods, cleaning supplies, and sacks of flour, sugar, and coffee. A large steel sink was being used as a grain bin; it was filled with ears of corn.

I stepped beyond the pantry. The hallway ended in another open area. There were racks of folding chairs, a blackboard, and some miscellaneous furniture. No doors, no windows.

"Looking for something?" Norma asked.

I turned around. "The knife was a little dull. I was looking for another."

"All you had to do was ask."

"Didn't want to interrupt."

She eyed me suspiciously. "Very considerate of you." After leading me back to the kitchen, she supplied me with another peeler and I went back to work. The women resumed their talk about suffrage. I noticed that Margie spoke knowledgeably about the status of the amendment and that Connie was attentive to Margie's opinions.

After I'd produced a sizable pile of peels, I offered to take them out to the trash. "I hear it's what we do best," I said.

Margie laughed, and Norma said, "It's around the corner out back. Prop the door open, so we don't have to let you back in."

I dumped the peels into a tin bucket and hauled them to the back door. Before stepping outside, I stopped to give the door a thorough inspection. It nestled firmly against the jamb; there was no room to slide anything in to lift the cross bar from the outside. The steel bar pivoted on one side; the other rested in a bracket. Surrounding the bracket was an additional piece of metal. I pulled at the entire assembly; it was all strong and secure. When I lifted the bar, I felt the resistance of a spring in the pivot end. The spring prevented the bar from being left in the up position. I opened the door, wedged a doorstop in the bottom, and went outside, where I tossed the potato peels into a trash bin.

From my examination, it was clear to me that to get in through the back door, you had to be let in. Somebody inside either had to open it for you or leave it propped open. So how did Calvin Garrett get in? If he saw the killer leave, surely the killer didn't leave the door propped open. And I couldn't imagine the Wobblies opening it for him.

When I got back to the kitchen, Whitey Boggs was there inspecting the work of his Relief Committee. Most of his "supervision" involved remaining in close proximity to Norma. Margie and I stayed until dinner was cooked and served.

Just before we left, Boggs ducked his head close to me and whispered, "We appreciate the help, but you sure picked an odd way of spending your last night alive."

**T**here were too many threads that I couldn't tie together. I had nothing definitive, not even any new theories that I could offer to Leo Hyman as justification for another deadline extension. It was time to call the smartest guy I knew, and see if he could come up with any answers.

Saturday morning, I placed a call to Karl Landfors in Boston, and gave him a rundown on where things stood. I told him that Siever had been both shot and stabbed, and I reported on my visit to Calvin Garrett and my talks with Leo Hyman and Stan Zaluski.

The line was silent for some time after I finished my account. Then came Landfors's assessment of the situation: "I must say, this is really most puzzling."

Jeez. Okay, if he can't give me answers, maybe he can at least give me information. Among the issues that remained unclear to me was Calvin Garrett's function in the GID. "Could you explain to me about the Justice Department's General Intelligence Division?" I asked. "Some of what Garrett told me doesn't make sense."

"I'll try," Landfors said. "But the GID is less than a year old, and it doesn't exactly publicize its activities. I don't know much."

That was probably the first time in his life Karl Landfors had uttered that sentence. "Calvin Garrett is a special agent, based in Washington, DC," I said. "So why was he up in Detroit spying on some little IWW hall? I mean, there are probably hundreds of union halls and labor organizations they keep tabs on. Does the GID use their agents to stand in alleys watching these places?"

"Hmm. No, the GID is only supposed to maintain and organize intelligence information supplied to them by other federal agencies and local police. I don't think they were originally intended to be in the field at all. I hear their director makes a habit of exceeding the bounds of his authority, though, so perhaps he does use his agents in more active roles."

I remembered the stubby little man I'd seen. "Hoover?"

"That's right. John Hoover. Calls himself 'J. Edgar' now. An ambitious man, and ruthless from what I hear. You're right, though: even if Hoover was putting agents in the field, it doesn't seem likely that he would waste one of them on routine surveillance. As far as *why* Garrett was in Detroit, it could have something to do with Mitchell Palmer losing the primary election there. After the loss, Palmer said 'Detroit is the largest city in America in population of radicals and revolutionists.'" Landfors issued a humorless laugh and said, "I have a lot of friends in Chicago and New York who would like to claim that title for their own cities. Anyway, Palmer has to redeem himself for what happened to him in Michigan.

One way is to hit back at the people he thinks hurt him there."

That was pretty much what I'd suggested to Garrett. "Okay, so you think the Justice Department was going to start a major crackdown on Detroit 'Reds'?"

"Seems likely."

"Would a crackdown include the out-and-out murder of a labor leader?"

Landfors breathed out a whoosh of air. "You're asking if Calvin Garrett murdered Emmett Siever."

"Yes."

"I have a hard time believing that. Even if the GID was to go to that extreme, I believe they would be more subtle about it. Pushing Andrea Salsedo out a window and pretending he jumped is one thing. Shooting a man is something else."

"I don't see much difference between the two, Karl."

"Not in effect, but in technique. I think shooting is too direct for the GID."

"But if the plan was to assassinate Siever, that might explain why Garrett was there instead of some beat cop or two-bit detective."

"Oh!" Landfors's tongue tripped over itself getting out the next words. "There's a problem with that theory: if Garrett shot Siever, why didn't he leave? Remember, you said yourself he could have simply left the building."

That's right. And my recent examination of the door confirmed that there was nothing to prevent someone from going out. "I guess I still have some digging to do," I said finally. "How are things going there?"

"Not good. These men are going to be railroaded, and it's all politics."

"I'm sorry."

"I'll do what I can to stop it, but I doubt that writing about the case will be enough."

"Wish I could help," I said.

"Wish I could have been more help to you," he responded. "Oh, uh, you haven't by any chance seen Connie lately?"

"Last night. She and Margie are becoming pretty chummy."

"Did she ask—"

"Yes, she asked about you. Call her."

"You think?"

"I'm positive."

"Very well. I'll trust your judgment on that."

Trusting my judgment regarding women was like taking fashion advice from Hub Donner, but I didn't want to disillusion Landfors.

○ ○ ○

If Whitey Boggs was correct that last night was to be my last one alive, then today would be my last game. There was perfect weather for it: a high clear sky, warm with low humidity, just enough of a breeze to flutter the flag in center field. There were plenty of fans on hand as well. The Tigers had been showing signs of life lately. Instead of allowing our spirits to remain as low as our place in the standings, we were taking one game at a time, playing for pride and respect. And we'd been winning. The fans, the press, the entire city was starting to get behind us.

All that was missing was Margie Turner. I'd asked her not

to come to the game, and I wasn't going to see her tonight. If somebody was going to come after me, I wanted it to be me alone. I didn't want Margie in the line of fire. Of course, that wasn't the reason I gave her; I mentioned only that I had "things to do."

I'd already taken batting practice and was watching Chick Fogarty take his turn in the cage. Ty Cobb, who'd been first to hit, stood between home plate and the seats, talking with reporters and photographers.

I looked at St. Louis Browns starting pitcher Elam Van-gilder warming up outside the visitors' dugout. There were odd feelings running through me. The notion that it could be my last game made me determined to play a good one. But there was too much fight in me to accept that it was my last. I still had to get a hit off Walter Johnson, after all. No way was my last major-league at bat going to be against Elam Vangilder.

Fogarty unleashed a mighty swing at a half-speed fastball, and missed it by a foot. With an angry curse, he clubbed home plate with the head of his bat. It occurred to me that I might have to watch for more than the men from Fraternity Hall. What if the Wobblies decided to use somebody from the players' union to get back to me for Siever's death?

It would help if I knew for certain who on the Tigers team was unionizing. I shot a look at Cobb. I might not know who the head of the union was, but the leader of the team was easy to identify: Ty Cobb.

I made my way toward the Georgian. He was working his Southern charm on the press, laughing and joking. I knew he could explode with no warning, so I tried to get his attention with subtle gestures.

"What are you twitching about, boy?" he demanded.

"Need to talk to you," I said.

Cobb scowled, then dismissed the reporters. "Give us a minute, will you please, gentlemen?" When they dispersed, he said, "Well, kid, what is it?"

I didn't like being called "boy" or "kid" but didn't correct him. Pick your battles, I told myself. "It's about the union. I know you were one of the vice-presidents of the Baseball Players Fraternity—"

He cut me off. "That was strictly honorary."

I wasn't sure if Cobb wanted to distance himself from the current union or if he'd changed sides. It was well-known that his investments in Coca-Cola and General Motors had already made him a rich man. Could a capitalist also be a union man? "Well, I thought you might know who's involved with trying to unionize now," I said.

"Might be," he said. "Where you going with this?"

"I want whoever is involved to know that I'm not against the union. I won't do anything to hurt it, and I don't want any trouble. Could you pass that message along, please?"

"If the occasion comes up, I expect I could do that for you."

I nodded at the batting cage. Tiger players were yelling for Fogarty to get out and give them a turn. "By the way," I said. "I hear Chick Fogarty's the team's union leader."

"Where's your head, boy?" Cobb snapped. "Would *you* trust him in a job like that?"

Fogarty had missed another pitch and was pounding the plate, apparently trying to drive it into the ground. "No, I guess I wouldn't," I said. But I *would* trust him to do an effective job of beating someone up.

○ ○ ○

I'd spent a peaceful Saturday night alone in my apartment. No one came to the door and no shotgun pellets came through the window. I didn't even get a phone call. By Sunday morning, I'd decided they'd had their chance. I was going to get on with living normally. As normal as it ever got for me, anyway.

I left Navin Field after another win over the Browns, and turned up Trumbull to stop home before going to meet Margie at the Rex. I was dressed in my cheeriest red necktie and a cream-colored poplin suit. I had my straw boater tilted back to catch the sun on my face. Although determined not to let the Wobbly threat affect my actions, it still hung over me, causing me to look at every passerby with misgiving.

While I was casting a suspicious glance at a peanut vendor, two large men in old work clothes caught me by surprise, stepping out from behind a parked ice wagon. I was fairly certain that I'd seen them before in Fraternity Hall.

One of them said, "Gonna take you for a little ride," and gestured at a black hardtop Dodge moving slowly along the curb.

The other man had an overcoat draped over his forearm; he pulled back the coat just enough to reveal the twin barrels of a sawed-off shotgun.

The rear door of the Dodge opened and the first man started to push me toward it. My effort to resist was brief, lasting only until I heard the sound of a hammer being cocked. One of the first rules of staying alive is don't argue with a loaded gun. The second rule is assume that any gun pointed at you is loaded.

I was hustled into the backseat, where Whitey Boggs was waiting. "Your time is up," he said. The other two men hopped in, one in the front and one in the back, and the driver hit the gas to send us speeding south.

"Where we going?" I asked. My situation didn't look promising: there were four of them, and I was wedged between a man pressing a shotgun against my ribs and Boggs, who I was sure had his razor.

"To administer a little justice for Emmett Siever," Boggs answered.

I turned to the man on my right. "Mind pointing that thing to the side? I don't want to die just from hitting a bump."

The gunman said to the driver, "Try not to hit any bumps, Pete. Don't want a mess back here." The barrel remained where it was.

Whitey Boggs said nothing more. I started to wish that he'd put a blindfold on me. Either wherever they were taking me wasn't a secret, or I wouldn't be alive to identify it anyway.

After a right turn onto Jefferson, we crossed the railroad tracks. I silently cursed the driver for taking them so hard— the car bounced and lurched when he hit the rails. We proceeded about half a mile on a dirt road, until we were near the Wabash Freight Depot. The driver pulled up to a small, run-down brick building that looked like it had once been a warehouse.

"Last stop," said Boggs.

The driver killed the engine, and I was led out of the car. I spotted a slow-moving freight car rolling along the tracks. The idea of bolting for the train was tempting, but I knew I couldn't outrun buckshot.

The four men ushered me into the abandoned warehouse. It contained a few crates and barrels and a great deal of dirt. The walls shook and the floor rumbled from activity in the freight yard.

I was starting to feel numb, frozen. I wanted to fight, or to flee. But every option seemed more likely to hasten my death than prevent it.

"Okay," said Boggs. He fluffed out his clothes. "Got some good news for you. We're not going to kill you."

I took that as very good news indeed. "Then why'd you bring me here?"

He smiled. I wanted more than anything at that moment to punch him in the nose, never mind the consequences. Before temptation could get the better of my judgment, one of the men grabbed my arms and pinned them behind my back. "That's the bad news," Boggs said. "We *are* going to hurt you."

The man who'd held the shotgun put it on top of one of the boxes and picked up a short-handled sledgehammer from the floor.

Boggs went on, "We're gonna show you what it's like to be out of work for a while. Maybe then you'll appreciate what a union can do for you." He turned to the man with the hammer. "Your choice, Marty. Hands or legs?"

"Hands," was the reply. "They're easier."

Boggs nodded and turned back to me. "But first—" He pulled the straight razor from his pocket and flicked it open. "It's my turn." He nodded to the men behind me. The grip around my arms tightened as I tried to squirm out of it. One of the men pulled my tie to the side and tore open my shirt.

Boggs smiled. Then his hand flashed toward me and a searing pain ripped the center of my chest. I tried to back away and got nowhere. His hand came at me again. Another biting cut, and again the awful sound of tearing flesh. I braced myself to show nothing when the third slash came. The blade of the razor was now streaked with red, but I refused to look down to see what it had done to me.

The glee started to fade from Boggs's expression; I don't think I was giving him a satisfactory reaction. He lashed out twice more and was preparing for another, when a screech of tires outside gave him pause. "Go see who it is," he said.

Marty exchanged the sledge for his shotgun, went to the door, and peered out. "It's okay," he said. "It's just Leo."

Leo Hyman waddled through the door a moment later. His face was red and his whiskers quivered like they had static in them. "I heard you boys were coming here. Bunch of goddamned, thick-skulled hotheads is what you are. Let him go."

"But Leo—" Boggs said.

"Shut up and do what I say!"

My arms were freed. As they swung forward, the skin of my chest stung anew from the movement. I was no longer forcing myself not to look down, I just didn't want to.

Boggs pulled a handkerchief from his jacket and carefully wiped my blood off his razor. "He had it coming, Leo. You know what he did to Emmett."

Hyman walked over to me. "He didn't do anything to Emmett." He pulled the handkerchief from Boggs's hand and pressed it on my chest. "Doesn't look deep," he said to me. "Just messy." Turning to Boggs, he said, "Do you have to use that goddamned razor, Whitey? That thing is more bloody, and does less good, than anything else."

Boggs slipped the weapon back in his pocket. "I like it."

"Okay," Hyman said. "No real harm done here. All of

you beat it. And listen: everything's on ice for a while. Mind your manners till I say otherwise."

The four men skulked out of the warehouse, leaving Hyman and me alone. He continued to dab at my chest until the handkerchief was dripping blood. I thought his diagnosis of "no real harm done" might have been premature. I took out my own handkerchief, and finally looked to see what Boggs had done. From my upside-down perspective, the cuts read MI. To somebody looking at me, it would be IW.

"Least I got here before he did the next 'W,' " said Hyman. "You'd think it was his own monogram, the way he goes carving them letters on people."

"Thanks for stopping him."

He dismissed my gratitude and examined the cuts again. "Doubt if you need stitches. But I know a doctor if you want him to check it."

I looked again. The cuts were each only an inch or two long. "No," I said, "I've done worse than this shaving."

"Thatta boy," Hyman chuckled. He picked up my tie. "I'll take you home."

During the drive to my apartment, neither of us spoke. I sat with my arms folded across my chest, as if that would contain the flow of blood.

When he pulled up to the curb, Hyman said, "You'll be safe for a while. From us, anyway."

"You told them I didn't do it," I said. "What *do* you know about what happened that night?"

He shook his head. "Not enough—yet. Now go on in and clean yourself up."

Clutching my hat over my shirt, I sprinted up the stairs.

○ ○ ○

# Chapter Twenty-Three

In the locker room before the Memorial Day doubleheader, I took a fair amount of ribbing about the thin, dark scabs on my chest. Harry Heilmann advised me to stay away from "wild dames," Donie Bush suggested that I grow some hair to cover them up, and Bobby Veach said I should know better than to try to give a cat a bath. I thought maybe I should be grateful to Boggs for what he'd done—this was the most my teammates had said to me all season.

The only "wild dame" I knew still wasn't aware of what had happened. I'd told Margie only that I'd gotten into a "bit of a scuffle." Partly, I was embarrassed by having been on the losing end of it.

Our trainer taped gauze over the wounds and told me to avoid moving too much or I might break them open. Since I was slated to play shortstop, there was no way I could do as he advised—only first basemen can play baseball without moving.

Sure enough, the bloodied bandages had to be replaced between games, and then again after the second half of the double header.

With fresh bandages and clean clothes on, I left Navin Field and walked to the Empire Theatre. Stan Zaluski had mentioned he'd be working at the theater all weekend.

Judging by the density of the pipe smoke in the projectionist's booth, he must have been in there literally all weekend, puffing away round the clock. He'd appeared somewhat surprised at my unannounced appearance, but didn't hesitate to let me in.

Once I was settled on a stack of film cans, I asked Zaluski, "You hear about what happened yesterday?"

"Yep. You all right?"

"I been spiked worse than that. What I'm wondering is: will there be more of that coming? Hyman told Boggs and the others to 'mind their manners' and 'everything's on ice for a while.' Will they listen to him?"

"That's the way he put it?"

"Yes."

Zaluski nodded. "They'll leave you alone. 'Mind your manners' means don't get involved in anything you wouldn't want the cops to know about. It's a phrase we use when there might be an infiltrator. Sometimes the cops or the government plant somebody in the organization to stir up trouble—*agents provocateurs,* they're called. The *agent* incites other people to do something that they end up getting arrested for. 'Everything's on ice' means nobody will make a move on you until Leo says otherwise."

"You think there is one of them *provocateurs?*" I couldn't make the word sound foreign the way Zaluski did.

"Doubt it. Leo probably just wanted to make sure they'd back off."

Hyman and Boggs had mentioned something about

plants when we'd spoken in the Rouge shack. "You have a lot of trouble with spies in the IWW?" I asked.

"Not anymore." He pulled the pipe from his mouth. "We found a couple of ways to discourage that sort of thing. For one thing, we test anybody who seems too nosy or a little too eager for trouble. And then of course there's the penalty."

"Death," I said.

"That's it. Marvelous deterrent."

I pondered that while Zaluski performed a reel change on the projector. After he completed it, I asked, "How can you tell which side somebody is really on?"

"It's not easy. You know, I'd swear there are some people who could be on one side of an issue just as easy as on the other. They get involved in a cause more to feel like they belong to something than because they believe or understand the philosophy. Sometimes those are the ones who become the worst fanatics."

"If it's so hard, how do you go about testing them?"

"Oh, give them some information and see if it gets passed on. Something like that. Can't really tell a person's belief, but we can check for behavior."

*Provocateurs.* I couldn't believe I hadn't thought of this before. "What about Whitey Boggs?" I asked. "Seems he's always inciting the others—against me, anyway."

"What about him?"

"Could *he* be a government plant? Why is the guy who's in charge of the *Relief* Committee so violent?"

Zaluski chuckled. "I think it's because of someone else who's on that committee. Whitey's trying to make a good impression on Norma. I wish he'd realize that feeding people is more impressive than beating them up."

"Oh."

"Besides when an infiltrator joins, he usually wants to get on a committee where he can learn secrets. Boggs joined the Relief Committee right from the start. And he's been tested—and he passed."

"Was Emmett Siever tested?"

"Hmm. I don't rightly know. I expect his daughter vouching for him was enough."

"Why would she vouch for him? Based on what? He abandoned her when she was a baby. What did he ever do to show she should trust him?" I was getting angry at Siever for some reason.

Zaluski asked, "Would *you* want to be judged based on what you did when you were young?"

"It should be included in the judging, yes. I may not be proud of everything I've done, but I'll take whatever comes because of it."

"Well, I think the slate should be wiped clean after a while. But then, my way of thinking might be a little different. I spent four years in Jackson paying for what I did when *I* was young."

"Jackson?"

"State prison."

Hyman had mentioned that Ford hired ex-convicts. He hadn't told me that Stan Zaluski was one of them. "What did you do?" I asked.

"I paid my debt. The slate is clean. End of story."

"Okay." I wasn't going to push him if he didn't want to say. "Back to Siever and his daughter . . ."

Zaluski sucked at his pipe. "I don't know how Emmett and Connie got back together. That's between them. I do know he tried to make up for his past. He left her well provided for."

"How did she—"

"If you want to know about Connie Siever, you'll have to ask her. I ain't gonna speak out of turn about a lady."

"All right."

I dropped the questioning. To repay him for his time, I took over at the projector for an hour or so while Stan Zaluski went out for dinner.

It wasn't until he'd returned and I left the theater that I thought to ask: where did Emmett Siever get the money to leave his daughter "well provided for"?

○ ○ ○

The new month began with a new problem. Not brand-new, but not one that I expected to have to face again, either.

Tuesday morning, Calvin Garrett phoned before I was half-awake. "I'm in Detroit," he said. "Thought you might like to get together."

"Why would I want to do that?"

"Because you can use a friend, somebody who'll watch your back."

I didn't want Garrett as a friend; I only wanted him to be truthful about what he knew. "Will you tell the police—and the papers—that I didn't have anything to do with Emmett Siever's murder?"

"No. Afraid I can't do that."

"Then what good is it having you watch my back?"

Garrett snorted. "I hear you got carved up."

"I don't know what you're talking about."

"Don't play dumb with me! You do *not* want to get on my bad side." He paused, and sounded more controlled again when he went on. "It's time for you to decide which side you're on. To make the choice clearer for you, I'll point out that *our* side doesn't cut anybody with razors."

I wished for my own sake that he hadn't called so early in the morning, because I was too grumpy to be diplomatic. "You just push 'em out windows," I said.

"Don't sass me! Salsedo was a suicide, and that's all there is to it."

"Right, just like I killed Emmett Siever in self-defense." Mickey, I warned myself, you're going to get yourself in trouble.

"Okay," Garrett said. "Let's start over. No sense going into things that can't be changed. The present situation is that the IWW sees you as their enemy, and that means they're going to come after you. You want me for an enemy, too, or you want to cooperate? You help me out, and I'll give you some protection."

"What kind of 'cooperate'?" I wasn't at all interested, but curious as to where he was heading.

"That's more like it. The business I mentioned last time we talked. I want to know if baseball is going to be taken over by Reds."

I was tempted to say that, no, I didn't think Cincinnati was going to win the World Series again. What I did say was, "You sound like Hub Donner."

"Who?"

"Now who's playing dumb? You're in Detroit, trying to crack down on unions, and you don't know a union buster like Donner?"

I listened to Garrett's ragged breathing. Abruptly, he said, "I'll be in touch," and hung up.

I had no doubts that Garrett and Donner must have known each other. I considered it while I treated myself to a full breakfast in Kelsey's Cafe. Then I thought of a way to do something about Hub Donner.

Back in my apartment, I phoned Karl Landfors and asked him if he still knew any reporters from his newspaper days.

○ ○ ○

Wednesday morning, I visited the *Detroit News* building and met with an editor named Malcolm Bingay. Landfors had made a few calls for me and arranged for me to give my first newspaper interview. Bingay was a baseball fan, a former sportswriter, and an influential newsman. He was easy to speak to, and except for one minor detail, I told him the exact truth.

Hub Donner and the team owners weren't going to like what I had to say, but if the article came out as I hoped, there might be fewer people after my hide. My teammates would learn where I really stood on the players' union, and Donner would be out of the picture. Then I could focus my efforts entirely on solving Emmett Siever's murder and clearing myself with the Wobblies.

Wednesday night, I was with Margie again, in her hotel room, in her bed. I'd filled her in on my encounter with Whitey Boggs and his friends.

She traced the *IW* on my chest with her fingertip. "Doesn't look bad," she said. "It'll leave a scar, though."

I still had hope that some hair might eventually grow over it. Could it still come in after age twenty-eight, I wondered.

"What you need," Margie said, "is a girlfriend with the initials 'I.W.' Do you know anyone named Irma Worthington?"

"No."

"Ingrid Westinghouse?"

I smiled. "No."

She began tickling me. "Iris Wolechesky?"

"No! I give!" Margie always won.

She laughed at her quick victory. "Oh! Sit up a second." I did so and she examined the top of my head, parting the hair to check my scalp. "Here it is!" She ran a finger over an old scar. "Do you remember when you got this?"

"How could I forget?" A bottle had been smashed over my head while I was acting in one of Margie's movies six years ago. It had taken nine stitches to close the gash.

"Those were fun times, weren't they?" she said.

"You have a strange idea of fun. But, yeah, except for getting conked on the noggin, they were great times." I lay back down, and she nestled her head on my shoulder. "Wish we could go back to those days. Everything seemed easier then. Easier to understand, anyway. The world made sense."

"Can never go back," she said. "Times change."

"Well, I want them to change back to the way they were when we first met. I thought that was the reason for going to war: defeat the bad guys and then everything would be peaceful and happy again. Sure as hell didn't turn out that way. All that happened was some boundary lines got changed and a whole lot of kids got killed in the process. What was the point?"

Margie draped her arm around me. She asked softly, "Something happened, didn't it?"

"Yes."

"Do you want to tell me about it?"

Until she asked, I hadn't realized just how much I did want to talk about it. I told her about me killing the German boy, and some of the things I'd seen during the war. Then I went on to tell her things that I hadn't mentioned to Karl Landfors. I told her that I felt guilty about taking the life of another human being. And that I hated being called a "hero" because of shooting that boy. I said that I regretted having gone to war at all, and at the same time resented the fact that it had ended so soon after I'd joined the battle—I was there long enough to be horrified but too briefly to become hardened to the bloodshed.

Margie uttered some soothing words, then said, "You can't expect to go through something like that without being changed forever. Both you and the rest of the world are going to be different. Can't pretend it never happened and simply set the calendar back a few years. Everything changes. You can't go backward." She stroked my arm with her fingertips. "Forward can be a nice direction, too, you know."

"I suppose. Just seems so hard to make sense of things sometimes."

We were silent for a few minutes. Then Margie said, "Speaking of change . . . and going forward . . ."

Helluva time to tell me about her show closing its run, I thought. "Yes?"

"I want to go to Tennessee with Connie Siever. Help get the Suffrage Amendment passed. Some changes are good, and I think women getting the vote is one of them."

"When? I mean, so do I, but what about— When would you go?"

"Noon tomorrow. I'll be gone a week."

I calculated the date. "But then I'll be on the road again. We won't see each other for at least two weeks. And what about your show at the Rex?"

"They got another actress to fill in for me. Theda Bara. Poor thing's trying to make another comeback. But vamps are another thing that's gone forever."

"You're right," I said. "Some changes *are* good."

Margie laughed. "You don't mind me going?"

"No, not at all," I lied.

Then we proceeded to make the most of the last night we would have together for a while.

**M**argie and I woke early Thursday and went down to the hotel restaurant for a breakfast of pie and coffee. On the way, I picked up the morning edition of the *Detroit News*.

As soon as we'd given the waitress our orders, I flipped open the paper. My interview was prominently featured in the sports section, under the headline *Rawlings Won't Buckle*. I'd told how Hub Donner was working for the American League and pressuring me to go public against the players' union. I swore in the article that I would never do so. I even mentioned that I'd turned down Donner's offer of a bribe.

The piece came out exactly as I'd hoped, and I gloated to myself that Hub Donner was not going to be at all happy when he read it.

I showed the article to Margie, who shared my delight with the results. "I think it's wonderful that you exposed what Donner was doing," she said. "The players are sure going to be happy with you now."

"I hope so." I wouldn't have the chance to find out until tomorrow since this was an off day.

She frowned slightly. "But this says he only offered you $500. You told me it was $1,000."

"It was." I'd adjusted the figure downward when I'd spoken to Bingay.

We hurriedly finished the meal, then headed back to Margie's room so she could pack for her trip. The telephone rang shortly after we stepped inside.

Margie answered and listened for half a minute. Then she passed me the phone, whispering, "It's for you. Frank Navin. He sounds angry."

"Hi, Mr. Navin," I said. "How'd you know I was here?"

"Never mind that. What the hell were you doing talking to the press?" Margie's choice of the word "angry" was an understatement; the Tigers' owner was furious.

"I didn't have much of a choice," I said. "Donner kept pressing me and wouldn't let up. I talked to you about it first, remember? And I figured if you couldn't get him to leave me alone, nobody else could. After he planted those stories about me in the paper, it seemed only fair for me to fight back the same way."

"It is *not* wise to publicize internal baseball business," he said.

"Well, I never mentioned you or Ban Johnson. Just Hub Donner. And everything I said about him is true."

"That's another thing. It says here Donner offered you five hundred dollars. Is *that* true?"

"Cash. In hundred dollar bills. I counted them."

*"Five hundred* dollars?"

"Like I said, I counted. Then I handed it back and told Donner to go to hell."

"This is a very serious situation," Navin said. "I'll have to speak with Mr. Johnson about it."

"I'm sorry, Mr. Navin. I felt I had no choice."

"Actions have consequences. I'll call again and let you know whether to show up at the park tomorrow."

I suddenly didn't feel so smug about what I'd done.

○ ○ ○

After seeing Margie off at the train station, I went home to wait for Frank Navin's call and fret about possible "consequences" that Navin and Ban Johnson could subject me to.

As the afternoon wore on, the telephone remained silent. I started to debate whether Navin had meant I *should* come to the game tomorrow if I didn't hear otherwise, or I *shouldn't*. I decided that I'd show up at the ballpark unless he called and explicitly fired me.

I was about to go out for dinner when the phone finally rang. On about the eighth ring, I warily picked up the receiver.

In a thick Italian accent, a man asked, "Mickey Rawlings, please?"

I exhaled in relief that it wasn't Frank Navin. "This is me."

"Aldino Felicani is my name. I am with the defense committee for Sacco and Vanzetti in East Boston."

"Yes?"

"Karl Landfors tells me you are the person to telephone if anything happens to him."

"Why? What happened?"

"He was arrested this afternoon. He is now in the jail."

"*Arrested?* For what?"

"He has been of great help to us. I believe that is the true reason. But what the police will say, I do not know. They have not yet decided on the charges."

Jeez. Karl Landfors in jail. "What can I do to help?"

"Sadly, I do not think there will be any help. We will do what we can here, of course. But he only wanted me to tell you what happened. There is nothing you can do for him."

"Well, will you let me know if there *is* anything I can do? I mean it, *anything*. And please call me if anything else happens, okay?"

Felicani agreed he would, and we hung up.

This was a new one. How do you go about getting somebody out of jail? The only thought that occurred to me was to call someone who might know.

First I thought I should call Connie Siever, but she and Margie were probably into Ohio by now. The next person who came to mind was Leo Hyman. My guess was that he'd had lots of experience with arrests and jail.

I tried Hyman's home number. No answer. Then Fraternity Hall. Hyman wasn't there, either, so I asked for Stan Zaluski.

When Zaluski got on the line, I said, "Karl Landfors has been arrested."

I could hear his pipe stem clack against his teeth. "Damn. Where?"

"Boston."

"For what?"

"Not sure. The fellow who told me about it said there aren't any charges yet. I think it has to do with him helping a couple of anarchists. I was trying to reach Leo Hyman. I thought he might know how I could help Karl."

"Leo hasn't been here all day. You have his home number?"

"Tried it. No answer."

"Try again. He works in his cellar sometimes and might not hear the phone."

"All right."

"But Mickey . . ."

"Yeah?"

"There might not be *any* way to help Karl."

"I'm gonna try anyway, Stan. Thanks."

I tried Hyman's number for an hour without success. Then I grabbed my jacket and headed for Black Bottom.

○ ○ ○

The exterior of Hyman's house benefited from the fading light of dusk. It appeared less like an outhouse, but still not quite as elegant as a toolshed.

My repeated knocks on the front door went unanswered. There was no sound of movement inside, and no lights.

I walked around to the rear of the house. The cellar was closed and padlocked; I pounded on the door, again getting no response.

Back to the front door. I knocked once more, then tried the knob. It turned and the door eased inward. It seemed odd that Hyman would lock his cellar, but not his front door. I figured he must be home.

I pushed my way into the dark parlor, calling his name. Dodging around the workshop junk, I searched for a light switch. When I found one, and clicked it on, I saw why he didn't answer.

Leo Hyman was sprawled belly-up on the floor near the back wall. With his red shirt, the blood that soaked his chest wasn't obvious until I leaned over him. It looked similar to the wound that I'd seen on Emmett Siever.

I quickly checked for any sign of life. Hyman's eyes were open and dull; I touched his arm and found it to be a bit stiff. He must have been dead for some time.

I had an impulse to call the cops, but immediately stifled that notion—no way was I going to give them a chance to tag me with another "self-defense" killing.

While I considered what to do, I looked around the room. Everything appeared to be in the same disarray as I'd seen it last. No sign of a fight, just the mess of a sloppy tinker.

Perhaps I could call Detective McGuire. I felt I could trust him, but what about his superiors? Or maybe I should call Stan Zaluski.

Eager to get out of the house, I elected not to use Hyman's phone at all. A couple of blocks away I stopped in at small hotel and used the public phone to call the police and report the body.

I didn't give my name.

**F**rank Navin didn't need to call me. The Friday morning newspapers carried a statement from American League president Ban Johnson that said it all: "Mr. Hub Donner served merely as an advisor regarding the possible infiltration of the baseball players' union by radical elements from outside the game. At no time was Mr. Donner authorized to represent the American League, certainly not in the manner recently alleged by Mr. Rawlings of the Detroit Tigers. After reviewing the matter, my office has determined that Mr. Donner acted inappropriately, and the League has therefore severed all relations with him. The League further apologizes to Mr. Rawlings for any misrepresentations that, unknown to my office, may have been made to him by Mr. Donner. I consider this matter closed."

I was sure that Hub Donner's dismissal had more to do with Ban Johnson thinking Donner had tried to pocket five hundred dollars for himself than that Johnson was surprised at the union buster's conduct.

When I got to Navin Field, one of the articles about Donner was taped to the shelf of my locker. Someone had written across the top of it: *WAY TO GO!* As I dressed, every one of my teammates except Ty Cobb made a point of speaking to me. It seemed they were trying to make up for shunning me all season in one burst of clubhouse banter.

Only two of the players' comments weren't friendly. Dutch Leonard grumbled, "You just like getting your name in the paper. It ain't gonna happen with the way you play, so you make up a tale about this Hub Donner fellow being after you. Lot of malarkey, if you ask me."

Chick Fogarty piped up, "Lot of hooey."

Leonard and Fogarty were quickly told to "can it" and "stuff it" by the other players. I was bewildered by the two men. The articles should have been enough to convince them that I wasn't opposed to the union. So why continue the antagonism—was there some other reason they'd been riding me?

Once we were on the field, I didn't give Hub Donner—nor Leonard and Fogarty—another thought. I played second base, making no errors and going 2-for-5 in a hard-fought, ten-inning victory over the White Sox. Throughout the game, I reveled in the fact that I was no longer treated like an outsider.

Donner didn't come to mind again until I left the clubhouse, stepped out to Trumbull Avenue, and was confronted by his ugly face.

I braced myself for whatever retaliation he might be planning.

He took his time, looking me up and down slowly, before he spoke through clenched teeth, "You must think you're real smart, don't you?"

I wanted to say yes, to rub his nose in it, but that would have made him angrier than he already was. Be a gracious winner, I told myself. "Didn't do anything you wouldn't do," I said.

"It ain't over," he answered. "You may have given me a little setback, but I won't be the big loser. That's gonna be you." He tugged at his cap, then stepped into a waiting Ford and drove off.

○ ○ ○

I already had three of the Detroit papers at home. Before I went back to my apartment, I stopped at the newsstand for every other local paper they had. There had been no mention of Leo Hyman's death in the ones I'd read this morning. I wondered if the cops were being more patient before making his death public. Perhaps they wanted to be sure whether the cause of death was a stab wound or a bullet. Or, perhaps the delay was because they hadn't yet decided who to credit with his death.

I'd studied two of the city's minor papers without luck, when I got a call from Stan Zaluski. "What happened?" he asked.

"I'm sorry, Stan. When I got there he was dead. Really, I didn't have anything to do with it."

"Didn't think you had. That's what I told the fellas. You don't strike me as being dumb enough to call and tell me you were going to see Leo if you were planning on killing him."

"No, I wouldn't—uh, what do you mean about telling the fellows? They know I was there?"

"We got a description of a young man visiting his house. The description matched you to a tee, and there was some talk around the Hall that you might have done it. First Emmett Siever, then Leo Hyman. I told them I knew you were visiting him, and I think I talked them out of doing anything rash. For the time being, at least."

"Thanks. I really *didn't* kill him."

"*I* believe you. But things are a little crazy now. With Leo gone, there's gonna be a struggle to take his place. Some of our more hotheaded members might think that killing you will make them the leading candidate for Leo's job."

I didn't need to ask for names. "Well, I hope *you* end up in charge, Stan."

He gave a dry laugh. "I ain't running for anything."

"You got any advice what I should do?"

"Keep your back to the wall and stay away from windows."

○ ○ ○

For the next few days, I followed Stan Zaluski's advice. On Saturday, Leo Hyman's death finally hit the papers. The accounts were brief and vague; they referred to him as a "local radical" and simply reported that he was "found dead in his home of a gunshot wound." There was no mention of suspects or motive.

Monday morning, I paid a visit to Dr. Wirtenberg's filthy office. I was curious how long Hyman had been dead before I'd found him, and I figured Wirtenberg would be an authority on the conditions of corpses—a lot of his patients had probably died after being treated by him. I described to the doctor the stiffness of Hyman's arm and asked him how long it would take for that to happen. Wirtenberg hedged, telling me *rigor mortis* depended on a number of factors. After I agreed to pay him two dollars for the "consultation," he said it usually took at least several hours for rigidity to set in.

That relieved one of my concerns: that I might have been set up. It had been no more than an hour from the time I'd called Zaluski looking for Hyman to when I found Hyman's body. I thought of other details of the murder scene—the lack of a struggle, and the fact that Hyman's body had been far from the door. My guess was that he'd let the killer in, and that it was someone he knew and trusted.

Since the Tigers had a road trip starting Tuesday night, there was little more that I could do about looking into Siever's or Hyman's deaths for the time being. That was fine with me. Staying out of Detroit for a week seemed one of the more worthwhile things I could do for myself.

# Chapter Twenty-Six

**T**hree days in New York was exactly what I needed, and Harry Heilmann was just the fellow to spend them with. He knew every speakeasy in Manhattan that served up cold beer and hot music. Now that I was accepted as part of the team, he let me join him on his nightly outings. I stayed up too late, drank a little too much, and danced with women whose names I never asked.

In the daytime, I played two of our three games at the Polo Grounds, my home field when I'd been with John McGraw's Giants. The park was also presently home to the New York Yankees, who had been spending a lot of money buying baseball players, mostly from the Red Sox. I thought that if they could afford to buy players, the least they could do was build their own ballpark for them to play in.

Carl Mays pitched the opener for the Yankees. The right-hander was a submarine spitball pitcher with a reputation for headhunting. More for protection than strategy, I batted lefty against him. In the second inning, I beat out a bunt for a single. In my next at bat, I faked a bunt and when the third baseman moved in I poked a bloop single over his head. The next two times up, Mays hit me twice, once on the thigh and once on the shoulder. It was as successful as I could hope to be against Mays: two-for-two, with no broken bones.

Altogether, I had a better series against the Yankees than Ty Cobb did. Cobb's hatred for Babe Ruth got the better of him, and he played foolishly, trying to take extra bases, bunting in the wrong situations, and getting thrown out stealing in four out of five attempts. Meanwhile, Ruth hit two mammoth home runs, beating us twice in three games. At the rate the Babe was going, he'd break his own season home run record of twenty-nine before the end of July.

While Cobb cursed the demise of "inside baseball," I still had some hope that the kind of strategy he and I loved would survive the current rage for home runs. There was only one Babe Ruth, and I didn't see how one man could revolutionize the game, not even with the help of a livelier ball.

○ ○ ○

I gave up the recreational pursuits when we got to Boston. I'd had my little respite, and now it was time to get serious again.

The first morning in town, I took a cab to a forbidding stone fortress located between Massachusetts General Hospital and the foot of the Longfellow Bridge. It was the Charles Street Jail, and I was there to pay a call on Karl Landfors.

The process of getting to him wasn't a simple one. I was questioned by a surly officer, my clothes were inspected, and then I had to wait nearly an hour until the designated time when the prisoners could receive visitors.

When that time came, I was led through a series of cold, dank corridors to a cell that wasn't much bigger than a batter's box. Landfors was alone, seated on his bunk, reading a small book.

"Land*fors!*" the guard bellowed. "Ya got a visitor."

My friend sprang up at the sight of me, and a wan smile crossed his face. "What are you doing here?"

"I figured since you can't get out to the ballpark to see me, I'd just have to stop by to see you."

The guard unlocked the cell door. "Talk to him inside. Ya got fifteen minutes." He then stomped away.

The instant the door clanged shut behind me, breathing became difficult. I had to force my lungs to keep working.

The cell contained few furnishings: a wooden water bucket, an enamel pail for a toilet, and a single bunk covered by a thin blanket and no mattress. The air was thick with the smells of excrement, disinfectant, and cigarette smoke. I couldn't imagine Landfors surviving a locker room, much less a place like this. "At least you have lots of time to read," I said.

"Yes, but it's expensive. I have to bribe the guard to let me keep books—and if they look like they're on a subject he wouldn't understand, he charges me extra." He forced another smile. "It turns out that he doesn't understand much."

"What *I* don't understand, Karl, is what you're doing here. What happened?"

"I'd like the answer to that question myself. I still haven't been charged with anything."

"Don't they have to charge you or let you go?"

"Only if they're concerned about legalities. Apparently,

they're not. All I've been told is that the charges will probably have something to do with conspiracy."

"What conspiracy?"

"Whatever one they decide to invent. The authorities don't like it that I'm writing about Sacco and Vanzetti. And they especially don't like the fact that I'm reporting the truth. That's what this is really about."

"Jeez. What about bail? I'll give you whatever I have for bail. Can probably borrow some, too, if you need it."

"Thank you. But they can't set bail until they charge me. So . . . here I sit. And sit."

We both sat down on the bunk, which was hard and uncomfortable. "I got some bad news for you, Karl."

"Darn, and just when things were going so well," he joked.

"It's about Leo Hyman."

"I heard. He's dead. Any word on who did it?"

"No. Nothing in the papers, anyway. And I haven't wanted to appear overly curious about it. You know, after what happened with Siever."

"It's probably wise for you to stay out of it. Is there anything new about Emmett Siever?"

"Not really. I did wonder though . . . It's just an idea . . ."

"Yes?"

"What if somebody's knocking off labor leaders? First Emmett Siever, then Leo Hyman."

"It's a possibility. You think Hub Donner or one of his ilk?"

"Could be. That GID man—Calvin Garrett—he's back in Detroit now. He was there when Siever was killed, and now he's back in town when Hyman's killed. Coincidence?"

Landfors pursed his lips. "Perhaps not entirely. But I don't think he was sent there to assassinate labor leaders, either. It probably has to do with Mitchell Palmer's presidential aspirations. Palmer was badly hurt by the Michigan primary in April. He'd been such a favorite, that the other candidates conceded him the state. Not only did Palmer end up losing, though, he came in *fifth*, and Herbert Hoover—a Republican—won the Democratic primary! Since Palmer blamed the loss on labor, I can imagine him sending GID men to Detroit to crack down on unions. And I can understand him sending Garrett back now: it's only two weeks until the national convention, and if Palmer has any hope of getting the nomination, he has to do something dramatic to redeem himself for the loss in Michigan."

"And for predicting the May Day revolution that never happened," I put in.

"Yes, that too. However, killing labor leaders doesn't do Palmer any good. He needs to uncover them hatching some evil plot or something—even if the GID has to create the plot itself."

I followed the political motives Landfors had outlined, but there was one thing I didn't understand. "Why did Garrett want to know about the baseball union, though? How would that help Palmer?"

"Well, let's see . . . Oh! I've got it! Palmer saves the national pastime from the clutches of Bolsheviks. It strikes a nice patriotic chord."

I was skeptical. "That sounds like a bit much to me."

He looked at me over the top of his spectacles. "You haven't listened to many political speeches, have you?"

"Not when I can help it."

"Take my word for it, I've heard campaign slogans based

on far less." He shook his head sadly. "I am truly disappointed in Mitchell Palmer. He was a Progressive when he was in the Senate. He introduced the Suffrage Amendment, child-labor laws, was a strong ally of labor. I don't understand how he could have changed ideology so dramatically. It seems he got the bug to be president and decided to ride the Red Scare all the way to the White House. I don't know if I'm angrier at him for his policies or for changing sides as he did."

Steering the conversation away from national politics, I said, "I had another idea about Leo Hyman getting killed. Remember, there were *two* attempts to kill Emmett Siever— he was shot *and* stabbed. I think Hyman might have known who one of the killers was, but not the other. That's why he kept giving me time to look into it."

"And he was killed to silence him for what he did know about Siever's death?"

"Exactly."

The prisoner in the adjacent cell made noisy use of his toilet pail. Landfors's nose wrinkled as the smell drifted over to us.

It struck me as ironic that Landfors and I were sitting in a jail cell on Boston's Charles Street. It was on this same street that I had first made his acquaintance eight years ago. The same street, but a different neighborhood: it had been in a Beacon Hill town house. "You remember when we first met?" I asked.

He smiled. "Yes, at . . ."

"At Peggy Shaw's house." She had been a friend of Landfors and a sweetheart of mine when I was with the Red Sox. "Have you talked to her since you been in town?" I asked.

"Would you really want to know if I have?"

"No, I guess not. I was just thinking about her lately."

"Why? I thought you and Miss Turner . . ."

"I think Margie's going to do to me what I did to Peggy. I left Peggy for a baseball career. After the Sox released me, I wanted to be free to go wherever I could catch on with a team. Peggy wanted to be settled down, so . . . that ended it between us. Now I think Margie's going to be leaving—and maybe not even tell me. There's a new show starting at her theater July 4, and she hasn't even mentioned it to me." I sighed. "She's going to leave me the same as I left Peggy."

The guard appeared at the cell door. "Time," he said.

I stood. "I'll do whatever I can to get you out of here, Karl."

"Thanks," he said. "But no cakes with files in them, please. I don't want to be shot in an escape attempt."

I was glad he was still trying to maintain some humor. I reminded myself that Landfors had survived as an ambulance driver during the war, and if he was strong enough to get through that, he could handle this place.

○ ○ ○

I visited Landfors every day during the Boston series. I didn't bring him anything with a file in it, but did bring cookies, sandwiches, bottles of Moxie, and most of the current magazines. The guard thoroughly examined each item and charged me what he called a "tax" for allowing them through; he also took bites from much of the food.

Landfors and I didn't talk about Leo Hyman or Emmett Siever any more. Instead, in an effort to brighten his spirits,

I asked him to explain socialism to me; he always seemed happiest when talking politics. The effort didn't succeed. Each day, he looked a little more haggard. The food I gave him went uneaten, except by the guard and by the next-door prisoners—Landfors bribed them with sandwiches to move their slop buckets to the far side of their cells. I vowed to myself that I would find a way to get him out of this place.

Whenever I left the jail, it didn't seem that I could breathe properly again until I got onto the field at Fenway Park. I played all three games against the Red Sox, and we swept the series—it probably would have been different had Boston not sold Babe Ruth to the Yankees.

Our last night in town, I ran into Chick Fogarty in the hotel elevator. There were only the two of us, and he looked sheepish when he saw me. Just like in the army, smart alecks are different when it's one on one, when there's no crowd on hand to egg them on or applaud their antics. I asked him straight out, "What's your problem with me?"

He lowered his head. "Ain't nothing personal."

"Then what is it?"

"Dutch Leonard don't like you."

"And you go along with him."

"Got to. See, I figure if Leonard likes me, maybe he'll keep me as his personal catcher." He looked up, appealing to me with his eyes to understand his point of view. "Like Cy Young had Lou Criger. I know I don't got a lot of time left to play ball. If I can get an extra year or two by staying on Leonard's good side, even if it's mostly on the bench, I'll take it."

"What does *Leonard* have against me?"

Fogarty's face turned thoughtful, which was a pretty

pathetic sight. "He never did mention that. He just took to riding you, and I went along. I won't do it no more though. Okay?"

"Okay, Chick."

When the elevator reached the floor where the Tigers were staying, we took off in different directions.

Later, several hours after curfew, when Harry Heilmann returned to our room, I asked him about Dutch Leonard's antagonism toward me. "It's not Leonard," Heilmann explained. "It's Ty Cobb."

*"Cobb?"*

"Yeah. Cobb thinks nice guys don't win ball games. Got to light a fire under them, get them riled, then they'll get a fighting spirit to them. That's what I been doing with Bobby Veach. Feel kind of bad about it, but got to admit the kid's playing better lately." He fixed his bloodshot eyes on me. "And you been hitting pretty good, too. So maybe it works."

"Why would Ty Cobb care how I play? He only cares about himself."

"No secret that Jennings ain't gonna be in charge of this team much longer. And ever since Tris Speaker started managing Cleveland, Cobb's decided he'd like to do it, too. He wants the team in good shape for when he takes over."

I went to bed that night thinking that sometimes baseball could be just as underhanded as politics.

○ ○ ○

On the Pullman train back to Detroit, I thought about Chick Fogarty. It was ludicrous to believe he was in charge of anything; he certainly wouldn't be the Tigers' representative on a labor union. Which led me to the question: who would be? It should be somebody smart and a fighter. Ty Cobb? No, it shouldn't be a maniac. After some deliberation, I decided that the Tiger best qualified for the position was Donie Bush.

I found Bush in the club car, his thick, dark brows poking above the top of *The Sporting News.* I settled into the armchair next to him. "You got a minute?"

"Sure." He closed the paper. "What's up?"

"It's about the players' union. The way I understand it, each team has a representative trying to organize."

"That's the way I understand it, too."

"Somebody told me Chick Fogarty was the Tigers' organizer."

Bush snorted so hard that he quickly rubbed a handkerchief under his nose in case it had been a little too hard.

"Yeah, that's what I thought, too," I said. "And when I tried to figure out who it *would* be, I decided it would be you. Smart, scrappy, a veteran player. And if it isn't you, you probably know who it is."

He nodded, accepting the compliments as matters of simple fact. "You're partly right," he said. "If there was anything happening, I'd be organizing the Tigers. But it's pretty much fallen apart."

"You mean because Emmett Siever got killed?"

"No, long before that. There just hasn't been much interest. With the Ball Players' Fraternity folding, and the war, and the rumors about last year's World Series, it seems most of the fellows just want things to go back to normal and not stir up any kind of fuss."

I certainly understood that point of view. "Is that why Siever hooked up with the IWW? To light a fire under them?"

"Don't know for sure. Emmett Siever seemed to have his own reasons for doing things. Didn't ask any of us about joining with the Wobblies as far as I know."

"Okay, thanks Donie. And if it does start up again, let me know. I think I'd be interested in joining. If you guys trust me enough to let me in."

"I would," Bush said. "I liked how you handled things after Hughie Jennings gave you the wrong sign that time. You didn't embarrass him by telling the guys about his goof, you just took the benching. Showed class, in my book." He smiled. "But mostly I like what you did to Hub Donner."

That reminded me: what had Donner meant when he said that I'd be the big loser?

# Chapter Twenty-Seven

**O**ur Sunday outing started out sweet and carefree, with a basket lunch on the picnic grounds of Belle Isle Park. The sky was clear, the breezes soft, and the temperature balmy. I had no game scheduled, and Margie had called in sick at the theater, giving us a chance to spend the entire day together.

During the leisurely meal, we talked about the high points of our trips: the progress the women had made organizing in Tennessee and the progress the Tigers made moving up in the standings to seventh place. Then the two of us walked down to Lake Takoma. We sat on the grassy bank and watched the canoes and rowboats slowly moving through the water. We struggled for a while longer to keep the conversation light, but eventually we gave it up and became serious.

"Is your friend Karl in real trouble?" Margie asked.

"I'm afraid he might be—and it might get pretty bad. If it was going to be simple, they'd have filed some kind of charges. They're just keeping him in a cage to keep him quiet and out of the way. I feel useless—I don't know how to help him."

"Connie's worried, too," Margie said. "He called her shortly before he was arrested, and the two of them made up. She's going to contact everybody she knows who might be able to do something. Between Karl being in jail and Leo Hyman getting murdered, Connie's terribly upset—I think even more than when her father was killed."

That wouldn't take much, I thought. I said, "That government man, Calvin Garrett, is back in Detroit. He seems to always be around when people get shot."

"You think he's the killer?"

"I think there are some connections that just aren't clear right now. Tell me if this makes sense: Calvin Garrett gets sent up from Washington to crack down on the labor people that Palmer blames for losing the election. But how does Garrett know who the union leaders are here? How does he know where to start?"

"Maybe he asks the local police?" she suggested.

"Could be. Or, he contacts the man whose job it is to stop the unions—Hub Donner. Donner has been keeping tabs on organized labor in this area for years. Wouldn't he be the first one Garrett would talk to?"

"I suppose so."

"And if Donner had any spies or plants working for him, he'd let Garrett use them, right? That way Garrett does some of Donner's work for him, and Garrett owes Donner a favor for having helped him out."

"That sounds reasonable. But why do you think there was a spy?"

"Stan Zaluski told me they have problems with them from time to time. Somebody comes in, new to the cause, starts making a lot of noise, inciting the other Wobblies . . ."

"Go on."

"Well, to me, that sounds a lot like what Emmett Siever was doing."

*"What?* You're kidding."

"Wish I was. But it seems to fit. And there's another thing. Siever left Connie 'well provided for' the way I heard it. But he'd been broke for years. Where did he get the money? Maybe he was paid by Donner."

"I think you're completely wrong," Margie said.

"There's more. Just a possibility. I mean, all sorts of things have been going through my head about what might have happened ..."

She gave me a look that said, You're not really going to go on are you?

I went on. "You said yourself Connie wasn't too broken up over her father's death. And that's bothered me ever since I first met her. Even if he did abandon her when she was little, I'd expect her to have *some* reaction to his murder. So what I wondered is: what if she knew about her father being a traitor, and she knew about him being killed?"

Margie said derisively, "You think she had her father killed to inherit from him?"

"Not for herself, but maybe to help finance the cause. Or maybe she was loyal to the IWW and angry that he betrayed it."

"I promised Connie I wouldn't tell anyone about this," Margie said. "But I think I better tell you before you go and cause her any pain. You're right about her father's interest in labor being recent. It was mostly because he wanted to please her. And to make up to her for what he'd done in the past. As far as inheriting, it was on an insurance policy that

her father took out a year ago—he didn't leave any money
other than that. And as for why she wasn't devastated by his
death, it was because she was relieved that he was out of
his suffering. Her father was dying of cancer."

# Chapter Twenty-Eight

I was convinced that I could ultimately get to the truth if the individuals who knew bits and pieces of the story would reveal what they knew. I was close, I felt, but the final answer was just out of reach. If I could only extract a little more information from the right people . . .

Monday morning, I placed a call to Detective Francis McGuire at police headquarters. "I want you to set up a meeting with Calvin Garrett," I said.

"What makes you think—"

"I know he's in town, and I'm sure you know how to contact him. How soon can you set it up?"

There was a pause. "I'll see what I can do," he said.

"Thanks. And I want you to be there, too."

"Me? Why?"

"Because I don't trust him enough to be alone with him."

○○○

McGuire came through. Ten o'clock the next morning, the three of us got together in a small, second-floor Griswold Street office that might have been decorated by my landlady.

Calvin Garrett sat behind a battered pine desk; McGuire and I occupied mismatched chairs. There were no other furnishings, and the top of Garrett's desk was bare, leading me to believe that this room was used only as a meeting place, not a working office.

"Well, what is it, Mr. Rawlings?" Garrett asked, with a nod of his head.

"I'd like you to tell me the truth about what you were doing at Fraternity Hall."

"I already did."

"Your story doesn't wash. You didn't let yourself in the back door. I checked it. Somebody had to let you in—or you were already inside when Siever was shot. I think you must know who shot him, and I want you to tell me."

Garrett cast a glance at McGuire, who squirmed in his overcoat. The main reason I'd wanted the detective here was as a bluff, so that Garrett might suspect he'd told me more than he actually had. "Unless you have proof to the contrary," the GID man said, "I'll stick to what I told you earlier."

"Well, I can't *prove* much right now. But I suppose I could go to the papers with what I know so far. I can put you on the scene when Emmett Siever got killed. And I can *suggest* a lot more. Might be an embarrassment for you, the GID, and Mitchell Palmer. I don't expect he'd want a lot of publicity like that with the nominating convention next week."

"I don't believe you'll do that," Garrett said.

"Ask Hub Donner if I won't."

"Hub Donner was unprepared. I'm not."

"What do you mean?"

"You already have a friend in jail—Karl Landfors. I'd be happy to arrange similar accommodations for Marguerite Turner if you insist on pressing the issue. Traveling interstate with known radicals to incite trouble in Tennessee . . . Could get her quite a few years behind bars."

"You would go after Margie to get at me?" I couldn't believe he'd sink that low.

"Apparently, putting Landfors in jail wasn't enough."

"You . . . ?"

Garrett bobbed his head and leaned forward. "Now, let me tell you what *you* are going to do for *me*. You are going to use your new friends in the IWW, and you're going to talk to your teammates. And you're going to find a connection between the players and the Wobblies."

"What if there isn't one?"

"Then *suggest* one, and I'll take it from there."

"You must be a big baseball fan," I said facetiously, "to be so worried about the game's welfare."

"Can't stand baseball," Garrett answered seriously. "Football is my sport. Played a bit in college, matter of fact."

McGuire piped up, "I was a tennis man myself."

"Who cares?" said Garrett.

Maintaining an amused expression, McGuire shrugged and nestled a little deeper in his coat.

"You have work to do," Garrett said to me. "Now get out of here."

"And if I don't go along?"

"Miss Turner will suffer the consequences."

"Real gutsy going after a lady. Why don't you come after me?"

"No need to. According to my information, the Wobblies will take care of you very nicely. They still haven't settled on a new leader. Apparently, the unfortunate deaths of Emmett Siever and Leo Hyman have them concerned about security. Whoever can show they take care of their own will probably end up in charge. And your scalp would make a nice trophy for one of their candidates to show how strong he is."

Defeated, I made a vague promise that I would see what I could do. I didn't mention that what I'd be seeing *about* was how to stop Garrett.

Apparently satisfied, the GID agent called the meeting to an end.

When McGuire and I left the building, he said to me, "Nice try, but you're out of your league."

○ ○ ○

Hughie Jennings, completely ignoring reality, had decided that by pulling ourselves out of last place we were in contention for the American League pennant. He wanted to settle into a regular lineup, so I was out for the series against the Washington Senators.

We dropped Tuesday's game, 7–4, to the Senators' Tom Zachary. Wednesday, Jennings made a minor adjustment to the lineup: with Dutch Leonard facing Walter Johnson, Chick Fogarty got the start as catcher.

I was frustrated watching the game from the dugout. I wanted another chance to bat against Johnson. I kept getting up and down, changing my seat, and pacing along the bench. I finally succeeded in attracting Jennings's attention. "If you don't sit down and stay put, I'll nail your ass to the goddamn bench," he said.

My frustration grew as the game turned into a tight duel. By the bottom of the seventh inning, the score was 2–1 in favor of Washington. When Bobby Veach led off with a sharp single to left, a rumble rose from the stands as fans tried to inspire a rally.

Jennings gave the bunt sign and Babe Pinelli tried to execute it. But he popped up to the catcher, who threw to first, doubling up Veach. Two outs.

The groans were audible when Chick Fogarty stepped into the batter's box. He worked Johnson to a full-count before lifting a drive over the center fielder's head. Anyone else on the team would have had a triple, and Ty Cobb would probably have stretched it to an inside-the-park home run, but the slow-moving Fogarty had to settle for a stand-up double.

Dutch Leonard was next at bat, with a chance to help his own cause. Fogarty was almost anchored at second base, taking only a short lead off the bag. Then, on Johnson's first pitch, Fogarty tried to steal third. He'd barely reached shortstop by the time the ball was waiting for him at third base. The entire ballpark fell silent as we watched him lumber the rest of the way and be tagged out to end the inning.

Hughie Jennings went off like a pack of firecrackers, screaming at Fogarty for his blunder.

"Thought I'd catch 'em by surprise," was the catcher's explanation.

The curses piled up on Fogarty, with teammates and fans joining in the abuse. I was grateful to him though. He'd just given me one of the answers I needed.

○ ○ ○

Margie Turner pulled up in front of the ballpark in a rusty old Hudson. I hopped in and she asked, "Which way?"

"Down to Fort Street, then west."

She'd made good time. I'd called her immediately after the final out of the game, then showered and changed. I hadn't had to wait more than a couple of minutes before she met me outside the park.

"Where'd you get the car?" I asked.

"George, the stage manager. Sweet old man."

"You gonna be in trouble for missing the show?"

"No more than usual." She laughed.

I admired her driving skills as she maneuvered the automobile through the heavy postgame traffic. It was something I thought I should learn myself sometime.

Once on Fort Street, she picked up speed. Margie drove as if she considered the brake pedal to be a needless accessory, not bothering to slow down for turns or potholes. From the side of my eye I looked at her profile—chin tilted up, prominent nose looking like she could sniff out whatever was ahead, bright eyes eager to see everything. I loved the determined fix to her features, and the way she went into life head-on, with no apologies.

I directed her along the same course Leo Hyman had driven, through Woodmere Cemetery and across the shaky bridge to the shack on the other side.

Margie screeched to a stop in front of the dilapidated structure, raising a cloud of choking dust. "What do you hope to find here?" she asked.

"Not sure," I admitted. "I know there was *something* going on, though."

We proceeded to the door. Damn. I'd forgotten about the lock. I grabbed the padlock and shook it, an effort of total futility.

"Wait a minute," Margie said as she ran back to the car. She popped the trunk and came back brandishing a crowbar. "I found a key!" Instead of giving it to me, she shoved the end of the bar behind the latch and popped it off herself.

I'd also forgotten to bring matches for the lamp. When we stepped inside, we left the door open, so the interior was illuminated by the waning daylight.

"Yech!" Margie said. "What a mess."

I began to prowl the room, kicking at the boxes and cans and rapping on the warped walls.

"If you're looking for anything besides junk, I think you're out of luck," Margie said. "Tell me what you're looking for and I'll help. There isn't much daylight left."

"What I'm—" That's it! I looked closer at the walls. Three of them had sunlight squeezing through the cracks. The fourth was dark. Why would one wall be better constructed than the others? I went to the dark wall and ran my fingers over it; there were gaps between its boards too. "Can I have the crowbar, please?"

Margie handed it to me and I dug its tip between two of the boards. The thin wood pulled away easily. I could see that about two feet behind the first wall was a second. There was just enough space between the walls for a man to stand and listen to conversations in the shack.

I led the way outside and circled to the back wall. I felt around the edge and found it was secured to the rest of the structure by simple hooks. I grabbed hold of the wall and pulled it away. There was a small stool in the hiding space.

Calvin Garrett didn't have to stand when he eavesdropped on my conversation with Boggs and Hyman.

○ ○ ○

# Chapter Twenty-Nine

**A**fter a night's thought and a long discussion with Margie, I decided I had to keep squeezing—harder. Nothing more was going to come out of Calvin Garrett—nothing positive anyway—so it was on to the next candidate: Detective Francis "Mack" McGuire.

So far, McGuire had been the most forthcoming person in this whole mess. In my mind, that made him one of the good guys, so I hated to put the screws on him the way I was planning to. But since he'd already told me some things, he seemed the most likely to respond to pressure and come out with additional information. It seemed as unfair as the way nice guys lose close calls from umpires because the umps know they won't squawk. But I could see no alternative.

Okay, I told myself as I picked up the phone, you're just gonna have to play hardball.

When McGuire got on the line, I said, "You noticed I didn't say anything to Garrett about you showing me the files in your office."

"I noticed. And I didn't think you would anyway."

"Well . . . There's still more to this that you're not telling me. And I don't have time to get it from you one crumb at a time. I'd like you to tell me everything you know about the night Siever was killed."

McGuire's voice grew frosty. "I thought I was doing you a favor letting you in on anything at all."

"You were. But teasing me with a little information and then going quiet on me doesn't help. Either you open up to me, or I go see Garrett again—and I might not be as discreet this time."

"You got an interesting way of showing your appreciation."

"If you were in my position, what would you do?"

"I don't know . . . But I hope I'd know better than to try to blackmail a police officer."

"Give me another option," I said.

The line was silent for several moments. "I guess I did push you into this. Gimme your number. I'm gonna use another phone."

While I waited for McGuire to call back, I thought Ty Cobb would be proud of me. I was playing the game exactly as he would.

Five minutes later, the detective telephoned. I could hear noise in the background; it sounded like he was calling from a hotel lobby.

"Cautious, aren't you," I said.

"Can't be too careful with the GID involved. You better be cautious, too."

"That never seems to work for me."

"Well, it's probably too late for you now anyway. Garrett wants you kept quiet, and he'll find a way to do it."

"Including killing me?"

"No. I don't think so. I've seen my share of killers, and Calvin Garrett isn't the type."

"All right. What else do you know about what's been going on?"

"Not as much as you seem to think. I *can* tell you who shot Emmett Siever though."

"Who?"

"Calvin Garrett."

*"What?* But you just said—"

"Garrett swears Siever pulled a gun on him, and he shot him in self-defense."

"And you believe him?"

"I'm inclined to, yes. Hard to tell when these GID fellows are telling the truth—I think they're trained to lie. But Garrett was shaken by what happened, said he'd never killed anyone before."

"And then it turned out that maybe he *didn't* kill him, that Siever was also stabbed."

"Right. And I haven't a clue as to how that happened."

"Wait a minute. I thought GID agents aren't allowed to carry guns."

"Right. Not legally. But they all do."

"Okay. If Siever pulled a gun on Garrett, where'd it go? Why did you have to plant one?"

"Well . . . Sometimes it happens in a shoot-out that a gun gets dropped and skids off someplace. Garrett panicked when he went back to the body and the gun wasn't there. That's why he wanted me to bring one."

"Why did he go back to the body in the first place? Why didn't he just leave?"

"Told me he tried to but couldn't get out."

That didn't make any more sense to me than the story about how he'd gotten in. "Okay, so he panicked when he didn't see Siever's gun and told you to plant one. You must have searched for the one Siever dropped."

"We tore the place apart. Looked every place a gun could have gotten into. Never found it."

Jeez. "Then Garrett shot him in cold blood."

"It's a possibility. But in my professional judgment, he didn't. Partly it's just my read on Garrett. And then there's the phone calls—they support his story."

"What phone calls?"

"Garrett called me twice that night. The first time was right after the shooting. He told me to order a raid on the hall to create some confusion. We'd had cops standing by near the hall that night—at Garrett's request—so I sent them in. Then he called again. Told me Siever's gun had disappeared and to bring one to plant on him. If Garrett had shot him in cold blood, there would have been no need for the second call."

"Huh."

"And there's the fact that Siever was shot only once. Most of the time when somebody uses a gun in a murder, they fire several shots. Which brings us to Leo Hyman's death."

"You know what happened there?"

"Only that he had three slugs in him. Other than that, I'm staying out of it. I'm not assigned to that case and don't intend to get into it."

"Anything else you think I should know?"

"Well, this would have been a whole lot easier if you came up with something strong enough to turn the case back over to me. If you come up with some solid evidence, I'll go to my captain and try to get it reopened."

"Believe me, I'd like nothing better."

"You getting anywhere?"

It seemed fair to tell McGuire what I had, although I was embarrassed at how little it amounted to. "I have a connection between Garrett and Hub Donner. A shack outside the Rouge Plant."

"How's that?"

"A shack where I met a couple of the Wobblies—Hyman and Whitey Boggs. There's a false wall, and Garrett was behind it listening."

"You sure?"

"Yes. The Wobblies were pressing me for who was organizing on the Tigers. I said Chick Fogarty—it was a joke. Hyman and Boggs could tell I was kidding, but Garrett— who wouldn't know Chick Fogarty from Honus Wagner— must have taken it serious." It was when Fogarty had made his blunder trying to steal third that I realized what must have happened. The idea that the dull-witted catcher could be a union leader was ludicrous, so how did Calvin Garrett get the notion that he was? Only by having overheard what I'd said in the shack.

"And how's that a connection with Donner?"

"The shack was a couple of years old. I figure Donner used it to listen in on Ford workers, and he told Garrett about it."

"You still don't have anything I can take to my captain."

"No, I guess not."

McGuire then gave me a couple of telephone numbers where I could reach him, and again urged me to be cautious.

OOO

The movie flickering on the screen of the Empire Theatre was D. W. Griffith's *The Idol Dancer.* I'd have much preferred to be spending this Friday night seated next to Margie Turner, watching Clarine Seymour doing the hula in her grass skirt. Instead, I was with Stan Zaluski watching him crank the projector. He was the next person I thought I could get a little more information from.

"There's something I didn't think of till recently," I said.

"And what might that be?"

"After Emmett Siever got shot, there were two people back there: me and Calvin Garrett—the guy who called himself Detective Aikens. After Aikens let me go, I went into the hall, and there were people yelling that Siever had been killed. My question is: how did they know? I was the only one who'd heard the shot, and Garrett and I were the only ones who saw he was dead."

Zaluski drew at his pipe, long and slow. "Well, I reckon the message got through somehow."

*"How?"*

He thought it over, then shook his head. "With all that's been going on lately, I think the best thing is for me to keep quiet."

"It's *because* of what's been happening that you should talk to me."

"How you figure that?"

"Siever killed. Hyman killed. How confident are you that you won't be next? If I can find out what happened, and who the killer is, that might make things safer for both of us."

He took a few more puffs before answering. "A little electric light. We have some buttons and lightbulbs set up in the building, to let people know if there's trouble coming. I got one at the front desk; if the cops bust in, I push a button, some lights go on, and maybe some things we don't want the cops to see get hidden."

"Okay. So the signal came from somebody in the back offices. From Hyman? He was in the hall after the murder. What did he do—come out and mix with the rest of the crowd in the confusion?"

"That would be my guess."

"Don't guess. Just tell me. Hyman's dead—it can't do him any harm."

Zaluski shot me a look. "For one thing, I don't *know* all the answers. For another, there's people still alive who *can* be harmed—or who might *do* harm."

I thought of Whitey Boggs. "You still think one of the guys who wants to take Hyman's place might come after me?"

"Hell, they're acting so crazy, I don't know who the hell they'll be going after. Acting like a bunch of goddamn robber barons instead of socialists." His hand started to tremble.

"Want me to take over some?"

He nodded, and I spelled him at the crank. It gave me some time to think. When a reel change came, I waited for Zaluski to perform it, then asked, "I'd like to take a look in the back of the hall. Is there any time when the place is empty?"

"What do you want to do that for? Think you're going to

find something the cops haven't? Or that we haven't already looked for?"

"I might. If I do, I promise I'll let you know what I come up with." I didn't mention that I already knew who killed Leo Hyman. If that became known to the Wobblies, it might trigger actions that I couldn't deal with just yet.

"If you get caught," he warned, "there's nothing going to save you."

"When's the best time I can go in?"

"Sunday afternoon we're having a rally in Campus Martius. We want to remind everyone that we beat Palmer in here in the primary election—embarrass him just before the convention starts. I expect everybody will be at the rally, so the Hall should be empty. You got a game Sunday?"

"No, I can make it."

"It's gonna be locked." He fished in his pocket and handed me a key. "If things blow up, you swiped this from me. Got it?"

"Got it. Thanks."

was determined to make the most of the opportunity. If it
worked out, I'd be able to prove that I hadn't killed Emmett
Siever. If it didn't work out . . . Well, I was taking every step
possible to avoid that outcome.

I went over my plan with Margie, talking out every possibility. And I reviewed it in my mind a dozen times, mapping
out my movements once I got into Fraternity Hall. I wanted
to establish ahead of time exactly where I would go and
what I would do—the faster I got in and out, the better.

In case things didn't go according to plan, I stopped
at home Saturday morning. With McGuire's admonition of
caution and Zaluski's warning that I was on my own echoing
in my ears, I pulled out the biscuit tin from under my bed.
At the bottom of the container, wrapped in a white silk
handkerchief, was my army Colt .45. I unfolded the cloth
and looked at the automatic pistol with sadness; it wasn't
something I'd ever hoped to touch again.

After a quick outing to a hardware store for oil and fresh
ammunition, I cleaned the weapon thoroughly enough to

pass a drill sergeant's most critical inspection. Then I slipped seven rounds in the magazine and snapped it into the grip.

I waited impatiently for twelve-thirty. The rally was supposed to start at noon, which gave me a half hour time buffer in case anyone was late leaving the hall.

Assuming that Calvin Garrett had told the truth about Siever having had a gun, it must still be somewhere in the hall, I thought. If Siever had simply dropped it, the weapon would have been found. I believed that somebody hid it. And if the gun didn't turn up in the police search, it should still be there—what safer hiding place than one that has already been searched?

At half past twelve, I stepped out onto Grand River Avenue. I took a quick inventory of what I had: a key for access, a gun for protection, and as good a plan as I could come up with.

○ ○ ○

Using the key, I opened the front door to Fraternity Hall quickly and quietly, and stepped inside the vestibule.

I first poked my head into the meeting area; it was empty and still.

Next I looked around Stan Zaluski's desk. I found a small lightbulb and a button attached to the desk's left leg, and thin wires that ran from them up to the ceiling. The wires were painted the same color as the walls, but were visible if you looked for them. One thing about concrete block construction: it's tough to hide the wiring.

I then made a beeline through the hall, and carefully

opened the door to the back offices. Still no sound or sight of anyone.

I started in the kitchen and tried to retrace Calvin Garrett's movements from the moment of the shooting. The first thing he would have done is try to leave. I followed the corridor from the kitchen to the back door, the same as Garrett must have. I'd originally thought that he'd been lying about trying to get out, but perhaps he hadn't. One thing I'd noticed during my earlier inspection of the door led me to believe it warranted a second examination.

I lifted the crossbar, pulled the handle, and the door opened easily. I quickly shut it again. Then I took a closer look at the bracket that held the bar. The metal plate around the bracket surrounded it like a light switch plate. They weren't attached, and I could see no structural reason for it.

With a screwdriver from one of the tool boxes, I removed the plate. When I lifted the bar again to pull the plate free from the bracket, the bracket also moved up a good half inch. And the door wouldn't open.

I pressed down on the bracket, feeling the resistance of a spring, and the door opened freely. Lifting my finger, the bracket rose, and along with it, a metal plug rose out of the saddle. The work of Leo Hyman the tinker, I was sure. With the plate screwed in to hold the bracket in the down position, the door and crossbar work exactly as they should. Without the plate, lifting the crossbar causes the bracket to rise and a plug to go into the bottom of the door. Calvin Garrett had been intentionally trapped in the building.

As I replaced the plate, I thought over the next step: Garrett found he was trapped, then called McGuire to order a raid—no doubt to create a ruckus so that he could escape in the confusion. I opened the door of the nearest office. Like the one Hyman had shown Landfors and me, it was in a shambles. But the phone on the desk worked.

Okay, Garrett calls McGuire and returns to the kitchen. He finds me there, and Siever's revolver gone.

What happened while Garrett was trying to leave? Somebody—presumably Hyman—took Siever's gun and hid it. Purpose: to make it seem like Garrett killed an unarmed man.

I walked back to the kitchen, wondering *where* he would hide the gun. I took myself out of Garrett's shoes and stepped into Hyman's. Where would *I* hide the weapon? Not in the offices—that's the direction that Garrett would be coming back from. The other direction, then. The pantry.

The mess in the pantry was discouraging; searching through the clutter could take all afternoon. All right, I reminded myself, I could eliminate all places large enough to hold a pistol since the police would have already checked them. But then where *do* I look?

I put myself in Hyman's place again. I'd have already been in hiding when Garrett shot Siever. Then when Garrett tries to leave, I come out, grab Siever's gun, and go back to my hiding spot. Then I signal Stan Zaluski.

I looked up at the pantry ceiling and spotted wires running along the edge. They came down next to the sink. Taking care not to bump my head on the trap, I crouched down and found the button on the wall underneath.

Okay, now how did I know *when* to come out and get the gun? Footsteps? Maybe, but I'd want a better way to tell what was happening than simply listening for footsteps. I examined the wall between the pantry and the kitchen. Near the button, I found a peephole that had been taped over.

Sitting under the sink, I considered the question of where the gun would be. I'd have stashed it close to where I was hiding. There was only one possible place within arm's reach, and it was right in front of my nose. The trap. But it wasn't big enough to hold a revolver.

I gently hit the trap with the heel of my palm, and heard a rattling inside. Using both hands, I grabbed hold of the pipe and pulled down. It slid off easily. I turned the "U" over, dumping its contents on the floor. There were two pieces to a gun, a *model* gun; one section was the barrel, and the other the butt. I fitted the pieces together. It looked realistic, but would never fire. I remembered Hyman's words about his model ship: *Ain't never gonna sail, but she's sure gonna look seaworthy.*

Why did Siever pull a gun that wouldn't work? Did Hyman give it to him?

I weighed the fake weapon in my hand. It wouldn't fool anybody trying to use it. Siever must have known it wasn't real. Why pull a gun that you know won't fire?

Jeez. And what about the ice pick? I put Siever's gun in my pocket and banged the trap on the floor. It was empty. Then I probed inside the pipe hanging from the bottom of the basin. My fingers felt a piece of rag stuffed inside. I pulled it out and unrolled it. A blood-encrusted ice pick fell out.

"You got to be the noisiest burglar in the business."

I looked up at Whitey Boggs standing in the pantry doorway. Then I lowered my gaze to the revolver in his right hand.

"You're making it easy for me by coming here," he said. "This way I'm protecting the place against an intruder."

Okay, I thought, the good news is that he didn't simply

shoot me. "How'd you know I was here?" I asked, trying to swallow the fear that was percolating in my chest.

"Same way I know you bought a box of bullets this morning. Keep your hands where I can see them."

I raised my arms slightly so he could see I was making no moves for my gun. "And how's that?" I asked.

"Hub Donner. Been keeping tabs on you. So I also know you went to the Rouge shack—and you ripped it apart."

"Yeah. I found out why you insisted on going there that night with Leo Hyman: because you wanted Calvin Garrett to hear what we talked about. Same way you'd bring men there when you worked for Ford—so Hub Donner could listen in and find out what the union plans were."

"It wasn't what *I* wanted. It's what they made me do, Donner and Garrett. Yeah, I worked for Donner at Ford. Then he had me infiltrate this place to see what the IWW was up to."

"But you decided you *liked* the Wobblies. You really changed sides."

"Damn right I did. People here treated me with respect. Hub Donner never did. He paid me, yeah, but to him I was scum, a stoolie—he called me his 'White Rat.' I told him months ago I wanted out, but he wouldn't let me off the hook. He said he'd let the Wobblies know I was a plant if I tried to quit. Then when Garrett came to town, Donner lent me to him like I was some goddamn ballplayer he could just trade to another team."

"You're really caught in a tough spot," I said, trying to sound sympathetic.

"Not anymore I'm not. I'm sticking with the IWW and I'll cut down anybody who can tell about my past."

330 Troy Soos

"Like you cut down Leo Hyman?"

Boggs started to answer, then caught himself. "Like I'm going to do to *you,*" he said. "But first, I want to know what you've been telling people."

Since he wanted information from me, I figured that gave me a chance to stall him. What I'd be stalling *for* I didn't know, but when somebody's planning to shoot you, just getting a little more time seems important. "You want information from me, you answer a few of my questions first," I said.

"All right," he agreed. "A *few.* But take out your gun."

I was about to reach for my .45, then paused, shifted, and slowly went for the model instead. "I thought you'd be at the rally today," I said.

"Real easy," Boggs ordered. "Put it on the floor and slide it over."

I did as he said, and Boggs kicked the fake pistol down the hall. His body relaxed, as did his grip on his revolver. He went on, "That's why this is the perfect time to finally take care of you. There's dozens of men who'll swear I was at the rally. Now: who else have you talked to?"

"No, I go first. I never figured you for a plant. Why the Relief Committee, for one thing?"

"That was Donner's idea. He's a bastard, but he's a smart bastard. He figured by joining the Relief Committee, nobody would suspect me. But just by being a committee head, I'd get to hear a lot of things from the other leaders. Worked pretty well for a time."

"Until you thought Hyman was onto you. At the warehouse, when he told you to leave me alone, he said something suggesting there was a spy in the group."

"You got it. He also said you had nothing to do with Siever's death. I thought maybe he knew about Garrett. And if he knew about Garrett, maybe he knew about me. Couldn't take the risk of letting him live."

"Donner and Garrett know what you've been doing. Are you going to kill them, too?"

"Damn right. Donner first."

"Well, what about—"

"No," said Boggs. "Enough of your questions. Now it's time for answers."

"Uh-uh. You want me to talk, you got to tell me some more."

With his free hand, Boggs pulled the razor from his pocket. "No, I got another way to get you to talk."

I tensed, ready to take advantage and go for my gun if he switched the razor to his other hand.

My eyes stayed on his hands. Suddenly an urgent pounding rattled the door to the alley. Boggs turned to look down the hall. "Who the hell?"

In a second, I had the Colt in my right hand. "Drop it!" I said.

The hammering at the door continued. Boggs started to fall to a crouch, spinning toward me. The muzzle of his gun exploded. I squeezed the trigger of mine as a bullet crashed into the sink over my head. I fired again. And a third time. I kept shooting as Boggs kept dropping. Splotches of red were bursting on his white clothes.

More knocks on the door. I caught my breath and stood, slowly walking toward Boggs, my eyes and pistol still trained on him. It didn't require much of an examination to realize that there was no need to keep him in my sights. I picked up his revolver and carried it with me to the alley door. "Who's there?"

"It's me!" came Margie's voice. "Whitey Boggs isn't at the rally!"

I pocketed my weapon and let her in. "He's here," I said. "I had to shoot him."

"Is he—"

"Dead."

"Oh." She took a few deep breaths. "I'm glad it's not you."

"You better not stick around here. Can you go back to the rally and ask Stan Zaluski to meet me in the front of the hall?"

After Margie left with the message, I used the office phone to call McGuire and asked him to meet me in the same place.

# Chapter Thirty-One

I sank into Stan Zaluski's chair in the front entrance, feeling shaky, my energy sapped. I thought of the way McGuire had described Calvin Garrett, saying that he'd seemed shaken at having shot Emmett Siever. But when Garrett had talked to me immediately after, he'd seemed composed, in charge. Now I understood. I was fine while I had to act and think; not until I was left alone in the quiet building did the jitters hit me. I tried to quell them by concentrating on what should be done next.

Stan Zaluski got to the hall first. He had worry on his face and his hand trembled when I returned his key.

"Whitey Boggs is dead," I said. "I killed him."

Zaluski stiffened. "Explain."

"Boggs was a spy, planted by Hub Donner. He thought Leo Hyman suspected him, and so he killed Leo. He tried to kill me in the pantry. I had to shoot him. It was self-defense."

"I don't understand how—"

There was a rap at the door. I opened it to let McGuire

in. For the first time, he looked warm, with rivulets of sweat coursing over his freckles. He and Zaluski eyed each other suspiciously.

I made the introductions and gave McGuire the news about Boggs. Then I said, "Here's the thing: nobody's going to believe that I killed *another* Wobbly in self-defense. Especially not in the same place where I'm supposed to have killed Emmett Siever. Do either of you have an objection to saying Boggs was killed by a burglar? And that I was never here?"

They both chewed on my proposal. McGuire spoke up, "Considering the way everything's been twisted around the last couple of months, I think that just might the best way to put an end to it."

"No," said Zaluski. "It won't wash."

Damn.

"You'd still be on the hook," he explained. "Having the cops say a robber did it doesn't help since most of us don't trust what the cops say. There's fellows who are still gonna jump to the conclusion that you killed Whitey, the same as they think you killed Emmett and Leo. And if they believe you killed *three* of their comrades, it's only a matter of time until they get revenge." He tapped his pipe stem on his teeth. "How about if *I* killed him. I found out about him killing Leo, and had to shoot him when he drew on me." Directing the question to McGuire, he said, "Self-defense okay with you?"

McGuire thought for a moment. "Hell, I just want this mess over with. I'll be damned if I ever let myself get caught up in anything like this again."

"Boggs's gun is probably the same one that killed Hyman," I said. "Sounded like he had a long list of people to kill, and I don't expect he'd have been buying a new gun for each one."

"What about yours?" said Zaluski. "I'll need the gun that killed Whitey."

I pulled the .45 from my pocket and promptly handed it over. It wasn't a memento that I really wanted to keep. "Got this in the army," I said. "There might be a record that it was issued to me."

McGuire spoke up. "No problem. We'll match the bullets that killed Boggs to this gun—*Zaluski's* gun. That'll be enough to confirm his story. Then the gun will disappear from the evidence room."

"Sounds good," I said.

Zaluski nodded. "Let me go back there and see what it looks like. You two better get out of here."

McGuire started to protest to Zaluski, "I'll have to take you in. Just until we can determine it was 'self-defense.'"

"No," I said. "We have to go. There's somebody else we have to see."

His freckles sagged. "I remember when the police got to give the orders." He said to Zaluski, "All right, turn yourself in at headquarters."

"I'll be there," Zaluski answered.

○ ○ ○

Less than an hour later, Calvin Garrett and I were crammed into Detective McGuire's fetid office. With the IWW rally taking place, I was sure that Garrett would be nearby, and McGuire had no trouble getting in touch with him. McGuire had insisted to Garrett that he meet us, and that the meeting be in his office at police headquarters. The detective was finally taking charge, something I wished he'd done in April.

"I am reopening the Emmett Siever case," McGuire informed the GID man. "As a murder investigation."

"You're *what?* Who the hell do you think— I'll— You'll—" Garrett's voice trailed off into incoherent sputtering.

"There's been some new evidence," McGuire said. He gave me a nod. "I believe you have something to say."

I turned to Garrett. "Whitey Boggs is dead. I killed him."

Garrett's eyes darted about; it looked he was trying to figure out what the ramifications of Boggs's death could be.

I immediately suggested some. "Before we started shooting, we had a nice chat. Boggs was working for *you,* on loan from Hub Donner. He knew what happened between you and Emmett Siever, and he told me all about it."

Garrett's entire body drooped. "Siever pulled a gun on me," he said. "I had to shoot him."

I asked McGuire, "Did you search the hall?"

"Thoroughly."

"Find a gun?"

"No."

To Garrett, I said, "Then you must have killed an unarmed man."

He started sputtering again.

I cut him off. "Here's the deal. No matter what really happened between you and Siever, I'll keep my mouth shut and drop the whole thing. The official story can remain that I killed Emmett Siever in self-defense. You're off the hook."

"Sounds good so far . . ." said Garrett.

"Actually I should say you'll *be* off the hook after you do something for me: you get Karl Landfors released from jail."

"Hell no! I'm not making any deals."

"Ask yourself two questions," I said. "Do you believe I know enough to cause you serious trouble? And, with the convention starting Monday, is this the time Mitchell Palmer would want your name all over the papers for assassinating a labor leader?"

McGuire added, "Which is exactly the conclusion my investigation might lead to."

Garrett took his time thinking it over. It was an excruciating process to witness. Finally, he said, "I don't like it, but it's a deal." He then added, "But I'm going to keep a file on you."

That didn't sound like much of a threat—how could a file hurt me? "One more thing," I said. "Boggs told me that you and Hub Donner were next on his list to be killed. So be sure to mention that to Donner—and that I expect him to leave me alone from now on. If he does start trouble for me again, I'll make sure we're *all* in trouble."

"I'll pass along the message. And I'm sure he'll be agreeable to letting this entire matter drop."

"Anything else?" McGuire asked.

"Just a question," I said. I asked Garrett, "Why did you go to Fraternity Hall in the first place?"

"It's the only place Siever would meet me. Said he was going to give me information on how the IWW rigged the primary vote. I *had* to meet him."

"I have one more thing, too," said McGuire. He leaned toward Garrett. "Don't you *ever* try to interfere with my department again."

Garrett gave an affirmative grunt.

McGuire shuffled some papers on his desk. "Well, I think this investigation is closed."

Over the next few days, events settled down much more quickly than my insides did. There is something awful about killing a man, whether justified or not. It's a human life that's been ended, and I didn't feel I was the one who should be making the decision to end it.

I talked it out with Margie, repeating myself endlessly. She was patient in listening, told me that I had no choice in what I'd done, and continued to be patient when I repeated myself yet again. I knew what she was telling me was correct, but I couldn't get my head to convince my heart.

I started to pull out of the doldrums when Karl Landfors phoned on Monday with the news that he'd been released from jail. He was back to his old arrogant self, crowing that, "They finally realized how futile it was to try putting a *journalist* behind bars. Not even the GID can impede freedom of the press!" He sounded like the Landfors I knew and liked, and I wasn't about to spoil his mood by telling him about my deal with Calvin Garrett.

There was no uproar among the Wobblies over Whitey

Boggs's death, and I started to feel I was safe from them. Margie heard from Connie Siever that Stan Zaluski had earned a kind of hero status for discovering Boggs's treachery and killing him.

The more I thought about it, I grew to accept what I'd done as necessary. I wasn't going to lose any more sleep over Whitey Boggs. He wasn't going to haunt me like that young German kid I'd shot.

◯ ◯ ◯

Wednesday was the last day of June, an off day for the Tigers. I called Stan Zaluski and I asked him if he wanted to catch the Stars game at Mack Park.

The two of us watched the first four innings, concentrating solely on the game, until each team had made a hit. The Kansas City Monarchs' Bullet Joe Rogan had yielded a home run to Pete Hill, and the Stars' Bill Holland was nursing a two-hitter and a 1–0 lead.

"Things going okay for you?" I asked Zaluski. "None of Boggs's friends trying to get back at you?"

"What friends? By now everyone of them is claiming that he always knew Whitey was a rat. Some are even speculatin' that he was really the one behind Emmett Siever's death." Zaluski shook his head. "Still don't know how Whitey fooled me. He passed every test we gave him."

"That's because after Donner planted him in the IWW, he really changed—he crossed over to your side."

"Hmmph. Pretty big jump."

"Any bigger than Charlie Comiskey switching from being a pro-union player to being the worst owner in baseball?

Or Mitchell Palmer going from supporting labor causes to ordering the raids?"

"You really think Whitey came to believe in the cause?"

"Maybe. A little, I think. Or he could have been one of those you were telling me about, who can be on either side of an issue just to feel like they belong."

"Yeah, that sounds like Whitey."

We watched the Stars execute a flawless, fluid double play on the Monarchs.

"You still haven't told me all you know," I said to Zaluski.

He pulled his pipe from his mouth. With a laugh in his eye, he said, "Son, it would take years to tell you all I know."

"Be time well spent, I bet!" I took a swallow of ginger ale. "When we were here with Leo, I told him he knew I didn't kill Siever because he was the only one not to accuse me of it. Everybody else did—including you. Remember when Landfors and I first went to the hall? That threw me."

He nodded. "I remember. As I recall, it was just after Whitey Boggs and the others came out and said you did it. Figured I better join in."

"But you *knew* I didn't kill him. You knew exactly what did happen."

"You sure about that?"

"Yes. The night Siever was killed, people in the hall were yelling 'Siever's been shot!' Even if Hyman signaled you, how would you know from seeing a lightbulb go on that there'd been a shooting—and that Emmett Siever was the one who'd been shot?"

"Hmm. You got me. That was my part in the plan. And it was about the only part I knew about. Hyman didn't tell me most of what happened until afterward."

"Calvin Garrett told me that Siever asked for the meeting so that he could give him information on the primary vote being rigged. Is that true?"

Zaluski laughed. "It's true that that's what Emmett told him. But the vote wasn't rigged—it's what the GID wanted to hear, so Emmett used it to coax him into the hall."

"But why?"

"It was a trap, set by Leo and Emmett. The idea was that Garrett would be caught 'red-handed' having committed an assassination. It would be a blow to the GID and maybe win us some sympathy."

"Emmett Siever knew he was going to die that night."

"He *wanted* to. Part of the change *he* went through, I suppose. Wanted to make up to Connie as best he could for what he did when she was a youngster. He didn't have long to live, anyway."

"I heard he had cancer."

"You heard right, but don't let it get around."

"Why?"

"He took out a life insurance policy after he got the diagnosis. Lied about his health to get it. By getting shot, the insurance company paid off to Connie. Emmett called it her 'inheritance.'"

"He got himself killed in order to leave her money?" My read of Connie was that money wasn't so important to her.

"No. That was just part of it. Mostly he wanted her to be proud of him. He thought getting killed by a GID man would make him some kind of martyr."

"Did Siever know Leo was going to stab him, too?"

Zaluski lowered his eyes. "No. Neither did I. Leo told me afterward. Even with setting up Siever to be shot, how do you know the bullet's going to be fatal? So when Leo went into the kitchen to take Emmett's gun away, he stuck an ice pick in his heart just to be sure."

"I don't understand how Hyman got out. I know there was a lot of confusion in the hall, but how did he get past Garrett in the back?"

"That's something he *didn't* plan real well. I swear nine out of ten guys I was in prison with were there because they figured out how to get *into* a place but forgot to plan how they were going to get *out.* Hyman got out when Garrett went into one of the offices to make a phone call."

That must have been Garrett's second call to McGuire, I thought, the one in which he'd told him to bring an extra gun. "You never told me what you were in jail for," I reminded Zaluski.

"That's right." He clamped his pipe in his mouth to show he wasn't going to.

I went back to what happened in April. "Do you agree with what Hyman and Siever did?"

"Nope. That's probably why Leo didn't tell me most of it till later. I don't believe in martyrs; I believe in live fighters. But that was Emmett Siever's choice to make, and under the circumstances, who knows, maybe it was the right one for him. Who am I to judge?"

I decided I wasn't the one to judge either.

○ ○ ○

That night I finally asked Margie directly about her plans. "When you came to Detroit," I reminded her, "you said you had an 'unlimited engagement.' I've known for weeks that you're leaving town. Why haven't you said anything?"

"What makes you think I'm going anywhere?" Her wide eyes had a look of exaggerated innocence.

"It's in the papers, posted at the theater . . . Your show is moving on."

"Oh, that. When I said 'unlimited engagement' I didn't mean the show."

"You didn't?"

"No. I meant you and me. I was leaving things open."

"For . . . ?"

"For in case you asked me to stay, you numskull!"

"Oh. Oh!" I took her hand, and promptly added, "Please stay with me."

# Chapter Thirty-Three

**B**etween games of the Labor Day doubleheader against visiting St. Louis, while the groundskeepers were applying fresh lime to the foul lines and watering down the infield dust, I was having a catch with Bobby Veach near the Tigers' dugout.

The season had turned out to be much like that simple activity: easy, enjoyable, but to no great purpose. There was zero chance of us going to the World Series, and not much hope of climbing higher than seventh place. A calm had settled over the team. We played one game at a time, with no pressure and little strife.

I'd become more relaxed, too. No longer having to protect myself from my teammates, I directed my attention to learning from them. I studied the strategies of Ty Cobb and Donie Bush, picked up a few new tricks, and kept my batting average around .260. Most of all, I'd learned to appreciate simply being on the turf of Navin Field, in the sunshine, with my body intact and a friend or two on hand to watch me play. Karl Landfors, back from Boston, would be in the stands this day. He and Connie Siever were spending the morning at an IWW parade, but had promised to be at the park for the second game.

Even the Labor Day parade was expected to be without incident. There'd been enough of a backlash against Attorney General Mitchell Palmer that the labor crackdowns had pretty much ended.

The last two months had been eventful ones on the political front. Palmer failed in his bid to get the Democratic nomination for president. His party instead chose James Cox to face Republican Warren Harding. Harding was promising a "return to normalcy," a notion which had strong popular appeal. He wasn't going win me over on a slogan alone, though. I'd taken John Montgomery Ward's advice to heart and done something to further a cause that I cared about: in July, I'd joined the National Committee on Child Labor, and wrote to both Cox and Harding asking them to support legislation to protect children from exploitation by industry. Until I got a positive response—so far, I hadn't heard from either candidate—neither would get my vote.

Nor would they be getting Margie's, she'd told me. And she now had the constitutional right to cast a ballot. The suffrage issue had been settled in August, when Tennessee ratified the Nineteenth Amendment.

Fresh off that victory, Connie Siever had directed her efforts toward getting Stan Zaluski elected the new head of the IWW local; she'd succeeded in that goal in less than a week.

Of all the recent changes, the one that affected me most was a personal development: Margie had moved into my apartment and it had become *our* home.

It had certainly been a turbulent year for me since I'd arrived in Detroit, but I thought I came through it pretty successfully, and was adjusting nicely to the new circumstances.

From several rows behind the dugout, I heard Margie start to chant, "Raw-lings! Raw-lings!" When Landfors's and Connie's voices joined in, I dropped a throw from Veach.

Well, living with Margie Turner was still going to take some getting used to. But the important thing was that I was no longer yearning for things to go back to the way they used to be. I was now looking forward to whatever was coming next.